TIBERIUS BOUND

WALTER SIGNORELLI

ISBN
978-1-958690-29-1 (Paperback)
978-1-958690-30-7 (eBook)
978-1-958690-28-4 (Hardcover)

TABLE OF CONTENTS

Forward vi

Chapter One 1

Chapter Two 13

Chapter three 25

Chapter four.. 31

Chapter five 39

Chapter six.. 45

Chapter seven... 53

Chapter Eight.. 65

Chapter Nine 75

Chapter Ten 81

Chapter Eleven.. 89

Chapter Twelve 97

Chapter Thirteen 105

Chapter Fourteen 113

Chapter Fifteen 127

Chapter Sixteen... 137

Chapter Seventeen..145

Chapter Eighteen 153

Chapter Nineteen...165

Chapter Twenty 177

Chapter Twenty-One 191

Chapter Twenty-Two..197

Chapter Twenty-Three 205

Chapter Twenty-Four 213

Chapter Twenty-Five 231

Chapter Twenty-Six 241

Chapter Twenty-Seven 253

Chapter Twenty-Eight 261

Chapter Twenty-Nine 273

Chapter Thirty 285

Chapter Thirty-One 295

Forward

Tiberius Caesar, the second emperor of Rome, was a complex character whose life spanned ancient Rome's transition from the Republic to the emperorship. He played a prominent part in the political and social upheaval of that period, and, as interesting as were the public aspects of his life, his private life was even more interesting.

Born in November 42 BC, he was named after his father Tiberius Claudius Nero, not to be confused with the later Roman emperor Tiberius Claudius Nero, who was infamous for allegedly fiddling while Rome burned in 64 AD.

As with all the emperors, we know the historical facts of their public lives, but, for Tiberius, we have so much more. We know more about his private and inner life than any other emperor. Because of the unusual and surprising turns of his life, ancient writers and historians delved deeply into his thoughts and motivations. Suetonius and Tacitus painted a portrait of a physically and intellectually gifted man, but a troubled man, a man who felt unappreciated for what he had accomplished for Rome, and also felt that he wasn't living the life he truly wanted to live.

His childhood was tense and unsettled. The divorce of his parents, the initial separation from his mother, the death of his father, and then the move to the household of his step-father, Augustus Caesar, the *princeps* and first emperor of Rome, were all traumatic events.

In Rome, marriages were often used for political purposes, and Augustus had ordered Tiberius' father to divorce Tiberius' mother, Livia Drusilla, so that Augustus could marry her. Tiberius was greatly affected by the divorce, by the separation from his mother, and by what he saw as his father's betrayal and cowardice. The circumstances of the divorce left emotional scars for Tiberius that remained his entire life. Perhaps these scars accounted for the erratic conduct of his later years.

His position as the step-son of Augustus set the course of his life. He was considered a leading candidate to succeed the *princeps*, and he wanted to prove himself worthy. At a young age, he accepted his responsibilities to train and study hard, and he went on to excel as a magistrate and military commander.

At the same time, he had other interests and ambitions. Like many Roman aristocrats of the time, he was a Hellenist, enamored of Greek culture and arts. He had a true penchant for history and philosophy, and aimed to excel in those fields. His first wife, Vipsania, whom he loved deeply, had the same interests, and they enjoyed studying together.

However, in 11 BC, just as Augustus had ordered Tiberius' father to divorce Livia, he now ordered Tiberius to divorce Vipsania in order for him to marry Augustus' daughter, Julia. Tiberius obeyed, but this act of obedience devastated him. Miserable in his marriage to Julia, he left Rome and retired for seven years to the Island of Rhodes, where he immersed himself in philosophical studies.

He was content for a time on Rhodes, but he was still bound to Rome, and hearing that Augustus considered him a traitor for abandoning his post and leaving Julia, he felt compelled to return to Rome to redeem himself and reclaim his position in the imperial hierarchy. He returned, led successful military campaigns, and, at forty-seven years old, was adopted by Augustus as his son, making him the heir-apparent.

When Augustus died, Tiberius became the emperor, and was immediately confronted with political intrigues and mutinies in the legions. He dealt with them forcefully and proved to be a capable and successful emperor though he often found his duties unpleasant and distasteful. To distance himself from Rome, he moved to the Island of Capri and ruled Rome from there until the end of his life at age seventy-seven.

◆

This is a book of historical fiction based on the facts of Tiberius' life and those of his family and associates. The story is enhanced by fictionalized accounts of conversations and scenes, which I have tried to make compatible with the known facts and consistent with human experience.

As often happens when reading history, one recognizes parallels to modern times. The political and social issues experienced in ancient Rome are clearly relatable to our own world, and the stories and personalities of some of the characters in this book are comparable to some of our most prominent modern-day characters and leaders. What these issues are and who these characters are, I will leave to the reader to decide.

TIBERIUS BOUND
By Walter Signorelli

CHAPTER ONE

On the 16th of November 42 BC, at a time when Rome was still reeling from the assassination of Julius Caesar two years before, Senator Tiberius Claudius Nero, forty-three years old, dressed in his finest white toga, walked down the shining marble steps of the Temple of Jupiter Maximus Optimus on the Capitoline Hill of Rome to the Forum below.

Nero had just offered prayers and a sacrifice to ask the gods for the good health and safety of his soon-to-be-born child. Surrounded by his freedmen and slaves, he descended to the Forum, where he saw people rushing from place to place, looking warily at one another, a sense of impending catastrophe and worry on their faces. The Forum was less crowded than usual on such a clear, fall day; missing were the regular groups of spectators who normally gathered to hear political speeches or watch trials. These kinds of activities had been disrupted by the ongoing civil war that had made it unsafe to give a political speech—one faction or another would take offense—and it was too dangerous to hold trials because they had become flashpoints. Verdicts one way or the other could spark violence.

Nero continued along the Via Sacra in the direction of the Palatine Hill where the villas of the most prestigious citizens stood overlooking the city. Reaching the foot of the Palatine, he took the pathway up to his own villa near the top ridge. He climbed as fast as he could, anxious to see his young wife, Livia Drusilla, who was in labor with her first child. He was worried. Childbirth was a dangerous matter with high mortality rates for both mother and child. Nero was concerned for the child, but more concerned for Livia, frightened that something would happen to her. To lose her, he thought, would be too much to bear.

If the child lived and was a boy, he would name him after himself, but that was getting ahead of things. It was considered bad luck to assume what hadn't yet occurred.

By the time he reached the villa, he was perspiring and out of breath. He sat on a bench in the portico and asked a slave to bring him a wet rag. As he wiped his face, a piercing scream came from Livia's room. He grimaced, and when more screams came, he grimaced again and clenched his fists.

He couldn't go into the room; custom didn't allow it. A slave brought him water and a plate of food. He took the water but waved away the food. The screams grew louder and more frequent, then stopped. There was a long silence. Nero held his breath, then heard the baby cry. After a while, the midwives came out with the child in swaddling clothes.

"Well?" Nero demanded.

"It's a boy."

"How's my wife?"

"She's fine."

"Thank the gods."

The midwives placed the baby on the floor, as required by custom, and opened the swaddling clothes so that Nero could inspect the child. This was the moment when the father decided whether the child would live or die. If the child was deformed, if the child didn't seem normal in any way, it would be exposed and left to die on the side of a hill or in the forest.

The boy was fine.

The next step was for the father to either accept or deny the child as his own. Accepting the child had major legal significance. It would invoke obligations and responsibilities for both father and child, entitling the child to inherit a portion of the family estate and requiring the father to preserve the estate as well as he could.

If the father had reason to believe that the child was not his, he could deny the child. Physical characteristics that differed from those of the father might be grounds for denial. Information that the wife had been unfaithful might also be grounds. That wasn't the case here. Nero picked up the child, signifying that he accepted him as his progeny, and named him—Tiberius Claudius Nero. The boy would be called "The Younger."

Nero carried the boy into the bedroom, and gently placed him in Livia's arms.

"Thank you for giving me a son," he said.

Livia nodded and tried to smile.

◆

The next morning Nero went back to the Temple of Jupiter to pray again and to make another sacrifice. He was grateful that his son was healthy and that Livia had survived, but now he prayed for peace and for guidance. The guidance he asked for regarded the civil war. He was unsure whether to align himself with the Caesarian faction, led by the trio of Octavian, Caesar's adopted son, Marc Antony, Caesar's righthand man, and Marcus Lepidus, Caesar's longtime ally, or whether he should align himself with the senatorial faction that had supported Marcus Junius Brutus and Quintus Longinus Cassius, the assassins of Caesar, the so-called "liberators." This was a dilemma with life and death consequences.

The events leading up to his quandary began with the assassination of Caesar and the revelation that Caesar had adopted his eighteen-year-old grandnephew Octavian as his son, leaving three-quarters of his estate to him. Octavian took the formal name Gaius Julius Caesar Octavianus, and using Caesar's name and money, recruited a private army with the intention of seizing power and avenging his adoptive father's murder.

In August 43 BC, Octavian encamped his army on the Campus Martius outside the walls of Rome and sent armed centurions into the Senate to demand that he be allowed to run for consul, Rome's highest executive office. The Senate capitulated, Octavian was elected consul, making him, at nineteen, the youngest in history.

In October 43 BC, Octavian, Marc Antony, and Lepidus formed a triumvirate under the authority of a law passed by the citizens' assembly. Their goals were, first, to avenge Caesar's death and, second, to restore stability. They declared the assassination a crime and appointed a tribunal to convict the assassins in absentia.

Although the triumvirate appeared united, each member strove for preeminence. Octavian, to enhance his own position, convinced the Senate to declare Caesar a god. This done, it followed that Octavian was the son of a god, and the people apparently believed it. His star was rising, and many nobles rushed to attach themselves to him.

One who didn't attach himself was Livia's father, Marcus Livius Drusus Claudianus, who was in Greece fighting on the side of the assassins. This was the dilemma Nero faced. If he didn't take the side of his father-in-law, Livia would surely divorce him. But the triumvirate was in the stronger position, and Nero couldn't decide.

Time and events solved his problem. A month later, in October 42 BC, the armies of the triumvirate defeated the armies of Brutus and Cassius at the Battle of Philippi in Greece, an enormous battle on the north shore of the Aegean Sea, with perhaps two hundred thousand soldiers in the field. The armies had been evenly matched, nineteen versus seventeen legions, but Octavian and Antony's armies were quicker and more decisive. They were victorious, and Brutus and Cassius each committed suicide.

The triumvirs showed no mercy to their beaten foes. They had the severed heads of Brutus and Cassius sent to Rome and thrown at the foot of Julius Caesar's statue in the Temple of Venus.

After Philippi, Livia's father, with no expectation of clemency, also committed suicide, falling on his own sword. Although that was terrible news for Livia, it made it easier for her husband Nero to side with the triumvirs, and he sent a message to them, saying that they had his full support and that he would provide troops and funds.

The triumvirs divided the empire among themselves. Octavian took control of Italy and the West; Antony went to the East to reclaim the wealthiest provinces of the empire; Lepidus lost prominence and was given control of North Africa, the least important province.

To cement their ties, Octavian married Antony's teenage stepdaughter, Clodia Pulchra. As important as the marriage was for Octavian's connection to Antony, it was more important for the connection to Clodia's mother, Fulvia Flaccus, a formidable woman, who was a powerbroker in her own right. She previously had been married to Publius Clodius Pulcher, the infamous radical tribune. Clodius had a large following of trade union and street gang members. When he was killed in 52 BC, Fulvia instigated a riot and had the rioters build his funeral pyre inside the senate-house, using the wooden benches for firewood. The building was burnt to the ground.

In the aftermath of the riot, Clodius' followers became Fulvia's followers, and Antony married Fulvia to gain her supporters and strengthen his position.

Since Clodius' death, Rome had suffered several bouts of civil war, and the treasury was depleted. To raise money, the triumvirs published proscription lists of those whom they believed had sided with the assassins and were now considered enemies of the state. Proscription meant death or exile and confiscation of property. The proscribed person was "interdicted from fire and water," meaning no one could harbor him. Anyone who did risked being proscribed themselves.

Any citizen could kill a proscribed person and claim a reward for doing so. To prove their deed, they had to bring the severed head of the victim to the Forum to receive the reward. Most of the proscribed chose exile, but they still lost their property, which reverted to the state.

Although the revenues raised by the proscriptions were substantial, the triumvirs found that they needed more money to pay their soldiers and fund the government. So, they added names to the proscription lists, finally reaching two thousand names. It was still not enough, and Octavian imposed heavy taxes, which incited complaints and unrest.

While Antony was in Egypt consorting with Cleopatra, his wife Fulvia stayed in Rome. She saw the unrest over Octavian's taxes as an opportunity. With or without Antony's knowledge, she instigated a rebellion against Octavian, hoping to draw Antony back to Rome, and hoping to pave the way for Antony to become Rome's uncontested ruler. She raised an army and convinced her husband's brother, Lucius Antonius, the consul of 41 BC, to lead it.

When Octavian learned what Fulvia was doing, he divorced her daughter, Clodia Pulchra, signifying that the triumvirate was breaking up and Rome was moving toward another civil war in which the two most powerful triumvirs would fight each other.

Nero, Livia's husband, though he had been wise to side with the triumvirs, now made the mistake of siding with the Antony, Fulvia, and Antonius faction against Octavian. He joined Antonius' army, supplying troops and funds to him. But Antonius lost several battles, and had to retreat to the City of Perusia in Umbria.

Nero and Livia, carrying the one-year-old Tiberius, also retreated to Perusia and were trapped there when Octavian's army cut off supplies to the city. After months of siege, the people inside the city were starving, and, in February of 40 BC, Antonius surrendered.

As Octavian's soldiers plundered and destroyed Perusia, Nero and Livia escaped the city and found their way back to Rome. But they weren't safe there because Octavian had proscribed Nero. The proscription warrant read:

Since Tiberius Claudius Nero has committed treason by aligning himself with the rebel Marc Antony against the People and Senate of Rome, it is hereby ordained that he be interdicted from fire and water to a distance of four hundred miles from Rome, that nobody should harbor or receive him on pain of death, and that all his property and possessions be forfeit.

The couple had to flee to Sicily. Nero wanted to leave the baby with a nurse in Rome, but Livia insisted on taking him with them.

In Sicily, they weren't safe, so they fled by ship to a safehouse in Sparta, Greece. There, a reward-seeker betrayed them. As soldiers closed in on them, the couple escaped just in time and fled through a raging forest fire to safety. It was a close call as Livia's hair and the baby's blanket were singed by the fire.

While the family was fleeing from place to place, political events changed their circumstances. Antony disavowed Fulvia for instigating the rebellion against Octavian, and she either committed suicide or was murdered. With her out of the way, Octavian and Marc Antony agreed to a reconciliation. To solidify their agreement, Marc Antony married Octavian's sister, Octavia. As part of the agreement, the proscriptions that had been imposed on those who had sided with Antony against Octavian were lifted, allowing Nero and Livia to return to Rome.

In 39 BC, Octavian, who had divorced Clodia, strengthened his political position by marrying into the wealthy Pompeius clan. He married

Scribonia, a cousin of the late Pompey the Great, and she immediately became pregnant.

The marriage lasted several months until Octavian met Livia at a festival. She was with her husband Nero the Elder, Tiberius' father. It was an awkward meeting, as the older man, dressed in an unflattering loose-fitting toga, introduced his young wife to the conquering hero. Octavian was twenty-four, Livia was nineteen. He was dressed in an armored cuirass, designed to mimic an idealized male body. His heavy-soled soldier's boots made him look taller than his average height.

As Nero talked, Octavian looked past him as though he weren't there and straight at Livia. She was beautiful, with large striking eyes and brown hair pulled back in the republican style. Octavian instantly fell in love, enamored with everything about her.

She was equally taken with him, not only with his handsome appearance, but, more importantly, with his striking confidence and his Olympian presence. He had outmaneuvered the Senate to become the youngest consul ever and had since taken command of half the empire.

Despite both being married, and despite Livia having her three-year-old son, Tiberius, and being quite pregnant besides, Octavian and Livia began an intense affair. Within weeks, he proposed to her.

"But we're already married," she said.

"I'll take care of everything," he said.

Octavian took control of family matters with the same iron will with which he had taken control of the state. He waited for Scribonia to give birth, and as soon as their daughter was born, he divorced Scribonia. He named the child Julia, after Julius Caesar's daughter, who had died in childbirth.

Next, Octavian asked Nero to meet him at the Temple of the goddess Venus, who was considered the mythical goddess-mother of the Julian family. Octavian thought that meeting there would have an intimidating effect on Nero.

Inside the temple, Octavian led Nero to a bench next to the statue of Julius Caesar. Above the statue's bronze head was a star-shaped symbol that represented the comet that had been seen streaking across the sky after Caesar's death, a comet that was said to be Caesar ascending to heaven to join the gods.

Octavian stared up at the statue, not saying anything.

"What did you want to talk to me about?" Nero asked.

Octavian put his right hand on Nero's left forearm. "I'm going to ask you to do something that will be good for all of us, for you, for me, and for Livia."

"What do you mean?"

"You've been very fortunate. You've had a son with Livia, and, the gods willing, you'll have another child with her. But Livia's young, and should have the chance to marry someone closer to her age."

Nero winced as though he had been slapped in the face.

"After all, you are much older than she is," Octavian said.

"She's not unhappy."

Octavian removed his hand from Nero's forearm. "I believe she is."

"She has never told me that she's unhappy."

"She's a good wife," Octavian said.

"What business is this of yours? Is this for some alliance? I don't think Livia should be used that way. She can't be just given away."

"You've misunderstood me. I'm not giving her away."

"Then what do you want?"

"I want her for myself."

Nero began to get up and raise his fist; Octavian was up faster and pushed him back on the bench. "Listen to me. It's best for all of us."

"It's not best for me," Nero said.

"Yes, it is," Octavian said. "I'll be sure that you're well taken care of. Appointments. Governorships. Contracts."

"I don't care about that. I'm well off. I have as much as I'll ever need."

"And you want to keep it, don't you?"

"You have no right to threaten me. I'm a Roman citizen, a Roman senator. The laws don't leave me without recourse."

"Sir. I call you, sir, because I respect you. But remember, you didn't side with the triumvirate until after Philippi, which, to our minds, means you were with the assassins. The people may have forgotten, but they can easily be reminded."

"But I, I. . . . I had. . ."

"To make matters worse, you sided with Antony and Fulvia against me. You were proscribed once, and you can be proscribed again."

Nero slouched on the bench and put his hand to his forehead. "Does Livia know what you're asking?"

"She does."

"I'll have to talk to her. If that's what she wants…"

"Yes. Ask her."

Nero agreed to the divorce, and in January 38 BC, Octavian married Livia. Nero gave the bride away as though he were her father.

Two months later, Livia gave birth to her second son, Drusus Claudius Nero. People whispered that the wedding was in violation of Roman law, which imposed a ten-month period before it would be acceptable for a widow or divorced woman to marry again. The interval was to keep clear the paternity of any children. But no one was courageous enough to accuse Octavian of defying the law.

As for the custody of Livia's children, she and Octavian complied with the law that sons of divorced parents should live with the natural father. Tiberius and Drusus were sent to live with Nero on his countryside estate in the Sabine Hills northeast of Rome.

It was not a happy time for either boy. In Nero's home they lived under a reign of strict discipline. Nero spoke to the boys as though his only function was to punish them, and, as the *pater* of his family, he conducted himself almost as a tyrant. This was not uncommon in Roman society, which was built on the foundations of a *paterfamilias* system wherein the *pater* exercised absolute authority over his natural and adopted children. The *pater* controlled the family's estate and was responsible for the preservation and proper distribution of the family property. He also controlled the property acquired by his unemancipated descendants, no matter the descendant's age or marital status.

The *pater* decided family business, disputes, disciplinary matters, and, within legal constraints, had the power of life and death over his family members. The Laws of the Twelve Tables of 450 BC proclaimed patriarchal authority:

> A father has absolute power over his legitimate children
> throughout their life: he may imprison, flog, chain, or
> sell them, or even take their life, however exalted their
> position and however meritorious their public services.

Not surprisingly, disobeying the *pater* was treated harshly, and the worst punishment was reserved for anyone who killed his or her father, either a natural or adoptive father. The Twelve Tables prescribed:

> A parricide was flogged with blood-colored rods then
> sewn up in a sack with a dog, a dunghill cock, a viper,
> and a monkey; then the sack is thrown into the depths
> of the sea.

Although this archaic punishment was rarely imposed, the law sent an undeniable message that underpinned a culture of discipline and obedience throughout Roman society.

Tiberius, as the older brother, was subjected to the more rigorous discipline. His military instructor, Barbonius, pushed him hard with physical training and combat exercises. Barbonius said that training for battle should be so strenuous that an actual battle would seem easy in comparison.

Tiberius' history and Greek language tutor, Menelaus, drilled him for hours on the history of his Claudian ancestors, explaining that the Claudians were the most prestigious family in Rome, and instilled in him an obligation to preserve the honor of his family.

Prestigious aristocratic families functioned as *paterfamilias*, and each family member lived by the rules of obedience and loyalty to the family. Like a pride of lions, the family members were fiercely loyal to each other and competitive against other families.

In military endeavors, family members fought for love of honor and glory, subordinating their desire for safety and comfort to the desire for praise. They believed that their place in the afterlife depended on how they would be judged by their ancestors and how they would be remembered by their descendants.

Although the families competed with one another, they maintained their loyalty to the nation. Their traditional values held them together and provided the strength for Rome to fulfill what they saw as their destiny— conquering the world from Gibraltar to Egypt, from Britain to the Black Sea, from North Africa to the North Sea.

The Claudians had many illustrious members. The first was Appius Claudius Sabinus, the leader of the Sabine tribe, who in 504 BC, merged his tribe with the Romans, and was accepted into the patrician order and given a seat in the Senate, beginning a long line of Claudian magistrates.

Another prominent Claudian political leader was Appius Claudius Crassus, a patrician consul who quelled a rebellion among the soldiers led by tribunes of the plebs. In a famous speech to the Tribal Assembly in 403 BC, he pointed out the dangers created by the tribunes:

Death by cudgeling is the wage of him who forsakes the standards or quits his post; but those who advise the men to abandon their standards and desert the camp gain a hearing, not with one or two soldiers, but with whole armies, openly, in public meetings; so accustomed are you to hear with complacency whatever a tribune says, even if it tends to betray the City and to undo the state.

He persuaded the assembly to reject the calls of the rebellious tribunes, pointing out their treasonous nature. His speech was often quoted as an exemplar of traditional Roman values and standards.

The most famous Claudian of all was the great builder, Appius Claudius Caecus, the Blind (he became blind in his old age). He began the construction of the Appian Way in 312 BC, a road that ran 132 kilometers south from Rome to Capua. It was fifteen feet wide, paved with close-fitting basalt stones so precisely set that no cement was needed. By 300 BC, the road was extended to Brundisium on the heel of the Italian boot, for a total of 366 kilometers. Appius also began construction of the Appian Aqueduct, the engineering marvel that brought water from the Sabine hills to the city.

Appius was also respected as a wise political leader. In 280 BC, when King Pyrrhus of the City of Epirus in Greece invaded Italy, won several battles, and offered Rome peace terms, the Senate debated the terms, and, as it was about to accept them, Appius, now old and blind, rose to speak and chastised the senators for contemplating the peace treaty. He began by saying that he wished he was deaf as well as blind so that he couldn't hear Romans accept such humiliating terms. Due to the respect that they had for him, the Senate rejected the terms, and the war went on. Pyrrhus won battles, but lost so many soldiers in these battles that the expression "Pyrrhic victory" was born. In 278 BC, Pyrrhus was defeated and retreated to Greece.

Like all Claudians, Tiberius was most proud of Appius the Blind, an ancestor who would never surrender, proud that the blood of such a Claudian ran in his veins.

There were many other illustrious Claudians, and Menelaus taught young Tiberius about every aspect of their victories and defeats. His father expected him to know every detail of his family history and to be able to recite passages from important speeches. He pointed to death masks of his ancestors on the walls of his villa, and told Tiberius that they were watching him, whether he was at home or away, and that it was his duty to live up to the honor of his ancestors.

Tiberius internalized the discipline he received in his father's house, and he became a model of self-discipline. Time was not to be wasted. He studied hard and engaged in extra physical training. In competitive games with other boys, he usually won. On the rare occasions when he lost, he'd try harder to win the next time.

In 33 BC, when his father died, the young Tiberius delivered a eulogy from the *rostrum* in the Forum. Although only nine-years-old, he spoke clearly and confidently, and many people commented about how precocious he was and what a bright future he would have.

CHAPTER TWO

After their father's death, Tiberius and Drusus moved to the Julian-Claudian domus of their mother Livia and their step-father Octavian. Tiberius was nine, Drusus six. Their tutors, Barbonius and Menelaus, and their personal slaves moved with them.

The domus, on the highest ridge of the Palatine Hill, consisted of seven buildings that Octavian had combined into a compound. The main house looked like most aristocratic homes of the time with an atrium surrounded by small private sleeping quarters and walls covered with brightly colored paintings and mosaics depicting landscapes and mythological scenes. Octavian's study and office were in the rear. To the right, a staircase led up to the master bedroom. Through a doorway to the left was the kitchen where all work was done by slaves.

The other buildings of the compound were separated by narrow roads and alleys. A shrine to Vesta, the goddess of the hearth, and a fountain topped by a statue of the god Neptune stood in the garden and next to the complex was the Temple of Apollo and a library.

From their first day in their new home, life changed for Tiberius and Drusus. Their mother began making up for lost time. Her commitment to her duties as the first matron of Rome now came second to her role as mother of her two boys, and she treated them with great affection. Their new home was livelier than their father's house, and the brothers charged into their new lives with the enthusiasm of typical, growing boys.

Julia, Octavian's daughter from his previous marriage to Scribonia, lived in the domus as well. She was seven years old and excited at the prospect of the brothers coming to live with her but was disappointed to find that Tiberius ignored her.

Drusus was more fun-loving and friendly, and he always played with her and never did anything to hurt her feelings. He seemed the more gifted brother, with natural talent for everything he tried and an easy manner that made people like him. He was a quick learner, too.

In contrast, Tiberius was known for his perseverance. He might not learn as fast as Drusus, but he would study until he had mastered a subject and always seemed to have important matters on his mind. Like other young nobles, he studied the classic Latin and Greek texts, memorizing their famous quotes. Since Romans didn't read silently, people who passed by their homes could hear them reading out loud. Reciting the words improved their enunciation and was good practice for when they'd be making speeches in the courts or the Senate. They were also required to study and know the Twelve Tables of Laws.

The differing personalities of Drusus and Tiberius fueled rumors that they must have had different fathers. People speculated that while Tiberius was the son of Nero, Drusus was the son of Octavian. They asked, why would Octavian marry the six-month pregnant Livia if she weren't pregnant with his child?

Octavian was glad to have the boys living with him, and enjoyed spending time with them when he wasn't traveling or too occupied with matters of state. It was disappointing that he had to spend most of his time dealing with the ramifications of the Perusian Civil War and the treaty that had ended it. The difficulty with the treaty was that it included an agreement for Antony to marry Octavian's sister, Octavia. When the two married, it was assumed that Antony would break off his relationship with Cleopatra, but Antony continued to live openly with Cleopatra, fathering two sons. This was an outrageous insult to Octavian and the Julian family.

A propaganda war between Octavian and Antony ensued, and a claim circulated that Cleopatra was using Antony to restore Egypt to its ancient preeminence. Cleopatra had previously charmed Julius Caesar, and now she charmed Antony. She was beautiful, brilliant, and, among her many talents, spoke seven languages. Of pure Graeco-Macedonian descent, she was believed by many to be descended from the line of Alexander the Great.

Octavian saw Cleopatra, with her extravagant, eastern ways, as the antithesis of the ideal Roman matron, and considered Antony's subservience to her obscene. He delivered a speech in the Senate criticizing their illicit affair and accusing Antony of treason. Octavian produced a copy of Antony's will, which showed that Antony had bequeathed legacies to Cleopatra's children and had directed that when he died, he should be buried beside her in Alexandria. The will spawned wild rumors, and Octavian used it as a pretext for war. To further stir up war fever, rumors circulated saying that Antony and Cleopatra intended to conquer the west and transfer the capitol to Alexandria. Antony responded by accusing Octavian of wanting to make himself a king.

In late 32 BC, with accusations hurled back and forth, Antony divorced Octavia, and Octavian declared war. For the second time Octavian and Antony would fight a civil war against each other. Huge armies and navies were assembled on both sides. Octavian recruited an army of one hundred and fifty thousand, and, with his top general Marcus Agrippa, sailed east to confront Antony.

In September 31 BC, at the Bay of Actium on the west coast of Greece, Octavian's navy lined up for battle against Antony and Cleopatra's Egyptian navy. Hundreds of triremes and quadrireme ships, manned by thousands of rowers and sailors, approached one another for a fight that would determine whether the empire would be ruled from the West or the East.

Surprisingly, the battle, although anticipated to be a monumental one, was over in a day as the Roman ships outmaneuvered the Egyptian ships, and the battle quickly turned in Octavian's favor. Cleopatra fled in her ship and Marc Antony followed, leaving their navy to be sunk or captured. They fled to her palace in Alexandria, where they eventually committed suicide.

When Tiberius heard of Octavian's victory, he was thrilled. Everyone in Rome was talking about it. Uncertainty had passed and the people could look to the future. Tiberius had no doubts about his own future. His stepfather was now the undisputed ruler of the empire, a giant in most everyone's eyes, although to Tiberius he was only a distant giant because he had been away for so much time.

While Octavian was solidifying his hold on the empire, Tiberius kept to his disciplined routine of study and physical training, pushing himself hard. He excelled at whatever he tried, and his self-confidence continued to grow. But an incident occurred that shook his confidence and raised questions about his heredity and status.

He was taking a chariot lesson with his instructor, Barbonius, in the Circus Maximus along with several older boys. The Circus Maximus was Rome's largest stadium, about two thousand feet long and five hundred feet wide, located between the Palatine and Aventine Hills. The stands curved around like an elongated horseshoe, and could seat more than 100,000. The race course was divided by a spina, a massive masonry barrier, about a thousand feet long, with goal posts at either end.

On racing days, the stands were always packed, but on this day there were only a few hundred spectators. During the lesson, Barbonius had the boys compete in practice races, driving two-horse chariots around the track. The goal of the practice wasn't to drive the horses fast, but to keep them running straight and under control, something that Tiberius did well. It was unusual for a twelve-year-old to be given chariot lessons, but Tiberius was strong and capable beyond his years.

A crowd of spectators watched from the stands, and after winning his practice race, Tiberius paraded his chariot past them. He stood regally, holding the reins of the two white horses, nodding and waving to the crowd, and imagining that he was parading before a fully-packed stadium. As he dismounted from the chariot, his slave, Pometius, smiling at Tiberius' pose, took the reins of the horses and said, as though making a proclamation, "Octavian the Younger, descended from the gods, has arrived."

"What?" Tiberius said.

"Oh, I didn't mean anything," Pometius said.

"You meant something," Tiberius said.

Although a slave, Pometius had been Tiberius' playmate since they were small. Pometius' father, a learned Greek slave in the Claudian household, had managed to have his son chosen as Tiberius' first playmate. They were the same age, and when Tiberius moved to Livia and Octavian's house, Pometius went with him.

The boys had no difficulty playing their roles as equals but not-equals. They competed in sports, raced, and wrestled as equals, but they could revert to their master-slave relationship in an instant.

"Tell me what you meant!" Tiberius said in his already commanding voice.

"People say you will be the next Octavian. You will continue the Julian line of the divine Julius Caesar."

"Why would they say that?"

"I, I don't know."

"Tell me," Tiberius commanded.

"People. . . they say that your real father was Octavian, not Tiberius Claudius Nero."

"That's not true," Tiberius said emphatically. "You know my name. It was the name of my father. When my mother and Octavian met, she divorced him, but he's still my real father."

"Yes, of course."

"Why do you say it like that? Tell me."

"I can't. It was just talk."

"Tell me."

"Master, I'm sorry, but some of the others were saying—I don't believe it—that when your mother was married to Nero, she got pregnant by Octavian, and Octavian forced Nero to divorce her. He married Livia and even made Nero oversee the wedding. That's what some people were saying. I didn't know if you knew."

"Pometius, we've been together every day of our lives. You know what I know and what I don't know."

Since he could remember, Tiberius had been troubled by his parents' history. Most of the time, he put it out of his mind and concentrated on his studies and training, but what Pometius had said brought it all back.

They unhitched and stabled the horses and walked in silence to the Julian-Claudian domus. At the front gate, they banged the clapper until a slave opened the gate. They entered the main house and headed straight to the kitchen, looking for a snack. They passed through the reception hall and the atrium, went into the kitchen, and began picking up any food available. Pometius took as much as Tiberius.

"Don't spoil your appetite," said Matea, the plump slave woman who oversaw the kitchen.

"Don't worry," Pometius said, taking a handful of honeyed-barley cakes.

The boys bathed and sat for dinner. Their kitchen raid hadn't been spoiled their appetites. Tiberius sat on a couch with his mother while his brother Drusus and his stepsister, Julia, sat across from them. Everyone was talking but Tiberius wasn't listening. All he could think about was what Pometius had said.

The next morning, Tiberius and Pometius walked down the Palatine Hill to the Forum and sat on the steps of the Temple of Concord to wait for their tutor, Menelaus. The Temple of Concord was an important landmark in Roman history, built in 367 BC by the consul Marcus Furius Camillus. It was designed to commemorate the peace between the patricians and the plebeians and the law that allowed plebeians to become consuls. It was still in use more than three centuries later.

Five boys from the noblest of families waited on the steps for their Greek language lesson. Each had a slave in attendance. Four had older male slaves; Tiberius had Pometius. The boys bantered with one another, but Tiberius remained silent. Pometius whispered to him, "I'm sorry about what I said yesterday. It was just people gossiping."

"Forget it," Tiberius said. "But I'm going to find out for sure. Menelaus knows everything about everything."

"He probably won't say anything."

"He'll tell me the truth."

Menelaus arrived at the temple. He was a tall, gaunt man who carried a walking stick. Although he sometimes threatened his students with it, he never hit them. He immediately began lecturing and, at one point, said to the students, "Now we will speak only Greek. I will ask you a question in Greek and you will answer in Greek." Tiberius hated this exercise, but he was determined not to get anything wrong. He wouldn't be embarrassed by making a mistake. Even at this young age he was a perfectionist. When his turn came, he thought about his answers and spoke carefully and correctly.

During a recess, the students began kidding each other and gossiping about the latest news. Every day in the Forum, official statements were posted on bulletin boards and Senate heralds made announcements about the latest news and latest wars. By the time the information passed from one person to the next, it was often no better than a rumor. Besides the official announcements, the people posted unofficial announcements on the city walls. Much of what they wrote was scurrilous and defamatory. Tiberius wasn't interested in what the boys were saying. He asked to speak to Menelaus privately.

Most Greek tutors were slaves but Menelaus was not. His grandfather had been enslaved by the Romans at Corinth in 146 BC, but Menelaus' father had been manumitted from his slavery for his long service to the Claudian family. This meant that Menelaus was born free. He was an outstanding teacher who idolized Polybius, the Greek historian who had become a Roman hostage in 167 BC under a peace treaty with the Arcadian League. The treaty called for a thousand Greek nobles to be sent to Rome as an assurance that the Arcadians wouldn't rebel or start another war. The nobles weren't exactly hostages; they had freedom of movement within the city, but they weren't allowed to leave.

As a highly-educated noble, Polybius was treated with respect and became the tutor of the illustrious general Publius Cornelius Scipio Aemilianus, the adopted grandson of Scipio Africanus who had defeated Hannibal in the Second Punic War.

During the Third Punic War, Polybius accompanied Aemilianus when he led the assault against the city of Carthage. Aemilianus blockaded the harbor and built extensive siege works around the city. In 146 BC, after three years of war, the final battle took place. The Carthaginians fought furiously, but after fierce house-to-house fighting, the Romans overwhelmed them. Thousands were killed, fifty thousand survivors were sold into slavery, and the rest were forced to settle inland.

The Romans set the city ablaze, and as Aemilianus watched the city burn, he cried. When Polybius asked him why, he replied, "A glorious moment, Polybius, but I have a dread foreboding that someday the same doom will be pronounced on my own country."

Now, more than a century later, Menelaus wanted to emulate Polybius by also writing a first-hand history. He hoped to stay with Tiberius as the boy rose in prominence just as Polybius had stayed with Aemilianus.

With Octavian away more than he was home, Menelaus became somewhat of a father figure, but not as much as other tutors who were *in locus parentis* to their charges. Most tutors of young Roman nobles could discipline their pupils, but Menelaus didn't discipline Tiberius, not because he was prohibited from doing so, but because of Tiberius' serious, austere nature, it would have been inappropriate. If discipline were needed, Menelaus would tell Livia what had happened and she would do the disciplining. That was only necessary the few times that Tiberius lost his temper and started breaking things. Other than those incidents, Tiberius conducted himself properly and upheld the standards expected of a young noble. He looked forward to putting aside the *toga praetexta* of a boy and putting on the *toga virilis* of a Roman citizen.

Menelaus followed the standard curriculum of the time, having his pupils learn by rote the definitions of the virtues essential for a Roman noble: courage, firmness, frugality, loyalty, honesty, veritas, and piety. These virtues were foundations of Rome's secular religion, and people were judged by how well they lived up to them.

Menelaus went beyond the standard curriculum. He developed his own teaching materials, relating historical narratives to his pupils. Tiberius was his best student, and Menelaus gave him all his books and materials to read, even some rare papyrus scrolls. He drew diagrams to illustrate the connections between people and events, and continually quizzed Tiberius to make certain that he understood their nature and importance. "As a leader of the Republic," Menelaus always said, "you must know history and how past conflicts and events arose, so that when a new problem arises, you can use your knowledge of old events to help you determine how to handle the new one." Menelaus concentrated on past history, staying away from anything recent, which could be controversial and even dangerous to discuss.

Menelaus agreed to talk with Tiberius, and they sat on a bench inside the temple. Tiberius came right to the point. "Tell me about my father and step-father," he said. "People are saying that Octavian is my real father"

Menelaus was reluctant to talk about it, but Tiberius pressed him.

"You should ask your mother," Menelaus said.

"I will, but I need to know some things first."

Menelaus, knowing how strong-willed the boy was, decided he had to tell him something. He pulled Tiberius a little closer and whispered. "The story going around is confused. You were three when Octavian married your mother."

"Then why are they saying these things?"

"That's all I can tell you now. For anything more, you must ask your mother," Menelaus said.

"But why would my father allow Octavian to steal his wife? And why would my mother let Claudius Nero raise us in his home, not hers?"

"That's the law. You know that when there's a divorce the male children stay with the father, females go with the mother," Menelaus said. "It was your brother Drusus that was the question."

"What do you mean?"

Whispering again, Menelaus told the story. "Your mother was pregnant with Drusus when Octavian decided to marry her, even though he too was married at the time, and his wife, Scribonia, was also pregnant."

"Scribonia was pregnant with Julia?"

"Yes, Julia."

"So, Julia and I are not related."

"Not by blood."

Menelaus continued, "Octavian waited until Scribonia gave birth to Julia, and on the very day Julia was born, he divorced Scribonia. At the same time, he ordered your father to divorce your mother."

"How could he order him to do that? Did they agree?"

"Livia certainly agreed. Nothing against your father, but he was many years older than she was. Octavian waited until Drusus was born, then he married your mother. And your father agreed. He even gave Livia away at the wedding. It was for the best. Octavian and Livia have a wonderful marriage."

"That's true," Tiberius said calmly, although inside he was agitated.

Menelaus continued. "But still the rumormongers have mixed you up with Drusus. You're surely the son of your father Tiberius Claudius Nero. And Drusus is also his son, but people could speculate that he, in fact, is the natural son of Octavian. They might say that Drusus might only be your half-brother."

"I'm sure we're full brothers. We look so much alike."

"You have the same mother."

"Yes. And we should have stayed with her."

"Your father did what he thought best," Menelaus said.

Tiberius abruptly stood up from the bench, raising his right fist, "But at the time my father was as powerful as Octavian. What about his *dignitas*? The honor of the Claudians? My honor?"

Menelaus raised his forefinger to his lips as though to say, "be quiet," and pulled Tiberius by the arm to sit down again.

"Nobody would cross Octavian," Menelaus whispered. "He had just seized power by intimidating the Senate, formed the triumvirate with Antony and Lepidus, and crushed the assassins of Julius Caesar at the Battle of Philippi." Menelaus continued holding Tiberius' forearm, "Anyone who opposed him was exiled, and their property was confiscated."

"Still, I don't understand how my father could do it" Tiberius said. "It's one thing to give up power to Octavian; it's another to give up your wife."

"He had some consolation in that you and Drusus were sent to live with him to be raised."

"Doesn't that go against the law of nature that a mother is best to raise her children?"

"In Rome, at the highest levels, some things are complicated," Menelaus said. "When you're older, you'll come to understand."

"I have a question," Tiberius said. "If the law was that when a divorce happens, the boys go with the father and the girls go with the mother, why does Julia live with us?"

"Well, there's the law, and then there's Octavian. Julia was his only natural child, and he decided that it was better for her to be raised in his home under the care of your mother than to stay with Scribonia."

"I see," Tiberius said. "But if Octavian was the leader of the nation, how could he disregard its laws?"

"That's a good question. The answer is that leaders tend to change the laws for their own benefit. You might ask Titus Livius the next time he comes to dinner. He might give you a better understanding of the inner workings of Rome."

"You mean Livy?"

"Yes. He's your mother's favorite historian."

"Why aren't you her favorite historian?" Tiberius asked.

"I'm merely a tutor. Livy has written a monumental history of Rome. He's thought to be far above all other historians, and his lectures are always interesting. But they can be difficult for him."

"How come?"

"There's a friendly rivalry, or maybe not so friendly, between the Julians and the Claudians, for the position of preeminent Roman family. Octavian, of course, advocates for the Julians; your mother holds that the Claudians are the backbone of the nation. So, when Livy lectures, he has to please both your step-father and your mother without offending either one."

"Rome is a complicated place," Tiberius said.

CHAPTER THREE

Octavian finally returned to Rome after the Battle of Actium, and the Senate granted him a triumph—a ceremonial parade through the city to the Temple of Jupiter Optimus Maximus on the Capitoline Hill.

Preparations for the triumph took precedence over all other matters. Three days were set aside for it, and a million city residents, plus more people from the countryside, packed the streets. When the bugles were blown to begin the triumph, Octavian, wearing a purple toga and a crown of laurels, entered the city at the head of the procession, riding in his four-horse gold and ivory chariot. His face was painted crimson to signify that he represented Jupiter, the supreme god of the city, the real victor.

Tiberius and Marcus Claudius Marcellus, Octavian's nephew, rode white horses on either side of his chariot. They were fourteen years old.

Drusus and Julia, both now ten, rode in the chariot with Octavian.

The magistrates and five thousand soldiers marched behind them, followed by the captives and the plunder taken from the defeated enemy.

Setting out from the Campus Martius, the procession followed the Via Flaminia to the Circus Maximus, around the racing track, through the arch of the Servian Wall onto the Via Sacra, and to the foot of the Capitoline Hill. From there, Octavian dismounted, walked up the hill, and laid a laurel wreath in the temple of Jupiter Optimus Maximus.

Most citizens were proud of the victory and enjoyed the pageantry. Others saw Octavian's triumph as unjustified because he hadn't defeated a foreign enemy but fellow Romans. Octavian was aware of the criticism, so he tried to present the triumph as a victory over Cleopatra, the Egyptian Queen, rather than over Marc Antony.

He knew that the best way to allay the criticism was to give the people what they enjoyed most—a spectacular celebration. And they celebrated, playing games, singing songs, chanting insults at the captives, eating and drinking with abandon, and marveling at the riches and stacks of gold taken from Egypt's treasury.

Tiberius was more interested in the soldiers—how they behaved, how they dressed, their discipline. He was particularly interested in the captives. Only Egyptians and other mercenary troops were shown as captives, no Romans. Usually, a defeated monarch or general would be marched in chains in front of the captives, but Cleopatra was dead. Instead, several Egyptian generals were chained together. When the parade was over, they would be strangled, unless they could be ransomed.

As the captive soldiers marched, most stumbled along as though in a trance; others walked with their heads erect, proudly defiant. A few chastised the ones who were crying, telling them to behave like men. Some captives spit at the people who jeered or threw things at them.

Tiberius thought of Publius Cornelius Scipio Aemilianus crying at the destruction of Carthage. He understood that one could be victorious today and in chains tomorrow. He remembered Menelaus quoting the Greek playwright Euripides, "Never count a man fortunate while he still lives."

After Octavian's triumph, Rome took a three-day holiday. Tiberius was glad to stay around the compound with Pometius and his younger brother Drusus. With no lessons or training scheduled, they played *harpastum*, a soccer-type game with a linen ball filled with feathers. The three of them played just for fun until some teenage friends showed up and the play got rougher. Although Drusus was younger than the teenagers, he was tall and fast and could hold his own with them.

Julia wanted to play with the boys, but they wouldn't let her. She sat on the sidelines, watching. After a while, Drusus said he would play with her, and they went into another garden to have a catch.

The name "Julia" had historical significance for the Julian clan; every generation had a Julia. The first Julia was Julius Caesar's aunt. She married the great plebeian general, Gaius Marius, and the marriage shifted the alignment of the Julians toward the *populares* and away from the *optimates*.

The second Julia was Julius Caesar's daughter Julia. She married Pompey the Great to cement the ties between Caesar and Pompey in the First Triumvirate. Even though he was much older than she was, the marriage was a success, but, in 53 BC, Julia died in childbirth. Her death diminished the marital link between the two triumvirs. The child (who would have been Pompey's son and Caesar's grandson) died within a few days of his mother, a tragedy that altered history.

The third Julia was Octavian's daughter from his marriage to Scribonia. When Octavian divorced Scribonia, Julia was brought to live with him and Livia. In 37 BC, when Julia was just two-years-old, Octavian betrothed her to marry Marc Antony's son, Julius Antonicus. The subsequent civil war between Octavian and Antony precluded that arrangement.

Livia had been kind to her but very strict. Julia had a rebellious streak, and when she didn't get her way, she'd throw a tantrum. Once in the midst of a tantrum, she shouted at Livia that she hated her and wanted to go back to live with her real mother.

When the boys took a break from playing *harpastum*, two slaves brought drinks and fruits out to them at Neptune's fountain. Spray from the splashing water cooled the boys while Julia sat on the edge of the pool, dangling her feet in the water.

◆

On the second day of the holiday, Tiberius and Pometius walked down the Palatine Hill and across the Forum to the Capitoline Hill. They often did this because Tiberius loved the sight of the Temple of Jupiter and the other great buildings and monuments on the hill. He thought that one day he would construct great buildings there himself.

On these walks, Tiberius and Pometius were not like master and slave but like boyhood friends. They talked about things that average boys would talk about, and Tiberius talked openly about his dream to be a builder.

"I'll have to study architecture and engineering," he said.

"I could study with you," Pometius said. "Some slaves have been great architects."

"Certainly, you could," Tiberius said.

At noon, they walked back to the compound where Drusus was in the garden with a half-dozen boys playing *harpastum* again.

"Can we join in?" Tiberius asked. One of the boys, Marcus Galba, the son of Senator Galba, was the leader of this little gang of teenagers. He was a year or two older than Tiberius, and said, "Sure. You can play, but your slave boy can't."

"Don't be stupid," Tiberius said.

"By law, we don't compete with slaves," Galba said.

"It's only a game," Tiberius said. "It's just for fun. It doesn't mean anything."

Galba stood in front of Tiberius, "He's not allowed to play."

"I'll tell you what," Tiberius said, pointing at Galba. "He's playing and you're not"

Pometius interceded. "That's alright. I don't need to play. I don't want to play."

Tiberius and Galba circled one another getting ready to fight. The other boys got between them. Galba was in a difficult situation. Could he fight with Octavian's stepson? What if he won?

Tiberius guessed what Galba was thinking. "Don't worry, whoever wins, wins fair and square. And then it's forgotten."

"There's no point in fighting," Pometius said. "I'm not playing, even if you invited me. I'm leaving. Fight if you want to, but leave me out of it," he said as he turned and walked toward the domus.

Galba and Tiberius stared at each other until Galba said, "The game was almost over anyway. I guess there was really no reason to fight."

"Let's forget it," Tiberius said while thinking that maybe there really was a reason to fight. Should slaves be treated like such dirt? They're property, but still should be treated with respect if they deserved it. And Pometius deserved it.

◆

On the third morning of the holiday, Tiberius was expecting Menelaus to come to the domus. When he didn't come, Tiberius walked around to the side of the Palatine Hill to Menelaus' modest house. He wasn't home. His wife said that he had gone out on an errand and wouldn't be back until later. Tiberius was disappointed and wondered where Menelaus could have gone. He hadn't said anything about being away.

Tiberius walked home and found Drusus, Pometius, and a few other boys playing dodgeball with a linen ball filled with sand. Julia was watching them.

Tiberius joined in, and within a few minutes the play turned to wrestling. Tiberius and Pometius grappled with each other. They stumbled and fell together into the pool of Neptune's fountain. Drusus laughed at them. They climbed out of the water and chased Drusus through the courtyard and around the house. He was fast, but they cut him off and tackled him. They picked him up and carried him back to the fountain and dumped him into the pool. Julia came behind Tiberius and pushed him into the pool, too. Then Tiberius grabbed her and pulled her into the water with them. They were all soaking wet and laughing. As Julia climbed out of the pool, her clothes clung to her.

Livia came into the garden, "That's enough," she said, trying to be stern. But the boys' laughter was contagious, and Livia laughed at them as they ran around the fountain. To Julia, she said, "Get inside and change those clothes."

"Why can't I stay with the boys?" Julia said.

"Get in the house," Livia answered.

Julia flung her head to the side, smirked at the boys, and walked slowly and deliberately into the house.

Later, Tiberius overheard Livia talking to Julia.

"You must not tease the boys," Livia said. "They might get ideas. Then you'll have a problem. It's better to keep your distance. If a boy likes you, you can talk to him, but not alone."

"How are you going to really have a conversation if you're not alone?" Julia said. "Without having a real conversation, how am I going to decide if a boy is for me or not?"

"Your father will decide who is best for you," Livia said.

"Well, I'll tell you, and I'll tell him right now, I'm not marrying some old goat just so he can make some political alliance," Julia said loudly as though wanting her father to hear.

"That's enough," Livia said. She was taken aback by Julia's impudence.

Julia stomped away.

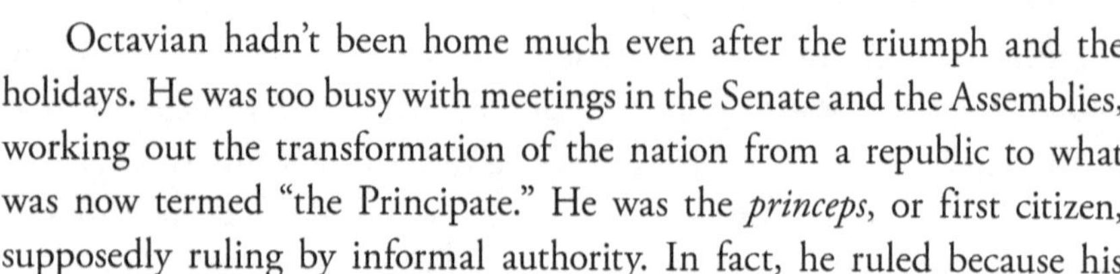

Octavian hadn't been home much even after the triumph and the holidays. He was too busy with meetings in the Senate and the Assemblies, working out the transformation of the nation from a republic to what was now termed "the Principate." He was the *princeps,* or first citizen, supposedly ruling by informal authority. In fact, he ruled because his armies had defeated the armies of the assassins, the Senate, and then the army and navy of Marc Antony and Cleopatra.

Tiberius knew of the powerful political maneuvers Octavian was making, maneuvers that only an extraordinary man could accomplish, but one evening when Octavian came home for dinner, Tiberius was struck by Octavian's ordinary appearance. He watched him as he took off his cuirass, washed in a basin of water, and put on his tunic. Without his cuirass, he didn't look extraordinary. He was fine looking, lean and moderately muscular with his light brown hair combed forward in the style of Julius Caesar, but Tiberius didn't think that he looked like the ruler of Rome.

The dinner was pleasant. It was one of a few times that the whole family had dined together. Livia seemed quite content and even patted Julia's head as though to say all was forgiven. Tiberius wanted to ask Octavian about when he could wear his toga *virilis,* but thought his stepfather seemed too preoccupied.

Octavian sat erect on his couch. "I've heard that you're all doing well with your studies, and I'm so proud of you," he said. "It's good to be home with you, but tomorrow I have to meet with the legion commanders at Ostia."

"Can I go with you?" Tiberius said.

Octavian shook his head. "No, not tomorrow."

Livia asked, "Will you be back by Saturday? I've invited Livy to dinner and for him to give one of his history lectures."

"Yes. Of course," Octavian said. "That should be interesting."

CHAPTER FOUR

History Lessons 1

The next day as Octavian was meeting with the legion commanders at Ostia, Tiberius and Pometius were sitting with Menelaus on the steps of the Temple of Concord. Tiberius had asked Menelaus whether Pometius could listen to his history lesson since he, too, was interested in the subject.

"My father was a slave," Menelaus said. "So, alright, but the two of you can't gang up on me."

"Thank you," Tiberius said. "And can I ask you something else?"

"Of course."

"Your father was a slave, but Menelaus is not a slave's name?"

"That's right. Do you know who Menelaus was?"

"It sounds familiar, but I can't remember."

"Menelaus was the husband of Helen of Troy, the king of Sparta. When the Trojan warrior, Paris, seduced Helen and carried her off to Troy, Menelaus and other Greek kings went to war to get her back, which is why it has been said that Helen's face launched a thousand ships. Indeed, she caused the ten-year Trojan War."

"Now I remember."

"In the war, Troy was destroyed, and King Menelaus got Helen back."

Tiberius was struck by the king's determination to get his wife back. "Not like my father," he whispered to himself. But he quickly put that thought out of his mind, and said to his tutor, "So, you might be descended from a Spartan king?"

"It's possible. If it's true, the lesson is that kings can become slaves, and, conversely, slaves can become kings."

Pometius interrupted, "So there's hope for me yet."

"Anything is possible," Menelaus said.

"Perhaps life goes in a circle and your descendants will become kings again," Tiberius said.

"Unfortunately, I have no children," Menelaus said. "But I view my students as my children, and I hope by teaching them history, I set them on the right course."

"I'm glad you do," Tiberius said.

They walked along the Via Sacra and, as they passed below the Temple of Jupiter where Octavian's triumph had ended, Tiberius stopped to ask a question. "Do you think we should still have triumphs?"

"Why do you ask?"

"It doesn't seem right to treat the captive soldiers like chained animals. They're ordinary people who were just doing their duty. Why humiliate them?"

"A good question, my boy."

"I could understand dragging their kings and generals in chains, the ones who were responsible for the war, but not the ordinary soldiers."

Menelaus paused for a moment. "Our citizens expect it. It makes them feel part of the victory."

"That's another question. Who gets credit for the victory? Octavian takes all the credit when it's well known that Marcus Agrippa led the campaign. I heard people saying that Octavian was sick in his ship's cabin when the battle was fought."

Menelaus stopped walking, clasped Tiberius' hands, and led him a distance away from Pometius. "Listen to me. Don't say things like that out loud. Don't even think them. You're young, but people listen to everything. They remember everything you say. And someday, if things go wrong, they could use it against you. They can twist your words to claim you insulted the *princeps* or that you were part of a conspiracy against him."

Tiberius was taken aback. "You think Octavian would ever believe that, or would ever turn against me—his own step-son?"

"No one can predict the future."

"Octavian would never turn on me."

"But others might. You'll be assuming your manhood soon, putting on the white toga. With that comes responsibility and accountability. Be careful what you say, be careful what you do."

Menelaus waved for Pometius to join them, and they walked silently until they reached the Colline Gate, the northern entrance of the city. They went through the gate and out of the city. Across the road, they sat on a fallen tree trunk and looked up at the Servian Wall, built five centuries before by the Etruscan king Servius Tullius to enclose and protect the city. It was more than ten meters high, built of large stone blocks, each two cubic meters, set in two rows, making the wall four meters thick. The iron gate fit perfectly in the archway. The entrance was open now, but when the heavy iron gate closed, the city was impregnable.

Menelaus pointed to the Colline Gate, "This is where Lucius Cornelius Sulla defeated the Marians."

"I know," said Tiberius.

"How much do you know?"

"I know that when Sulla was in the East fighting the armies of Mithridates, he was betrayed by the *populare* consul, Cinna, who invited Gaius Marius to come back to Rome with an army of slaves. Marius set his army loose, and they killed Sulla's friends and supporters. When Sulla learned of this, he marched back to Rome with his army and defeated the Marian army right here outside this gate."

"That's the second part of it. Do you know what led up to it?"

"I'm sure I don't know everything."

Menelaus sent Pometius to buy lunch from a pushcart near the gate—three cups of goat cheese and grapes. As they ate, he began a lesson.

Menelaus taught history and politics by narrating historical facts then asking "what if" questions—what if one of the prominent actors of history did something differently or made a different decision, how would that have changed history? He would ask Tiberius what he would have done in that same situation to avoid the mistakes that were made.

He believed that a rising young noble had to know the history of the Marian-Sullan conflict to understand present-day Rome. Everything occurring now had its roots in that conflict. The civil war between Julius Caesar and Pompey had its beginnings in the Marian-Sullan conflict, just like the civil war between Octavian and Antony. Menelaus explained that young leaders must learn the lessons from that conflict.

"You must know about it in order to understand how ambitious, dangerous, and treacherous people can be, and how failing to deal sternly with such people can lead to disaster," Menelaus said. "Marius and Sulla personified the two halves of Rome. There was bad blood between them, and for two decades they circled one another, vying for supremacy, competing to be the most acclaimed man of Rome."

Menelaus explained that Marius was a *populare*, a "new man," who claimed to represent the common people, the plebeians. As a great soldier, he had made his way up the ranks of the legions, and, when he turned politician, he often gave rousing speeches criticizing the patricians or the so-called *optimates*. In almost every speech, he lifted his tunic to show the wounds he had suffered fighting and winning battles for Rome, contrasting himself to the aristocratic officers who, because of their family connections, were given military commands without having ever fought in battles.

Marius claimed that Sulla was installed as a commander only because he was a member of the illustrious Cornelius clan, and a descendent of Publius Cornelius Scipio Africanus, Hannibal's conqueror. But that was unfair. Sulla was a great soldier and had earned an excellent reputation.

The bad blood between Marius and Sulla began during the war against Jugurtha, the Numidian King, in North Africa when Marius was in command of the legions and Sulla was his lieutenant. The war was going badly until Sulla, on his own initiative, captured Jugurtha, effectively ending the war. Then Sulla turned his prisoner over to Marius who took Jugurtha to Rome, displayed him in a triumph, and took all the credit for the capture.

"What if Sulla had not turned his prisoner over to Marius but instead took him back to Rome himself?" Menelaus asked.

"That wouldn't have worked," Tiberius said. "It would have broken the chain of command, and Sulla would have been branded a usurper. But, he should have been smarter and sent the news to Rome before Marius got there. Then people would have known who deserved the credit."

"Very good, you're thinking strategically," Menelaus said.

Menelaus continued, "Their next conflict occurred ten years later during the Social War. The war was precipitated by your grandfather, on your mother's side, Marcus Livius Drusus. He was an advocate for Italian citizenship at a time when some of the Italian tribes wanted complete freedom from their obligations to Rome, while others wanted full Roman citizenship. The largest tribe, the Samnites, wanted complete independence."

Menelaus went on to explain that when Drusus was assassinated in 90 BC, the Italian tribes revolted. They formed a federation and assembled a formidable military force that was equal in fighting capacity to the Romans; their soldiers had trained and fought with the legions. Three years of war followed, spreading throughout Central and Southern Italy. The Italians won several hard-fought battles, but when Marius took command in the north and Sulla in the south, the Romans began to win. In 89 BC, Sulla led a lightning campaign against the Samnites, inflicting a decisive defeat on them.

Because of his victories, Sulla was elected consul for 88 BC, but the war continued, depleting the treasury and leaving both Italy and Rome drained. Prudently, the Romans made concessions, agreeing to confer Roman citizenship on all Italians who had remained loyal and any of the rebels who would put down their arms. This concession satisfied most of the Italians and weakened the impetus of the rebellion, which gradually came to an end. Italians south of the River Po gained full citizenship and the right to vote, hold office, and access the courts.

Menelaus stopped lecturing for a moment to take a drink, then asked, "Was it a good decision to grant full citizenship to the Italians after they had rebelled and killed Roman soldiers?"

"They had no choice," Tiberius said. "It was either that or go on with the war, which would have left them weakened and vulnerable to attack by either the Gauls or Mithridates. It was the smart thing to do."

"Right again," Menelaus said. "In the end, making the Italians full citizens made Rome a far stronger nation than it would have been if it had relied solely on its own people."

"Now, you can't tell them apart," Tiberius said.

"That's a good point," Menelaus said. "Let's walk back."

Pometius hadn't said anything during the lesson, and Menelaus turned to him. "Do you know about Mithridates?" he asked.

Pometius was surprised by the question but quickly answered. "He was a king from Pontus on the Black Sea who challenged Rome in Asia Minor and Greece. In 88 BC, while Rome was fighting the Social War in Italy, Mithridates slaughtered thousands of Romans and Italians, anyone who spoke Latin."

"You're right," Menelaus smiled, surprised by such a definitive answer from a slave.

He continued the lesson, saying that for Rome, not only did justice call for vengeance against Mithridates, but, if its empire was to stay intact, retaliation was imperative. Rome declared war and the Senate chose Sulla to lead it. He was the best choice. At fifty years of age, he had proved himself many times. He had captured Jugurtha and defeated the Samnites in the Social War, and was described by an adversary as "cunning as a fox and brave as a lion."

After Sulla left Rome to join his five legions in Capua that were waiting to embark to the East, Marius tried to convince the Senate to replace Sulla and, instead, appoint him to lead the legions. He would have been a poor choice; at seventy years old, he was not in good enough physical condition for what certainly would be an arduous campaign against the formidable king.

Failing to get the Senate to give him the command, Marius and his supporters were able to pass a law in the assembly that rescinded the Senate's assignment of Sulla and gave the command to Marius.

The assembly sent a messenger with the order to Sulla. He read it, tore it up, and, with his legions that included many of his loyal veterans from the Social War, marched on Rome. For the first time, a Roman army marched to Rome not to protect it from external enemies but to free it from internal tyrants.

Waiting in Rome for the attack, Marius put many of Sulla's supporters to death. He called for recruits and offered freedom to slaves who would fight on his side, but his calls were largely ignored. With limited troops, Marius wasn't able to stop Sulla's army from taking the city, so he fled to North Africa.

Though he surely could have, Sulla chose not to seize absolute power for himself. He held elections instead. Lucius Cornelius Cinna, a *populare*, and Cornelius Octavius, an *optimate*, were elected as co-consuls for 87 BC. Although Sulla could have imposed his will as to who would be his successor, he accepted the results of the election; but only after extracting a solemn oath from Cinna, in the Temple of Jupiter, that his laws and reforms would be left intact He was confident that the co-consul, Cornelius Octavius, an *optimate*, would uphold his laws.

Menelaus asked, "Was Sulla wise to hold elections?"

"I think that instead of holding an election," Tiberius said, "he should have made the Senate declare him a temporary dictator so that he could restore order."

"What about Mithridates?"

"That could have waited until everything was settled in Rome. You can't send the legions off when there's turmoil at home."

"Well, you're right, my boy. That would have saved a lot of trouble. But, of course, it's easy to say in hindsight. Do you know what happened?"

"I know in general what happened, but I don't know all the details."

Menelaus explained how, when Sulla led his legions across the Adriatic Sea to confront Mithridates, Cinna broke his promise to uphold Sulla's laws, and the co-consuls fought each other with Romans killing Romans. The violence was horrific with beheadings, the wanton slaughter of entire families, and hundreds of heads stuck on the ends of pikes.

"I knew it was bad, but not that bad," Pometius said. "How could such a madman have gotten people to slaughter so many people?"

"That's the point I've been trying to make," Menelaus said. "Humans can be incredibly vicious. Polybius once wrote that 'malignant lividities and putrid ulcers often grow in the human soul and no beast becomes at the end more wicked or cruel than man . . . sometimes there is nothing so abominable or so atrocious that they will not consent to it . . . at the end they are utterly brutalized and no longer can be called human beings.'"

Pometius let out a breath and said, "I guess that's true. People can be worse than savage beasts."

"Far worse," Menelaus said., "And remember, society is always only a few massacres away from a descent into chaos."

Turning to Tiberius, he said, "As a leader, it's your job to maintain stability, and never underestimate the hatred that the lower classes harbor for the rich. Always beware of those that exploit these hatreds, promising land or money if the upper classes are destroyed and their possessions confiscated."

"Don't the rich hate the poor just as much?" Pometius said.

Menelaus looked inquisitively at Pometius but continued the lesson, explaining that the bloodbath lasted until Marius died in 86 BC. "Marius' reign was a tragedy for Rome," he said, "and it was also a tragedy for the man. Marius had begun as an outstanding soldier. He was loved by the people, elected consul six times, but then something went wrong. Power went to his head, and he went mad. But, because he was so powerful and ruthless, no one thought or dared to confine him in a madhouse."

"It seems to me that the mobs were as insane as Marius," Tiberius said.

"Yes, that's what happens with mobs," Menelaus said. "When individuals join a mob, they lose their identity and blindly follow a demagogue who claims he will solve all their problems. They think that they won't be singled out from the others and will be able to get away with murder."

"And no one dared to topple Marius," Pometius said.

"No. His was a reign of terror," Menelaus said. "Meanwhile, Sulla, still in the East, was on the verge of defeating Mithridates but, instead, he signed a peace treaty with him so that he could return to Rome to restore order for the second time."

Tiberius interrupted, "Sulla must have been furious that he couldn't finish off Mithridates."

"Yes. He was. And when he marched on Rome this time, he made many people pay. A year of fighting culminated when his troops destroyed Cinna's army right here at the Colline Gate. After that, Sulla had the Senate appoint him dictator."

"Did they have any choice?" Pometius asked.

"None at all," Menelaus said.

"Maybe he should have done that the first time he marched on Rome," Pometius said.

"You might be right," Menelaus said. "When he died, do you know what he inscribed on his monument?"

"I do," Tiberius said "No friend has ever done me a kindness and no enemy a wrong without being fully repaid."

"Very good."

"I think that should be Rome's motto," Tiberius said. "And I think Sulla wasn't as bad as they say."

"I suggest you keep that to yourself."

CHAPTER FIVE

On the evening of Livy's lecture, the imperial family assembled at the Julian-Claudian domus. Livy stood on a platform to deliver his speech. He was a small man with brown hair brushed up from the side to cover his baldness. He had a pleasant, moderate voice and spoke with the confidence of a master, not at all intimated by the presence of either Octavian or Livia. He lectured about the fame and accomplishments of the Claudians and repeated almost word for word great speeches that the Claudians had made in the Senate. With dramatic flair, he told the story of Gaius Claudius Nero, who was instrumental in defeating Hannibal Barca and the Carthaginians during the Second Punic War. Livy told how, in 216 BC, when Hannibal had destroyed a Roman army at the battle of Cannae, killing 50,000 Roman legionaries, and bringing Rome to the brink of complete defeat, he was ready to attack the city itself. But Hannibal needed reinforcements, so, in 207 BC, his brother, Hasrubal Barca, marched with an army from Spain across Gaul into Italy to join up with him. This posed a deadly threat, but Gaius Claudius Nero, in command of four legions, snatched victory from the jaws of what could easily have been Rome's defeat. As Hasdrubal marched south to join his brother, he sent a courier with a letter giving Hannibal the location where they should meet. Fortunately for the Romans, the courier was intercepted. Armed with the information about the meeting place, Gaius Claudius Nero marched his legions for six days to cut off Hasdrubal at the Metaurus River, surprising him and annihilating his entire army.

The Battle of Metaurus prevented Hannibal's troops from being reinforced, destroyed his chances of conquering Rome, and set the stage for Publius Cornelius Scipio Africanus to invade North Africa and draw Hannibal out of Italy. The war ended when Scipio defeated Hannibal at the Battle of Zama in 202 BC.

When Livy had finished his speech, all applauded, and Octavian said, "The lecture was wonderful, thank you. But, perhaps, next time you can tell us about the accomplishments of the Julians."

"Of course, Caesar," Livy said as he bowed.

Hearing about the great history of the Claudians reignited Tiberius' resentment toward his father. He wanted to get away from everyone and went outside into the garden, thinking about his heritage and his illustrious ancestors. He pictured their death masks mounted in the antechambers of the Claudian homes. He couldn't accept that his father had betrayed the Claudian honor by allowing Octavian to take his wife without a fight.

Later that night when his mother came to his room, Tiberius, still resentful and angry, didn't want to talk to her and pretended to be asleep. After she left, he pounded the mattress with his fist, asking questions out loud to an imaginary audience. *What kind of man would give away his wife? Couldn't he have fought to keep her? How could he do it without a fight or even a protest? The Claudians were the most powerful family in Rome. They were there at the founding of the Republic; they represented the great traditions of Rome. They had thousands of tenants and clients loyal to them. My father should have put up a fight.*

He half-remembered the day his mother left his father's house to live with Octavian. He was only three at the time, and although he didn't remember much else from that age, he was always sure that he really remembered his mother leaving. Whether it was a real or an imagined memory, it was with him always, and the thought of it made him angry. He had pictured the wedding many times, with his father giving Livia away to Octavian as though he was her father, not her husband. Tiberius swore to himself that he would never be humiliated that way.

◆

The next morning, Tiberius stopped at Menelaus' house and asked him what he thought of Livy's lecture.

"It was certainly very good, and very detailed," Menelaus said. "But, you know, he has to paint the history of Rome in glowing terms. He has no choice. He wouldn't be invited to speak at all the major houses of Rome again if he didn't."

"I was amazed at how he memorized all the speeches," Tiberius said.

"That's because he wrote them."

"What do you mean?"

"Livy recreates the speeches that he puts in his histories. Don't get me wrong. They're very good. But he couldn't know exactly what the senators said. The Senate notes were sparse, so he has to speculate about what was said. I think he gets very close to the truth, but he embellishes the language. As you'll notice, his speeches, though from different eras, sound similar, with the same rhythms."

"You think he makes them up?"

"No, I'm not saying that. He paints a picture of the past as best he can, based on the information we have. His great contribution is making history so interesting, more like stories with lessons, very valuable lessons."

"You don't do that," Tiberius said.

"No. I'm afraid I have a more mundane style and a skeptical approach. I see victories, but I also see defeats. I think we can learn more from being realistic than by gilding the past."

Tiberius left Menelaus' house and continued down the Palatine Hill to the Campus Martius for a training session with Barbonius. A dozen boys would participate in a strenuous session of running sprints, throwing javelins, and carrying boulders. Tiberius thrived on the training. He had grown to above average height, with wide, muscular shoulders. His hair grew down to the nape of his neck, in the Claudian tradition. When he smiled, he was handsome, but he frowned more often than he smiled. People told him that he should smile more.

During the training Tiberius kept thinking about asking his mother about who his real father was. It was clearly a difficult question for her, but he was determined to get an answer. He asked Barbonius if he could end the lesson early so that he could see his mother before she left the house. Barbonius always kept to a rigid schedule. "Can't you talk to her later?"

"No, she's going out," Tiberius said. "It's important."

"Well, if you complete all of your exercises, you can leave when you're done."

"Alright," Tiberius said, and he pointed to one of the other boys in training. "Let's do the clash and sweep exercise." Within two seconds, he had swept the boy to the ground.

The boy jumped up, "Let's try that again."

"No," Tiberius said. "Do the overhead block and thrust." With his right hand the boy swung his wooden sword overhead. Tiberius blocked it with his shield, spun the boy's arm around, pulled him off balance, then thrust his wooden sword to the boy's shoulder, hurting him slightly.

That done, he turned to two other boys, tripped them both, and pretended to thrust his sword into their chests.

Barbonius watched the exercises and gave Tiberius permission to leave.

Carrying his wooden sword and shield, Tiberius walked up the Palatine to the domus. He found his mother sitting in the atrium, spinning yarn. Here was the first lady of Rome, doing as she always had done, even in desperate and dangerous times. It calmed her.

"Mother, may I talk to you?" Livia was an extraordinarily beautiful woman, but it was not simply her beauty that earned her praise. She was considered the ideal Roman woman—decent, loyal, and honorable. In public she always wore the *stola*, the long wraparound dress that was the symbol of feminine modesty. She was noble but at the same time approachable, an understanding counselor, who either could instruct a person, or chastise him, without humiliating him.

"Of course."

"I wanted to ask you about something."

"I know. Menelaus told me."

"He did?"

"Of course. And you are indeed Tiberius Claudius Nero's son," she said.

"Yes. But why did he divorce you?"

"What Claudius Nero did, he had to do," Livia said. "Your step-father was like a charging bull with sharpened horns. No one could defy him. If Claudius had tried, he would have lost everything—all his property and your property. He was protecting me, and he was protecting you."

That was a powerful argument, but Tiberius wasn't satisfied. "He could've assembled an army from his tenants and clients."

"Your father already tried that and lost."

"What do you mean?"

"I mean, the civil war was terrible. Everyone was afraid. The *populare* and plebeian parties were demanding radical changes, and the *optimates* were fighting to keep the status quo. Anyone aligned with the losing side could be destroyed even if they hadn't fought in battle. It didn't matter how illustrious your family was."

Livia stood, put her arm around Tiberius' waist, and they walked him into the garden. "My father, your grandfather, Marcus Livius Drusus Claudianus, sided with the assassins. He was with the *optimates* Brutus and Cassius at Philippi. On the day you were born, we learned that he had been killed in battle. Not killed, actually. Seeing that the battle was lost, like Brutus, he fell on his sword. He did the honorable thing."

"I didn't know that," Tiberius said. "Where was my father?"

"Fortunately, your father, instead of siding with the assassins, as your grandfather had, sided with the *populares* and the Caesarians led by Marc Antony and Octavian. He thought that siding with them would make him safe from the proscriptions. But later, when the civil war between Antony and Octavian began, your father's good fortune ran out. He thought Antony was the stronger of the two and made the mistake of going over to his side. Fighting broke out everywhere, and we were eventually trapped by Octavian and Agrippa at the hilltop town of Perusia in Umbria."

Tiberius was puzzled. "You said 'we were trapped,' what did you mean by 'we'?"

"I was there, and you were there. We got out before the onslaught. Fifty of us fled through an avenue of escape that had been left open for us."

"How old was I?"

"Just a baby, about a-year-and-a-half."

"Did I know what was happening?"

"You sensed something was wrong. You never stopped crying."

"Then what happened?"

"Octavian put your father on the proscription list, so we fled to Sicily. We weren't safe there, so we fled to Sparta in Greece. We had to. Anyone who caught your father could have killed him and collected a reward. Many good people were murdered. It was a very frightening time. Your father was afraid, not so much for himself, but for you and me."

"Were you safe in Sparta?"

"Not really. At one point, we were hiding, and you were crying so loudly you almost gave us away. We had to flee because there were gangs of soldiers looking for us. We escaped by running through a forest fire. My hair got singed by the flames."

Livia lips quivered. "The irony is that Octavian's men were chasing his future wife and step-son. We could've been killed, and he would've never known us."

Tiberius stared into space for a minute. "But how is it that everything turned out okay?"

"A peace treaty was arranged, and Octavian granted clemency to some of the people on the proscription lists, including your father. We returned to Rome. We were very fortunate. Cicero wasn't so fortunate. He was on a proscription list and was caught on his way to Greece and executed right there and then."

All this stunned Tiberius. It changed everything. He had heard that when Cicero was caught, they cut his tongue out, cut his hands off, and nailed them to the rostra in the Forum. This was the kind of fate that his father might have faced. Had he been too hard on his father? Judged him too harshly?

CHAPTER SIX

Tiberius tried for several days to ask Octavian for permission to begin wearing his toga *virilis*, but Octavian was too busy to see him, frustrating Tiberius, who took his frustrations out during a military training drill on the Campus Martius. While practicing hand-to-hand combat, he knocked three boys to the ground, one after another, and while throwing javelins, he threw one so far that it almost reached a crowd of onlookers. Barbonius shouted at him to be careful. "No matter who you are, if you hurt someone, they're entitled to compensation. That's the law."

When the training drill was over, Barbonius told Tiberius to be more careful, and also that Octavian was holding a meeting at a nearby conference hall. The meeting was about changes being made to the Praetorian Guard. Instead of the Praetorians being dispersed outside of Rome to protect generals in the provinces, they were going to be the personal guard of the *princeps*, stationed in and around Rome.

Seeing an opportunity, Tiberius went directly to the conference hall hoping to see Octavian. He waited outside until the meeting ended and the participants began to leave, then he walked into the hall and approached his step-father, "Father, may I talk to you for a moment?" Octavian was surprised to see him, and looked angry for a second before he smiled.

"You're getting bigger every time I see you."

"Yes, I am. And I'm ready to wear the white toga and assume the rights of manhood. May I?"

Octavian thought for a moment. "Tomorrow we're going for a ride south with the Praetorian cavalry. It will be arduous. Are you up to it?"

"Yes. What time?"

"Dawn. Tell your mother."

At dawn, Tiberius was ready to go even though he hadn't slept much during the night worrying about waking up on time. Livia had packed a lunch basket for him. "I don't want that," Tiberius said. "The soldiers will laugh at me."

"No, they won't," Livia said. "Put it in your knapsack."

Horses were brought up to the domus. Octavian, Tiberius, and ten Praetorian Guards mounted and then rode down to the Via Sacra and through the south gate to the Circus Maximus where a hundred more Praetorian Guards were waiting for them. They joined up and galloped south on the Appian Way, four abreast, with Augustus and Tiberius in the middle of the formation.

"Father, where are we going?" Tiberius asked

"To the coastal town of Antium to dedicate a temple to Apollo," Octavian said. "Do you know how far this road goes?"

"It goes all the way to Brundisium on the Adriatic coast," Tiberius said proudly. "My great ancestor Appius Claudius Crassus built it almost three hundred years ago."

Octavian looked sideways at Tiberius as though examining his motive for saying that the way he did. "Building it was a great achievement," Octavian said, "Appius Claudius was a great man."

Tiberius had studied maps and books about the Roman roads. The Appian Way was fifteen feet wide, paved with close-fitting basalt stones. It stretched from Rome southeast to Brundisium on the heel of Italy, for a total of six hundred kilometers. Other roads branched off it, reaching every region in Italy, and outside to the foothills of the Alps, Southern Gaul, the Iberian Peninsula, Macedon, and Greece. In all, eighteen roads radiated from Rome like the spokes of a wheel.

Galloping south, the cavalry kept up a steady rhythm. Tiberius, although a good rider, wasn't used to this pace for this long, but he kept up, exhilarated to be part of this elite contingent of Rome's best soldiers. He felt the history of Rome's forward march. It seemed that nothing could stop the Romans from spreading their power, their hegemony, and their law, culture, and religion.

After two hours of hard riding, Octavian called a halt, and everyone dismounted in front of a dilapidated building, a two-story inn that was undergoing repair as part of a plan to upgrade the Roman postal system.

During the Republic, Rome had a privately-run messenger system that used relay-stations spaced every twenty kilometers along the main roads. At some of the stations, like this one, inns were available for travelers to rest. Water was available for them and for their horses and oxen. When Octavian came to power, one of his first acts was to order the conversion of the private postal system to a public system, the *cursus publicus*. He wanted to improve its speed and efficiency.

While the soldiers tied their horses to a railing and relaxed, Octavian led Tiberius to the entrance of the inn and pointed to an oblong stone that had a chiseled inscription: "In memory of Publius Clodius Pulcher, Friend of the People, Murdered on this Spot."

"This is where your relative, Clodius, met his end," Octavian said almost triumphantly. "Milo's men chased him into that inn, dragged him out, and killed him."

"Every family has a black sheep," Tiberius said. "And when he changed his name from Claudius to Clodius, he was disowned."

"That was a good answer."

"I didn't know you were testing me," Tiberius said.

"You're a proud young man," Octavian said. "Rest here for a while. I have to take care of a few things."

Tiberius sat on a stone wall, opened his lunch basket, and began eating. He thought about Clodius, an ancestor who hadn't made the Claudians proud. An arrogant and unsavory character, Clodius was an associate of Julius Caesar. He could mobilize gangs and trade guilds for strikes and demonstrations. Tiberius' father said Clodius was the worst scoundrel that ever called himself a Roman. He thought Clodius represented the decay that was creeping into Rome and destroying its morals.

Tiberius' father had ranted about the scandal that had erupted when Pompeia, Julius Caesar's wife, hosted a religious ceremony of the Vestal Virgins at her residence. No men were allowed. But before the ceremony began, Clodius slipped into the house dressed as a woman and mixed with the guests. During the evening, he was found out and he fled. The story going around was that his purpose was to consort with Pompeia. As a result, Caesar, in his role as *pontiff maximus*, charged him with sacrilege, and a trial was held. Clodius claimed that the man who fled wasn't him, and that he was out of the city on the day in question. Cicero contradicted his alibi, testifying that he had met with him in the city on that same day. Despite Cicero's testimony, Clodius was acquitted, most likely through bribery.

Shortly afterwards, Caesar divorced Pompeia, proclaiming that there had been no consorting, but "Caesar's wife must be above suspicion."

Tiberius' father called Clodius effeminate. "What kind of Roman would dress up in women's clothes? What a disgrace. What would our ancestors say if they saw this kind of silliness? What would they say about all the promiscuity and all the divorces?"

On one occasion, Tiberius overheard his father talking with some men who claimed that Clodius slept with his sister Clodia.

When the soldiers got back on their horses, they galloped for another hour until they arrived at Antium. The townspeople were waiting for them in the town square. As Octavian rode into the town in front of the soldiers, the mayor welcomed him and the people cheered.

At the ceremony to dedicate the temple to Apollo, the cornerstone was laid, a priest recited a prayer, and a lamb was brought to the altar for sacrifice. Tiberius watched the priest lift a long, silver-plated knife over his head, and thrust it downward straight into the animal's heart. The lamb trembled and fell sideways without a whimper.

The townspeople provided a banquet of food and wine and mingled with the soldiers. Tiberius heard one of Octavian's legates talking to the mayor about confiscating farmland so that it could be given to soldiers who had been released from the legions. The legate asked the mayor to prepare a list of landowners who were suspected of siding with Antony.

Tiberius guessed that the real reason for the trip was not to dedicate the temple, but to intimidate the local authorities into identifying parcels of land for Octavian's soldiers. He noticed that although the town people acted in a friendly manner, there was an unmistakable sense of apprehension. When Octavian and the Praetorians departed, the people clearly were relieved.

On the way back to Rome, Octavian rode next to Tiberius. "I hear you've been studying history."

"Yes, I have. I enjoy it; lots of great stories."

"Tell me about my father," Octavian said.

Tiberius instinctively realized that this could be an important test for him. He knew a lot, and knew that Octavian's natural father was Gaius Octavius Thurinus, a wealthy plebeian senator, whom Octavian never mentioned. He only referred to his adoptive father, Julius Caesar, so Tiberius would only talk about Caesar. He had a lot he could say about him, some of it not complimentary, but he would avoid those parts of the story.

"Where should I begin?"

"Wherever you like."

He began a memorized speech: "Caesar first came to prominence when he married Cinna's daughter, Cornelia. This was the time when Cinna was in control of Rome and Sulla was still in the East fighting Mithridates. Fortunately for Caesar, he did not fight in the battles against Sulla, so he was not put on the proscription lists. But he was no fool, and fearing that his marriage to Cinna's daughter would mean he could be added to the list, he left Rome and joined a legion in Asia Minor, keeping a low profile until Sulla's retirement."

"Are you implying he was hiding from Sulla?" Octavian said.

"It was the smart thing to do," Tiberius said.

"He wasn't in hiding or afraid of Sulla," Octavian said. "In fact, when Sulla insisted that he divorce Cornelia, he refused, demonstrating his courage and independence, like a true Julian. Nobody was more courageous in the face of danger than Caesar. As a young man sailing in the Mediterranean, his ship was captured by pirates who demanded a ransom of twenty talents for him. He told them that he was worth fifty talents, not twenty. For thirty-eight days as a captive, he conducted himself as though he were still in command, joking with the pirates and ordering them about. When the ransom money arrived and he was released, he announced that he would come back and crucify them all. His captors laughed.

"Not long after, he came back with ships and captured the pirates. He delivered them to a prison at Pergamum where he had them crucified as he had promised, though he exercised a degree of mercy by ordering that their throats be cut first."

Tiberius realized that he had displeased his step-father and sensed that to say anything even remotely negative about Caesar was risking his wrath.

"Yes, he was never needlessly cruel," he said.

"He was never cruel," Octavian said. "He did what he had to do to save the nation. Continue."

"When Caesar returned to Rome, he entered the political arena," Tiberius said, "and at the funeral of his aunt Julia, he displayed the images of her husband Marius, which had been hidden since their disfavor in the reign of Sulla. This was a courageous act that sent a strong message about where Caesar stood."

"Right, tell me more."

Tiberius began again, but Octavian interrupted him. "I have a better idea. We're having a dinner on the first of the month. Livy will be there to give another one of his lectures. You know that he never talks about anything unless it's about something that happened more than a century ago. Since you know history so well, why don't you give a talk about the Julians, and you can bring us up to date?"

"I'm a Claudian."

"That's good. You can give an objective assessment. It will be a fine introduction to public life for you, and it will be great practice among friends. It will be your coming-out speech."

"Won't I be stepping on Livy's toes?"

"That's alright. We'll let him follow up. And it will put him on the spot. He'll have to address recent history."

"Well, in his defense, older history is more complete and an historian can study it with full hindsight," Tiberius said.

"Menelaus taught you that."

"Yes."

"Older history is good, but you need to study more recent history, too," Octavian said. "Let me ask you something. Does your study of the past tell you what we should do about the standards that Crassus lost to the Parthians? Should we retrieve them?"

Tiberius knew the importance of military standards. Legions, cohorts, and centuries carried standards, which originally were flags used in battle to communicate rallying points and signal tactics and formations. The standard bearer lowered, raised, or pointed the standard to signal orders from the commander. Over time, the standards became symbols of pride, and soldiers would fight to the death to protect them. This pride encouraged the soldiers to fight as an indivisible team alongside their comrades in arms. Unity among the legionaries discouraged flight and lessened the sudden panic that often overwhelms individuals facing death. The soldiers fought because those around them fought. A soldier's confidence in his comrades, knowing that they wouldn't panic and flee, strengthened his own resolve, and the resolve of the legionaries was the basis of Rome's military success.

Tiberius began to say something but was startled to see the walls of Rome ahead. He had been so engrossed in the conversation that he had not paid attention to how far they had come.

"We're back already," he said.

"Yes, we're back. So, what's your advice about the standards?" Octavian asked.

"I'd have to think about that before giving you a good answer," Tiberius said.

"You're definitely a smart young man," Octavian said.

Tiberius felt the conversation ended well. He was elated to think that although he hadn't even come of age yet, he had conversed, on equal terms, with the most powerful man in the world.

As they dismounted at the south gate, Octavian said, "I'm looking forward to your coming-out speech. Don't let me down."

CHAPTER SEVEN

For two days after the ride to Antium, Tiberius' muscles were sore. He had ridden horses around the Circus Maximus and the Campus Martius for some time, but he had never ridden on a journey as arduous as the one he had just taken. Julia laughed at the way he was walking, and teased him by daring him to catch her. Drusus laughed at him and challenged him to a race. "I can beat you any day of the week."

"Have your fun while you can," Tiberius said. "I don't have time to play kids' games, I've got work to do." He went to his room to get a handful of scrolls and notebooks, and took them to a bench in an alcove in the garden. The alcove was surrounded by high, thick bushes and a trellis covered in vines.

He worked on the speech he was to give at the dinner with Livy, writing it and practicing it out loud, trying to make it perfect. He studied the scrolls and notebooks, but he also thought about what he would say to his step-father about invading Parthia. He didn't know too much about Parthia. He'd go to Menelaus to find out.

As he thought about what to say, he was interrupted by voices coming from another alcove not too far off to the left. He parted the bushes to see who it was, but he couldn't see anyone. He left the alcove, and walked toward the voices. He recognized Julia's voice but not the other.

As he got closer, he heard her, "You can kiss me here on the neck."

"Leave me alone," the other person said, and Tiberius realized that it was Drusus.

Tiberius pushed the bushes aside and entered the alcove. "What's going on?"

"Nothing," Drusus said, clearly embarrassed.

"Oh. It's you," Julia said. "What do you want?"

"I want you to behave yourself, and stop teasing Drusus. He is your brother, you know."

"He's only my step-brother."

"No matter who he is, you should behave yourself."

"It's none of your business," Julia said.

"If you don't stop your nonsense," Tiberius said, "you're going to find yourself in a lot of trouble."

"Who made you the lord and master around here?" Julia said.

Tiberius turned to Drusus, "A word to the wise."

Drusus walked back to the house with Julia following him. Tiberius thought of what Julia had said and realized that if Octavian was Drusus' real father, then Drusus and Julia were half brother and sister by blood.

The next day, Tiberius went to Menelaus' house. "Can I talk to you about something?"

"Of course, Come in," Menelaus said.

It was a small house. The main room had several tables and desks, all cluttered with scrolls, boxes, and papyruses.

"What do you want to know?"

"On the ride back from Antium, Octavian told me that Livy has been invited to give another speech at the domus."

"If he's invited, he'll attend."

"Octavian also wants me to give a speech about recent Julian history."

Menelaus was surprised. "That's quite an honor."

"Will you help me write it?"

"Of course."

"I'm already nervous."

"Don't worry about it." Menelaus said, "You know more history than the whole crowd of them, except, of course, Livy. We'll put something together."

"He also asked my opinion about whether Rome should retrieve the standards that Crassus lost to the Parthians."

"That's a tough question. What did you say?"

"I said I'd have to think about it."

"Good answer."

"But I'm sure he's going to ask me again."

"Yes, let's think about this." Menelaus took a chair and motioned for Tiberius to take a seat next to him.

Menelaus leaned back and thought for a moment. "We know Crassus invaded Parthian territory to prove he was a military commander as great as Caesar and Pompey," he said. "But he shouldn't have gone."

"That's not the question," Tiberius said. "The question is what should we do now?"

Menelaus smiled at what from any other student would have been impertinence. "You're right, but first you need to know what's brought us to where we are today."

Menelaus moved to a desk, and, using a stylus and a sheath of papyrus, made notes as he talked. "Let's draw up an outline of what points we'll cover. First, before you get to the Parthians, emphasize the best of Julius Caesar's career and how much he accomplished. Remember, you must also mention some small setbacks, otherwise they'll think you're a sycophant. Then you can talk about bringing back the standards. And it's important to remember that Caesar was preparing to invade Parthia when he was assassinated. Octavian should take heed of that."

"Yes. But should we invade or not?" Tiberius asked.

"I can advise, but I can't make that decision for you. Let's list the pros and cons, then you decide," Menelaus said.

They spent the rest of the day talking about Parthia and working on the outline of his speech. Every day for the next two weeks, Tiberius went to Menelaus' house to practice it. Some days, he brought Pometius with him to listen to the speech as it developed. Finally, he felt that he was well prepared.

Tiberius' speech was to be given at the Julian-Claudian domus where most of the imperial family and friends would be present. After dinner, the group moved to the atrium where couches were arranged in rows. Octavian, Livia, and Octavia were seated together on the first couch in front of the speaker's rostrum. On the couch behind them were the young people—Drusus, Julia, and Marcellus. Then came several senators and their wives.

On the right side of the room was the great general, Marcus Agrippa, Octavian's life-long friend and right-hand man. On the left side was Gaius Maecenas, another life-long friend, confidant, and advisor, who was a wealthy equestrian and a patron of the poets Virgil and Horace. Sitting with him was Livy.

Barbonius, Menelaus, and a few freedmen were in the back of the room.

Octavian stood. "We have a special occasion this evening. Before our honored guest, Titus Livius, speaks, my step-son Tiberius, who will put on his white toga in a few weeks, will give us a short history of the accomplishments of the Julian clan."

When Octavian nodded, Tiberius promptly stood up and began his lecture. He began with the story of Caesar's capture by the pirates and his return to fulfill his promise to capture them. It was well received, and when Tiberius said that Caesar showed mercy by cutting the pirates throats before crucifying them, the audience laughed and applauded.

Taking Menelaus' advice, he made only brief mention of the First Triumvirate of Caesar, Pompey, and Crassus. He skipped to the Gallic Wars, explaining that as proconsul, Caesar conducted perhaps the most astounding military and political campaign in history, defeating several large and formidable Gallic and Germanic tribes.

Tiberius explained that the Gallic tribes viewed one another as adversaries. By dividing and conquering them, Caesar established Rome's domination over Gaul and extended Rome's reach to the Great Ocean. He was not only a great military tactician, but also a brilliant diplomat and an astute manager of people. His superb oratorical skills and the pure force of his personality won the loyalty of his troops. On several occasions, his self-confidence made the difference between victory and defeat. Remarkable, too, were his construction and engineering projects, which were unmatched in history.

Tiberius paused for a moment then said that Caesar's success was not necessarily permanent. The Gauls had learned that divided they could not resist Rome, and Vercingetorix, the king of the Arverni tribe of southern Gaul, emerged to unite them. He was a gifted and imposing chieftain, and traveled the country to organize a coalition of more than twelve Gallic tribes to revolt against Roman rule. He had closely studied Roman tactics and designed ways to defeat them. With a united tribal army, he invaded the Roman province of Narboensis, cut off the Roman armies from one another, blocked roads, and set fire to farms and villages in a scorched-earth campaign to prevent the Romans from obtaining supplies.

Vercingetorix won battles and came close to defeating Caesar. But when he entrenched his army of 80,000 soldiers in Alesia, a fortified town in central Gaul that stood on a plateau and seemed impregnable, Caesar built a siege wall surrounding the town that was twelve-feet-high and eleven miles long. The wall was topped with a walkway and turrets every eighty feet. But without enough men to occupy the entire fortification, Caesar devised other means to contain the Gauls, digging deep trenches and filling them with water that he had diverted from a nearby river. Behind the trenches, he built palisades augmented with pits, sharpened stakes, and traps. To protect his army from the Gallic reinforcements that were sure to come to relieve Vercingetorix, he built additional walls and fortifications behind his army. It was one of military history's most astounding feats.

Meanwhile, inside the town, Vercingetorix was running low on provisions. To preserve food for his fighting force, he expelled the women, children, and elderly. These people had no choice but to approach the Roman lines to offer themselves as slaves in return for food. When Caesar turned them away, and Vercingetorix wouldn't allow them back into the town, they camped outside the walls where many starved to death.

Soon a Gallic army of tens of thousands arrived to relieve the siege and attack the Romans from the rear. At that moment, Vercingetorix sent his soldiers out to fill up the Roman trenches with branches and earth so that they could charge at the Romans. Three days of ferocious fighting followed until the fortunes of war shifted in favor of Caesar.

Vercingetorix was unable to break the siege and with his soldiers facing starvation, he capitulated. Wearing his best shining armor, he rode out of the town alone to the Roman camp to surrender himself. Caesar chastised him, chained him, and sent him to Rome where he was eventually executed at one of Caesar's triumphs.

Tiberius finished his lecture saying, "After subjugating Gaul, Caesar built a bridge across the Rhine and invaded Germany to discourage the tribes there from invading Gaul. He then turned his attention west, built a fleet, and twice crossed the sea to invade Britain, planting the seeds of a Roman colony."

The audience applauded, and Octavian smiled and said, "That was an excellent presentation. You've got a great career ahead of you in the Senate. Let's open the floor up for discussion. Livy, what did you think?"

Livy responded, "It was a wonderful narrative, but I think, perhaps, we should talk about the civil war between your father and Pompey the Great, and what led up to it."

"Go right ahead," Octavian said.

Livy stood up and explained that the time leading up to Caesar's assassination was a time of turmoil. "After Pompey the Great suppressed the riots in the wake of Clodius' death, Pompey's star continued to rise with the *optimates*, and Caesar's declined. A block of *optimate* senators, led by Cato the Younger, announced that they would prosecute Caesar for what he had done during his earlier consulship. However, while he held imperium, he could not be prosecuted."

Tiberius was surprised that Livy would talk about such recent history, particularly such controversial history. But Livy continued, "For Caesar, it was imperative that he win the next election for consul to avoid a break in his imperium and the loss of immunity from prosecution that came with it. The dilemma he faced was that his governorship of Gaul was scheduled to end, but no one could run for consul from outside Rome, so he proposed to run for consul *in absentia* while keeping command of his army. A year of negotiations and political intrigue followed. Caesar sent a letter to the Senate promising that if his demand was met, he would disband his soldiers. When Pompey was asked his opinion of Caesar's promise, he famously replied that 'actions speak louder than words.' As expected, the Senate rejected the proposal and did not renew Caesar's command or allow him to run for consul *in absentia*.

"The Senate passed a *senatus consultum ultimatum*, an emergency decree, authorizing Pompey to take control of all the legions, including Caesar's legions, and to take whatever actions necessary to protect the Republic. The Senate ordered Caesar to retire his command and return to Rome, decreeing that if he refused to comply, he would be judged an enemy of the Republic."

At that point in Livy's speech, Tiberius noticed that Octavian didn't look pleased. Nevertheless, Livy continued, "When Caesar learned of the *senatus consultum ultimatum*, he was infuriated that the Senate had disregarded all the conquests he had made in the name of Rome; and it was clear that he was in personal jeopardy. With his most loyal troops, he crossed the Rubicon River. This was a gamble for either survival or destruction, and as he gave the order to cross, he said loud enough for all to hear, 'The die is cast.'

"Caesar had eleven legions that were fresh from their battles in Gaul, confident in both their superiority and invincibility. On the other side, Pompey had seven legions in Spain and two in Italy, but since his veterans, although loyal, hadn't fought in twelve years, he retreated to Greece to enlist reinforcements from among his allies.

"With Rome abandoned by Pompey, Caesar entered the city, solidifying his authority through both force and clemency. He had the twenty-two remaining senators appoint him as temporary dictator, declared martial law, and forcibly seized the treasury. When a tribune protested that the seizure was against the law, Caesar responded, 'Laws and arms have each their own time. If you don't like what I am doing, get out: war doesn't permit of free speech. When I've finished the war, and made peace, come back and talk as much as you like.'"

Tiberius was surprised again that Livy would say something so controversial and that could reflect so poorly on Caesar. He could tell that Octavian even less pleased.

Livy noticed that, too, so he switched to more positive points. "On the conciliatory side, he released many whom he had captured in return for their oath not to take up arms against him. Liberally dispensing clemency helped Caesar win the public over to his side and many recruits joined his camp. Of course, he knew that public sentiment would swing to the one who proved his point by military victories, and in a surprise move, instead of following Pompey to Greece, he led his troops to Spain. His plan was to fight Pompey's allies there and prevent them from joining Pompey. As he set out, he said, 'I am off to meet an army without a leader; when I return, I shall meet a leader without an army.'

"Caesar fought several battles in Spain, maneuvered Pompey's generals into an unfavorable position, and sent word to Pompey's troops that, in exchange for surrender, they would receive clemency and a discharge from the legions. The troops demanded that their generals accept the surrender terms, and the generals had no choice but to agree."

Agrippa interjected, "I think that was Caesar greatest gift, gaining an advantage and then negotiating a settlement to avoid unnecessary bloodshed."

"Very true," Livy said. "With Spain secured, Caesar returned to Rome. He took the initiative, and in December, rather than waiting for Pompey to invade Italy, he transported his army of 26,000 across the hazardous winter seas to Greece where Pompey was waiting with twice as many soldiers.

"After several skirmishes, the two armies finally clashed near Pharsalus in an enormous battle. Caesar's forces won a decisive victory. When Pompey realized that the battle was lost, he fled to his tent where he was found by his aides dazed and disconsolate. He had never lost a battle before. His aides whisked him away, and he fled to Egypt where he believed he had allies. When he arrived at Egypt, his ship anchored off shore. He saw what he thought was an Egyptian welcoming committee waiting on the beach. He left his wife and son on the ship and with three guards took a rowboat to the beach. When he landed, the welcoming committee assassinated him within sight of his wife and son.

"Unaware of Pompey's death, Caesar followed him to Egypt intending to capture him. Pompey's death made the trip unnecessary and he could have returned to Rome. However, while in Egypt, he became involved in a power struggle for the Egyptian throne between Cleopatra and her brother Ptolemy III. Caesar sided with Cleopatra.

"And you know the rest of that story. Thank you," he said as he sat down to applause.

Octavian stood. "Perhaps, there are some questions?" No one responded.

"What about you, Tiberius?" Octavian said, moving his open hand up as though to say "stand."

Tiberius stood at his seat. "I have a few questions. First, why didn't Pompey make a stand at Rome? Giving up the city without a fight made him look weak. And it gave Caesar the advantage of being in lawful control of the city."

"That's a good point, my boy," Livy said.

"He's not going to be a boy much longer," Octavian said. The audience laughed.

"Yes, I can see that," Livy said. "And he's absolutely right. Pompey should never have abandoned Rome. He should have stayed secure behind the walls, and should have called for reinforcements from around the empire. And your second question?"

Tiberius stood again. "Do you think that if Caesar hadn't crossed the Rubicon and seized sole power, someone else would have seized power?"

"That's hard to say," Livy answered.

"I mean," Tiberius said, "Was it time for a change from a republic to a single strong leader or did the change come about simply because of the will of Caesar?"

"Interesting question, I think the former," Livy said. "One person or one event doesn't change the direction of history but a combination of many factors establishes the trend. One person isn't enough. Apparently, the hidden hand of history determined that it was time for the Republic to have a strong leader. If it was not Caesar, I believe someone else would have filled the leadership vacuum."

Tiberius did not fully agree with the idea that history is beyond the control of individual men. On the contrary, he thought that it wasn't general events and trends that made history but the will of powerful men. He thought Caesar was destined to assume absolute power, and particular events along the way could have changed, but the end result would have been the same. The question was always who among the leading citizens would gain supremacy over the others. His step-father Octavian had succeeded and Tiberius took some pride in that; however, his real father had lost, and that still gnawed at him. He chose not to voice his opinion, but changing the subject, he asked another question. "Was the empire too big to be ruled by a senate from Rome, a senate that tended to debate for months before making a decision?"

"Debate is good when the issues are confined to a manageable topic," Livy said. "But, you're right. With the empire so big, there may be too many diverse interests and opposing factions to settle issues. That's why one-man rule or a small unified committee is more efficient than a large body of debaters."

Octavian stood, "Thank you both for explaining Caesar's story so well."

Tiberius thought that Octavian had signaled the end of the lecture, but Gaius Maecenas spoke for the first time, addressing Tiberius. "You didn't tell us how the First Triumvirate was formed."

Tiberius looked to Octavian to see whether he should continue, and Octavian nodded for him to continue. So, he repeated the history of the First Triumvirate that Menelaus had taught him: "Pompey joined the alliance of Caesar and Crassus, and the three agreed to support one another's interests and divide control of the empire between them. To cement their ties, Pompey married Caesar's daughter Julia, and Caesar married the daughter of a close associate of Pompey. The three-way partnership was called the First Triumvirate, though it was not an official body. However, the triumvirate collapsed seven years after it was formed when Crassus was killed invading Parthian territory."

Octavian said, "Probably what was more important was that Julia died in childbirth. The child also died. He would have been Pompey's son and Caesar's grandson. This was a great loss that gravely weakened the alliance.

"My father attempted to reaffirm the alliance with Pompey, offering another member of his family to be Pompey's next wife. Pompey rejected the offer and instead sold the people out, marrying into the heart of the *optimate* nobility, aligning himself with the old-line reactionaries rather than his triumvirate partner. Everything might have been different, but speculation about the past doesn't solve today's problems."

At that moment, Tiberius was struck by another point. He thought that if Julia's son, Caesar's grandson, hadn't died, Caesar wouldn't have adopted Octavian. And it follows that Octavian would not have been in such a powerful position to demand that Nero divorce Livia. He would not have married Livia, would not have become Tiberius' step-father, and a thousand more other "would-not-haves" would have followed.

He thought about how chance events could change the course of history. Even, small, seemingly insignificant events, can cause people to act in ways they otherwise would not have. How can anyone claim to predict the future, when random, unexpected, unseen events can change the course of the world?

Tiberius began to say something about that but thought better of it. He said only, "Studying the past can help solve today's problems."

"Indeed, it does," Octavian said. "But as for the present, I've asked you this before. Should we retrieve the standards that Crassus lost to the Parthians? Have you thought about it?"

Everyone in the room was astounded that Octavian would ask a boy such a question. Roman leaders usually asked such questions of generals, priests, or augurs.

No one spoke. They looked to Tiberius, who answered, "Yes, I have, and I would advise against it."

Gaius Maecenus laughed out loud, and continued laughing as if a great joke had been made.

Agrippa said, "What's so funny?"

"Are we to make decisions on the word of a fourteen-year-old boy," Maecenas said, "even such a precocious one?"

"Why don't you hear him out before you laugh at him," Agrippa said.

"I'm listening," Maecenas said. "Should we or should we not? Isn't it important to get our standards back?"

"It is important. But you remember Crassus was annihilated in the East because he was overconfident and his troops weren't prepared for the scorching desert," Tiberius said. "Unless you find a way to beat the desert, it could be a disaster. Marc Antony found that out. He was lucky to retreat with his life when he invaded Parthia."

"So, young man," Maecenas said. "You just want to abandon the standards? You don't want to avenge the disaster?"

Everyone was staring at Tiberius. He was not intimidated and leaned toward Maecenas, "If it's going to cost fifty thousand of our soldiers, it's not worth it. Find some other way to get the standards back. Hire some barbarian desert army to get them back. Let them fight amongst themselves, and when they finish killing each other, we'll pick up the pieces, and our standards."

Agrippa said, "He makes a lot of sense. Maybe we should listen to fourteen-year-olds more often."

Octavian stood up and smiled. "I agree," he said. "And congratulations young man. I'm proud of you."

Octavian asked Menelaus to come up front, put his hand on his shoulder, and said "And I also want to congratulate you, Menelaus, for having taught Tiberius the lessons of history so well."

CHAPTER EIGHT

The Toga *Virilis*

On the day he was to wear the pure white toga *viriles* of a Roman citizen for the first time, Tiberius collected his childhood toys and placed them at the altar of the household god, Lares, at the front of the domus. He left them there as a sign that he was leaving his childhood behind and becoming a man. He took off the *bulla* amulet from around his neck, the one that boys wore as protection against evil spirits, and put on his new toga that had been perfectly measured for him.

All the members of the household watched him leave the domus and walk with Octavian to the Tabularum Registry in the Forum to have his name entered on the citizenship rolls.

Walking with them were Octavian's *lictors*, guards, each holding a *fasces* on his shoulder (a *fasces* was an ax surrounded by a bundle of wooden rods that symbolized the imperium power to judge and punish). Consuls had six lictors; Octavian's superior imperium authorized him to have twelve, as temporary dictators had in the past.

Outside the Tabularum, a large group of people gathered and cheered. Octavian raised Tiberius' arm, and together they waved to the crowd. When they went inside, all the clerks stood at attention as Tiberius signed the registry book.

Tiberius considered this a solemn event, and kept a serious expression. When he turned after signing the book, he was surprised by Octavian's hand on his shoulder. "Come on," Octavian said. "You can smile. This isn't a funeral."

Tiberius smiled, but it wasn't genuine.

"I don't know what we're going to do with you," Octavian said.

They returned to the domus, and later that morning Tiberius overheard Livia and Octavian in the atrium making up the guest list for the banquet in his honor. The list began with Marcus Agrippa. Tiberius was glad that Agrippa was the first name on the list. If he admired anyone, it was him. Although Agrippa didn't have the lineage of an elite family, he had attained the highest honors because of his hard work and merit. A robust, no-nonsense, get-things-done type, he possessed all the attributes of a great leader and was most responsible for the defeat of Antony and Cleopatra at the Battle of Actium. It was well known that Octavian had taken sick during the battle though no one spoke aloud of that.

Next on the list was Octavia, the princeps' older sister. With the exception of Livia, she was the most respected matron of Rome. She had led an eventful but not always happy life. In 55 BC, at fifteen, she was married to Gaius Claudius Marcellus, a member of the Claudian family. They were happily married for a year until her great uncle Julius Caesar asked her to divorce her husband and marry Pompey the Great.

This was thought to be necessary because Caesar's daughter Julia, who had been married to Pompey to solidify the alliance of the First Triumvirate, had died in childbirth. To preserve this alliance, Caesar asked Octavia marry Pompey.

It would be a crucial decision. If she said no, it would incur the anger of Caesar and have an adverse effect on her husband's career. Octavia nevertheless refused, and she and Marcellus stayed together. They had three children. Unfortunately, in 40 BC, Marcellus died. Now, Marcellus, Jr., was ready to wear the toga *virilis* of manhood.

As a widow, Octavia became highly valued in the game of marital alliances, and, at Octavian's request, she married Marc Antony to solidify the alliance of the Second Triumvirate. The marriage took place even though it was widely known that Antony had been consorting with Cleopatra and had children with her. It was assumed that he would end that relationship.

Octavia was an upstanding woman, who, like Livia, always wore the *stola* in public. Having lived a dignified life, she and Antony seemed to be a mismatch. He had lived his life flagrantly disregarding conventions. In addition to Cleopatra, Antony consorted with actresses and dancers. Nonetheless, Octavia had a strong influence on him, and often played the role of peacemaker between Antony and Octavian, helping to bring calm when military conflict seemed imminent. She even helped broker a peace treaty between the two men.

She raised seven children: three from her marriage with Marcellus, two step-children from Antony's previous marriage, and two daughters from her marriage with Antony. But while she continued raising the children, Antony continued spending his time in the East with Cleopatra. People said he was under some mystical Egyptian spell.

In 32 BC, Antony divorced Octavia, breaking the alliance with Octavian and precipitating the civil war that ended with the Battle of Actium and, eventually, Antony and Cleopatra's suicides.

—————◆—————

Octavian and Livia continued discussing the guest list.

"Maybe we should have the banquets for Tiberius and Marcellus at the same time," Octavian said. "They're cousins and both the same age."

Livia shook her head. "That would diminish the event for Tiberius."

"It shouldn't. I think it will strengthen their relationship."

"Whatever you wish," Livia said.

"Good. It's agreed. We'll celebrate their coming of age together."

Also on the guest list was the adviser, Gaius Maecenus. Tiberius didn't like him. He thought of him as a political schemer, less interested in the nation's success than in collecting fine objects and literary men. Tiberius' dislike of him had grown since Maecenas laughed at him during his coming-out speech.

Several prominent senators who had been helpful to Octavian were invited, along with other senators who hadn't been so helpful but were too important to ignore.

Livia asked Octavian about inviting Tiberius' relatives from his father's side, the Claudian Neronian branch of the family.

"As few as possible," Octavian said.

"But they're his blood relatives," Livia said.

"Blood relatives who delayed coming to my side for as long as they could"

"As you wish."

After a pause, Livia asked, "What about my relatives from the Claudian Drusii side?"

"Some of them were not exactly my friends either," Octavian said.

"It's true that my father sided with Brutus and Cassius, but Tiberius' father sided with you."

"But later he sided with Fulvia and Antony against me."

"Darling," Livia took his hand in hers, "those were difficult times. People didn't know what to do. You can't blame them. You can't take it personally. People made the best decisions they could for themselves and their families. They didn't know who would come out on top. A few chance occurrences, a few surprise turns, and it could have been Antony, not you."

Octavian stared into Livia's eyes. She stared back until he said, "I suppose you're right."

"And we need to unify the Republic; we need all the allies we can get," she said. "There's no telling what's going to happen, some new catastrophe could come along tomorrow."

Octavian nodded, "Invite whomever you think best."

◆————◆————◆

At the banquet for Tiberius and Marcellus, dozens of guests gathered at the Julian-Claudian domus. As they arrived, they were entertained by musicians, jugglers, and acrobats.

The guests were assigned by name to couches in the large banquet room. There was an exact order to the seating arrangements. Octavian and Livia sat together on the main couch. On the couch to their right sat Agrippa with his wife, Claudia Marcella. With them was Agrippa's daughter from a previous marriage, Vipsania Agrippina, who was eleven.

Tiberius sat across from Agrippa and Vipsania. No one else knew it, but Octavian and Agrippa had secretly betrothed Vipsania to Tiberius. The arrangement was made when Vipsania was a one-year-old. Now she was eleven, and the fathers were only waiting for the right moment to make the arrangement public.

On Octavian and Livia's left sat Octavia and Julia. Across from them sat Marcus Marcellus, the other honoree. Marcellus didn't know it, but in another secret arrangement, Octavian and Octavia had agreed to betroth Julia to him even thought they were cousins.

On a couch farther to the left sat Maecenas and his portly poet friend, Horace. Maecenas had rescued Horace from financial ruin after the poet had been proscribed for writing favorably of the assassins. He lost his property for it, but Maecenas, because he appreciated Horace's poetry and wit, secured his amnesty and bought him a country villa

When the speeches began, Octavian, Livia, and Octavia talked about the young men, their fine character, good manners, and loyalty to their families. Octavian praised Tiberius' learning. "He has taught me a few things about our history, and about my own, some of it not so complimentary."

Octavian praised Marcellus in the highest terms, talking about his considerable talents and the good he would do for Rome in the future, saying that "Marcellus has all the strength of character and ability to lead Rome to new heights."

Horace gave a speech. He began by reciting lines from his poems, including his most famous line: "It is sweet and glorious to die for one's country." He finished with a sycophantic line, "This day, truly festive for me, will drive away black cares. I shall fear neither the uproar of civil strife nor death by violence as long as Caesar is holding the earth."

Tiberius barely listened. He was thinking about Octavian's speech praising Marcellus. Octavian obviously favored Marcellus, and Tiberius felt slighted. It was clear that he was looked upon only as a step-son; Marcellus was a nephew, and favored nephews were often the equal of sons. Octavian was the grand-nephew of Julius Caesar, and Caesar left his fortune to him. To whom would Octavian leave his fortune?

Tiberius also noticed how friendly Marcellus and Julia were. He wondered who had decided that they should be seated across from one another. Whoever made the choice, it was apparent to all that they would make a highly attractive match.

After the main course was served, the guests circulated around the room. Marcellus and Julia walked into the garden. As they did, Pometius nudged Tiberius and nodded toward the couple.

"Marcellus doesn't know what he's getting into," Tiberius said.

Pometius laughed, "I wish him luck."

"He's going to need it," Tiberius said.

After the banquet, Livia and Octavia strolled in the gardens. It was a bright moonlit night, and they talked about what a perfect day it had been. Octavia talked about her hopes for Marcellus, Livia talked of the present. She said that she hoped the Senate would cooperate with Octavian's plans for rebuilding Rome and with his plans to replace Rome's bricks with marble, an expensive undertaking but one that she thought was worth the cost. It would establish Rome as the preeminent nation in the world.

Two dozen guests stayed overnight. To make room for them, Marcellus shared Tiberius's room. With a torch burning on the wall above them, they talked into the night. Before this, the two cousins hadn't engaged in many one-on-one conversations; now, as co-honorees, they became closer, and they talked openly and comfortably.

"Did you see those Greek girls in the marketplace, yesterday?" Marcellus asked.

"I did. They thought they were something special," Tiberius said. "But they weren't that good looking."

"Maybe not, but I wouldn't throw them out of bed."

"Neither would I."

"Talking about pretty girls, did you see they put me sitting across from Julia?" Marcellus asked.

"Yes, I noticed. But you know who's prettier than Julia?" Tiberius asked.

"Who?"

"Vipsania. She's going to be a real beauty."

"She's only eleven," Marcellus said. "You'd better be careful."

"Don't be stupid," Tiberius said.

Marcellus changed the subject. "How's it going with that slave driver, Barbonius? He made us run for an hour last week, then swim back and forth across the Tiber."

"He hasn't been that bad to my squad."

"Really? He told us that you guys trained harder than we do."

"He told us the same thing about your squad. I guess he's trying to push us all."

"Yeah, he can be a real bastard," Marcellus said.

"He must have been one tough soldier," Tiberius said. "Someone said he was an ex-gladiator."

"Being an ex-gladiator says something," Marcellus said. "Did you see that scar on his back? We've asked him, but he won't tell us how he got it."

The boys sat quietly for a few minutes, then Marcellus asked, "When you gave your speech at the dinner with Livy, why'd you stop at Julius Caesar and not talk about the rise of Octavian?"

Tiberius thought that maybe he should give an evasive answer to that question, but he was forthright. "What could I say? If I told the whole truth, I could've ruffled feathers, if you know what I mean. It's a dangerous subject."

"I think you were right to be careful," Marcellus said. "So, what do you think will happen in the Senate? Some people say that they're going to try to take Octavian's powers away. You're the historian, how did he get so much power? I mean when he became consul, he wasn't much older than we are."

"It's an incredible story." Tiberius said, and then explained what had happened as though he were Menelaus telling it. He was glad to show how much he knew, saying things that he couldn't talk about during his speech in front of an audience or the *princeps*.

"I'd say it began when he was twelve and his grandmother, Julia, died. Octavian was chosen to deliver the funeral oration, and that's when Caesar noticed his potential."

"Like when you were chosen to give the eulogy at your father's funeral," Marcellus said.

"I guess so," Tiberius said. "And Caesar took him on campaigns with him to Spain, always teaching him about the army and politics. Then, when Octavian was seventeen, Caesar sent him to Greece for his studies. He secretly adopted him as his son, and, in his will, left him three-quarters of his estate.

"When Caesar was assassinated, Octavian took his adopted name, Gaius Julius Caesar Octavianus, and put himself forward as Caesar's heir apparent. The name was important,"

"Not as important as the inheritance."

"You may be right, but it took more than money to do what he did. Although Octavian was only eighteen, he steered perfectly through a web of political intrigues. Some people say it was Maecenas who advised him about what to do, or maybe it was Caesar's generals. They wanted to keep their positions close to power. Anyway, when Octavian came back to Rome, Marc Antony was consul. Octavian knew Cicero hated Antony, so the first thing he did was visit Cicero to get his support.

"He succeeded in getting Cicero's support, then openly challenged Antony for the leadership of the Caesarean faction. He accused Antony of doing nothing to avenge Caesar's murder, and asked why he hadn't paid the citizens the stipend that Caesar had promised them in his will. He let that question simmer until the people began demanding the payment. Then at the right moment, he announced that he would pay the money from his own funds."

"That bought him a lot of support."

"Yes, and Octavian had other built-in advantages. Because of his adoption, Caesar's freedmen and clients became obligated to him as their new patron. And he had the family right to avenge Caesar's murder. More important, he had the money to recruit a private army, promising to pay a bonus of two thousand sesterces per soldier, far more than the four hundred that Antony was paying. Two of Antony's legions promptly defected to Octavian."

Tiberius recounted how Marc Antony refused to give up his army after his term as consul expired, and how the Senate declared him an enemy of the state and sent five legions against him under the command of the two new consuls, Aulus Hirtius and Vibius Pansa. At that point, Cicero convinced the Senate to legitimize Octavian's private army by making him a pro-praetor. Octavian then combined his army with the consular armies to march against Antony near the City of Mutina in Gaul.

During the battle that followed, both of the Senate's consuls fought bravely while leading their legions. They forced Antony's army to retreat, but both consuls were killed, leaving Octavian in *de facto* control of their legions plus his own legions. At that point, the Senate made the mistake of ordering Octavian to turn over the consular legions to another general for the remaining campaign against Antony. Realizing that he had been used and was being dismissed, Octavian defied the Senate and, in violation of the law, marched on Rome.

On the 19th of August, 43 BC, with his army camped on the Campus Martius, Octavian sent armed centurions into the Senate to demand that he be allowed to run for consul. The Senate capitulated. Although Octavian was under the required age of thirty-two, he was elected consul—and at nineteen years old, became the youngest consul in history.

"You were right," Marcellus said. "It's an incredible story, and you know every detail."

"And it gets more incredible. Once in power, Octavian acted quickly, declaring the assassination of Julius Caesar a crime and appointing a tribunal to convict the conspirators in absentia. Then, with great fanfare, he gathered his armies and returned to the north to confront Antony's army. The Senate put their hopes in him, but they were disappointed. As the armies approached one another, Octavian made an astounding reversal. He switched sides, double-crossed the Senate, and negotiated an alliance with Antony and Antony's ally, Marcus Aemilius Lepidus. The three met near Mutina on an island in the Lavernus River.

"They formed the Second Triumvirate. This triumvirate wasn't arranged in secret like the First Triumvirate. It was entitled 'Three Men with Consular Powers for Confirming the Commonwealth.' The tribal assembly ratified the agreement and gave each triumvir a province with imperium for five years. The triumvirs were to be superior to all other magistrates. Octavian had outmaneuvered everyone, including the Senate and Cicero."

Marcellus interrupted. "Is it true the triumvirs ordered the execution of Cicero to get him out of the way?'

"That was Antony's doing," Tiberius said. "He wanted revenge against Cicero for some insulting speeches he had made against him."

"Octavian was right, you are quite the historian," Marcellus said. "I don't know if I should say this, but my uncle was quite the schemer. First, he gets Cicero and the Senate to authorize his army against Antony. Then, after the two consuls are killed, he takes control of their legions. When the Senate recalls him, he marches to Rome and gets the Senate to make him consul so he can go to war with Antony. Then, he double-crosses the Senate and makes a deal with Antony to divide the Republic between them. Quite a trick."

"You can say that again, but we should keep it to ourselves," Tiberius said.

"And when Antony took up with Cleopatra," Marcellus said, "That gave Octavian the excuse to crush him and take control of everything."

"That's why I don't think the Senate is going to take away any of his powers. He's too smart for them," Tiberius said.

"Then we can rest easy," Marcellus said as he turned to go to sleep.

Tiberius snuffed out the torch, but couldn't sleep. He was thinking about how past events shaped today's world, how history could be understood in retrospect, but the people who lived through it couldn't predict what would happen in the future or what the best course of action was to take. Many of them made mistakes and took a wrong course, like his father and grandfather had. He was determined not to make the same mistakes.

CHAPTER NINE

The year Tiberius and Marcellus came of age was a prosperous one for Rome. With the civil war between Octavian and Antony over, with funds no longer needed for the disbanded legions, and with taxes and tribute pouring into Rome, the treasury surged. Octavian used the extra funds to rebuild the city.

He built the Temple of Julius Caesar; the Curia Julia to house the Senate, and the Julian family mausoleum, the latter, an imposing three-tier circular building on the banks of the Tiber. He also built the Temple of Apollo high on the Palatine Hill, a monumental white marble structure with gleaming doors of gold and ivory. The temple was topped with a bronze statue of the god driving a four-horse chariot.

Agrippa was even more productive than Octavian. Freed from his duties as military commander, he began building several major projects, including the Basilica of Neptune, the Baths of Agrippa, and the Pantheon. He repaired and improved the Appian Aqueduct and began building the Augusta Aqueduct that supplied water to the cities around the Bay of Neopolis from Pompeii to Puteoli. He also built a naval base at Misenum, which became the home of the Roman fleet.

Both Augustus and Agrippa owed much to Vitruvius Pollio, Rome's greatest engineer and architect, who designed not only their temples, buildings, and aqueducts, but planned the layout of the city. Vitruvius had begun his career designing catapults and siege towers for Julius Caesar, but he was more than a military man. Broadly educated, he wrote a ten-book treatise on architecture in which he described the rules of proportion and symmetry. He described the properties of stone and cement, and the strength of walls and buildings. In his designs, he acknowledged the obligations to the gods, and considered the direction of the winds, the movement of the sun, and the health of the people.

Tiberius took a great interest in Vitruvius' teachings, and decided to record the progress of all the constructions projects in the city. He walked to Agrippa's home on the south side of the Palatine Hill, and entered the anteroom where Agrippa held morning interviews with his clients. When Agrippa appeared, Tiberius stood up before anyone else. "I'd like to go with you to watch the construction projects."

"Don't you have lessons?"

"I'm way ahead in my lessons."

Agrippa smiled. "Alright, you can watch, but be careful. Don't get mixed into the cement."

Over the next months, Tiberius saw the Pantheon taking shape. The building, which was to house the statues of all the gods of Rome, had an enormous dome on top of a rectangular base. The dome was an engineering marvel, held together by the pressure of its own weight. At its center was an oculus that allowed light into the interior of the building. The oculus was an adventurous concept, and though many doubted that the dome would hold together, it did.

Tiberius was amazed at the ingenuity of the engineers and also the herculean efforts of the workers. He watched as they lifted eight huge stone columns into place at the building entrance.

Inside the building, scaffoldings reached the domed ceiling, fifty meters high. Tiberius looked up at the workers walking across the beams, and thought that these were the men who built the empire.

Agrippa and Tiberius spent much time together, and formed a bond, like father and son, but also on an informal level. Agrippa encouraged Tiberius to ask questions about anything, even personal matters.

While Agrippa concentrated on great building projects, Octavian rebuilt the government. In 27 BC, he solidified his control of the state in what was called the First Settlement. While keeping up the charade that Rome was still a democratic republic, he absorbed all of its real powers. The Senate and the assemblies continued to exist, but Octavian controlled them, and they mechanically agreed to all his decrees.

Step-by-step, he reorganized and strengthened the legal foundations of his authority, taking for himself the offices of consul, tribune, proconsul of provinces, augur, and pontiff. With these executive, military, and religious powers, none could refuse his commands. His word was law.

He was called the *princeps*, or first citizen, but, in fact, he was the first emperor of Rome.

He removed the proconsuls from the most important provinces, taking their positions for himself, and had the Senate appoint him to ten-year terms as proconsul of Spain, Gaul, Cyprus, Cilicia, Syria, and Egypt. This gave him command of almost all the legions, and for the three remaining provinces, he assigned his close associates as proconsuls. For Egypt, with its extraordinary wealth and treasury, he banned any officials from even visiting it without his permission.

He courted the *equestrian* order, promoting and encouraging them to become magistrates and senators. The *equites*, or knights, had originally been the cavalry of the legions. They were citizens wealthy enough to equip themselves with a warhorse, weapons, and armor. Over the centuries, the equites grew into a distinct order with membership based on wealth, and were transformed from calvary soldiers into businessmen, merchants, and financiers. At census time, to remain in the order, they had to show that they had assets of more than 400,000 sesterces. The equites wore gold rings and distinctive tunics with a narrow border. In the arenas, they had the privilege to be seated in the rows next to the senators.

A group with such wealth was politically influential, and the *princeps* made them his most important constituency, a counterweight to the senatorial order.

Even with all the power and control he had established, the *princeps* still worried about resistance to his actions in the assemblies. Voting in the assemblies required the physical presence of voters, and citizens from outside the city were often unable to attend to cast their votes. In such cases, legislation was decided by what some referred to as the city rabble, often with unpredictable results. To fix the problem, Octavian transferred the legislative powers of the assembly to the Senate, which he could more readily control. To maintain the illusion that the Republic still existed, he left the election of magistrates in the assembly, but preapproved who could run for office.

The consolidation of Octavian's authority enhanced his power, but to rule as he wished, he still needed the support of the people. All means of persuasion were employed to enhance the *princeps'* personal stature. He enlisted poets, historians, and pontiffs to present him as the savior of the nation, one who enjoyed the special favor of the gods. Statues depicting him as young, handsome, and robust were erected in city centers and at main crossroads. On coins, he was identified as "Caesar, the son of the deified." The deification of his adoptive father implied that he was the son of a god and would assume his own apotheosis.

The poet Virgil moved into the Julian-Claudian domus. Like Horace, he had been saved from bankruptcy by Maecenas. Virgil's property had been confiscated, not for anything he had written, but because the people of his region in Mantua had sided with the assassins of Julius Caesar during the civil war. As punishment, their lands had been confiscated and given to Octavian's veterans. Maecenas interceded to have Virgil's property restored, earning his gratitude and loyalty.

Virgil's task was to write an epic poem to commemorate the ascendancy of Octavian. Using *The Illiad* of Homer as his model, Virgil wrote *The Aeneid*, recounting Rome's founding when Aeneas fled from the burning city of Troy with his family, and how, with the aid of the goddess Venus, he crossed the Mediterranean, settled in Italy, and established the nation that would become Rome. The story was designed to identify Octavian as the descendant of the god-like savior Aeneas.

Each night after dinner, Virgil read excerpts from his poem. One he often read was a homage to Octavian:

Just as often happens when in a great nation turmoil breaks out and the base masses go on a rampage; firebrands and stones fly, and madness supplied the weapons: then, if they have caught sight of some man who carries weight because of his public devotion and service, they stand silent, their ears ready to listen. Then he prevails in speech over their fury by his authority, and placates them.

As the city was being rebuilt and Octavian was being deified, Tiberius and Marcellus were being groomed as possible successors. New Greek tutors of literature, philosophy, and rhetoric were hired, and Valerius Messalla Corvinus, a former consul and close ally of Octavian, taught them law. Customarily, new tutors hired for students coming of age replaced their childhood tutors, but Tiberius wouldn't let that happen to Menelaus. He would learn everything the new tutors had to offer, but he would continue to rely on Menelaus for history lessons and common-sense advice.

To teach them politics, Octavian began taking Marcellus and Tiberius to the Senate to hear speeches and debates, letting them sit in the front row with the most senior senators. At first, Tiberius was greatly impressed with the dignity of the senate proceedings, the high-level of debate, and the magnificence of the oratory. However, after several sessions, he began to see what he thought was rampant hypocrisy, and he became disgusted with some of the senators who engaged in outlandishly sycophantic flattery. A senator proposed to give Octavian the name "Father of the Republic." This was discussed at length until it was decided to give him the exulted name "Augustus," meaning the one who is to be venerated. From this point on, Octavian would be called Augustus.

To Tiberius, it seemed that most of the senators were afraid to disagree with or even slightly affront Octavian/Augustus. This was understandable since proscriptions were still possible for anyone suspected of having sided with Antony during the civil war or having engaged in seditious acts or speeches. The senators knew how ruthless Augustus could be, how, after defeating Antony and Cleopatra, he had wiped out anyone who might have had a claim to power in the East, children included.

Cleopatra had a seventeen-year-old son with Julius Caesar named Caesarian. Seeing Caesarian as a potential threat because of his blood ties to Julius Caesar, Augustus ordered the boy's execution.

Marc Antony had two sons with Fulvia Flaccus who could also have been threats. After Fulvia's death, their seventeen-year-old son, Antyllus Antonicus, lived in Alexandria with Cleopatra. Augustus had him killed.

Their other son, Jullus Antonicus was thirteen-years-old. Augustus spared him, treating him differently because he lived with Octavia, and she was fond of him. It was a decision that would have unexpected consequences in the future.

CHAPTER TEN

First Military Campaign

In 26 BC, Augustus and Agrippa planned a military campaign into the mountainous area of northwest Iberia. This became necessary in order to quell an insurrection by the local tribes, who had never fully accepted Roman domination since the Second Punic War in 209 BC when Scipio Africanus expelled the Carthaginians from the peninsula. The problems in Iberia had persisted for two centuries, and Rome had regularly sent armies to suppress the rebels, protect trade routes, and secure Rome's interests in Iberia's rich silver and copper mines. This new campaign was also to keep the legions fit. Agrippa told Augustus that an army cannot be maintained unless it has a purpose, unless it has something to do. "The Rome was the army, and the army must be on the move," he said.

There were twenty-eight legions with a total of 150,000 men still active even after the end of the civil war with Antony. The legionaries served for twenty-five years and expected bonuses at the end of their terms. The campaign would occupy the soldiers and direct their energies.

As Augustus and Agrippa discussed the campaign, Agrippa suggested that they take Tiberius with them so that he could get some first-hand military experience.

"I know he's precocious," Augustus said, "but I don't think it would be worth putting him in that kind of danger."

"Life is dangerous," Agrippa said.

"I could get the best military men to teach him without taking him into the wilds of Iberia."

"Scipio Africanus learned by going with his father and his uncle on campaigns."

"And the father and uncle were both killed."

"Not on the campaign that they took Scipio."

"But if I took Tiberius, I would have to take Marcellus," Augustus said.

"Take them both," Agrippa said.

"Too dangerous, they're the next generation."

"We'll keep them separate. Since it's too dangerous for us to march together, Marcellus can march with you, Tiberius with me."

"We'll have to ask their mothers."

"They're going to say 'no.' You have to make the decision."

"We'll see."

At a dinner that evening, they asked Livia and Octavia to let Tiberius and Marcellus go on the campaign with them.

"I suppose I have to say yes," Octavia said. "I can't tie my son to my apron strings. And if I don't let him go, he'll probably get in worse mischief here without either of you around to control him."

"If Marcellus goes, Tiberius has to go too," Livia said.

Both women made the men promise that their sons would be safe.

"I'll be sure that they're well protected," Augustus said.

"I'll protect them with my life," Agrippa said.

Eight legions were assembled and split into two groups. Agrippa and Tiberius would travel with the first, and Augustus and Marcellus with the second.

Despite their youth, Tiberius and Marcellus were enlisted as military tribunes so that they would have the authority to issue commands if necessary.

For Tiberius, riding with the cavalry into battle was exhilarating. Barbonius, at the insistence of Livia, was with him to give support and direction, and Tiberius watched and copied everything he did.

Starting from Rome, the troops marched for twenty-five days covering between thirty and thirty-five kilometers per day. They marched north on the Via Aurelia into Gaul, west on the Via Domitia, and through a mountain pass in the Pyrenees into Iberia.

Each night the legionaries built a camp protected by trenches and palisades. Building camps was one of the secrets of Rome's success; the soldiers were never idle; they worked continuously, building up their stamina.

In Iberia, they camped at the market city of Emporion to resupply before heading to the northwestern mountains. Along the route, they either negotiated with locals for additional supplies or foraged for food, water, and firewood.

For three days they marched through the mountainous terrain without incident until they were suddenly attacked by the Cantabrians, who hurled spears and rocks at them, and rolled giant boulders down on the Roman line. This was the type of guerilla warfare they had used against invaders for centuries, making lightning quick strikes and then retreating high in the mountains.

The Romans didn't chase them into the mountains. They were careful about proceeding through narrow mountain passes and steep gorges. During the Second Punic War, Hannibal had taught them hard lessons in this same kind of terrain. He had lured them into traps and untenable fighting positions, and had defeated several Roman armies.

Agrippa knew all of Hannibal's tricks, so he kept his army under strict control, marching in a tight line. He sent scouting parties ahead to secure the high ground before entering any pass, and sent cavalry to the other side of ridges to see whether enemies were lurking there.

After another day of marching and as the Romans set up camp, their scouts spotted a contingent of enemy forces through a thickly wooded area. Without being seen themselves, the scouts relayed the information back to camp.

Agrippa ordered his soldiers to continue building the camp as though they didn't suspect anything. Then, during the night, he sent troops to hidden ambush positions on either side of the enemy. At sunrise, the Cantabrians launched what they thought would be a surprise attack, but they were surprised to find themselves quickly surrounded and defeated. The Romans killed several hundred soldiers and took two hundred captives without suffering many losses themselves. The Canabrians who escaped retreated to a settlement on Mount Vindius. The Romans surrounded it, and demanded surrender.

Within days, the Cantabrian chiefs asked for peace terms. Agrippa demanded assurances that the rebellion would stop, and an agreement was reached and signed by both sides. With mutual assurances of peaceful conduct, the Cantabrians supplied the Romans with provisions in exchange for the Romans releasing the captives.

The Romans moved to higher, defensible ground where Agrippa ordered that another camp be built so that the legions could rest before marching further west to subdue the Astures and Galician tribes.

Unfortunately, three days after the peace arrangement, Cantabrian representatives appeared at the camp to complain that Roman soldiers had wandered into the countryside, raped two Cantabrian girls, and killed one girl's brother who had tried to defend her.

Agrippa personally took charge of the investigation, and Tiberius stayed with him throughout. Agrippa questioned centurions, legionaries, and Cantabrian witnesses. Three soldiers were identified. Two of them had scratches on their faces and bodies. They were placed in three separate tents for questioning, and a team of investigators went to the area of the alleged rape. They found a faceplate that had broken off from a Roman helmet. One of the legionaries was missing a faceplate. Confronted with the evidence, he changed his initial denial to a claim that the girls had consented.

One of soldiers claimed that he wasn't guilty but saw the others committing the rapes.

Agrippa presented the results of the investigation to Augustus who found all three soldiers guilty.

An assembly was called, and the troops were arranged in a large circle. On horseback, Augustus and Agrippa inspected them. Then the three prisoners with their hands tied behind their backs were brought to the center of the circle and made to kneel before a ditch. They were lashed with bullwhips as the other soldiers watched. The three prisoners only grunted at first but soon began screaming in pain.

Tiberius, standing behind Agrippa, was close enough to see the whips cutting into their flesh. He winced each time they were struck.

After a drumroll, three legionaries, wearing black masks, approached. The masked legionaries each carried long, curved swords. Standing behind the prisoners, they waited for Augustus to give the signal. Augustus nodded to them, and, in unison, they raised their swords high and swung them down on the necks of the prisoners. Two heads were cleanly cut off. The third required another stroke. Tiberius stood with his mouth and eyes wide open as the blood from the prisoners' necks spurted meters into the air, like geysers. He had seen bodies and gaping wounds before, but this was another dimension—blood and more blood. He felt his stomach cramping.

Agrippa rode into the center of the circle and addressed the legionaries. His voice boomed, "These men disobeyed orders. They committed a crime against the people we just pacified. We made a peace treaty under oaths with these people, and these so-called soldiers violated the treaty, bringing dishonor on all of us. Remember, you all took an oath to obey the commands of your generals. These men violated their oaths. If we didn't punish them, the gods would punish us."

Pointing to a group of centurions, Agrippa shouted, "Drag those bastards to the cliff, and throw them off."

Turning his horse around, he shouted to the others, "Dismissed!"

As the prisoners were dragged away, the other legionaries dispersed, silently at first, but then began chattering, and soon they were going about their regular duties.

Camp was dismantled, and the legions continued westward to find the Astures and Galicians. Tiberius rode next to Barbonius, asking him question after question. He asked about the decision to execute the soldiers.

"Couldn't they have been held in custody? What about a citizen's right to a trial?"

"In the legions, you're under military law. You don't have a right to a trial. During war there's no time for that."

"How do we know that they were all equally guilty?"

"No matter who committed the actual rape, there's no question that they were all guilty of leaving their posts and breaking the peace treaty," Barbonius said. "A treaty must be honored."

"But did that warrant execution?"

"It's about discipline," Barbonius said. "You can't let the troops run wild. There are beasts among them. Strict discipline keeps them under control. Without it, we would have chaos."

"I know," Tiberius said. "Someone once told me that soldiers can get so wild and crazed that they can't even be called human."

Barbonius pulled his horse to a halt," That's right," he said. "Remember the lesson of Scipio Africanus, when during the war against Carthage, a false rumor spread that Scipio had died, and his soldiers threw off all discipline, ejected their military tribunes, and plundered the native inhabitants. Scipio, using other troops, captured the mutineers. After identifying thirty-one ringleaders, he had them chained in front of the assembled soldiers."

Barbonius continued, reciting almost verbatim the speech that Scipio Africanus had given to the soldiers. "Scipio told them that 'every multitude is in its nature like the ocean, which can be excited by storms and winds. So, also, in yourselves there is calm and there are storms; but the cause and origin of your fury is entirely attributable to those who led you on. You have caught your madness by contagion from them, and have followed them to commit heinous crimes against your country, your parents, your children, and the gods.'"

Barbonius took a long breath after delivering the speech and continued, "To emphasize the importance of the duties that had been forsaken, Scipio had the thirty-one ringleaders scourged and beheaded in front of the soldiers. He showed leniency to the rest, allowing them to take another military oath."

"That must have been an unforgettable sight," Tiberius said. "But couldn't it have caused a mutiny?"

"No," Barbonius said. "Discipline comes not just from the consul in command but from the state. The sensible soldiers knew that if they overthrew Scipio, Rome would send another army to hunt them down, just as Crassus hunted down Spartacus and his rebels. They'd be crucified, and those with families knew their families would be punished."

Tiberius thought it was a powerful story and a powerful speech, but wondered whether the speech attributed to Scipio Africanus was actually his or one that Livy had invented.

The legions moved west, and after relatively easy battles, subdued the Astures and the Galicians. Peace treaties were signed, and a garrison assigned to the area to maintain a Roman presence. The legions, with their mission accomplished, began the march east back to Rome. The march went smoothly at first, but after two days, a powerful thunderstorm with driving rain swept over the Pyrenees, soaking everything and turning the road into mud. Augustus gave up his horse and was carried in a covered litter.

The legions kept marching through the drenching rain, and as they passed into the area in Cantabria where the convicted soldiers had been beheaded, a sudden lightning bolt cracked the air and struck the ground in front of Augustus' litter bearers, knocking them to the ground. The litter toppled over, and Augustus fell into the mud. One of the litter bearers was killed.

The soldiers near the scene stood aghast, not because of death or injuries, but because they saw it as a terrible omen. Within minutes the word spread that Jupiter was angry at Augustus for beheading the soldiers.

Word was sent to Agrippa, who raced to the scene with Tiberius following him. Soldiers were milling around. Agrippa shouted at them, "Double time, double time over the next two ridges. We'll make camp after that."

A group of soldiers didn't move right away. Agrippa ran his horse at them. "Centurions," he shouted, "get these men moving, now!"

Two centurions ran to the group and began prodding them to run double time. Agrippa rode back and forth on the line of soldiers, repeating, "Double time, double time, let's go."

Only after the line was moving did he dismount to check on Augustus.

Augustus was sitting on a rock. He seemed unhurt, though his hands were shaking.

"Are you alright," Agrippa said.

"I'm not sure," Augustus said.

"Can you stand up?"

"I think so."

With Agrippa's help, Augustus stood and, after a few minutes, regained his composure.

He decided that before moving on, a ceremony to pay tribute to the dead soldier was required. With the rain pouring down on him, Augustus conducted the ceremony, offering prayers, vows, and promises to Jupiter, the god that Romans believed cast lightning bolts as retribution. Augustus kneeled and asked Jupiter to protect the legions. The dead soldier was buried on the spot where the lightning had struck. Augustus relieved the other litter bearers, and rode on his horse for the rest of the march.

The march east was slowed by rain and mud, and after another two days, Augustus became sick. The doctors said his illness might have been brought on by the lightning strike. He was shivering with fever, and it was decided that he couldn't continue the journey on horseback. So, he returned to a litter, and a cohort of legionaries escorted him to a palace in Tarraco on the Mediterranean coast where he could convalesce. Agrippa and the main body of troops continued on to Rome.

Upon arriving at Rome, Agrippa proclaimed that Augustus had conquered the whole of the Iberian Peninsula, and that it was now completely under Roman control.

CHAPTER ELEVEN

As Augustus was recovering from his illness at the palace in Tarraco, he began to think about his successor. He favored his nephew, Marcellus. This became clear to all when he publicly announced the marriage of Marcellus to his daughter Julia. Marcellus was seventeen, Julia fourteen. It was legal for cousins to marry under Roman law, and Julia seemed almost old enough to produce the grandsons Augustus desperately wanted.

The wedding date was set for Augustus' expected return to Rome in 25 BC, but when he returned, he was still too ill to attend. In his place, Agrippa presided over the wedding. It was a spectacular affair with all of Rome greatly interested in the imperial couple. Marcellus, handsome, robust, and promising, had the lineage of the Claudians; Julia, beautiful and confident, made the perfect princess. No expense was spared for the three days of banquets and games. The couple could not have been happier, and Marcellus was sure that he would be designated as the successor to Augustus when the time came.

Augustus recovered from his illness and continued working on his building projects, administering his new constitutional structure, and stabilizing the empire's border, all to good effect. However, in 23 BC, he became gravely ill again. Thinking he was going to die, he summoned senior senators to his sickbed. Marcellus heard of the meeting and expected that he would be named the successor. Instead, Augustus gave his signet ring with the imperial seal to Agrippa. The *princeps* knew that Marcellus was not yet ready to rule; Agrippa had all but ruled already, and had proven more than capable. He would exercise the imperial power while Augustus was ill.

Most senators accepted this decision as the best for Rome, although some complained that Agrippa came from an undistinguished ancestry and should not supersede candidates from the most elite senatorial families.

Augustus overruled their objections, and plans were laid for the transition of power. But that became unnecessary. A Greek doctor treated him with a series of cold-water baths, and, defying expectations, Augustus recovered.

With the *princeps* back in good health, Agrippa gave back the imperial ring, then sailed for Greece and Syria to address problems there and negotiate with eastern rulers.

Meanwhile, Marcellus remained in Rome. He skipped over election to the office of quaestor, the usual first step on the course of honors, and with the approval of Augustus, was elected to the office of aedile, the usual second step. As an aedile, he was responsible for public works and festivals, and spent lavishly on games and festivals, winning popular approval. Backed by Augustus, he also laid the foundation stone of what would later become the grandest theater in Rome—the Theater of Marcellus.

With his popularity increasing, it appeared certain that he would be the choice to succeed Augustus; it was just a matter of time. However, three months later, Marcellus fell ill, suffering from an illness similar to the one that had stricken Augustus. The Greek doctor again tried cold-water treatments, but this time they didn't work, and Marcellus died.

The death of the nineteen-year-old prince was a devastating blow, and all of Rome mourned. After a grand funeral, Marcellus had the honor of being the first to have his ashes interred in the newly-built Julian mausoleum.

Julia was inconsolable and went into a deep depression. Livia frequently had to force her to leave her bed. Octavia, too, went into depression and stopped all public appearances.

Augustus, although also despondent, knew that he had to make new plans. It was a difficult period because of illness spreading through the population, fires in the city, and a grain shortage. He held a strategy meeting with Maecenas, his shrewdest adviser. They discussed Rome's current problems and those they were likely to face in the future, agreeing that if they weren't handled wisely, they might spur calls for new leadership. "Enemies are always lurking in the weeds," Maecenus said. "They'll take advantage of the bad times, and without a family member firmly in place as your successor, the ambitious will surface. They could move to replace you with someone they can control. They would support Agrippa, who is seen as someone who can fix all problems. You've made him very powerful, and the people would back him."

"Agrippa is like a brother to me; he would never go against me," Augustus said.

"Never say never," Maecenas said. "He could easily be convinced that it would be for the good of Rome. You must act first. Either kill him or make him your son-in-law."

Augustus was shocked by Maecenas' bold proposal. He thought about it for two sleepless nights, then summoned Agrippa back from Greece. When Agrippa arrived, they met in the atrium of the Julian-Claudian domus. They both wore black togas to signify that they were still in mourning for Marcellus.

"How was your trip?" Augustus asked.

"Going, everything went well; on the way back, the sea was monstrous."

"The sea can humble us all," Augustus said.

Servants brought a dinner of roasted lamb and an urn of wine, but Augustus waved them away. He served the meal himself. This was unusual to say the least, and Agrippa realized that something was going to be asked of him.

Both men remained silent until Augustus spoke. "I'm not going to live forever," he said. "Every time I have a bout of illness, it seems to get worse. Our brilliant doctors can only say it's a recurring thing. They're talking about bleeding me dry."

Augustus began to eat; Agrippa didn't.

"I'd advise against letting them bleed you," Agrippa said. "You just need to rest more. When you're out on a campaign, you don't take care of yourself. You've proved yourself. You don't have to be in camp. You can direct operations from here. Let others take the field."

"If I had more generals like you, I would do just that. But there's only one Agrippa."

"Thank you," Agrippa said and began to eat.

"Since the war with Antony, you and I have held the empire together," Augustus said. "But when I'm too old or gone, the factions will raise their ugly heads again. The people want a strong leader. Although they cling to the ideals of the Republic, they need someone they see as chosen by the gods. I believe that's why they follow me."

"Of course."

"So, we need a line of succession that the people will accept."

"Yes."

"Julia is our only hope," Augustus said. "The loss of Marcellus has cost us dearly."

"Yes."

"I have something to ask of you," Augustus said as he poured two more cups of wine and handed one to Agrippa.

"Yes?"

"You must marry Julia."

Agrippa put his cup down. "But my wife. . ."

"Rome needs you," Augustus said. "The people love you. But more is needed. You need to have an unassailable noble lineage to rule. As my son-in-law you'll become a member of the Julian family, and a child of yours and Julia will establish a bloodline that will be seen as anointed by the gods."

"You ask too much."

"It's necessary."

"It won't work. I'm twenty-five years older than Julia."

"You're in great health. It'll be fine. Remember, I once ordered Tiberius' father to divorce Livia, and the outcome could not have been better."

"Julia is not Livia."

"I admit that, but she's my best hope for a natural descendent. And if she produces children, our lines will merge, and your lineage will be the future of Rome as much as mine."

Agrippa thought about the idea, then said, "Julia might not want me as her husband."

"I'll make a promise to you," Augustus said. "If, after three years, there are no children, you can divorce her, and go back to your wife. We'll set the marriage for after the new year."

Agrippa stared intently at Augustus. "How am I going to tell my wife?"

"Gently."

Agrippa wanted to protest but begrudgingly nodded his assent, then rushed out of the atrium. As he was leaving, Tiberius was arriving. He saw Agrippa staggering down the front steps, ghostly white as if all the blood had drained from his body. He had never seen him like that before.

"Are you alright?" Tiberius asked.

"No. I'm not."

Tiberius began to follow him, but Agrippa looked back angrily. Tiberius stopped following.

◆

On the 15th of September 23 BC, Augustus convened the Senate and announced the wedding plans of Agrippa and Julia. The ceremony would take place after the appropriate mourning period for Marcellus. The senators shouted approval. No one mentioned that Agrippa was already married. Divorce would be no obstacle; it was common in Rome, especially to make political alliances.

Augustus also announced his Second Settlement of the nation's constitution. He proclaimed that from now on he would not hold the consulship year by year, but would take permanent pro-consular imperium in the provinces.

To compensate in part for not holding the consulship, he would take the power of a tribune for life. He would not have to run for office every year, but would permanently have the powers of a tribune, assuring him that he could never be prosecuted for any wrongdoing. His inviolability would never expire.

The senators overwhelmingly approved the settlement, and thus, twenty-one years after the demise of Julius Caesar's dictatorship, Augustus re-established a dictatorship far more comprehensive and absolute than Caesar ever had imagined.

Tiberius had known in advance that Augustus was going to make changes in the power structure, but hadn't known about the marriage of Agrippa to Julia. He was stunned by the news. When he learned that Augustus had ordered Agrippa to do it, he realized why Agrippa had been so upset when he saw him rushing down the steps.

He wondered whether Agrippa would go through with the marriage. Agrippa was happily married, and the thought crossed Tiberius' mind that if Agrippa divorced his wife, he was no better than Tiberius' father had been when he divorced Livia. Now the person he most admired was about to commit the same kind of betrayal that his father had committed.

He went to Agrippa's residence to look for him but was told that he was at the Pantheon construction site. Tiberius rushed there, and was surprised to see how much progress had been made. The portico, the columns, and the pediment at the entrance were complete. Masonry workers were on scaffolds cementing friezes onto the pediment.

Agrippa was inside the huge rotunda, directing construction. Tiberius asked to talk to him privately. "You'll have to wait," Agrippa said, pointing to workers hoisting a statue of Mars to a balcony high up in the rotunda.

The Pantheon was going to be a crowning achievement for Agrippa, even more impressive than his public baths and his Basilica of Neptune. Here, in one building, the statues of all the gods of Rome would be housed.

Agrippa signaled for Tiberius to come to him, "What do you want to talk about?"

Tiberius, with some trepidation, came right to the point. "I know it's not my place, but how do you feel about divorcing your wife and marrying Julia?"

Agrippa scowled. "Let's walk."

They went outside and walked around the perimeter of the building. As they walked, Aggrippa gave Tiberius an explanation, which seemed like a rationalization he was making to himself. "Julia is a fine young woman, your step-father's only child. She is his only chance for a male heir, and with Marcellus gone, it would be a waste to leave her without a husband."

"Excuse me for being blunt, but I don't see why you have to do it. There must be someone else who would be suitable," Tiberius said.

"No one that Augustus would trust to take charge of the empire."

"There must be someone."

Agrippa smiled wryly, "How about you?"

Tiberius began to say "No way," but thought better of it. That might be insulting. "Julia and I are like brother and sister," he said, "and I'm nowhere near ready for marriage."

"You're not brother and sister through blood."

"But we feel as if we are," he said while thinking to himself, like siblings who don't get along.

Finishing his explanation, Agrippa said, "It's my duty. I'm doing it for the good of Rome."

"Again, I hope I'm not being impertinent," Tiberius said, though he knew that he was being impertinent. He felt so strongly that he didn't care. "How do you know it's for the good of Rome? Breaking a marriage vow doesn't bring the favor of the gods."

Agrippa stopped, and grabbed Tiberius' shoulders with his huge hands, pulling him close, and staring straight into his eyes. "The gods have chosen Augustus to lead Rome, and they have given him good fortune. You know that's true from all his achievements, from the peace he has brought to the empire, from the prosperity he has dispensed to the people, and from the respect shown to us by all nations. And I believe that the gods have a plan for us. Rome is to bring peace and order not just to Italia but to the world. Augustus represents the gods. I'm just a soldier, and I have to obey my orders. Not to obey my orders would break a vow even greater than any marriage vow."

Tiberius could only say, "I see."

Agrippa released Tiberius and they began walking again. "I appreciate your concern, but it's something that must be done."

When they finished circling the Pantheon, Agrippa told Tiberius to wait while he went inside to give instructions to the workers. He said, "I have something to tell you. Wait here."

As Tiberius waited, he realized that Agrippa truly believed that the gods were directing Rome's destiny and this unconditional belief strengthened him. Menelaus had lectured many times about how the extraordinary strength of the Romans came from their disciplined adherence to the religious and civic practices of their ancestors. Romans prized devotion to the gods. They taught their children moral lessons through anecdotes and legends that often included the intercession of the gods. They believed that failure to abide by the will of the gods would invite catastrophe and that the entire community would suffer for affronts to the gods. Collective retribution might be meted out by an angry deity, and the Roman's made extraordinary efforts to appease the gods through sacrifices and vows. If Agrippa believed that Augustus represented the will of the gods, he would obey his commands as though they were coming from Jupiter.

What troubled Tiberius was that he didn't think Augustus was so devoted to the gods. From watching him, he didn't get the sense that Augustus had an unconditional belief that the gods even existed, and he suspected that Augustus only used the cover of religion to cajole and control the people and his followers.

Agrippa emerged from the Pantheon, and again held Tiberius' shoulders and looked straight into his eyes. "I am going to tell you something, but you can't say anything to anyone about it."

"I won't."

"Augustus and I have agreed that you and my daughter Vipsania will be married."

Tiberius felt as though he had been struck by a small jolt of lightning. Vipsania, the young girl whom he and Marcellus had been joking about, would be his wife.

"How do you feel about that?" Agrippa asked.

"I don't know. It's quite a shock."

"Just think about it, and don't say anything. I believe the gods will approve."

"Does Vipsania know?"

"I'll tell her soon."

"What if she doesn't want to marry me?"

"I've noticed that she likes you, so I believe she will."

"I assume I have to obey."

"Yes. And you'll be glad."

As Tiberius walked home, he realized that he was already glad, more than glad.

CHAPTER TWELVE

First Prosecution – Agrippa – Eastern Diplomacy

Tiberius didn't have much time to dwell on his prospective marriage. He was called to a meeting with Maecenas, who told him that Augustus had decided to accelerate his career. Augustus had authorized his election to the office of quaestor. Tiberius appreciated the advancement but was thinking that Augustus had allowed Marcellus to skip to rank of quaestor and go directly to aedile.

Maecenas interrupted his thoughts, saying "He wants you to prosecute a case, as soon as you're installed as a quaestor. Read these," Maecenas handed Tiberius a folder of legal papers. "Here's your first case."

Tiberius opened the folder and began reading with excited anticipation. His first case! But as he read through it, he quickly realized that it was a tainted assignment. Two senators, Licinius Varrones Murena and Fannius Caepio, had been accused of *perduellio*, or high treason, for allegedly plotting against Augustus. Before they could be arrested, they were warned, and they fled, which was taken as an admission of guilt. Augustus sent soldiers to track them down and summarily execute them. The soldiers followed his orders.

To retroactively justify the executions, Tiberius was to convict them *in absentia*. It was expected to be an easy prosecution for the new quaestor. But Tiberius was troubled by the case and objected on the grounds that citizens cannot be convicted after their deaths. Maecenas reminded him that treason was an exception and convictions in absentia were not unusual. Furthermore, in this case, the defendants were wealthy men who chose to avoid trial. Convictions were necessary to prevent their descendants from receiving their inheritances.

"Should we punish the children because their fathers did something wrong?" Tiberius asked.

"Those that contemplate treason must know the consequences," Maecenas said. "If their children suffer, it's because of them, not us."

Tiberius was also troubled because Augustus had ordered the defendant's executions without waiting for a trial or conviction. Although this case was for treason, he thought the basic right to a fair trial should not be so readily disregarded. It was too easy for Augustus to order executions and too likely to lead to tyranny, if it hadn't already.

Nonetheless, Tiberius was compelled by the command of Augustus. He accepted the assignment and prosecuted the case.

The case against the defendants had been built by *delatores*, or professional informers. In Rome, a citizen could bring criminal charges against other citizens, and, if they prevailed, they would be entitled to a part of the fine imposed, and in some cases, they would be entitled to substantial part of the defendant's property. This system worked effectively for centuries during the Republic, but from the time of Marius and Sulla, abuses of the system became rampant. *Delatores* often uncovered, and sometimes manufactured, charges against wealthy targets. They targeted senators and equestrians who had assets to confiscate if they were convicted of the crimes. The *delatores* claimed that their activities were for the public benefit, but most of them were working for their own benefit, and many became wealthy in the process.

The trial of Murena and Caepio was held in the Senate house with fifty selected senators sitting as jurors. Tiberius delivered an opening statement outlining the facts of the case and the argument for conviction. Advocates for the defendants' families delivered opening statements in rebuttal.

Tiberius called three *delators* to the witness stand, and they provided incriminating evidence against the defendants, testifying to three separate occasions when the defendants were overheard talking about removing Augustus and reestablishing the Republic.

Tiberius didn't have to do much lawyering to present the case. The *delatores* were professional witnesses and knew just what to say. There was no cross-examination, and the defense only called family members of the defendants as character witnesses.

After completion of the evidence, there were no closing arguments, the judge did not instruct the jurors, and the jurors did not retire for deliberations—they simply cast ballots, by marking a token: A for acquittal; C for condemnation. Verdicts required only a majority; a tie meant acquittal.

The senators dropped their tokens in an urn. The judge counted them, and the defendants were convicted 49 to 1. The usual penalty for treason was death, but that was not an issue here because the defendants had already been executed.

Senators congratulated Tiberius on his first victory. Some patted him on the back, but he didn't acknowledge it or smile. He didn't view the case as a victory. He viewed it only as a job he had to do. He wasn't proud of it because he was suspicious of the *delatores* and wondered whether they had made up what they allegedly overheard. Without cross-examination by the defense, there was no way of testing the witnesses' veracity.

He was also suspicious of something that he had learned while investigating the case: Maecenus' wife, Terentia, was the person who warned the defendants to flee. She had been sleeping with Augustus, who had let slip that the defendants were about to be arrested. For her own reasons, Terentiua warned the defendants.

Tiberius believed this was the reason the defendants were executed without trial. Neither Augustus nor Maecenus wanted the scandalous conduct to become public. At a trial, it might have come out. Although it was known that Augustus engaged in extramarital affairs, sleeping with the wife of one of his best friends was hypocritical to the fullest and an utter disgrace. It belied all of his preaching about marriage and morality. How could he condemn others for adultery when he was doing the same thing himself?

Tiberius had never liked Maecenas, and now he disliked him even more as he assumed Maecenas knew of and consented to Augustus sleeping with his wife.

In 21 BC, Agrippa and Julia married. At the ceremony, Agrippa gave a speech, making all the usual statements of appreciation and thanking

Augustus for giving him the privilege of marrying his daughter. He ended the speech by saying, "I have a reason for double joy today, not only because of my marriage to the beautiful Julia, but also because I am announcing the betrothal of my daughter Vipsania to Tiberius. Of course, he is already like a son to me."

Agrippa's marriage to Julia would take place in 20 BC, when he returned from an upcoming trip to the East. The trip was necessary to address a number of problems that had arisen between the nations of Armenia and Parthia. Augustus had ordered a military buildup, and legions had already been sent to strategic locations. Agrippa would go because Augustus, prone to illness, had curtailed his own campaigning.

Agrippa would take Tiberius as his deputy, and as they prepared for the campaign, they worked side by side, outfitting ships and training troops. Agrippa explained the purpose of each step of the preparations, and Tiberius listened to every word. There was no better teacher in the world. He appreciated the opportunity and was proud of his role as Agrippa's deputy.

But his high spirits were soon taken down a peg. Augustus and Livia announced the betrothal of Tiberius' brother, Drusus I, to Antonia Minor, a daughter of Octavia and a niece of Augustus. When Tiberius heard the news, he was glad for his brother, but he had the familiar feeling that he was second in line again. Augustus had clearly favored Marcellus over him; now it seemed that he favored Drusus over him. Augustus had always liked Drusus, as most people did, and marrying him to Antonia Minor, who carried the illustrious Julian blood, was a significant sign of favor. The Julian bloodlines were of paramount importance to Augustus, and if a choice had to be made as to who would be the next *princeps*, Drusus' Julian family relationship by marriage would weigh heavily.

Tiberius told himself that he would be glad for his brother, but what bothered him was the thought that Augustus didn't care for him. He thought that in either their discussions during their ride to Antium or in his coming-out speech, he might have said something that displeased him. Or, perhaps, Augustus disliked him because Tiberius' father, Nero, had fought on the side of Antony. Or, perhaps, he disrespected Nero for submitting to the divorce of Livia, and, in the recesses of his mind, he transferred that disrespect onto Tiberius.

In any case, Tiberius resented being bypassed by his younger brother while he was sure that he was the more competent and deserving. In a less than mature moment, he thought that perhaps Augustus would die soon, Agrippa would become the *princeps*, and would make him his successor. But he dismissed these thoughts. If it turned out that Drusus became the *princeps*, he would welcome it and would support him wholeheartedly.

In January 20 BC, Agrippa and Tiberius sailed to the East, landing at Pompeiopolis, a city established by Pompey the Great on the south coast of Asia Minor. From there, Agrippa sent Tiberius, now twenty-two-years old, to Armenia with two legions. His mission was to install Tigrandes, a Roman ally, on the Armenian throne. With the aid of experienced generals, Tiberius led the legions unimpeded into Armenia and placed the crown on the new king's head. This strengthened Rome's hand against Parthia, the successor nation to Persia with territory stretching from Syria to India.

In May, Agrippa was able to negotiate with the Parthians for the return of the standards that Crassus had lost at the Battle of Carrhae when his legions were annihilated. Agrippa sent the standards to Tiberius in Armenia for him to transport them to Rome. Tiberius was glad that they had been recovered without having to resort to war, as he had recommended in his speech to Augustus seven years earlier.

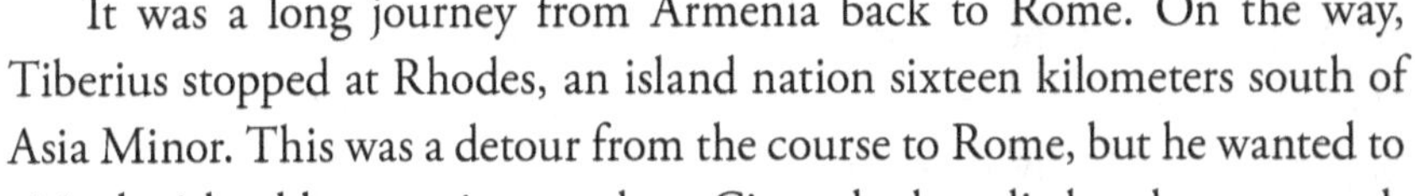

It was a long journey from Armenia back to Rome. On the way, Tiberius stopped at Rhodes, an island nation sixteen kilometers south of Asia Minor. This was a detour from the course to Rome, but he wanted to visit the island because it was where Cicero had studied and wrote much of his great book *The Republic*.

He was also eager to see the remains of the Colossus of Rhodes, a bronze statue of the sun god Helios that once stood thirty-three meters high, straddling the entrance to the harbor with a leg on each bank. Ships sailed through the statue's legs. It had been erected to celebrate a military victory in 304 BC, but was toppled by an earthquake in 226 BC.

Now it lay next to the harbor entrance, pitted and discolored. Seeing it reminded Tiberius of how even prospering civilizations can unexpectedly find themselves defeated and lying prostrate.

One of his tutors in Rome, Theodorus of Gadara, now lived on Rhodes. In his letters to Tiberius, he had described the intellectual activities and discussions that were part of Rhodian culture, and invited him to visit.

Tiberius attended lectures by his old instructor, and was surprised by his advice that for political oratory it was sometimes better not to be too clear, but to be equivocal, thereby allowing the politician to keep his listeners guessing about his true intentions and giving him room to backtrack from his promises.

While on the island, Theodorus introduced Tiberius to several Rhodian scholars and philosophers, including Jason of Nyet, who was the great grandson of Posidonius, one of the founders of the Stoic school of philosophy. Posidonius was a Syrian Greek, who lived on Rhodes. He was the most accomplished student of science, mathematics, and literature that Greece had produced since Aristotle. He had made important scientific discoveries, and wrote about the tides and volcanoes. He studied northern Europe, and wrote a continuation of the histories of Polybius.

Posidonius used his skills to prove his view that the world had a hidden, spiritual nature that could be experienced through mysticism. His views on mysticism were difficult to explain, but Jason could talk at length about the other accomplishments of his great-grandfather, and Tiberius enjoyed talking with him throughout his stay on Rhodes.

Tiberius loved the academic life at Rhodes, and would have liked to stay longer, but he had to return the standards, so he reluctantly departed. As he sailed away, he thought that he would return someday to converse and debate on equal terms with the many learned Hellenic scholars and philosophers who lived or studied there.

The trip back to Rome took a month. He entered the city with great fanfare, driving a chariot into the packed Circus Maximus. Five riders on white horses rode behind him holding the recovered standards high as the crowd roared approval. This was a proud moment for Rome; the trio of Augustus, Agrippa, and Tiberius had erased the stain of Crassus' defeat at Carrhae.

Tiberius remembered how he had practiced chariot racing here and how he had imagined the crowds cheering; now the cheering was real. With the success of his mission, he believed that it was just the start of a great career to come and that he would someday achieve tremendous things for himself and for Rome. The Senate agreed, and rewarded him with a praetorship. After Agrippa, he was now considered the most likely man to succeed Augustus.

As the fortunes of Tiberius were rising and the prospect of his marriage to Vipsania was so promising, Agrippa's marriage to Julia was troubled, and everyone knew it. Nevertheless, Julia became pregnant with the first of five children. However, even with the children, Agrippa's marriage to Julia was doomed; the longer it lasted, the more he would come to loath her. He felt like a prisoner in the marriage, and wondered what would happen if he divorced her. He had no doubt that Augustus would strip him of his position, and he couldn't accept that. He enjoyed his power too much. So, he stayed married.

Between 20 BC and 12 BC, the couple would have five children: Gaius, Julia the Younger, Lucius, Agrippina, and Agrippa Postumus.

In 17 BC, Augustus would adopt Gaius and Lucius, his two oldest grandsons, as his own sons.

CHAPTER THIRTEEN

In 19 BC, Tiberius and Vipsania married. He was twenty-three, she was seventeen. Both were elated. Tiberius, as the step-son of Augustus, and now the son-in-law of Agrippa, had a two-track path to leadership. Agrippa had become like a real father to him, and Vipsania was incredibly beautiful, vivacious, and fun to be with. He thought that if he had a choice between becoming the *princeps* and being married to Vipsania, he'd choose her.

Vipsania was the granddaughter of Titus Pomponius Atticus, an extraordinarily wealthy equestrian with whom Cicero had exchanged letters throughout his life. Atticus was a Roman who chose to spend most of his time in Athens because of his admiration for Greek culture. His household welcomed philosophers, artists, and poets. Whenever it could be arranged, he spent extended periods of time with Cicero discussing life and world affairs. In his library he had important literary scrolls and letters from Cicero. Vipsania read them all.

Atticus believed in educating his daughter just as he would have educated a son, and in her studies, she was the equal of any young man. She could quote long passages from Cicero's writings and brilliantly discuss any and all manner of cultural topics. She often read parts of Cicero's speeches to Tiberius. Some they found rather amusing.

One speech Tiberius found particularly entertaining was Cicero's closing argument in a murder trial. He said that the victim was so mean and miserable in his life and had so many enemies, that he should be glad to be dead. In another case that Vipsania found amusing, Cicero's adversary, Marcus Porcius Cato the Younger, was an advocate of an extreme form of Stoicism, and Cicero ridiculed Cato's Stoic beliefs. Vipsania read Cicero's words, "The Stoics say that all offenses are equal, that every sin is an unpardonable crime, and that it is just as much a crime to needlessly kill a rooster as to strangle one's own father."

Tiberius said, "I think there's more to Stoicism than that."

"Of course," Vipsania said. "Cicero was performing for a jury. He always said when you have the facts on your side, argue the facts; when you don't, distract. When you have a guilty client, change the subject."

While both admired Cicero for his genius, they were critical of his switching sides depending on the political winds. Vipsania had a letter of Cicero's, written in 54 BC, in which he tried to justify changing his mind from being against the triumvirate to supporting it. The letter shed light on his pragmatic character. She read: "I should like it to be clear to you that I should not be in favor of sticking fast to one set of opinions, when circumstances have changed and the sentiments of honest men are no longer the same. I believe in moving with the times. Unchanging consistency of standpoint has never been considered a virtue in a great statesman. At sea it is good sailing to run before the gale, even if the ship cannot make harbor; but if she can make harbor by changing tack, only a fool would risk shipwreck by holding to the original course rather than change and still reach his destination."

"He makes a sound argument," Tiberius said, "but he was only justifying his own hypocrisy."

"Most men do that at one time or another," Vipsania said.

"We agree on that," Tiberius said.

In addition to their discussions about Cicero, Vipsania introduced Tiberius to a wide range of learning. He was knowledgeable about history, politics, and military tactics, but she taught him about literature, drama, and philosophy. Although many people had considered him morose and sullen, his relationship with Vipsania was changing him, making him look almost cheerful. He thought of her as the ideal of young womanhood, not only for her beauty, but also for her unwavering efforts to bring happiness to their lives. She loved to do small things for him. She would bring him lemonade and his favorite snacks; she massaged his shoulders and combed his hair. This is how life should be lived, he thought. Unfortunately, he often had to be away from home on military campaigns; but when he could, he took Vipsania along; when he couldn't, it was hard to leave her.

Between 16 BC and 14 BC, he commanded legions either as a propraetor or governor in Gaul with his base of operations at Lugdunum. Nevertheless, whenever he could, he returned home to see Vipsania, even if only for a few days.

His brother, Drusus I, also became a pro-praetor and led legions in western Gaul.

The brothers had distinct styles of leadership. Drusus, handsome, eloquent, and charismatic, led boldly, inspiring his troops with his claim that he was destined to be victorious in all his battles. On the contrary, Tiberius was a methodical and cautious general. He checked every detail, and made sure supplies were in place and orders were clear before embarking on any operation. His troops considered him stern and unapproachable, but were confident in his leadership.

In 14 BC, Tiberius and Drusus combined their armies to battle warlike Germanic tribes on the northern side of the Alps. These tribes had built strongholds protected by deep defensive ditches, high mounds, and palisades. To assault these strongholds, the legions used catapults and *ballista* weapons to hurl rocks, boulders, and iron-tipped bolts at the defenders. Designed by Vitruvius Pollio, Rome's greatest engineer and architect, these weapons were superior to those of any other nation, and were capable of hurling their missiles farther and faster. They used the stored tension of twisted animal gut or horsehair to make a spring. A trigger released the tension in the spring to hurl an object several hundred meters at the enemy. Each legion had about sixty bolt-firing catapults or *ballistas* that could be adjusted up or down to change trajectories. Fired simultaneously, the hail of missiles had devastating effects.

One by one, the tribes were defeated, and the campaign was a resounding success. When it was over, the two brothers had extended the reaches of the Roman Empire to the banks of the Danube River.

In January 13 BC, Tiberius returned to Rome and became consul at twenty-eight years of age, not nearly as young as Augustus but still extremely young. Consuls were supposed to be forty-two, but so many waivers had been given that the rule became the exception.

With Tiberius in Rome, Drusus took command of Gaul. Augustus accompanied him, and both enjoyed some leisure time at the official residence in Lugdunum. All was not war and conflict. Augustus wrote a letter to Tiberius about the five-day festival of the goddess Minerva in March 13 BC. He wrote:

We had, my dear Tiberius, a pleasant time of it during the festival of Minerva: for we played the *tali* every day, and kept the gaming board warm. Your brother uttered many exclamations at a desperate run of ill-fortune, but recovering by degrees, and unexpectedly, he in the end lost not much. I lost 20,000 sesterces for my part; but then I was profusely generous in my play, as I commonly am.

In Rome, the public expressed great interest in the exploits of the three generals, Agrippa, Tiberius, and Drusus, and also in their wives and children, especially Julia and her five children.

Augustus had adopted Gaius and Lucius in 17 BC, and it became clear that in the event of the *princeps* death, Agrippa would temporarily hold the reins of power until either of the boys was old enough to assume power. Since they carried the Julian bloodlines, they had superior claims over Tiberius to be the successor. Once again, Tiberius felt relegated another step down the succession ladder.

Whatever his complaints were about his public position, Tiberius' private life was joyful. In 14 BC, Vipsania gave birth to a son, Drusus II, named after Tiberius' brother, Drusus I. When he saw the boy, Tiberius was thrilled, and, despite the Roman custom that fathers not become attached to their children until they reached the age of five, he spent as much time as he could with his son.

Meanwhile, Drusus I married Antonia, Augustus' niece, the daughter of Octavia and the deceased Marc Antony. Augustus had arranged the marriage in another attempt to unite the Claudian and Julian families. Eventually, the couple would have three children: Germanicus, Claudius, and Livilla.

With these children, the Julian-Claudian line was prospering, and Augustus was quite content believing that his aggregated family would rule Rome for a long time to come. He also made sure that these marriages were held up as examples for all to follow. He professed that marriage and the traditional virtues of fidelity, supported by the sanctity of vows, were the foundations of Roman society.

Blessed with all of these children, with the scars of the civil war fading, rebellions in the provinces suppressed, and the empire at peace, this was an era of good feelings for both Augustus and for Rome.

To memorialize the peace and the prosperity that came with it, Augustus commissioned the building of the *Ara Pacis Augustae*, the Altar of Peace, in honor of the Pax Romana, the world peace that he had made possible. The monument would take three years to build.

The gleaming, all white marble structure was erected on the Campus Martius. Ten steps led up to the open entrance. Inside the walls, the altar stood on a raised platform, and the roof was open to the sky.

The outside walls were embellished with friezes depicting recognizable figures—the Vestal Virgins, the *pontiff maximus*, the consuls, and their lictors.

Depicted on the inside walls on either side of the entrance were life-sized statues in a religious procession marching toward the steps leading to the altar. The figures in the procession represented members of the imperial family with Augustus leading the procession. Directly behind him was Agrippa. Livia was next, with her hand resting on the shoulder of a young girl, and after her came Tiberius, wearing a toga and looking stern. After Tiberius was his brother, Drusus, with his wife Antonia Minor, who held the hand of their son, Nero Claudius Drusus, the future Germanicus. Other family members followed.

Augustus believed that the monument symbolized the strength, honor, and piety of his family and of Rome. He intended it as an inspiration for the people.

Five years earlier, in 18 BC, he had enacted social reforms and strict morality laws to combat what he saw as the decadence that was spreading across the empire and the deteriorating morals of the citizenry, particularly among the wealthy and the elite. He believed that the decline was the result of the ever-increasing wealth and luxuries pouring into Rome that encouraged extravagance and licentiousness. The number of marriages were dwindling, and upper-class couples weren't having children. Adultery and divorce seemed more common than sound marriages. To counteract this trend, he encouraged both marriage and child rearing. His law, the *Lex Julia et Papia*, required men between the ages of twenty-five and sixty to marry; the age for women was between twenty and fifty. Anyone not in compliance lost certain privileges and rights. The law made adultery a crime punishable by exile and forfeiture of property. A father who caught an adulterer with his daughter in his home or the home of his son-in-law could kill the adulterer and his daughter with impunity. Husbands weren't allowed to kill their adulterous wives, but, for killing the wife's lover, the punishment would be lenient. To discourage sexual immorality, cuckolded husbands had to divorce their adulterous wives, inflicting severe financial consequences for the wives as well as a loss of parental privileges.

To insulate the nobility from libertine or degenerate influences, the law forbade any man eligible for the Senate to marry a freedwoman or an actress or the daughter of an actor or actress. Senator's daughters were forbidden to marry a freedman, an actor, or the son of an actor or actress. Also, no freeborn man could marry a prostitute, a procuress, or a woman convicted of adultery.

Augustus attempted to control the most personal aspects of his subjects' lives. He assessed heavier taxes on the unmarried and offered rewards for marriage and childbearing. Any senator he considered immoral or corrupt was removed from the senatorial rolls.

However, the morality laws didn't cure the problem. Divorces continued to increase and births continued to decline, especially among the nobility and gentry. Augustus became more and more frustrated, and took to lecturing senators, equestrians, and retiring soldiers about the duty to marry and have children. No ceremony went without his admonishing anyone who remained single.

On one occasion, he summoned the entire order of equestrians to the Forum for a lecture. He divided the group into the married and unmarried, and congratulated the married and urged them to continue having more children. "Rome has been built generation upon generation by proud Romans like you."

To the unmarried, he wasn't kind. He asked them if they thought they were Vestal Virgins, and, if they weren't virgins, then why did they squander their virility on prostitutes of all kinds instead of coupling with decent women of their own class? How many unknown children had they discarded in the brothels rather than producing and rearing healthy Roman citizens?

Augustus called them murderers of their own posterity and of Rome's. The army needed officers to protect the empire, and he warned that without enough officers to fill the ranks, Rome would soon find itself overrun by barbarians.

"Without descendants," he said, "what is the purpose of your lives— just to indulge yourself and leave nothing behind? Your fathers left you their hard-fought-for properties, so that you could live with dignity, not like brigands, not like rabble in the streets asking for handouts. And you must leave something for your children, so they can improve upon your legacy."

Many complained about his moralizing and the strictness of his laws, and some said that Augustus was atoning for his own indiscretions, reforming both himself and the state. Eventually, his morality laws would have unexpected consequences for him and his own family.

CHAPTER FOURTEEN

While Augustus stayed in Rome passing laws and addressing administrative and other problems, Agrippa traveled to the East, where he established the city of Mytilene as his base of operations from where he could oversee the region.

Mytilene was an ancient Greek city on the Island of Lesbos in the Aegean Sea between Greece and Asia Minor. It had a storied history. In 485 BC, it rebelled against the rule of Athens but was defeated. As punishment, Athens ruled that all the men would be killed and all the women and children sold into slavery. But, on the day that the executions were to begin, a ship arrived from Athens with a decree rescinding the order. The Mytilenes were grateful for the reprieve, but would forever harbor deep-seated resentments against Athens.

Since 86 BC, when Sulla conquered and took control of Athens, Mytilene became a staunch ally of Rome, and Roman generals often headquartered there.

King Herod the Great of Judea, Rome's most important ally in the East, visited Agrippa at Mytilene, and the two became friends. They traveled throughout the region together, touring cities and military posts. Herod introduced Agrippa to governors, kings, and important local leaders. The king showed him the vast building projects he had undertaken, including aqueducts, towers, and the port city of Caesarea, which he named for Julius Caesar.

Herod's projects combined architectural elements of Judea's ancient traditions with classical styles. The king needed to satisfy the tastes of his native orthodox citizens, but he also had a strong predilection to follow newer Greek and Roman models. Blending the styles worked well. An example was a project he called Herodium. It was a massive fortified palace on a huge artificial hill that was to become his mausoleum when he died.

The two men traveled to Jerusalem. Herod arranged a grand welcome for Agrippa there and had the entire population assembled in their finest garments to greet him. In return, Agrippa offered a hecatomb—the sacrifice of 100 cattle—to Jehovah, the god of the Jews, and provided a feast for the people. To commemorate the occasion, Herod had Agrippa's name inscribed at the top of the temple gate.

Agrippa's visit was in stark contrast to the capture of the city in 63 BC by Pompey the Great, when Pompey had sacrilegiously entered the inner sanctum of the temple.

In October 14 BC, Julia was in Athens and gave birth to her daughter, Agrippina. Agrippa wanted to visit them in Athens, but had to deal with problems between client kingdoms in the Crimea on the north shore of the Black Sea. Military force or threats of force were needed, so Tiberius and Herod combined their fleets and sailed north from Jerusalem to the Bosporus. The might of their combined fleets convinced the disputing kingdoms to negotiate a settlement.

From the Bosporus, Agrippa and Herod traveled south along the Aegean coast of Asia Minor to the port city of Ephesus. Along the way they stopped at towns and cities, settling disputes, granting pardons, and dispensing justice. It was said that they were in competition with one another to be the most generous. From Ephesus, they crossed to the island of Samos, where Herod arranged for a delegation of Jewish leaders to meet Agrippa. They had grievances with Greek city officials who had forced Jews to go to court on the Sabbath, required them to serve in the city militias, and confiscated the taxes that they had collected to send back to Jerusalem.

Agrippa conducted a hearing with both sides arguing their positions. He ruled immediately and sent an edict to the Greek city magistrates, writing:

The Jews have petitioned me that I also would confirm what had been granted by Augustus. I would therefore have you take notice, that according to the will of Augustus and Agrippa, I permit them to use and do according to the customs of their forefathers without disturbance.

The edict was received with great joy in the Jewish communities. This was a major accomplishment for Herod, raising his stature among his people. In gratitude, when Herod left Samos to return to Jerusalem, he promised that his next grandson would be named after Agrippa.

Agrippa spent the winter on Samos, and, in the spring, returned to Rome to meet with Augustus. They discussed how and where to deploy the legions. Revolts were ongoing in Illyricum, and the Roman commander there had made an urgent request for reinforcements. The question was who should be sent.

In earlier years, Augustus would have gone himself, but he was getting older and was not up to what promised to be a difficult campaign. Agrippa, although he, too, was tired, agreed to go. In November 13 BC, he left for Illyricum with two legions, hoping this would be his last campaign.

It took a year, but in 12 BC, Agrippa completed the military campaign in Illyria, subjugating most of the rebelling tribes there and signing peace treaties with them. It had been an arduous campaign, and he was uncharacteristically tired. In winter, not feeling well, he traveled to his villa in Campania where he fell seriously ill. In March, a messenger was sent to Augustus with the news. Augustus rushed to Campania to be with his greatest friend, but was too late. Agrippa was dead at fifty-one.

For the funeral, the body was dressed in ceremonial military attire. A priest slipped a coin under Agrippa's tongue to pay the underworld ferryman Charon to row his spirit across the river Styx to Elysium for an eternal afterlife. The funeral procession traveled for two days from Campania to Rome with thousands of people lining the road to see it pass. Augustus, Tiberius, and Drusus I rode on horseback behind the wagon carrying the body.

At Rome, the procession continued to the Temple of the Divine Julius Caesar where all the members of the family assembled. Julia stood with her four children—Gaius, now eight-years-old; Julia the Younger, seven;

Lucius, five; and Agrippina, almost two. Julia was also seven months pregnant with a child who, if it was a boy, would be named Agrippa Postumus.

Throngs of citizens filled the Forum and surrounded the mourners. Actors wearing death masks of Agrippa's ancestors stood on a platform above the mourners. Eulogies were delivered, and Augustus gave the last one, saying, "No one would have greater imperium that you. You were raised to the highest position with our support and through your own virtues by the agreement of all men."

The body was placed on the funeral pyre, the flames lit, and the body consumed. The ashes were mixed with oil and honey and poured into an urn, which Augustus carried to his family mausoleum, placing it next to the remains of Marcellus.

Augustus grieved, but, just as he had after the death of Marcellus, immediately began planning. He knew that one man couldn't rule the empire alone. Agrippa had ruled half of it for him and someone was needed to take his place. Since his grandsons Lucius and Gaius were too young, he had to decide which of Livia's two sons it would be? Drusus I was charismatic, charming, and flamboyant; Tiberius was thoughtful, methodical, and competent.

The *princeps* summoned Tiberius for a meeting at the Pantheon. Tiberius walked there through the Forum with a brisk step, projecting confidence, his shoulders squared and his chin high. He thought Augustus would name him as Agrippa's successor. If that happened, he might follow in the footsteps of his hero and eventually rule the Roman empire.

He arrived at the Pantheon first and waited on the steps. When Augustus arrived, his lictors and praetorian guards ushered the public out of the temple, and Augustus and Tiberius entered together.

"I thought it fitting to meet at Agrippa's magnificent building," Augustus said.

"It's a great monument to him," Tiberius said. "I'm glad he lived to see it finished."

They walked through the portico and around the rotunda, passing the statues of the gods that stood in the niches in the walls. They stopped at the statue of Apollo, the Greek god of music and poetry that the Romans had adopted as their own. He was believed to speak through the Oracle of Delphi at the temple of Apollo on the slopes of Mount Parnassus in Greece.

"Apollo taught that it is right and just to appreciate those who have done good works." Augustus said. "So, I appreciate all you've done for me and for Rome."

"Thank you."

Augustus had a chair brought to a spot in the center of the rotunda where a shaft of sunlight from the oculus shone on the floor. He sat in the chair with the sunlight encircling and illuminating him, making him look as though he were a god, while Tiberius stayed standing before him.

"I know how much Agrippa's death has hurt you," Augustus said. "He was like a second father to you."

"Yes, he was."

"But his death has hurt Rome more. There's a vacuum of leadership that must be filled. He had the same powers as I had, and together we kept the empire united. We owe him an enormous gratitude."

"We do."

"I brought you here because Rome needs you now. Do you think you're ready to take the responsibility?

"I am."

"I agree. But before that, I need your commitment to the Julian line. For you to be accepted by the people and to be seen as my possible successor, you must be part of the family."

Tiberius realized what was coming next. Augustus was using the same argument he had used on Agrippa.

"You must be seen," Augustus continued, "as the latest in the line from Aeneas and the Divine Julius Caesar, the line favored by Venus and Apollo." Augustus paused, took a breath, and said, "The only way to achieve that is for you to marry my daughter, Julia."

Tiberius wasn't surprised but nevertheless felt as though he had been hit in the head with a mallet. His life was being upended. He looked at the illuminated Augustus, and felt a shiver go through him. The talk of connections to the gods seemed strange, unreal, and he felt as though he was in a kind of dream-like state.

"Well?" Augustus asked.

Tiberius had to think without Augustus staring at him. He turned away and walked around the rotunda. He walked three times in a circle around Augustus, wondering what to say, what to do. For a moment, he felt revulsion toward Augustus. He really thinks he's a god, he thought.

"Well," Augustus said again.

Tiberius stopped in front of him, "Can I give you my answer tomorrow?"

"No, before you stop walking in circles and before you leave this building, I want an answer."

Without thinking, Tiberius made a sarcastic remark, something he had never done to Augustus. "Who do you think you are, Popillius?"

They both knew exactly what he meant. Famously, in 168 BC, the King of Syria, Antiochus IV, had invaded Egypt and was marching with his army toward Alexandria when he was met by a Roman ambassador, Gaius Popillius Laenas, who was accompanied by only a small contingent of troops. Antiochus held out his hand to Popillius, but the ambassador declined and instructed Antiochus to read a decree from the Roman Senate that forbade him to wage war against Egypt and ordered him to return to his own country. Antiochus read the decree and said he would confer with his council to decide what to do. He said he would inform Rome of his decision later. Then, Popillius, with a stick, drew a circle in the sand around the king, saying, "Before you step out of that circle give me a reply to lay before the Senate."

Astounded, Antiochus hesitated for a moment then said, "I will do what the Senate thinks right." He turned around and returned with his army to Syria.

Augustus first scowled at the remark, then said, "Antiochus made the right decision."

Tiberius understood what he meant. "What if I say no?"

Augustus scowled again. "Then someone else will be the next Agrippa; someone else will be my successor. And you know how these things work. You'll be seen as a competitor, perhaps an enemy to be feared. I don't know whether I ever told you this, but Maecenus once advised me about Agrippa—and Maecenus has always been right in these things—he told me to either kill Agrippa or make him my son-in-law. I made the right decision."

Tiberius was surprised to hear that, and wasn't pleased to hear that Augustus took such counsel from Maecenus. "What did he say about me?"

"This is a different situation. This is about Rome. It's about continuing all the accomplishments we've made. You must do this. Rome needs you."

"You know how much I love Vipsania."

"Yes. I'm sorry about that. But it must be done."

"Julia may not want it. She has children already," Tiberius said.

"Julia wants it. And your mother wants it," Augustus said. "Of course, you'll have to wait until Julia delivers her child."

Tiberius walked around in a circle one more time. His head was pounding. "Alright. But don't announce it until I tell you," Tiberius said, almost disrespectfully.

"But it must be soon. I want the wedding before you go to Illyria. The rebels there are still causing trouble. Without Agrippa, we need a strong hand."

Tiberius nodded, and left the Pantheon without asking permission to leave.

He walked randomly through the streets, thinking that he would get a ship and take Vipsania someplace where no one would know them. But that would never work.

As he walked, his guards cleared people out of his path. When he got home, he quietly entered the house. Vipsania was seated at her spinning-wheel, looking very much like Livia, the picture of beauty and womanly virtue.

He knew it was not right, but he had to have her. He thought it might be the last time that he'd make love to her. He'd do it before telling her that he was going to have to divorce her. Hesitantly, he asked, "Can we go to bed?"

"Of course, let's go," she said.

In the bedroom, she undressed while he closed the doors and shuttered the windows.

"You always like it so dark," Vipsania said. "You don't want to see me?"

"That's not so, my beauty. I always want to see you. I just want to escape the outside world. I want us to be alone in our own little world."

He lay next to her on the bed and stared up at the ceiling.

"What do you want to escape from?" she asked.

"Everything."

"Are you alright?"

"No. I'm not," he said.

"What's wrong?"

"Augustus stabbed me in the heart."

"What do you mean?" There was panic in her voice.

"He's ordered me to divorce you."

"Why?"

He didn't answer.

She looked closely into his eyes, "Oh, I see."

"Yes. He's doing to me what he did to Agrippa."

"What did you tell him?"

Again, Tiberius didn't answer.

"I see," she said. She didn't cry, but dressed quickly and left the room.

He punched himself in the face.

The next morning, Tiberius needed to talk to someone. He asked Pometius to bring Menelaus to him.

"He's been ill lately," Pometius said.

"Then I'll go to him."

Tiberius and Pometius walked down the Palatine Hill to Menelaus' house.

On the way, Pometius asked, "Is anything wrong?"

"It couldn't be much worse," Tiberius said. "Don't breathe a word of this to anyone. I have to divorce my wife."

"No! Why?"

"I have to marry Julia."

"I'm sorry," Pometius said, not knowing what else to say. Rumors had been floating around that Julia was openly promiscuous and had taken many lovers when Agrippa was away on campaign. There was even a rumor that she had used slaves. That part was probably not true, Pometius thought, but much of the rest could be. Her cover was that her children all resembled Agrippa, so how could she have had affairs outside of her marriage. But a story circulated that once when she was asked by a friend whether she was worried about getting pregnant by one of her lovers, she replied, "I never took a passenger on board unless the ship's hold already had a full cargo."

Pometius thought better of saying anything about it.

As they walked, Tiberius put his hand on Pometius' shoulder, "I have to do this terrible thing. I have to betray Vipsania. But I'm going to try to balance it out with something good. I'm going to get my mother to grant you your freedom. You've been a slave too long."

Pometius didn't respond at first, then, in a lowered voice, said, "I don't feel like a slave, but maybe I don't know any better. Maybe I don't know what it feels like to be free. I'd like to find out. If you can do that for me, I'll always be in your debt."

"I'm sure I can do it."

When they reached Menelaus' cottage, his wife let them in. The old tutor was sitting in a chair and didn't stand up. He had aged a lot in the past year.

"How are you, my tutor?" Tiberius said.

"I'm okay. My legs are giving me trouble, but my mind still works. For now, at least."

"Your mind will always work."

Menelaus pointed to a chair. "What can I do for you?"

Tiberius explained the situation to him. He told him that he had already said yes, but now he was having second thoughts. "I don't know if I can live through it. You know how tormented I was about my father obeying Augustus and giving up his wife, and then Agrippa, who was like my second father, giving up his wife to marry someone he didn't care for. I criticized Agrippa for doing it, for caving in, yet here I am about to do the same exact thing with the same exact woman. I'm the biggest hypocrite of all."

Menelaus looked at Pometius, "Could you wait outside?"

"Of course," Pometius said.

Menelaus rubbed his temples. "Why can't Augustus just give you the authority you need and let someone else marry Julia?"

"Augustus thinks that he has to maintain a straight line from the Divine Julius Caesar," Tiberius said. "He thinks that he must ensure that the next ruler is connected to the Julian line. Apparently, he believes all the tales about Venus and Aeneus and the touch of the gods on the Julian line. I'm beginning to think that he believes that he is a god himself."

"I take it you don't subscribe to the accepted views that our gods exist and favor chosen men over others."

"I'm not disavowing belief in the gods, but the names and forms we give them are probably just figments of our imaginations—more accurately, our collective imaginations. And I don't see why the gods, even if they really exist, would favor the Julian family above all others."

"That's a good point, my boy," Menelaus said, smiling. They both remembered the many times he had said those words to Tiberius during their lessons.

Menelaus shifted forward in his chair. "You must remember, it doesn't matter if the gods exist or not. They might; they might not. What matters is that men believe they exist. Men create myths that, in turn, create duties and obligations. Then they make vows and promises that they would rather die than break. This drives them to battle, to risk their lives, to conquest. You can't talk them out of it."

"True enough."

"Augustus believes in the destiny of the Julian line," Menelaus said. "He's going to preserve it. I think you have no choice. If you refuse him, he'll see you not as an ally but as an enemy. He'll punish you, or worse."

"Why can't I just leave?"

"Why give up everything you have, everything you've worked so hard for? Let's be practical; he needs you as a protector of Julia's sons until they are old enough. You're in a strong position now, and if you go along with his offer, you'll become stronger. He's not in good health. Time may solve the problem."

"Thank you," Tiberius said as he got up to leave. "Please be well. I'll come to visit you soon."

"Please do. And what have you decided?"

"I have one more thing to do before I decide."

Tiberius met Pometius outside and they walked to the Julian-Claudian domus. When they arrived, Pometius went straight to the kitchen; Tiberius went to the atrium and sat with his mother. He kissed her on both cheeks.

"Has Augustus told you?" he asked.

"Yes. And I'm so glad you agreed," she said. "It will finally end the competition between the Julians and the Claudians. The two greatest families combined into one."

"Perhaps, but I don't think you'll ever end the competition between families. Look at the Claudians, one family, but still divided into factions. It's man's nature to divide into factions. You have to have someone to oppose in order to get people to follow you and form a party."

"That's very cynical," Livia said. "Your marriage will help unify Rome."

"Mother, I hope you're right. But I have another issue."

"What?"

"I want to give Pometius his freedom."

"You'll have to ask Augustus."

"No, I don't. Pometius is your slave."

"Augustus is the pater of the family; everything is under his power."

"That's not true. When you married him, you weren't handed over *in manu*, but you were married *sine manu*, so you maintained your status in your father's *paterfamilia* and you maintained your own property, including your slaves, including Pometius."

"I'll have to ask Augustus."

"Ask him, but tell him if he doesn't free Pometius, I won't marry Julia."

"You don't mean that."

"I do. Make it clear to Augustus that before I do what he demands, my demands must be met."

"Son, let's not antagonize the *princeps*. If you say that Pometius belongs to me, if that's correct, and the registrars say that it's alright, it's fine with me. Give him his freedom."

"Thank you, mother." He kissed her cheek.

Tiberius found Pometius in the kitchen teasing the kitchen girls. Tiberius put his arm around Pometius. "It's all set," he said. "Tomorrow we go to see the registrar. You'll be free."

Tiberius was shocked by the reaction. Pometius fell to his knees and kissed Tiberius' hand. "Thank you, thank you." Tears ran down his cheeks.

Here was a man as big and as strong as Tiberius, yet totally overwhelmed. The girls all surrounded Pometius, kissing him again and again. Everybody was crying and laughing at the same time, even the stern Matea.

Matea kissed Tiberius, and some of the other girls kissed him, and they all began kissing and hugging Pometius again.

Two months after Agrippa's death, Julia delivered her fifth child, a boy they named Agrippa Postumus. Then, in March of 11 BC, Tiberius and Julia married. It was a solemn event, followed by a sedate banquet in the Julian-Claudian domus. Augustus gave a formal speech, explaining how the marriage of this wonderful couple would bring together their great, illustrious families, strengthen Rome, and secure its destiny far into the future.

The atmosphere lightened when Drusus, the best man, gave a toast. He talked about their childhood years and brought up several embarrassing but humorous moments. He talked about moving into the same house as Julia and told of more embarrassing moments. Nothing unseemly. He was tactful, knowing how strict Augustus had become about anything that might debase the character of his family, his circle of friends, or the Roman people in general.

Tiberius hardly laughed at jokes, and he was in no mood to laugh now; he smiled only slightly. Drusus said that he was going off to fight those "hilarious" Germans, and that when he came back, he'd bring some German jokes "that even my older brother might find funny."

The evening ended with everyone generally satisfied and sober. Tiberius and Julia were to spend the night in the guest cottage. He didn't carry her across the threshold.

The next day, Pometius drove the couple in a horse-carriage to Tiberius' country estate in Sperlunca in the Campagna region. Pometius had been freed, but still remained obligated to Tiberius, and, as a freedman, he would become the caretaker of Tiberius' properties and account books.

After two weeks of what they called their honeymoon, Tiberius and Julia returned to Rome, and lived in the villa where Agrippa and Julia had lived. The villa had been built by Pompey the Great at the height of his power; it was the most elaborate, ostentatious villa in the city. The people called it Pompey's palace, as though he were a king. After Pompey's beheading in Egypt, his villa was confiscated, and Marc Antony bought it at a discount price. When Antony committed suicide in Egypt, Agrippa acquired the property, and left it to Julia in his will. With her marriage to Tiberius, the ownership passed to him.

In his new home Tiberius did his best to play the part of a good husband. He told himself that, like Agrippa, he was a soldier following orders for the good of the nation, and kept up the appearance of a happy marriage.

CHAPTER FIFTEEN

In May 11 BC, the campaigning season opened. Tiberius took command of the legions in Illyria, and Drusus took command of the legions in Germany. They led their separate armies north, Tiberius taking a route east of the Alps, and Drusus taking a route west of the Alps.

Drusus quickly won several victories. He sent daily progress reports back to Rome, just as Julius Caesar had about his victories in Gaul. To his troops, Drusus announced that he intended to win the *spolia opina*, an award given for killing an enemy leader in single combat.

Tiberius moved more methodically. He was facing tribes that were not only rebelling against Roman hegemony, but were attacking allies of Rome. The most formidable and warlike were the Pannonians.

Although there was potential danger, Julia accompanied him on the campaign. Litter bearers carried her on a curtained platform, and each evening, her staff set up a tent with couches and a bath for her. She enjoyed her special status and stayed with the campaign until she realized she was pregnant. Returning to Rome, she gave birth to a son. Unfortunately, the boy lived only a few weeks. Julia had already had five children with Agrippa, and she probably wouldn't have any more. Tiberius was disappointed. The child's death was a fatal blow to the prospects of their marriage.

◆

Before venturing to meet the enemy, Tiberius drilled his soldiers in their formations and the maniple system, the system the Romans had developed in the third century BC when they were fighting the Samnites in the Apennine Mountains.

Prior to that time, the Romans had used the standard phalanx formation, grouping the troops in a single block of heavily-armed infantry many ranks deep. The phalanx operated best on flat, unbroken ground, but in mountainous terrain, it had disadvantages, and lacked the mobility to deal with fast-moving skirmishers. So, the Romans changed their formations from the phalanx to a more maneuverable maniple formation in which the maniples were arranged in checker-board patterns, each distinct maniple separated from the next by a space equivalent to its own size, which allowed greater flexibility and tactical deployment. This tactical system made great demands on the individual line soldiers who had to respond to orders and signals and move in unison with their comrades. Rigorous discipline and training were required, a Roman strength, and the soldiers quickly learned the new system, making their legions the most potent military force in the world.

Tiberius reveled in his command. He believed his destiny was to be Rome's greatest general, not the most popular or spectacular, but the most competent and efficient. He made sure that his military tribunes, centurions, and soldiers knew all the signals and what they were expected to do on command. To keep his army as mobile as possible without any hindrances, he personally inspected the centurions and checked their baggage to be sure they weren't carrying anything unnecessary. He ordered the centurions to do the same with each of their legionaries. He also banished camp followers, including hucksters and prostitutes; he wanted no distractions.

Although he was a stern disciplinarian, his soldiers respected him. He cared for them, and always paid special attention to the sick or wounded, putting his own doctors and provisions at their disposal. The soldiers could see that he was a hardworking general, who would never risk their lives unnecessarily or recklessly. They understood that following his orders would give them their best chance of survival.

With his army in battle condition, he moved north through rough territory to confront the main Pannonian army. Contact was made, and the two armies lined up on a field in opposing formations. Tiberius kept his cavalry behind the foot soldiers to be deployed as necessary. Riding on horseback among the maniples, he shouted instructions and encouragement.

The Roman legionaries moved forward. When they were close enough, Tiberius gave the signal to launch their *pilum* spears and charge. Hundreds of spears flew in the air at the same time, many striking and killing enemy soldiers. Many more penetrated the shields of the enemy, making the shields cumbersome to wield. While the enemy tried to recover, the Romans were upon them, attacking with their swords.

The Pannonians fought stubbornly but eventually gave ground. Tiberius believed the Romans were winning, but at one point when his legionaries were pressing forward, a contingent of enemy archers suddenly appeared on the Roman right flank. Tiberius saw the threat and immediately thought of the annihilation of Crassus' army by Parthian arrows at Carrhae. He wheeled his horse in front of the cavalry and shouted, "Charge! Charge! Charge!"

His first contingent of cavalry responded immediately and raced full-speed at the archers. The enemy archers aimed their arrows at Tiberius, the commander, and many arrows flew by him. He thought this would be his moment to die, but knew he had to lead the charge. One arrow caromed off the neck of his horse and struck Tiberius in the chest, but it didn't penetrate his plated armor.

The contest was whether the cavalry could reach the archers before being cut down by the flying arrows. Many men and horses were struck and felled, but enough survived to attack the archers at close range. Tiberius saw one of his men struck in the throat by an arrow from a nearby archer. The soldier tried to scream but made only a gurgling sound. Enraged, Tiberius charged at the archer and plunged his sword into the archer's neck before he could draw another arrow.

As the rest of the cavalry caught up, the archers turned and fled in disorder. Tiberius led the chase and his horsemen rode down the enemy, plunging their swords into one fleeing archer after another.

When the cavalry's charge was over, more than two hundred of the enemy were dead. Fifty Romans were dead or wounded. Blood was everywhere. Tiberius dismounted and stood for a moment, staring at the bodies, hearing the moans of the wounded. Covered in blood, he felt drained, as if all the pent-up rage and frustrations of his life had been released in a cathartic explosion. He looked around at the carnage, then sheathed his sword, remounted, and began shouting instructions at his troops.

With the menace of the archers eliminated, the legionaries defeated the Pannonians in a hard-fought battle. For Romans, the harder the battle won, the greater the glory of victory. The word spread through the ranks about how Tiberius had led the cavalry charge, and more than ever, the legionaries respected their leader, both as a great general and as a soldier as courageous as any man among them.

News of the fate of the Pannonians convinced other tribes in the region to capitulate, and Tiberius led his army to the Danube River without encountering much opposition. The campaign had taken three years.

In 10 BC, while Tiberius and Drusus were securing the northern reaches of the empire, Augustus continued implementing his plan to make Rome the most magnificent of all cities, surpassing Athens, Alexandria, and Antioch. The Ara Pacis on the Campus Martius was near completion, and Augustus wanted to embellish the Circus Maximus. From the City of Heliopolis in Egypt, he transported a twenty-four-meter granite obelisk weighing 263 tons that had been erected 1200 years before by the pharaoh Rameses in honor of the Egyptian sun-god. Augustus had a special barge built to transport it from Heliopolis to Rome. Hieroglyphics had been inscribed on the obelisk from top to bottom, and at the new base on which it would stand, Augustus placed an inscription that proclaimed he was the new ruler of Egypt.

In 9 BC, Tiberius returned to Rome, and was elected consul. Augustus had the Senate grant him extraordinary responsibilities and powers, effectively making him his equal in legal authority. For Tiberius, all seemed to be going well. Then, terrible news came from Germany—Drusus I, his beloved brother, was dying.

Drusus had fallen from his horse and broken his leg while riding back to Rome after a victorious battle. His leg became infected, and he was racked with fever.

Tiberius immediately set out on horseback to be with his brother. He rode through dangerous territories to reach him but arrived only in time to see him die. His death would not have seemed as terrible if he had been wounded in combat or while trying to win the *spolia opina*, but, instead, he was injured in an ordinary accident.

To demonstrate to the people how great the loss was to him and to Rome, Tiberius escorted Drusus' body back to the capital, following the casket for two hundred miles. As he rode, he wondered whether the gods were punishing Rome, the imperial family, or him. They had taken Marcellus, Agrippa, and now Drusus.

In Rome, the Senate posthumously awarded Drusus the agnomen name "Germanicus," meaning the conqueror of Germany. The name would pass to his descendants. His oldest son, Nero Claudius Drusus, assumed the agnomen and became known to the public as "Germanicus." The other son, Tiberius Claudius Drusus, didn't assume the name, and remained simply "Claudius."

Tiberius dealt with his grief by throwing himself into work. He undertook two special commissions—a reorganization of the grain supply and an inquiry into the conditions of the slave barracks throughout Italy. The slave inquiry found that travelers who had been kidnapped and sold into slavery were confined in the slave barracks. They protested that they were freeborn but had not been allowed to prove their true identity and status. Tiberius conducted extensive hearings and freed more than a thousand of these wrongly enslaved individuals. Many of those who were freed expressed gratitude to Tiberius for years afterward.

He also found a substantial number of individuals who were passing themselves off as slaves so that they could avoid service in the legions. He punished these men severely.

With his commissions completed, Tiberius was elected consul for a second time in 8 BC. In a grand gesture of gratitude, he announced that with his own funds he would restore the Temple of Concord where he had been mentored so often by Menelaus, renaming it the temple of Drusus and Tiberius.

In the spring, Augustus gave Tiberius command of the legions that Drusus had led in Germany. He marched the legions northeast toward the Elbe River, intending to engage each German tribe separately. But, while marching through a valley, Tiberius saw a huge mass of German warriors on the surrounding hills. He guessed that the Germans had combined their forces, probably under the leadership of the Cherubi, the most powerful of their tribes.

Tiberius had seen ferocious-looking tribes before, but he was shocked by the appearance of these warriors. Tall and strong framed with wild red hair, shaggy mustaches, and bodies painted with bright colors, they raised an incessant clamor of war songs and howls. Their women fought alongside the men. With their lime-stained shaggy hair, the women looked equally ferocious. They shrieked, making horrible, unnerving sounds that seemed as though they had come from some strange, evil place.

The Romans were on low ground in a valley, and Tiberius decided not to engage in battle at the spot if he could avoid it. He ordered his troops to set up a defensive camp and be ready for an attack.

The Germans, seeing that the Romans were not offering a battle, began taunting them, running partly down the hills, stopping, and hurling insults, rocks, and spears.

Sensing the fear among his soldiers, Tiberius did everything he could to convince them that they would easily defeat these disorganized tribes as long as the legionaries maintained their discipline and formations. He supervised the construction of the camp and told the troops to stay calm. "Let the wild barbarians waste their energy running up and down the hills and howling like animals. When they come, we'll be ready."

Night fell, and no attack by the Germans came. But, at dawn, they were back on the hills, shouting and chanting their war songs.

Tiberius didn't want to engage them by running uphill, so he devised a plan based on one of Hannibal's old tactics. He had the troops begin a march out of the valley. When the Germans saw what they thought was a retreat, they charged down the hills, many running a fast as they could to be the first to attack. They acted not as a disciplined unit but as individual warriors.

Once Tiberius saw this, he ordered an immediate about-face, and had the troops reorganize into tightly-grouped defensive maniple formations.

The Germans attacked but couldn't break up the maniples. The Romans stood shoulder-to-shoulder, using their shields to form a barricade and their swords to stop the attackers. As the Germans began to tire, the Romans began stepping forward in unison, simultaneously clanging their swords against their shields, creating the sound of an unstoppable war machine.

The Germans wearied of the attack and began withdrawing back into the hills, dragging their wounded and dead with them. The legionaries wanted to chase them down, but Tiberius ordered them to hold their places. No Romans were lost and only a few wounded.

The next day, the Germans were gone, so Tiberius returned to his original plan of finding and dealing with the tribes one at a time. During the next months, the legionaries won several small battles, and Tiberius completed Drusus' campaign, gaining total control of Germany to the Elbe River. He negotiated peace terms with the remaining tribes, getting them to pledge fealty to Rome in return for being allowed to establish settlements and maintain their own laws. This was the kind of accomplishment that had earned Julius Caesar so much praise, and in Rome it was said that Tiberius could someday be the equal of Julius Caesar. In 7 BC, for his successes in Illyria, Pannonia, and Germany, the Senate granted him a triumph.

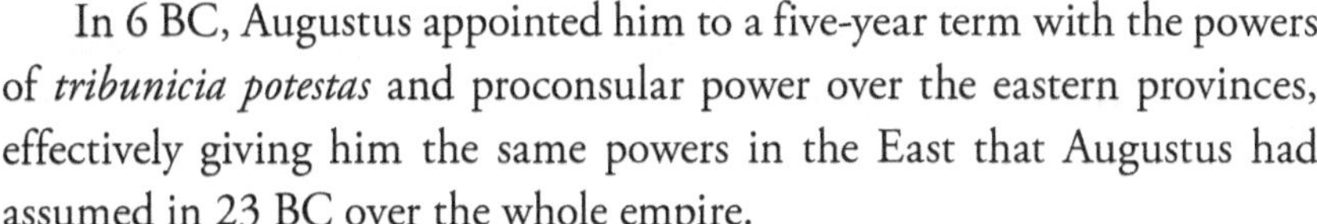

In 6 BC, Augustus appointed him to a five-year term with the powers of *tribunicia potestas* and proconsular power over the eastern provinces, effectively giving him the same powers in the East that Augustus had assumed in 23 BC over the whole empire.

Although Tiberius appeared to be the logical choice to succeed Augustus as *princeps*, Augustus had adopted his grandsons Gaius and Lucius as his sons, and wanted them to succeed him. Gaius was now fourteen and Lucius eleven.

Augustus raised and educated the two boys, personally teaching them everything from how to read to how to swim. He introduced them to administrative duties and took them on missions to the provinces. Augustus also issued an edict that allowed Gaius and Lucius to become magistrates at early ages, making it possible that they might become consuls at age twenty.

Allowing them to become consuls at such a young age made it clear to Tiberius that he was only holding their places until they were old enough to assume power.

No public comment was made as to why Augustus didn't adopt Julia's other son, five-year-old Agrippa Postumus. He had been born after Agrippa had died but within the nine-month period that gave a presumption of legitimacy, but questions about his paternity might have been the reason he wasn't adopted at that time.

Augustus reduced his role as a military commander and turned his attention to domestic matters. He intensified his efforts to improve Roman morals and to resurrect what he believed were the virtues of Rome's ancestors. It had been ten years since he passed the *Lex Julia et Papia* to encourage marriage and childrearing through tax penalties and incentives. The law sent a message, but had only been enforced sporadically in exceptional cases. Since Augustus hadn't seen improvement in marriages and morality, he began imposing punishments in earnest—exiling citizens, confiscating properties, and ordering husbands to divorce adulterous wives. The absolute authority Augustus exercised over such personal matters refuted the contention that the Republic still existed and that the People and the Senate of Rome still ruled. He increasingly used his Praetorian Guards to investigate violations of his morality laws. Ironically, an investigation led to his own family.

Rumors had circulated that while Tiberius was away, Julia had been having affairs with a series of lovers, just as she had done when Agrippa was away. When Augustus heard this, he said they were just rumors, but authorized an investigation.

Coincidentally, Maecenas was found dead in his gardens. How he died was undetermined. Some speculated that it was in connection with the scandal surrounding Julia, and because he was one of Augustus' oldest friends, he had been spared a public indictment and allowed to commit suicide. Tiberius had been away on a campaign in Germany when he heard about Maecenas' death, but didn't know about the rumors involving Julia.

✦

When Tiberius returned to Rome for a month-long stay, he noticed that Julia was frequently away from the house for hours at a time. When he asked about it, she told him that she had been attending a poetry club that the deceased Maecenas had organized. The club continued to meet in his honor. Poetry was popular among Roman elites who wanted to emulate or surpass the Greek poets. Even Augustus had tried his hand at it.

The club invited the best poets in the empire to speak at their meetings, including Virgil, Horace, and Publius Ovidius Naso (Ovid), the author of *Ars Amatoria (The Art of Love)*. Several young nobles were members of the club, including Mark Antony's son Jullus Antonicus, the son whom Augustus had spared from execution because he had lived with Octavia.

The meetings were at night, and on one occasion Tiberius sat by the fireplace waiting for Julia to come home. She was late and when she came in, Tiberius asked her where she had been. She showed him a leather case filled with the poems that the club was reading. He looked through them. "I don't see any by Virgil," he said.

"No, his poetry is not personal or emotional," Julia said, "it's more like made-up history."

"What's this?" Tiberius said, holding up a copy of Ovid's *Ars Amatoria*.

"Let me have that," Julia said as she tried to snatch it back from him.

He wouldn't give it to her and walked around the room reading it. "What is this—a book on how to commit adultery?"

"It's about real life," Julia said.

"Well, I don't want you reading this trash."

"I'll read what I want," she said.

"Who picked it out—that weasel Maecenas?" He tore the book in half and threw it into the fireplace.

"That's a terrible way to talk about the dead, the *princeps'* friend," Julia said as she pushed him out of the way and tried to retrieve the burning paper. She pulled it out of the fireplace and stepped on it, burning her foot.

"I should give you a good beating for that," Tiberius said.

"You wouldn't dare," Julia said.

"Don't be so sure," he said as he turned and went into his study.

All night he lay awake, thinking about his situation. "Here I am, the greatest living general of Rome, disrespected by this bitch of a wife." He knew that divorce would surely destroy him, but it might be worth it. He also thought that since he was no longer sleeping with Julia, he might be able to convince Augustus to let him divorce her. Augustus had promised that if they had no children in three years, they could divorce. She could get another husband who might provide another grandson for Augustus.

In the morning, he summoned Pometius. "Perhaps you could do something for me," he said.

"Of course."

"You're still friendly with all the slaves on the Palatine?"

"Yes."

"Without calling attention to it, see what you can find out about the poetry club that Maecenas ran. See where they meet. See who stays late. See who's sleeping together. But keep it quiet."

CHAPTER SIXTEEN

Early on a morning in 6BC, Tiberius was awakened by the noise of a horse-drawn wagon outside the house. Peering out, he saw servants loading a wagon with baskets of food. He saw Julia climb on the wagon, and as she rode off, he wondered where she was going so early. He went down to the kitchen and asked the cook about it.

"I believe she's taking food to some poor families as part of her charitable duties," the cook said.

"You're fooling with me," Tiberius said, wondering whether the cook really believed what she said.

He left her and went to his study to address some petitions, but couldn't concentrate. Instead, he paced about the study wondering where Julia had gone. At midday, he noticed Pometius standing outside the door, and waved for him to come in and sit down. He came in, but remained standing.

"What do you have to tell me?" Tiberius said.

"I've checked on the matters you asked about," Pometius said.

"And what did you find out?"

Pometius spoke reluctantly, "I was told by several people that while you were away, Julia and her poetry club friends spent almost every night drinking for hours late into the night."

"Anything else?"

Pometius took a breath. "People said that after some of the parties she went off with different men."

Tiberius grasped the sides of his desk. "Anything else."

Pometius didn't want to say anything more. He knew how quickly Tiberius could explode, and he saw the rage building in his face. Nevertheless, he continued. "She went off several times with Jullus Antonius."

Tiberius face reddened "That bitch. And with Marc Antony's son no less, the one Augustus let live after Actium. What a joke. That'll make the *princeps* happy. He'll be even happier when he learns that his enemy's son is screwing his daughter, a great example for his marriage and morality campaign. That bitch!" He stood up. "Where is she now?"

"I don't know," Pometius said.

Tiberius rushed to his dressing closet, put on his mail-armored cuirass, and strapped his gladius to his side.

"What are you doing?" Pometius said in a loud voice.

"I'm going to find her, and if she's with him, I'm going to finish them both. I'm entitled to. It's the law."

Pometius stood in his way. "No, you're not. You'd have to catch them in the act for it to be legal."

"Get out of my way," Tiberius said as blood rushed to his head. Everything appeared red to him. He pushed by Pometius.

At the front door, Pometius grabbed his arm. Tiberius spun around, threw him to the floor, yanked open the front door, and started down the steps, but Pometius lunged after him and grabbed him around the knees, begging, "Please, don't do this. It's not worth it."

Passers-by stood frozen, staring at them. No one dared to intervene.

"Let go of me," Tiberius shouted as he as grabbed the hilt of the gladius.

"Listen to me," Pometius said. "We can find another way to do this. Let Augustus find out. He'll have to do something."

"I said let go of me. I mean it," Tiberius said as he pulled the gladius from its scabbard. He looked down and saw the sword above Pometius' head. The sight stopped him. He pushed the gladius back into the scabbard, and lifted Pometius up.

"I'm sorry, my friend," Tiberius said. "You're right. Let the exalted Augustus deal with his slut of a daughter."

"That would be the best way," Pometius said.

"But he must know what she's been up to, why hasn't he done anything?" Tiberius said.

"People have tried to tell him," Pometius said, "but he ignores them."

"Maybe I should tell him," Tiberius said.

"That wouldn't be a good idea," Pometius said, "he would hate you for it. It's better that he finds out from someone else."

As they talked, a praetorian guardsman arrived with a summons from Augustus for Tiberius to attend that afternoon's session of the Senate. "What does he want now?" Tiberius said in front of the guardsman.

When the guardsman left, Pometius said, "Remember how Menelaus used to warn you about talking aloud in front of anyone? People listen and remember everything."

"I don't care. I'm fed up," Tiberius said as he started to walk to the Senate. He was still wearing his cuirass and his sword, and Pometius stopped him, "You can't wear the sword into the Senate."

Tiberius realized what a crazed state he had been in and how he hadn't been thinking clearly. He went back to his house, took off the cuirass and sword, put on his toga, and walked down the Palatine to the Forum and the Senate.

When Tiberius arrived at the Senate, Augustus was already speaking in the well of the chamber. He waved for Tiberius to stand next to him.

"I'm glad my son-in-law, Tiberius, is here for the next announcement," Augustus said. "He's going to lead an expedition to the eastern provinces to address several pressing problems out there. He'll make our wishes clear to our client kings in Syria, Armenia, and Judea. They'll have to understand that although Agrippa is no longer with us, we have a strong, capable commander to take his place."

Augustus went on the explain that a legion was waiting for Tiberius at the City of Ephesus on the west coast of Asia Minor. From there, he would be able to influence the eastern provinces. Augustus said that he hoped all matters would be resolved peacefully and that he wouldn't have to resort to military force.

Tiberius muttered to himself, "You could have told me in advance." But within a moment, he felt glad. This would get him away from Julia.

Augustus adjourned the session, saying that he had to get ready to leave the next day for Nola, the city of his birth in the Campagna region east of Neapolis. He left the Senate, but Tiberius stayed on, conversing with several senators who congratulated him. They wished him good fortune, and several offered their services to him. Tiberius spoke with Admiral Terullius of the imperial navy and confirmed that his ships and provisions would be ready for his departure to the East. As they were talking, a Praetorian guardsman delivered another summons from Augustus, calling Tiberius to a meeting at the Julian-Claudian domus.

He went directly to the domus, and when he arrived, he found Sejanus, the Praetorian Prefect, seated next to Augustus, a clear sign that Sejanus had gained the confidence of the *princeps*. Tiberius thought perhaps that's why Augustus was sending him to the East. Was he making room for Sejanus to replace him as second-in-command?

Sejanus, a dark-eyed Tuscan with ancestry going back to the mysterious Etruscans, was an articulate, engaging person, who knew a great deal about worldly affairs from the arts to politics to witchcraft. He was an avid collector of fine objects. His most prized possession was a bronze statue of the mythological Chimera—a fire-breathing lion, with the head of a ram protruding from its back, and a long, curved tail with the head of a snarling snake at its end.

People said that Sejanus could charm a snake. Apparently, he had charmed Augustus and had become powerful. Using his Praetorian Guards as investigators, he inquired into all matters of public and private life, and had obtained sensitive information about all the prominent Roman families.

Augustus told Tiberius to sit down while Sejanus reported about two cases. The first concerned the murder of a patrician, Pomponius, who was killed in his home on the Esquiline Hill, not far from Tiberius' house.

Under Roman law, when the master of a household was murdered, all the slaves of that household were executed. This was meant to ensure that household slaves would fight as hard as they could to repel invading criminals and would report slave plots. It was also meant to discourage slaves awaiting manumission-by-will from prematurely bringing about the master's demise.

After the murder of Pomponius was discovered, all twelve of his household slaves ran away. That didn't necessarily mean that they were guilty of the murder, but, aware of their fate, they tried to escape.

"We've captured four of them so far," Sejanus said, "and I'm confident we'll track down the others."

"Have they been executed?" Augustus asked.

"Not yet. We're interrogating them to get more information first."

Tiberius asked, "Could they be innocent? Maybe they tried to protect Pomponius."

"It doesn't matter," Sejanus said.

The second case involved an investigation into a group of senators who had openly discussed limiting the number of pro-consulships that Augustus could hold. The investigators were also checking into a report that this same group of senators discussed forcing Augustus to resign.

"What have you found out?" Augustus asked.

"We haven't been able to corroborate it so far," Sejanus said. "Slaves were present during the discussions but they can't testify against their masters."

"Why don't we buy them," Augustus said, "making them the property of the state. Then they can testify against their former masters?"

Tiberius was usually careful about disagreeing with Augustus, but he believed the subject was too important not to give his opinion. He thought it was a good thing that slaves were not allowed to testify against their masters, otherwise the entire structure of Roman society would break down.

"That would be a drastic mistake," he said. "The relationships between masters and slaves are too important to subvert. Masters couldn't function freely in their own households if they thought that their slaves could be bought away from them and made to testify against them. Our laws are designed to guarantee the loyalty of slaves to their masters."

"But this is an exceptional case," Sejanus said. "We could just do it now but not make it a general practice."

"The exception would soon become the rule," Tiberius said

Augustus raised his hand. "Alright, as of now, don't buy the slaves, but keep looking for the evidence we need. Why not place an informer in their midst of these so-called senators?"

"I've already done that," Sejanus said.

"Alright, that's settled," Augustus said, nodding for Sejanus to leave the meeting.

As Sejanus prepared to leave, Tiberius wondered how many informers Sejanus already had in place, and he wondered if Sejanus would torture slaves to manufacture evidence against the senators. He thought of Pometius being tortured to testify against him, and a sickening feeling came over him. He just didn't want to be part of this anymore, thinking that this kind of tyrannical government was neither moral nor honorable, but, at that moment, Augustus interrupted his thought. "When you get to the East, make it clear that we fully support King Tigranes in Armenia," he said. "After all, you crowned him; he's your client."

"Yes."

"I'm not sure that the one legion at Ephesus is enough," Augustus said.

"There are three others in the region that I can call upon if we need to," Tiberius said.

"I'm surprised. You usually ask for twice as many troops as I give you."

"Perhaps, you're right. I'll study it," Tiberius hadn't focused on his troop needs. He had other matters on his mind. "I want to ask you something."

Augustus waited.

As brave as Tiberius was, he was worried about what he was about to say. He took a deep breath. "With your permission, I want to divorce Julia."

Augustus stared straight at Tiberius. "Why is that?"

"We're not going to have any children," Tiberius said.

"You're not sleeping together?"

"No. We're incompatible," Tiberius said, leaving out that he loathed her. "Perhaps she should marry someone else. Maybe they'll produce a grandson for you."

Augustus rubbed his temples. "I don't need another grandson. I have Gaius and Lucius to continue my line," he said. "And I even have Agrippa Postumus, although I don't think he'll amount to anything but trouble," he said. "I also have my nephews, your brother and Octavia's boys, Germanicus and Claudius."

"I don't mean to demean him," Tiberius said, "but Claudius is lame and doesn't seem healthy. Julia produced strong boys. She could have more sons. She's only twenty-seven."

"That may be," Augustus said. "But you can't divorce Julia now. All my efforts to encourage marriage and morality would be undermined. Our family sets the example for the whole empire, and a divorce would make us look like hypocrites."

"But Julia is unhappy. Why make her suffer?"

"She'll just have to live with it. As my daughter, she has a responsibility. If she wants all the benefits of her position, she has to pay the price."

"As you wish," Tiberius said.

When Tiberius arrived home, Julia went into her rooms. He didn't bother to talk to her. Instead, he began drinking. He knew he was stuck with her. To make matters worse, he realized that his hope to be the *princeps'* successor probably wasn't going to happen. Either Gaius or Lucius would be the successor. Tiberius could only expect to be a caretaker until they were of age.

He had two more cups of wine before he went to bed; nevertheless, he had difficulty falling asleep. He thought about the future, about making changes, about resolving his dilemma. If I die, he thought, Augustus could marry Julia off without looking like a hypocrite. He's probably hoping that I die. I'd better be careful; he might sic that Sejanus on me to find some phony charges. I'm sure Sejanus would be happy to oblige. Then Augustus could then get rid of me and remain above it all, showing himself to be the great impartial statesman.

He mumbled to himself, something he had done a lot of lately, "Because Augustus wants to appear as the keeper of morality, I'm trapped. Although I owe everything to him, he drives a hard bargain. My life is not my own, it's his. Pometius has more freedom than I do. Even as a slave, he was happier than I am."

Tiberius drank another cup of wine, hoping it would put him to sleep. It didn't; he took another cup. As he became bleary-eyed, his thoughts became disjointed. If civil war returned and he was on the losing side, he could be executed. He remembered the soldiers decapitated in Iberia, and their blood spurting high into the air. He saw the faces of the Pannonian archers as he plunged his sword into them. He pictured his tunic soaked with blood and imagined a vicious fight with Sejanus. The wine finally overcame him, but in his sleep his mind was still working and he made a decision.

Pometius woke him in the morning. He rolled over slowly, still groggy, then bolted up from his bed. "That's it. I've made up my mind," he announced. "When I get to the East, I'm going to take a leave of absence, a long vacation."

Pometius was puzzled. "Why?"

"To get away from Rome."

"You can't do that."

"Oh, yes, I can."

"Who's going to run things while you're away?" Pometius asked.

"You're my first freedman. You'll take care of the houses, and I'm going to put you in charge of overseeing the payroll."

"I didn't mean that. I meant, who's going to run the government with Augustus?"

"I don't care," Tiberius said. "I'm going to go to the East as Augustus ordered me, and I'll take my leave from there."

"Where will you go?"

"Rhodes. I was there on my way back from Armenia," Tiberius said.

"What'll you do there?"

"I'll have plenty to keep me busy. But say nothing to anyone about where I'm going. On the day I leave, I'll give you letters to deliver to Augustus and the Senate informing them of my retirement. Don't deliver the letters for three days. They won't be able to react until I'm well on my way."

"What if they rescind your authorities?"

"My tribunate and proconsular powers are in effect for five years. I'm inviolate until they expire. One thing about Romans, they adhere to the law. Even if they want to kill you, they'll wait until your term is over."

"Tribunes and consuls have been killed in the past."

"Yes, but only when they overstepped their authority. I don't intend to do any such thing."

CHAPTER SEVENTEEN

Tiberius spent the rest of the day making arrangements for his voyage, then went to see his mother. He told her that when he reached the East, he was going to take a long vacation. He was exhausted and needed a rest.

"You can't. You have legions waiting for you at Ephesus," Livia said.

"I'll appoint legates to oversee them."

"Son, this is a terrible mistake."

"I have my orders to take command of the legion at Ephesus, and that's what I'm going to do. Once I fulfill my orders, I can take my leave."

"You should wait until Augustus returns from Nola to get his permission."

"I'm leaving tomorrow."

"If you do, you're going to regret it."

"That may be," Tiberius said. "But, as someone once said, 'the die is cast.'"

The next morning, a barge docked at a landing on the Tiber River. Tiberius was already there waiting with his quaestor, Senator Lucillius Longus, and his six lictors and ten aides. They would accompany him east and Longus would be in charge of the provisions and the treasury.

As the provisions were loaded onto the barge, Sejanus arrived at the landing. He asked to speak to Tiberius privately.

"What about?" Tiberius said.

"Augustus has forbidden you to take a leave," Sejanus said.

"Why?"

"He said it would be a dereliction of duty, almost treason."

Stunned that Sejanus learned of his plan so soon and angry that it was Livia who must have told him, Tiberius looked Sejanus in the eye. "How would Augustus know what I was going to do?"

"We sent messengers to Nola," Sejanus said. "And he said you shouldn't go."

"Unless horses can fly," Tiberius said, "I don't see how the messengers could have gotten from here to Nola and back."

"I'm just telling you for your own good. I know what Augustus will think," Sejanus said.

"So, you speak for Augustus."

"In this case, I believe I do."

"Tell Augustus that I need a rest."

"You can't keep your imperium if you don't exercise it. The Senate might strip you of your authority," Sejanus said.

"Not without a good reason. My imperium and my tribunician powers are good for five years. Taking a vacation is not a crime."

"Augustus is going to be angry that you're leaving Julia behind."

"Augustus can keep an eye on her for me. Make sure she behaves herself," he said sarcastically as he turned his back on Sejanus, and climbed aboard the barge. The barge headed Southwest down the Tiber towards the port city of Ostia, Rome's outlet to the sea.

The barge was propelled by a crew that used poles and oars. At times, the crew pulled it by ropes from the shore. In four hours, the barge reached Ostia, a city with shipyards, warehouses, and markets on either side of the river. This was where ships from Sicily and Egypt unloaded their cargoes of grain onto barges to be pulled up the Tiber to the city.

The two ships that Admiral Terullius had assigned to Tiberius were waiting to take him to Ephesus—a smaller trireme at the dock, and a larger quinquereme anchored out in the harbor.

Tiberius met both ship captains at dockside. The captain of the quinquereme, Cornelius Narbo, had a weathered face. A veteran of the Actium naval battle in 31 BC, he had chased Antony and Cleopatra to

Alexandria. The captain of the trireme, Licinius Strabo, a younger man, looked as though he had had much less experience.

Everyone boarded the trireme. The ship had two masts, and three banks of oars, one bank above the other, each oar rowed by a single oarsman. When Captain Strabo gave the command, they rowed the trireme out to the quinquereme.

The quinquereme, a massive ship, fifty meters long, had three masts and three banks of oars on each side. The highest banks had two men on each oar, the middle banks had two men per oar, and the lowest had only one man per oar, a total of 180 rowers in all. Besides the rowers, there were two drumbeaters, ten naval officers, thirty-two deck crew, eighty marine legionaries, and eight centurions.

Tiberius toured the ship, inspecting the crew and the rowers.

These were warships, each fitted with a bronze ram, a "rostra," attached to the front of its keel, just below the water line. The trireme was the better ramming vessel because it was more maneuverable and could accelerate faster. The quinquereme could ram another ship, but ultimately it would pull alongside an enemy ship and send its marines to board it. The quinquereme was equipped with grappling hooks and a *corvus* (a boarding bridge), that consisted of a walkway with iron spikes on the bottom side. One end was hoisted to a mast, and when an enemy ship was close, the *corvus* was dropped. The spikes impaled the planks of the enemy's deck, pinning the ships together, and the Roman soldiers raced across the walkway on the attack.

The *corvus* was a significant Roman invention that let their soldiers utilize their close-combat skills. In 241 BC, during the First Punic War against Carthage, they used the *corvus* to board enemy ships, and defeated Carthage at the decisive battle at Ecnomus on the southern coast of Sicily, taking Sicily, Sardinia, and Corsica from them.

Once the quinquereme was underway, Tiberius and Captain Narbo went to the captain's stateroom where Narbo rolled out a map of the eastern Mediterranean. He showed Tiberius the route that they would take to Ephesus. Pointing to the Straits of Messina, between the toe of the Italia peninsula and the northeastern tip of Sicily, he said that after passing through the straits, they would stop at Syracuse on the east coast of Sicily for supplies. Then they would cross the Adriatic Sea to Corinth, the city the Romans had destroyed in 146 BC, then rebuilt. After resting there, they'd take the canal through the Isthmus of Corinth into the Aegean Sea and sail to Piraeus, the port of Athens, where they would take on more supplies, release any injured or sick rowers, and hire replacements. After that, they would head straight for Ephesus to meet the legions waiting for Tiberius to take command.

"First," Tiberius said, "we're going to stop at my villa in Sperlunca in the Bay of Neopolis. We can rest there before we leave for Sicily."

"That's fine," Narbo said.

"And there will be another stop on the way before getting to Ephesus," Tiberius said. "I'll let you know later."

"Yes, Sir," Narbo said, looking displeased.

A day later, the ships docked at Tiberius' sea-side villa at Sperlunca. The villa had three tiers of terraces and enough rooms for the officers and centurions to sleep. Most of the sailors walked to the town looking for drinks or girls or both.

In the morning, Tiberius walked down the path to the dock where he was surprised to find a messenger who had arrived on horseback from Rome. The messenger had a letter from Sejanus, who wrote that Augustus was ill and Tiberius should postpone his trip to the East.

The news was a shock but Tiberius showed no emotion. He tucked the letter into his tunic, keeping the contents to himself. He didn't tell Captain Narbo or the others about it, but within a few hours the news of Augustus' illness had spread. Narbo heard the news and questioned Tiberius. "Excuse me, sir," Narbo said, "You didn't tell me that the *princeps* was ill?"

Tiberius was taken aback by the captain's question. He merely replied, "I didn't tell you because I don't believe it."

Narbo looked puzzled.

"We'll wait here for a day to see if there's any more news," Tiberius said.

"Yes, sir." Narbo agreed.

Tiberius didn't believe Augustus was really sick; he thought it was a ruse to get him to return to Rome. But, if he were wrong, and something happened to Augustus, it would be a mistake for him to be away. The intrigues would surely begin; the knives would be out. He was unsure of what to do, and had second thoughts about leaving. He stayed in his villa without inviting the officers or the centurions to stay with him. They stayed on the ships while he paced back and forth on the terraces.

At sunset, Tiberius took a cup of wine and sat on the highest terrace wall to watch the sunset. There were just enough clouds near the horizon to make it perfect. The sky lit up with gold, violet, aqua, and purple. Then, as the sun dropped below the horizon, he thought he saw a green flash above the waterline, a phenomenon sometimes reported when a bright sun touches the horizon. It was the most spectacular sunset he had ever seen. What an incredibly beautiful world; this is why the Romans build their villas here, he thought. At the same time, a feeling of sadness overcame him because he realized he'd hardly appreciated the world around him, he'd been too busy, too immersed in the politics of ambition and the quest for power and glory.

He thought the sky was painted by the gods. The beauty of it made him think that he should change his life, drop his responsibilities, and enjoy everything the earth had to offer instead. Perhaps he could convince Vipsania to enjoy it with him.

The next morning, he had second-thoughts about leaving, and as he looked over the terrace wall, he was startled by a flock of starlings bursting out of a tree, flying up and around in a circle, twisting left and right in perfect unison, then descending back into the same tree. Seconds later, the starlings burst forth again, making a circle in the other direction. They went higher, circled, then swooped back to the same tree. It seemed that each of the birds landed back on the exact branch that they had left. He thought it might be a sign for him to stay.

But the third time the birds rose from the tree, they flew away in a southerly direction. Was a sign to go or to stay? He stared at the sea for a moment, then walked down the path to the ships and gave the command to head south to the Straits of Messina.

"I thought we were going to wait until we hear news of Augustus," Narbo said.

"We'll make inquiries at Syracuse."

"Yes, sir."

"Captain, how long will it take to get there?"

"The wind is against us right now. We'll have to row, but when we get to Messina, we should be able to put up the sails," Narbo said. "We could make it in a day."

"Then how long to Athens?"

"Depending on the wind, maybe another three or four days," Narbo said. "Could you tell me what's the change in the route?"

"I'll tell you when we get to Syracuse."

Narbo was right. When the ships turned into the Straits of Messina heading east, the wind blew from behind them. The drumbeaters set an easy pace for the rowers, and a day later they arrived at Syracuse, a city founded by the Greeks on the east coast of Sicily. Its acropolis was an island-citadel connected to the rest of the city by a long causeway.

At the port, a full honor guard stood at attention for Tiberius. The provincial governor, Fabius Flaccus, welcomed the great commander and proconsul, and invited the officers for a luncheon at the palace.

"Any news of Augustus," Tiberius asked.

"No. We heard a few days ago that he was ill," Flaccus said. "But nothing since."

Tiberius was relieved. He concluded that the news of his leave of absence had not yet reached Syracuse.

They walked up the hill to the palace, an impressive structure but one that was clearly showing signs of its age. The palace had belonged to Hiero I, the king who, in 216 BC, during the Second Punic War, had resisted a Roman siege. At that time, the palace had been filled with bronze statues, marble fountains, and elaborate doors and arches, but now it was sparsely furnished and looked nothing like it had before the Romans invaded and stripped it.

Flaccus served an elaborate and sumptuous lunch to his guests. After the last course was served, a Greek historian, Theophrasus, described the siege of 216 BC. He told how Hiero had first aligned his city with Rome but later switched allegiance to the Carthaginians. In response, the Romans put the city under siege. After several attempts to take the city from the sea, they found that they couldn't gain entry because of the high seawall and defensive measures designed by the famous mathematician and engineer Archimedes, a native of Syracuse.

Eight Roman quinquiremes had approached the seawall and the ships' marines tried to scale the wall. To thwart the Romans, Archimedes had designed a set of large mirrors and prisms to reflect concentrated light into the eyes of the Romans, delaying and confusing them. He also had a system of chains, grappling hooks, and pulleys. The grappling hooks were thrown over the wall to ensnare the ships. Using multiple gears for leverage, the pulleys could raise a ship almost to the top of the wall then suddenly drop it back to the rocks below. This was how the Syracusans defeated the Roman naval assault.

The Romans, battered but not defeated, changed tactics, and invaded from across the causeway. They fought their way into the city. Syracuse fell, and Archimedes was killed. A legend took hold that a Roman soldier killed Archimedes while he was engrossed in the study of a complex mathematical problem.

Tiberius listened to this narrative without commenting. He thought it was the mythology of a conquered people hoping to salvage some dignity from defeat. It implied that the Greeks were actually intellectually superior to the Romans but had been overwhelmed only by barbaric force. Since he was a guest, he wouldn't insult his hosts by telling them what he really thought.

The governor invited him to sleep in the palace but when he was shown a luxurious bedroom, an uneasy feeling came over him about sleeping in the palace of a Roman enemy and where Archimedes had lived. It felt like a bad omen, and he returned to his ship for the night.

In the morning, when they set sail, Tiberius told Captain Narbo that they were not going to Ephesus but to Rhodes. Narbo was surprised, but quickly unrolled his maps and charted a new course. He suggested that instead of stopping at Piraeus, they could stop at the island of Crete for supplies. Crete was on a more direct route to Rhodes.

Crete had been the home of the ancient Minoan and Mycenaean civilizations. In 69 BC it was conquered by the Romans and made into a province.

"How long will it take?" Tiberius asked.

"I would estimate four days to Crete and another day or two to Rhodes," Narbo said.

"Good, let's take that course."

Again, Narbo's estimates about the number of days were correct, but it wasn't an easy trip. Strong winds turned the sails and pushed the ships off course, and the rowers and crew had to struggle to keep on course, while the drum beaters increased the speed of the rhythm.

The winds were called the Meltemi. When they came, they blew continuously, and it was said that on the Aegean islands, after thirty days of the Meltemi, murderers would be acquitted on the premise that they had been driven crazy by the unrelenting winds.

Tiberius stood at the bow of the ship, savoring the wind and the waves. When the seas got rougher and the waves pounded the ship, the salt water soaked him. He didn't care; he was escaping, putting the sea between him and Rome, putting distance between him and his contemptible marriage.

When the ships reached Crete, the rowers were exhausted. Narbo wanted to rest for two days, but Tiberius said no. He told him to hire as many new rowers as he could and that the soldiers could lend a hand rowing. "It will do them good, keep them in shape."

The ships embarked the next morning. A day later they reached Rhodes.

CHAPTER EIGHTEEN

As the ships sailed into the harbor of Rhodes, Tiberius stood on the foredeck of the quinquereme, and saw what was left of the Colossus of Rhodes, the great bronze statue lying at the harbor entrance where he had seen it fourteen years before. The wind had covered more of it with sand and soil, and he wondered how long before it would be completely buried.

Rhodes had a deep harbor, so the quinquereme was able to tie-up at the dock rather than anchor. Magistrates were waiting from the city council on the dock to greet Tiberius, saying that they were sorry that they hadn't known earlier of his visit. If they had, they would have arranged a splendid reception for him.

"I'm glad you didn't," Tiberius said. "I came here for rest and recuperation."

"The palace is at your disposal."

"That's kind of you," Tiberius said. "But I only need a modest house near the acropolis, and an equally modest house in the countryside. I'm going to need peace and quiet."

Arrangements for his housing were made, and Tiberius told Narbo that he was going to stay on Rhodes for some time. He told him that the admiralty would want the quinquereme back so he should return it to Rome, leaving only the trireme at Rhodes. Narbo was surprised and troubled. "With all due respect, I can't do that," he said. "My assignment from the admiralty is to transport you and protect you. When it becomes known that you're here, you'll be in danger from pirates and every other enemy of Rome."

"I think I'm safe here."

"Again, with all due respect, you can't depend on these Rhodians to protect you. If attacked, they might put up a fight for show, but they're not fighters, they're merchants, negotiators."

For centuries Rhodes had been a prosperous center of trade. Though it was not a military nation, it had never been conquered by Rome or any other power. Like all of Greece, it was no longer as prosperous as it had been, and its citizens looked more to the past than the future.

"If you're worried," Tiberius said, "you can send a letter to the admiralty to ask permission for you to return to Rome."

"That could take weeks."

"Then enjoy yourself while you wait."

Narbo and his crew did exactly that, first in the port's bars and the shops, then farther inland. They found Rhodes to be a marvelously pleasant island. The Meltemi winds were milder than in the Aegean, and the temperature was constant and moderate. The island had many interesting facets to explore, and the people were friendly.

Tiberius settled into a routine. He bought a horse and rode on the shore every morning. In the afternoons, he visited the acropolis and talked with the locals. He wanted his presence to remain as unobtrusive as possible, but a misunderstanding occurred when he told the Rhodian magistrates that, by tradition, such a visit as his required the dispensing of alms for the sick, and he wished to see those who were suffering. The next day, to his surprise, all the patients in the town were brought to the public square, many having to be carried there. They were arranged in groups according to their ailments. Embarrassed, Tiberius said that he had meant to visit the sick, not for them to be brought to him. He apologized to them for the inconvenience, asked about their illnesses, and gave each a silver coin.

Afterwards, Tiberius retreated to his country house where he spent time reading or writing in both Latin and Greek. To experience the island, he began going to the acropolis to see the auctions of Greek art and sculpture. What he bought he shipped to his villa at Sperlunca. He also attended lectures and debates that were a regular feature of Rhodian culture. In the city amphitheater a variety of teachers and philosophers gave talks that were followed by public debates. Stoics debated Epicureans, Sceptics debated Academics, Platonists debated Aristotelians, and they all took turns debating one another.

Well-versed in Greek, Tiberius was interested in Greek philosophy. He was typical of many Roman aristocrats who, over the course of the last century, had looked to Greece for new ideas. Many had adopted the ideas of Epicureanism or Stoicism. They read the popular Roman writer Lucretius, who expounded on Epicurean philosophy and explained the universe as comprised solely of atoms. It was an atom-based materialism that left no room for the gods, and most significantly, denied the existence of an afterlife. Lucretius ridiculed clinging to life for love of material pleasure or for fear of torment after death. Death was merely a relief from pain and affliction.

Epicureanism claimed many followers, including Julius Caesar, who, in his speech against the execution of the Catiline conspirators, argued that death was the end of everything, so criminals would not suffer in the underworld. Therefore, the death penalty, by itself, was an inadequate punishment, and it followed that the penalty for heinous crimes required severe earthly punishments.

Tiberius had studied Lucretius closely, but wasn't sure about the non-existence of an afterlife or whether it was wise to say that there was no afterlife. He believed that, in addition to fear of punishment in this life, fear of punishment in the next life was necessary. He thought Julius Caesar did a disservice by promoting the idea that there wasn't an afterlife. Fear of punishment in the afterlife was what kept people from breaking vows and committing crimes in this life. So, Caesar should have kept his opinion to himself.

Stoicism was another Greek philosophy adopted by Roman elites. A basic tenet of Stoicism was that the universe had no beginning or end. It moved in cycles that were interrupted by apocalyptic conflagrations, but it always recovered and continued. This belief helped individuals understand the small part they played in existence and helped them accept the temporary conditions of their lives. Some Stoics believed in reincarnation.

Cicero leaned toward Stoicism, and Tiberius remembered fondly when Vipsania read Cicero's writings to him. He remembered when they had laughed so hard at the murder case in which Cicero defended a man accused of murder, arguing that the victim was so hated and miserable in his life that he should have been glad to be dead.

Epicureanism and Stoicism were often portrayed as opposites, but they had much in common. Each proposed that the gods, if they existed at all, were not concerned with human affairs. Both philosophies taught that living a virtuous life was the sole end for man. Epicureanism emphasized the enjoyment of the simple pleasures of life; Stoicism emphasized that a virtuous man should calmly accept the vicissitudes of life and not be either lifted or diminished by extraneous events. In their purest forms, Epicureanism and Stoicism encouraged rationalism, the simple virtues, and intellectual pursuit. In any case, the practices and attitudes that arose from these philosophies tended to undermine the assumptions of traditional Roman religion and customs that had been so important to the development of Rome's character and strength.

These philosophies undermined the belief that the gods were watching and judging. Tiberius thought that the culture of Roman elites had evolved from one obsessed with appeasing the gods to one that had adopted materialistic explanations for the universe, bringing about deep and far-reaching consequences for society. Although he subscribed to the rationalism of Epicureanism and Stoicism, he nevertheless remained attached to the traditional Roman gods, still called out to Jupiter and Mars, and still kneeled at their altars. To him, religion and philosophy were not mutually exclusive.

After attending a few lectures, Tiberius began to ask polite questions, and he received polite answers. The more he went to the lectures, the more he was treated not as a visiting ruler, but as a citizen. People began to think that if they were circumspect, they could talk to him on an equal basis. His presence raised interest in the debates and drew large audiences. One day, after a lecture by the Stoic Jason of Nysa about Cicero's time at Rhodes, Tiberius joined in the debate, even taking a chair on the stage. He felt confident about the subject because of his own studies and because Vipsania had given him so much information about Cicero.

The debate focused on Cicero's arguments about the best form of government. Jason argued that all forms of government had advantages and disadvantages but the best form of government was a representative republic in which the oligarchy, meaning the senate, periodically selected the best person from among their ranks to be the leading citizen, either a consul or archon or some other titled person.

The historian Prytanius challenged Jason, saying that monarchy was the best form of government because of its stability. With a monarchy there was no need for frequent elections and the protracted conflicts and arguments that always occurred at the change of government. When a monarch died, a designated heir from within the imperial family quickly replaced him, and the nation went on with its business.

Jason responded that the whole concept of having hereditary rulers was absurd. "The ruler of a nation should be wise, fair, and capable. Hereditary rulers chosen by biological chance might be wise and fair, but they also might be idiots, tyrants, or mad. To be stuck with a king from the latter group, for a lifetime, is national insanity."

Tiberius commented that the monarchical system could be augmented by adoptions. When there were heirs who did not appear to be qualified, the monarch could adopt talented young men from among those of fine lineage to replace them, such as was often done in Rome. "Remember Scipio Africanus adopted Scipio Aemilianus, and Julius Caesar adopted Caesar Augustus."

Suddenly, to the surprise of those on the stage, people in the audience began shouting. "No monarchs here; no kings here. The people shall pick their own leaders."

Jason stood and raised his hands. "No need to shout. Who wants to say something?"

One of the men who had shouted approached the stage. He had long black hair and wore a green and blue cloak over his right shoulder. "Direct democracy is the Greek tradition," the man said, obviously talking to Tiberius. "We don't need outside rulers coming here to tell us how to run our country."

"If you're talking to me," Tiberius said, calmly. "I didn't come here to tell you how to run your country; I came here to vacation."

"I'll bet you did," the man said.

Jason moved to the front of the stage. "And it's also Greek tradition to be courteous to our visitors. I suggest that you sit down."

Tiberius raised his hand. "That's alright. Let him talk. It's a free country."

"Free, my ass," the man said. "Your Flaminius promised us freedom at the Games of Corinth; then you destroyed Corinth. After that, you enslaved everyone in Epirus. That's a strange kind of freedom you gave us."

Tiberius felt an urge to throttle the man, but he calmed himself. "That was a long time ago, almost two centuries," he said. "And Rome has had free and open trade with Rhodes. In fact, we changed our center of commerce in the Aegean from the island of Delos to Rhodes. And your economy has revived and prospered ever since, with more wealth than any other place in Greece."

"That's right," some in the audience shouted.

Jason took the opportunity to end the debate, saying, "That's all for today. Tomorrow we have another speaker."

Tiberius thanked all for an interesting afternoon, and walked home, proud of himself for keeping his temper and for so deftly undercutting the man in the cloak's insulting argument.

Narbo had been in the audience and walked with Tiberius. "I was impressed by your restraint," he said. "I wanted to club that arrogant showoff."

"That would have played into his hands."

As they walked, Narbo said, "I didn't want to interrupt the debate, but I have some bad news." He took a letter from under his tunic. "I received an answer to my letter to the admiralty. You were right, they want the quinquereme returned to Ostia."

Tiberius stopped walking, and immediately thought that Sejanus must have had a hand in it. In any case, the consequences of his leave of absence were taking shape.

"I can understand that," he said. "The expense of having a ship with a full crew just sitting idle is quite considerable. Someone must have brought the matter to the attention of Augustus."

"But no mention was made of the trireme," Narbo said, "and no mention was made of my assignment."

"That's interesting."

"With your permission," Narbo said. "I'll trade ships with Captain Strabo. He can take the quinquereme back, and I'll stay here with the trireme."

"You don't have to do that," Tiberius said.

"I'd like to. This is a nice place to settle down, and I'm getting close to retirement."

"Let me look at the letter," Tiberius said.

He read it twice. "You're right. All they've asked for is the quinquereme. So, I'm glad you're staying."

"Thank you."

Tiberius was indeed glad Narbo was staying. Without the quinquereme in the harbor, he would feel diminished, and realized what giving up the bulk of his forces would mean. It was hard to be a proconsul and tribune of Rome without an army. He felt some trepidation, not for his safety, but for being disrespected or humiliated. The incident with that man in the green and blue cloak could be just the beginning.

The speaker for the following afternoon was Thrasyllus of Macedon. He was introduced as the foremost astrologer in the world, a well-known scholar, and a philosopher of the Aristotelian school.

His lecture was not just about astrology, but also about recognizing one's fate, accepting it, and embracing it. "We cannot choose our initial place in the universe," he said. "We cannot choose our parents or our physical attributes. However, we can revere our parents. We can honor them and help them if necessary. We can preserve our health and strengthen our bodies. If we have mathematical abilities, we should apply ourselves to that study. If we have other abilities, we should do the best with them. Our stars are in their given constellations; they cannot change their positions; but they can shine as brightly as possible, and so can we."

Thrasyllus spoke for an hour. He talked about predictions he had made based on astrology and natural phenomena, giving many examples from comets, lightning, birds, animals, and even plants. "The world sends us signs," he said, "we have to read them and follow them."

At the conclusion of the lecture, Tiberius invited Thrasyllus to his house where they dined and talked for hours. Tiberius was greatly impressed by Thrasyllus' knowledge of so many subjects. Thrasyllus drank several cups of wine, but they didn't seem to affect his speech or his mental faculties. In fact, as the night wore on, his social and philosophical points took on even more complexity and sophistication.

As Thrasyllus rose to leave, Tiberius said, "In your lecture, you said that we should follow the signs of nature."

"Yes, if they are clear."

"When I was at my villa in Sperlunca, still deciding whether to come here or not, I saw a flock of starlings rise up all at once from a tree, fly into the sky, turn together in unison, as if on command, form different patterns, then return to the tree all at once. They did this three times. Do you think that was a sign to me? Was it a sign for me to stay or go?"

"What you saw was a natural phenomenon called a murmuration," Thrasyllus said. "I'd have to know more. Did they use this tree often? Or did they suddenly appear at your villa? Were you the only person watching?"

"Yes. I was alone. And I never saw that before. Of course, I'm not always at the villa."

"I can't say for sure. I didn't see it. But my sense is that it was a sign that something special was taking place. It was a sign for you to come here. When an unusual event occurs in nature, especially with birds, it's a positive sign."

"Thank you," Tiberius said. "Let's talk again. Come any time."

"I will."

Captain Narbo and Captain Strabo switched the commands of their ships, and Strabo departed with the quirquereme for Ostia. Without the larger ship's crew and marines going in and out of the bars and shops, the port of Rhodes became quieter.

Tiberius, Narbo, and Lucillius Longus continued attending the afternoon lectures and debates in the amphitheater. For some of them, Tiberius sat on the stage to participate in the discussions that followed.

The man who wore the green and blue cloak also attended the lectures. He had a habit of jumping up and shouting questions at a lecturer or debater. Without fail, whenever Tiberius made a comment, the man was on his feet, contradicting and challenging him. He shouted at Tiberius, "Augustus, your ruler, has designated his nephews, Gaius and Lucius, as the next rulers of the world. Are we to be forever slaves to one family?"

Tiberius smiled. "You're not a slave. You're free to go wherever you please."

The man almost jumped in the air. "I may be free, but you're not. You're exiled here. You've been shoved aside to make room for Gaius and Lucius."

Clenching his fist, Tiberius rose and moved toward the front of the stage. He felt his rage building but calmed himself and went back to his seat. He nodded to Narbo who was seated in the audience. Narbo left and came back quickly with two of Tiberius' lictors.

Tiberius pointed to the man. "Bring that annoying fool to jail. And inform him that to insult a tribune of the people is a capital offense. See what he has to say about that."

The lictors removed the man from the audience. A few people began to protest, but when they realized they were outnumbered, they stopped. The audience fell quiet as the lictors dragged the man away.

Tiberius left the theater and went to his country house. He spent a day there alone until Narbo, Lucillius, and Thrasyllus came to stay with him.

Each morning, the four men walked on the shore engaged in conversation. They talked a little about personal matters and their feelings, but mostly about general topics. Thrasyllus explained the history of augury and how it developed. He thought of it as a science, no different than Aristotle's experimental science. He believed that over the centuries, men have observed patterns of phenomena and recorded what events followed. Although it was difficult to see the actual cause and effect, it must be assumed there are connections beyond human understanding.

"Yes, there's a lot we don't understand, either about nature or about ourselves," Tiberius said.

"What don't you understand about yourself?" Thrasyllus asked.

"Well, for one, why do certain things, certain things people say, send me into a rage? In a real battle against armed men, I can remain as calm as a mountain. But an idiot like that one at the lecture, who doesn't amount to an ant hill, ignites something in me."

"It's frustration," Thrasyllus said. "You can fight an equal opponent with honor, but you can't attack someone so far beneath you without demeaning yourself."

"To tell you the truth, I feel a bit ashamed about throwing him into jail. As Aristotle said, moderation in all things is best. I could have been more moderate."

"I think you did the right thing," Thrasyllus said. "Moderation doesn't mean ambivalence. Anger, or rage as you call it, is not necessarily a vice. Anger can be a virtue when it's acted upon for the right reason, at the right time, and directed at the right person. Timing is everything. If you had thrown him in jail the first time that he insulted you, it would have been petty. But after so many instances of insubordination, you acted at exactly the right moment."

Narbo asked what he should do with the prisoner. Tiberius asked about the prisoner's background, and Lucillius said that he had found out that the man's name was Suffrates. "He must have confused his name with Socrates, and he just goes around asking questions and criticizing people," Lucillius said. "Unfortunately, he doesn't have the brains of Socrates. He only knows how to bother people."

"Was he ever in the legions? Ever have a business?" Tiberius asked.

"No, his family supports him," Lucillius said.

"We should have a law that you can't go around criticizing until you've done something useful yourself. These smart-asses just cause trouble," Narbo said.

Thrasyllas said, "If you did, Rhodes would be a silent place. Criticizing is the national pastime."

"Let him go," Tiberius told Narbo.

The next two years went by in relative quiet, although, when it became known that Tiberius was at Rhodes, ambassadors and other officials traveling in the area began stopping at the port to pay their respects. He greeted them cordially but refused to render any decisions or opinions, emphasizing that he was on a much-needed vacation.

He regularly dismissed his lictors and strolled about the town without guards. He sat at shops talking with common people and asking them for their opinions, which he often found more sensible than those of some of the philosophers and orators he had heard. They talked about family as the most important thing and what gave meaning to their lives and their struggles. They believed that the gods favored those who honored their own families.

Sometimes Tiberius took long walks without his companions. On one such walk, on sun-filled morning, he was alone on the shore, thinking about his family, when he saw a father with a boy who was about the age of his son Drusus. They were skipping rocks across the surface of the water. The sun was behind the boy, and as Tiberius squinted to see, the boy disappeared in the sun's glow. He shaded his eyes with his hand and could see the boy again, but when he squinted again, the boy disappeared. It seemed to be a sign, and regret overcame him. He blamed himself for not thinking more about young Drusus. How could he have left him?

His walks with his companions helped him push aside his regrets. Their conversations went in many directions. Narbo talked of sea voyages. Thrasyllus pointed out many interesting aspects of the island, both natural and spiritual. Lucillius, who spent much of his time gathering information and rumors, talked of politics. He regularly sent and received letters about political affairs and about who was in or out of favor in Rome.

As time went on, the conversations became more intimate. When Tiberius said that the future was uncertain and impossible to predict, Thrasyllus assured him that his future would be great, that he was going to fulfill his destiny. There were many favorable signs, and he predicted that if Tiberius read the signs correctly, he would be the next *princeps*.

"I'll believe that when I see it," Tiberius said.

He appeared to be content and enjoying his surroundings, but at night he had trouble sleeping, frequently overcome by a feeling of impending doom. He wondered whether he had placed too much faith in Thrasyllus' optimistic advice. It was more likely, he thought, that sooner or later, there'd be bad news.

Then, one afternoon, Lucillius came to the country house with news. He told Tiberius that Augustus had castigated him in the Senate, saying that Tiberius had abandoned his responsibilities and that he took it as a personal betrayal, almost treason; "It was not fitting for a Roman," Augustus had said, "to leave his wife, his step-children, and his own son at a time when they all needed him. Under such circumstances it would not be fitting for Tiberius to return to Rome."

Tiberius asked what brought this tirade on. Lucillius said, "Augustus was frustrated because of a few military setbacks. He didn't have a competent general whom he could trust. And he blamed you for leaving."

Tiberius realized this was a warning of coming disaster. He knew that Augustus did not have to give direct orders; he only had to express his opinion and his will would be carried out. The *princeps'* statement was an invitation for others to denounce Tiberius; it was an invitation for *delators* and prosecutors to look for charges that might be lodged against him.

This jolted Tiberius into action. He told Lucillius to bring him the financial records for the ships, salaries, and expenses. He wanted to be sure that everything was accounted for and the records were absolutely correct. "I'm sure that to please Augustus, some bloody leech will try to suck my blood."

Forbidden to return to Rome, he now wanted desperately to return. He sent a stream of letters to his friends, supporters, and Augustus. He tried to justify himself by saying that his absence was necessary so that he wouldn't hinder the advancement of Gaius and Lucius as future leaders. It was not a convincing explanation. He received no answer from the *princeps*. He wrote to his mother asking her to convince Augustus to let him return. She soon answered that Augustus had refused her request and had said that leaving his daughter was an insult to the imperial family. "Please be careful. Don't do anything rash," Livia wrote in her letter.

Tiberius threw the letter on the floor. Exploding in rage, he kicked a table over and broke a vase. Stomping around the house, he shouted. "I've got a mind to go the Rome and confront that bastard. Tell him right to his face about his so special daughter—I'll tell him what a whore she is. He can execute me if he wants, but the world will know that he's a fraud and a hypocrite."

After a while, he calmed down, and decided that he'd write to Menelaus, who would give him the best advice. He was tired of listening to Thrasyllus with his wait-for-a-sign-and-everything-is-going-to-be-fine advice.

Matters worsened. Lucillius received reports that Tiberius was now widely referred to as "the exile" and was held in disrepute throughout the empire. He learned that at the town of Nemausus, which had been under the patronage of Tiberius' father, the people overturned all the statues and busts of Tiberius and other Claudians. Rumors of a conflict between the Claudian and Julian families became widespread. Lucillius said there was no truth to it, but speculations can turn into self-fulfilling prophesy.

A few days later, Tiberius received a reply to the letter he had sent to Menelaus. The reply said only that Menelaus had died. Tiberius felt this loss profoundly. It was as though his childhood and his past had been wiped away, and, now, only an uncertain and unpromising future awaited him.

CHAPTER NINETEEN

Tiberius didn't go to Rome but stayed on Rhodes. He kept to his same routine, taking walks and talking to people he met on the way. The months went by slowly. After four years on the island, he wondered whether anything would ever change and whether he would ever be able to leave.

Then, in March 2 BC, when he was at his country house with Lucillius, Narbo, and Thraysyllus, a messenger arrived with a letter under the imperial seal. Tiberius tore it open, read it, and read it again.

"What is it?" Lucillius asked.

Tiberius kept shaking his head.

"What is it?" Thrasyllus asked.

"Read it for yourselves." Tiberius threw the letter at them.

Julia had been banished. She had violated the law of *Papia et Julia* by committing adultery and other immoralities. She was banished to Pandateria, a small, mostly uninhabited island off the coast of Campania, where she was to be confined. Her mother, Scribonia, would accompany her.

Each man read the letter, then sat silently, not knowing what to say. Finally, Lucillius spoke, "I heard this rumor weeks ago. Several of her friends were also banished."

"Why didn't you tell me this?" Tiberius asked.

"It was just rumor. I wouldn't pass on something as serious as that unless it was confirmed. I thought it was just the usual scandalmongering," Lucillius said.

"I think it's been confirmed," Narbo said.

The second part of the letter related that since Tiberius was not in Rome to carry out the divorce, Augustus had it done on his behalf.

"I should celebrate," Tiberius said.

"No." Thrasyllus shook his head. "We've got to think this through. These are treacherous times, and you must be careful how you react."

After another long silence, Tiberius said, "You know, I should be happy. I should be ecstatic. I should be saying, 'I told you so.' I should be telling Augustus what a fool he was, and how wrong he was, forcing her on Agrippa—she probably caused his early death—then forcing her on me. I should be telling him that I've been vindicated."

"That wouldn't be wise," Thrasyllus said.

"True," Tiberius said. "But we can have a toast just the same: To divorce, to my freedom, and to Julia getting what she deserves."

Each of them took a cup of wine, and they sat and drank. They all knew Julia's history. Although Tiberius knew a lot, he knew less than his friends because the worst rumors and allegations about her had been kept from him.

The men kept drinking and talking about Julia's extraordinary life, how when she was happily married to Marcellus, she seemed chaste and respectable, but when he died, and Augustus forced her to marry Agrippa, she changed. Her behavior then could only be described as less than respectable. When Agrippa was away from Rome, she wouldn't sit quietly waiting for him to return but went out almost every night attending as many fashionable parties as she could, as often as she could.

When Agrippa was home, she was an attentive wife, and they had five children—three sons and two daughters.

In 12 BC, when Agrippa died and Augustus forced her to marry Tiberius, she reverted to her most notorious behavior, seeking out many male companions. She joined Maecenas' poetry club and became an avid reader of Ovid's *Ars Amatoria,* the book that she and Tiberius had fought over and that he had thrown into the fireplace.

In the book, Ovid included a disclaimer, stating that he was not advocating adultery—his women characters were not wives but mistresses. Ovid advised that wives should adhere to the familial values of proper marriage and raise children as the *princeps* demanded. But, he said that mistresses could engage in *amores* as they desired.

While Julia was married to Tiberius, she must have considered herself a mistress, not a wife. She had contact with many men, but was most interested in Jullus Antonicus, Marc Antony's son, a club member who wrote poetry of his own.

As Tiberius became aware of her behavior, he found himself in an untenable position. He had a disreputable wife but was unable to do anything about it since she was the daughter of the *princeps*. That's when Tiberius retired to Rhodes.

During his absence, Julia's conduct became even more brazen and notorious. She attended drunken parties where the guests celebrated Bacchus, the god of wine, and she became the talk of Rome. It was also known that she took several lovers, including Jullus Antonius. Rumors of various conspiracies circulated: one, that Jullus would marry Julia and supplant Tiberius as the potential successor to Augustus; another, that Julia had driven Tiberius away so that she could promote the careers of her sons; and, a third, that Julia's circle was plotting to oust Augustus and return the rule of Rome to the Senate and assemblies.

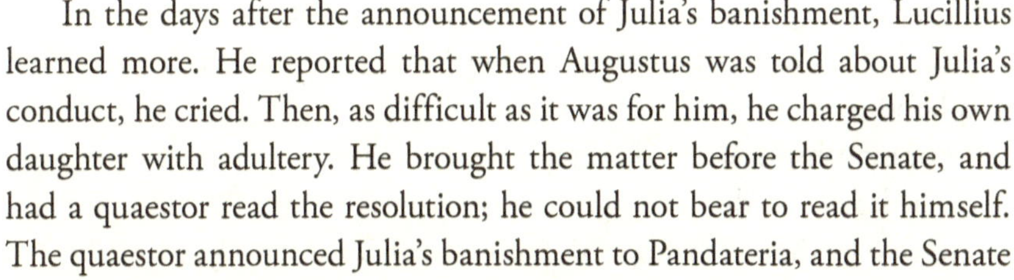

In the days after the announcement of Julia's banishment, Lucillius learned more. He reported that when Augustus was told about Julia's conduct, he cried. Then, as difficult as it was for him, he charged his own daughter with adultery. He brought the matter before the Senate, and had a quaestor read the resolution; he could not bear to read it himself. The quaestor announced Julia's banishment to Pandateria, and the Senate ratified it.

Julia was crushed. She threw herself on the ground and had to be tied up and carried to the ship that would transport her to the island.

Augustus also banished the poet Ovid to a village on the Black Sea coast, punishing him for his provocative writings.

Tiberius asked Lucillius, "Did you hear anything about Jullus Antonicus?"

"Yes," Lucillius said. "He's dead. Either he committed suicide or was killed by the Praetorians."

"How about her other lovers?"

"They were all exiled."

"How many?"

"A dozen, at least."

Tiberius slumped in a chair, "The question is, who's more ashamed, Augustus or me?"

Tiberius, Lucillius, Narbo, and Thrasyllus met regularly at the country house. They discussed Julia's plight and whether she would be able to survive the imposed solitude.

Tiberius said that she would survive, "Because evil always survives, and she's an evil bitch."

Thrasyllus advised Tiberius that although Julia deserved her punishment, Augustus must be suffering terrible anguish, and Tiberius should not add to it by insulting Julia or taking an adversarial position. "Despite your loathing of Julia," Thrasyllus said, "you should be seen not as an enemy but as a sympathetic friend."

Tiberius took Thrasyllus' advice and, during the ensuing months, sent a stream of letters to Augustus urging reconciliation and compassion for Julia, adding to each letter a request for permission to return to Rome so that he could be a parent to his son Drusus II who was approaching manhood.

For months he received no reply, then a sealed imperial letter arrived.

The letter was devastating. Augustus turned down Tiberius' plea and added that he should abandon all hope of visiting his family, whom he had been so eager to desert.

To add salt to the wounds, Augustus wrote that Gaius Caesar would become the proconsul of the East when Tiberius' term ended. Gaius was the son of Agrippa and Julia, the grandson and adopted son of Augustus, clearly in line to be the successor.

For Tiberius, the rejection was an outright denunciation. He didn't share it with anyone. It was too humiliating, and there was nothing he could do about it. He had escaped Rome for Rhodes; now he couldn't leave Rhodes. With his tribune power and proconsular imperium expiring at the end of the year, he was trapped, almost as though he were officially exiled. His thoughts went around in circles, and kept coming back to the same thing, the injustice of it all. Why did this happen? What if he had refused to marry Julia? What if he had stayed in Rome instead of taking this foolish leave?

For months he had had difficulty sleeping, now that became worse. The lack of sleep was affecting his thinking, and he realized he was losing control of his thoughts. It was hard to keep a focus on any one thought. His mind jumped from one question to another, then repeated those questions over and over. To stop the repetitions, he began leaving his house before dawn and walking to the shore. After a time, he began taking a fishing pole. He cast the line into the water, not expecting to catch anything. It was just a way to keep occupied, a way to mask his desperation. He would stay at the shore all morning, hoping to miss any visitors who came to his house. He didn't want to be seen. When he heard people walking his way, he'd retreat into a cave in a shoreline cliff, waiting until they passed.

To avoid the hot midday sun, he often stayed in the cave, just looking out at the sea. It kept him calm. One afternoon, he stayed in the cave for much longer than usual. He was thinking about the allegory of Plato's cave that Menelaus had taught him. How prisoners, who had spent their lives chained in a cave facing a blank wall with a burning fireplace behind them, could only see shadows on the wall in front of them. The shadows were cast on the wall from objects passing in front of the fire. The prisoners could not see the real objects, but only their shadows. They gave names to the shadows, and thought the shadows were what constituted reality. When one prisoner escaped and saw that what they saw weren't real objects but only shadows of real objects, he told the others that they weren't seeing the true reality. For exposing the fact that their beliefs were false, they killed him.

Tiberius lay in the cave thinking of what the allegory meant. He knew of Plato's dichotomy between ideal forms and distorted perception, but what did it mean for him? He was a prisoner of his exalted status, hiding in a cave, deprived of genuine and honest communication. He could see only the shadows of other men, but not their true natures; he could only hear their flattery and sycophancy, knowing that it disguised their true selfishness and hatreds.

Tiberius was sick of it all. Hiding in the cave, he thought of suicide. For Romans, suicide was an honorable end. He would no longer have to worry about everything he said or did. He would no longer have to suffer the shame of his exile. His suicide would make a statement. He thought of how and where to do it. In his house would be the best place. He began to plan it, but, as he thought about it, he heard voices. He looked out of the cave and saw a search party that was looking for him. Several slaves were walking in a line between the water's edge and the cliff line. Tiberius retreated farther into the cave, crawling into a small dark space in the rear. He felt like a rat hiding in a corner. One of the slaves looked into the cave. Tiberius crouched down. What if he saw him? What would people say? His heart was pounding. The slave kept peering into the cave, but it was too dark. The slave couldn't see him and continued walking.

Tiberius waited a little while then looked out to be sure no one was around before he left the cave. He walked back to his house, where a dozen men were waiting outside. "What's going on?" he asked. The men turned and looked questioningly at him. One man said, "The quaestor is inside."

Tiberius went inside. Lucillius, Thrasyllus, and Narbo were there. "Why are you here?" he asked.

"We were worried about you," Narbo said. "We were worried that you might have fallen off a cliff."

"As you can see, I'm fine. I didn't fall off a cliff."

They could see that he wasn't fine. He looked disheveled. He didn't make eye contact and his eyes darted back and forth.

Narbo began to take a letter from under his tunic, but Thrasyllus signaled him not to take it out. Obviously, Tiberius was in no condition to take more bad news. Tiberius noticed it and wondered what they were hiding. He sensed that everyone knew something that he didn't.

There was an awkward silence, then Lucillius called for the kitchen slaves to serve dinner.

They brought out several large trays of roasted pork.

"I have to apologize," Tiberius said, then paused. The others waited, expecting him to explain where he had been, but he said only, "I have to apologize that I wasn't able to catch any fish today. Otherwise, you could have had fresh fish."

The men all glanced at one another awkwardly as though they were thinking that Tiberius might be losing his mind. They sat down to eat, but no one could think of anything to say. Tiberius ignored them and ravenously began eating with his hands. After eating two large portions and drinking several cups of wine, he became animated. He began rambling, asking questions in rapid succession. He asked each of them what they really thought of the Senate; whether they thought Rome should keep expanding its empire; what they thought of Augustus.

Their answers were all crafted to be safe: The Senate needed to be purged of hangers on; Rome need not expand any farther; Augustus was the greatest ruler ever. Suddenly, Tiberius' demeanor changed completely. He laughed at each answer, and seemed remarkably relaxed and composed.

"You know," he said. "I wasn't feeling too well, but I'm much better now. I appreciate all of you, my great friends, being here with me. I mean that sincerely."

Tiberius called for more wine for everyone. "Let's have a toast. To good friends."

Narbo looked at Thrasyllus as he fingered the letter under his tunic. Thrasyllus shook his head indicating not to show it to Tiberius yet. But after an hour of relaxed conversation, Tiberius seemed okay. Thrysallus nodded to Narbo.

"I have a letter from the admiralty,' Narbo said.

"What now?" Tiberius said.

"They want the trireme returned to Ostia when your term ends."

Narbo handed the letter to Tiberius who threw it back at him, and laughed bizarrely.

"What do you think of that, my friend?" he said to Thrasyllus. "Is that a good sign or a bad sign?"

"You can't know until you see what follows," Thrasyllus said

"That doesn't help me very much." Tiberius leaned back and laughed oddly.

"Are you alright?" Narbo said.

"I feel great. I feel like a man who has hit rock bottom and there's nothing more anyone can do to me. I have my fate; I'm resigned; I have nothing more to lose; whatever happens will happen."

There was silence until Lucillius said, "I heard the ship was to be given to your step-son Gaius. When his pro-consulship starts next year, he will have command of the East and have imperium and tribune power."

Tiberius grinned. "How's that for your Greek irony?" he said to Thrasyllus. "Almost like a play by Sophocles or Euripides. No! Better yet, a comedy by Aristophanes! My step-son, a boy, will be my superior!"

They continued drinking and stayed the night, sleeping sprawled out on couches.

Tiberius woke before the others, and quietly went outside to look at the sunrise. As often happened to him when he awoke from a deep sleep, a new idea or a new solution to a problem would occur to him. His head was surprisingly clear, and he felt ready to begin again. Realizing that he been losing control, he took several deep breathes and talked to himself as though talking to another person, "You've conquered nations, led armies, passed judgments, and beat whomever they put against you. So now you're going to defeat whatever evil spirit has entered you." He went to the garden fountain, immersed his head in the water, then shook his head from side to side, as though trying to rid himself of whatever force had taken hold of him.

He put on his military cuirass, sword, and helmet. The others awoke and saw him. Thrasyllus said, "What are you doing?"

"Can't you see? I'm fulfilling my responsibilities as proconsul and tribune. That's what I am. Am I not?"

"Yes, Sir," Narbo said, observing that Tiberius appeared a thousand times more confident than he had the night before. He marveled at the transformation.

"Let's go to the ship," Tiberius said. "I want to thank the crew."

They walked to the port and boarded the trireme. Narbo called the crew to attention, and Tiberius addressed them. He told them that his term would be ending soon. He thanked them for their service, told them that he expected them to continue their fine work until his term was done, and assured them that at the end of it, those that were eligible for discharge or for bonuses would receive them.

That was how he conducted himself for the last months of his official term, wearing his military attire every day, performing his official functions, commanding his soldiers, and solving problems. He regularly assembled the legionaries and drilled them in military exercises. It was remarkable to see him in command and to see the soldiers, who had been idle for so long, respond so enthusiastically. Narbo told Tiberius, "I can see why they call you Rome's best general."

"Well, this is just practice," Tiberius said. "We won't really know if that's true until we get back on the battlefield."

Thrysallus heard this exchange, and wondered whether Tiberius was delusional or whether he was making plans for a military campaign.

On 15th of January, 1 B.C., the last day of Tiberius' imperium, Gaius Caesar took command of the eastern provinces.

Tiberius was now a private citizen. Captain Narbo, the trireme, and the soldiers, would have to return to Rome. Lucillius would also go as his term as quaestor was expiring, and Tiberius' lictors would leave with the ship.

As the ship got ready to depart, Tiberius, in military uniform, embraced both Narbo and Lucillius before they boarded. Then he walked with Thrasyllus back to his house where he took off his military gear and put on a civilian tunic.

"So, what's next, my friend," Tiberius said. "What do your signs tell you?"

"We'll have to wait and see," Thrasyllus said. "But while waiting, you should send a letter to your mother. Put your pride aside. Ask her to intercede. Augustus can't deny her."

Tiberius wrote to Livia. A month later, her efforts on his behalf succeeded, and he was given an appointment as an ambassador to Rhodes. It was half a loaf. He had an official status, which would provide more protection than he would have as an ordinary Roman citizen, but he still couldn't get back to Rome to see his son.

He sent more letters. Six months passed until a response from Augustus arrived, telling him to seek an audience with Gaius, the proconsul of the East, to ask his permission to return to Rome. Arrangements were made for Tiberius to meet Gaius on Samos, an island off the west coast of Asia

Minor. Tiberius commandeered a commercial ship at his own expense, and sailed north to the island.

Gaius Caesar was only eighteen years old, so Augustus had sent several advisors with him as overseers. The primary advisor and chief of staff was Marcus Lollius, not a friend of Tiberius. Years earlier, when Lollius lost a battle in Illyria, Tiberius stripped him of his command, and Lollius had hated him ever since. Now Lollius kept Tiberius waiting for two days for a meeting with Gaius. The waiting tested Tiberius' self-control. He found it insulting to have to wait to see this step-son, and wondered whether Gaius blamed him for his mother's disgrace. Did Gaius think that by abandoning Julia, Tiberius had caused her downfall?

The irony was not lost on him that while Julia was banished, her son was in command of half the empire.

A guard summoned Tiberius, saying that Gaius Agrippa Julius Caesar would see him now. When he entered Gaius' quarters, he was struck by how closely Gaius resembled Agrippa, but his officious manner would have been foreign to Agrippa.

The advisor, Lollius, stood in front of Gaius, "So how can we help you?"

Tiberius kept his request short. "The *princeps* suggested that I request Gaius' permission to return to Rome as a private citizen now that my imperium has expired."

"Is that all?" Lollius said.

"That's all."

"Couldn't you have made your request in a letter?"

"I followed the instructions of the *princeps*."

"What assurances do we have that you won't engage in political activities?"

"I have no intention of engaging in political activities," Tiberius said.

Lollius began to talk, but Gaius interrupted him. "It's good to see you. You look well. It seems your long vacation has done you good."

"I think it has. I definitely needed a vacation after my campaigns in Illyria, Pannonia, and Germany. And when we lost my brother Drusus, I had twice the responsibilities, and I had to avenge his loss."

Gaius didn't respond.

Lollius said, "The past has been settled. We have to be concerned with the present situation."

"There is no situation," Tiberius said to Lollius. "I simply want to retire to my home and my son." To Gaius he said, "Thank you, and I hope you will consider my request. And Gaius, good fortune to you, I hope you make your father proud."

Lollus spoke before Gaius could. "We'll send our decision to Rhodes. You're still staying there, right."

"Yes," Tiberius said.

He left the meeting, went straight to his ship, and sailed back to Rhodes.

Thrasyllus second-guessed everything that had occurred.

"You should have begun with some pleasantries, some small talk, before making your request."

"After they made me stew for two days, I should make pleasantries? And, Gaius, that pompous brat, he's hardly a commander. He's under the thumb of that intriguer Lollius, who never saw a fight he didn't run from."

"Gaius won't make the decision without approval from Augustus," Thrasyllus said. "You'll just have to wait until they get word from him."

"How long do they expect me to sit here doing nothing?" Tiberius raged in a way he hadn't in some time. "They're lucky I didn't run them through with my sword."

"I'm glad to hear you talk like that," Thrasyllus said. "That's the passion you're going to need when you're commanding legions again."

"Is that your prediction?"

"Yes. You were made to command armies. The stars only need to align."

"So, your signs tell you that?"

"Yes. You'll be in command as sure as the sun circles the earth."

"When?"

"Soon."

The prediction raised Tiberius' hopes, but it was premature. As the months passed without news, he began to complain that Thrasyllus' predictions were more often wrong than right. Then one evening, as the two men walked along the western cliffs, a ship approaching from the west was silhouetted against the sunset. Thrasyllus pointed to it and said, "That ship is bringing good news."

"Are you willing to bet your life on it," Tiberius said, in a half-joking manner.

"Every day, it seems, I bet my life," Thrasyllus said.

To Tiberius' amazement, a messenger from the ship delivered a letter from Livia. She wrote that Augustus had agreed to let him return to Rome. As he read it, Tiberius had to sit down. Thrasyllus danced around in a circle. He was ecstatic, not only because of the news, but also because his prediction had proven to be correct.

CHAPTER TWENTY

In 2AD, Tiberius returned to Rome after being away for seven years. His boat docked at the landing on the Tiber River, the same spot where he had embarked from. Pometius was waiting with three horse-drawn wagons to transport him and his baggage to his house.

"Good to see you, my friend," Tiberius said.

"It's been a long time," Pometius said, "but you don't look any older."

"You must be blind, but I did have a good rest."

Tiberius introduced Thrasyllus as his guest. Then, leaving the other wagons to be loaded, Tiberius and Pometius drove in the first wagon up the long incline to the city. Tiberius had come this way a thousand times, but he felt anxious, as though he was coming to Rome for the first time. Approaching the great walls, he said, "From the outside, it looks the same, just like I look the same; but on the inside, I'm sure it's changed."

"You're right about that," Pometius said. "It's been through a lot. I guess you've been through a lot, too."

"Yes, I have."

Passing through the south gate of the city, Tiberius was uncertain about how the people would receive him. Would he be considered a pariah for having abandoned his responsibilities and his family? Or would he be welcomed back like Cicero, whose return from exile was celebrated? Of course, he knew Cicero's celebration hadn't lasted, and his life ended badly.

When he reached the house, he saw Livia waiting in front. Standing beside her was his son, Drusus II, now fifteen, an athletic-looking young man, already much taller than Livia, and on his way to becoming ruggedly handsome like his father.

Tiberius kissed his mother on both cheeks, then approached his son, who put his hand out to shake. Tiberius shook it, then grabbed his boy and hugged him.

"I can't believe how much you've grown," Tiberius said. "We've got a lot of lost time to make up."

Standing behind Drusus was another young man. Livia introduced him. "This is Marcus Julius Agrippa Herod, the grandson of King Herod of Judea. He was a great friend of Agrippa, and named his grandson in honor of his friendships with Marc Antony, Julius Caesar, and Agrippa. Before the king died, he sent young Marcus to stay with us."

Drusus and Herod were being educated together and had become good friends, cementing the friendship between Rome and Judea. Agrippa Herod was thirteen, two years younger than Drusus. He had strikingly dark eyes, a high forehead, and a thick dark, curly hair. Tiberius put his hand on his shoulder. "I've heard good things about you. Of course, there could only be good things said about someone named after Agrippa. I was very close to him."

The group went inside and enjoyed a meal together. Tiberius asked Drusus question after question. Drusus was reticent and only gave short answers. Young Herod sometimes answered the questions for him. By the end of the meal, Herod was dominating the conversation, not in a negative way, for he was knowledgeable about many subjects, and everyone was interested in his views.

Tiberius asked him about the Jewish community in Rome.

"Since Julius Caesar proclaimed that they should be allowed to practice their traditions and religion unhindered," Herod said, "many Jews have immigrated here and settled in the Jewish quarter on the west bank of the Tiber."

The meal and the conversation ended with all expressing gratitude.

Afterwards, Livia privately told Tiberius that she had convinced Augustus to agree to his return for the sake of Drusus. The boy had been living with her and she had become very fond of him, but he needed a strong hand to direct him.

Tiberius asked Livia to stay overnight, but she said that she had much to do and needed to get home. As she left, he kissed her again and watched as she was carried away on a litter, surrounded by a dozen guards. Drusus and Agrippa Herod walked behind her.

In the morning, Pometius showed Tiberius the account books and gave him a financial report. Pometius had not only preserved Tiberius' assets, he had increased them substantially. He had also been successful on his own account. He showed his personal account books to Tiberius, because under Roman law a freed slave remained under the patronage of his former master and the master had a right to a portion of the freedman's assets.

"I'm so glad to see what a success you've made," Tiberius said, "when do I get to meet your bride."

"Anytime you wish."

"I'm sorry that I missed your wedding. Perhaps we can have a banquet here to celebrate it after the fact."

"My wife and I would like that. Thank you."

"We'll have to do it soon," Tiberius said, "because I'm going to sell this place and move into something less ostentatious, something more suitable for a retiree."

"As you wish, but where are you going to find someone to pay the price for all this?"

"There's got to be some fool who wants it. I want to get rid of it while times are good. I don't need a palace, and I don't want to be associated with Pompey's house. He had a very bad end, and so did the next owner, Marc Antony. You don't have to give me a sign three times."

Tiberius planned to live a quiet, private life without engaging in public or political activities. He put the palace up for sale and moved to a smaller, simpler house on the Esquiline Hill. He intended to use it only when he had to stay in the city. His intention was to spend most of his time at his villa at Sperlunca in Campagna, where he had shipped the sculptures that he had acquired on Rhodes.

Although he wanted a quiet life, he was still the *pater* of the Claudian family and the patron of many tenant and employee clients. When the news spread that he was back in Rome, people began visiting him each morning asking for audiences. The duties of the *pater* included approving marriages, divorces, adoptions, and manumissions; the duties of a patron included addressing business and legal issues. While he had been away, disputes had arisen, and petitioners now asked him to make rulings, either in his capacity as *pater* of his family or as patron of his clients.

Tiberius was surprised by the number of petitions brought to him and how willing people were to accept his rulings. He laughed and thought to himself: *Here I am, not long ago cowering in a cave, unable to think straight. Now, I'm the leader of one of the greatest families of Rome, making life-changing decisions for so many.*

Livia and Tiberius discussed where Drusus should live. When a divorce occurs, under Roman law the children live with the father. But Drusus had been living with his grandmother, Livia, for seven years, not with his step-mother, Julia, who was now in exile. Tiberius wanted to raise the boy, but without a wife to help him, he decided to leave things as they were. They agreed that Drusus would visit him three days a week so that he could train and educate him.

Tiberius trained his son in the same demanding way that his father had trained him, and he tried to pass on what he had learned from Barbonius and Menelaus. Drusus was not always properly receptive, and Tiberius found that it was hard to discipline him. He was reluctant to chastise or punish him since he felt so guilty about abandoning the boy for so long.

After a month, Drusus asked if Herod could train with him. Tiberius agreed, and the sessions improved, because Herod was enthusiastic about everything, and his enthusiasm was contagious. The boys trained and studied every day together. Physically, Herod was no match for Drusus, but was quick-witted and could challenge Drusus in other ways. When it came to academics, Herod was full of questions for Tiberius. Sometimes Tiberius didn't have a good answer, but he'd discuss the questions and the surrounding issues with the two boys. Herod could make a conversation go in any direction. They discussed history, philosophy, and religion. One subject they avoided was the notorious history of Herod Agrippa's father, who had executed several of his relatives, even two of his sons, because he had thought they might try to overthrow him.

Tiberius worried that Augustus had not invited him for a meeting or included him in any public or private events. He asked Livia, "Augustus hasn't contacted me, shouldn't I request an audience with him?"

"Not yet," Livia said. "Give him time."

Tiberius felt as though he were still banished. Without some formal acknowledgement that he had returned, most of the aristocracy ignored him, until one morning, at his smaller house on the Esquiline Hill, he was surprised by a visit from the Piso brothers, Lucius Calpurnius Piso the Younger and Gnaeus Calpurnius Piso. They were *optimate* aristocrats from a long-established and prestigious family. Lucius Piso had been consul in 1 BC, and Gnaeus Piso co-consul with Tiberius in 7 BC.

When Tiberius first saw the Piso brothers arriving at his door, his heart sank as he thought they might be coming to tell him that he was going to be charged with some crime or dereliction. Their family had a long history of deep involvement in the law, and had frequently participated in the prosecution of lawbreakers. But when Tiberius saw how friendly they looked, he relaxed and decided that their visit was just a courtesy call. Gnaeus Piso embraced him and called him "my favorite co-consul."

"Very funny," Tiberius said. "I was your only co-consul."

Over breakfast, they had an amiable talk, and neither brother brought up any issues of politics or the law. This surprised Tiberius because he knew that their ancestors had distinguished themselves in the law.

A hundred and fifty years earlier, in 149 BC, another Lucius Calpurnius Piso, a consul, passed the *Lex Calpurnia*, a law that established the *quaestio de repetundae*, or court of restitution, to investigate and prosecute charges of extortion by public officials and recover ill-gotten property. In 67 BC, another relative, Gaius Calpurnius Piso, proposed the *Lex Calpurnia de Ambitu* to address election bribery. This law enhanced penalties to include permanent exclusion from office, expulsion from the Senate, and a heavy fine. It extended liability not only to the candidate who was found guilty of bribery, but also to his agents. The plebeians, often the beneficiaries of the bribes, protested the bill and physically drove Gaius Calpurnius Piso from the assembly, but the Senate provided a bodyguard for him and he passed the bill at the next session.

The Piso Calpurnian family was known for its strict adherence to the law. The brothers' grandfather, Lucius Calpurnius Piso Caesoninus, had been a consul and a censor. Once, when presiding over a trial, he stated, "Justice must be done, though the heavens fall."

As the brothers got ready to leave, Lucius Piso invited Tiberius to visit him at his villa, the *Villa dei Piso*, at Herculanean, a small city in Campagna on the Bay of Neopolis about fifteen kilometers from the city of Pompeii. Both cities were in the shadow of Mount Vesuvius.

Construction on the villa was begun by the brothers' grandfather, and was recently completed by Lucius.

Tiberius gladly accepted the invitation, and spent a pleasant week there. Lucius was a gracious host and an interesting companion. He proudly conducted a tour of the villa and spoke about each stage of its construction.

The villa's property covered ten acres, with landscaped gardens along the shoreline that stretched for almost a kilometer. Five kilometers inland, Mount Vesuvius stood more than 1300 meters high with its majestic snow-covered peak.

The entrance to the main building led to a portico then into a high atrium. A large room on the east side of the atrium housed an extensive library of papyri, including collections of all the plays of Sophocles and the complete works of Aristotle.

An exit from the atrium led to an outdoor colonnaded peristyle that incorporated a pool, seventy meters long and eight meters wide. Beyond the peristyle, a footpath led to a terrace that overlooked the sea.

Each day, Lucius and Tiberius sat on the terrace discussing politics, sculpture, philosophy, law, and poetry. Lucius said that he had contacted Tiberius because he was interested in what Tiberius had learned about Greek philosophy during his stay on Rhodes.

Lucius was an Epicurean, Tiberius more a Stoic. Without arguing, they debated both philosophies, and agreed that there was room for both. They also discussed the Sophists and Cynics. Tiberius said these philosophers should suffer the same fate as Carneades. He was referring to the Greek Sophist Carneades, who, in 155 BC, was expelled from Rome by the censor, Cato the Elder, when Cato heard him take one side of an argument one day then the other side of the same argument the next day. Carneades did this to demonstrate that since both sides of the same argument could be proven, there was no such thing as truth, except the proposition that there was no such thing as truth. So, Cato expelled him and all the other Greek philosophers.

"Expelling them did not stop their ideas from spreading," Lucius said. "Some say the defeated Greeks, by their culture and philosophy, really conquered the Roman conquerors."

"I've heard that. But Cato had a point that I agree with. It's not their philosophies I'm against, it's the tricks of their sophistry, the way they twist words to prove a point. Too often, they convince the gullible of what might be the opposite of the truth."

"I can't disagree," Lucius said.

They talked about the famous statement of Piso Caesoninus that "Justice must be done, though the heavens fall." On this, they disagreed.

"What if punishment served no purpose?" Lucius asked. "What if, for instance, Rome abandoned a province, but left prisoners in jail who had committed crimes against Roman rule? What purpose would it serve to execute them? Deterrence wouldn't matter because Rome would no longer be responsible, and punishment without a purpose would only be cruelty."

"Deterrence is not the only purpose of punishment," Tiberius said. "Criminals must be punished because that's what they deserve," Tiberius said. "The magistrates have a duty to impose justice. It's the reason they're given authority."

"But perhaps the prisoners committed crimes only because they weren't under self-rule," Lucius said.

"It doesn't matter. They broke the law."

"You're a tough man."

"Exceptions to the rule can be made, but not too often."

Tiberius greatly enjoyed his week of conversation and when his stay at the villa ended, Tiberius and Lucius Piso parted as great friends.

The next months were relatively quiet, and Tiberius became resigned to his limited public role. But then, in August 2AD, news came that Lucius Caesar, Augustus' twenty-year-old adopted son, had died of a fever at Massilia in Gaul. It was another devastating loss for Augustus.

Tiberius was not asked to play a part in the funeral, but he composed and distributed a poem "A Lament on the Death of Lucius Caesar." He sent a copy to Augustus, and sometime later Augustus sent him a note thanking him for his condolences.

Lucius Caesar's death was a severe blow to Augustus' succession plans. Gaius Caesar still survived, but Augustus had entertained more hope for Lucius than Gaius. Lucius had shown himself to be the more intelligent; Gaius, although he was proconsul of the East, was prone to mistakes, and needed advisors.

Shortly after Lucius died, Thrasyllus approached Tiberius. "I have news from the East."

"Not bad news, I hope."

"It depends how you look at it, but I think you'll be pleased."

"Out with it."

"Remember Lollius," Thrasyllus said, "Gaius' advisor who was so rude to you."

"Yes."

"He got caught taking bribes and had to commit suicide."

"That's a reversal of fortune," Tiberius said.

"I knew it," Thrasyllus said. "Your star is rising, and your enemies are falling."

"I don't believe you ever told me that Lollius would fall by his own hand," Tiberius said.

"One can never predict the exact details, but your fate is unfolding just as I foresaw."

"My fate is unfolding, but that's all we know," Tiberius said.

"Lollius deserved his bad end after the way he treated you on Samos," Thrasyllus said. "I'm only sorry he was able to escape a whipping and the executioner's grip."

"You know I'm not a vengeful man," Tiberius said with a sardonic smile.

"Of course, you're not," Thrasyllus said, while trying not to smile.

The next news arriving at Rome was also bad. Gaius Caesar was dead. He had, indeed, been prone to mistakes, and made the mistake of meeting with rebels in Armenia. This was a trick, and Gaius was attacked and wounded. He barely escaped with his life. Though the wound didn't seem serious at first, it became infected.

Gaius was able to capture and execute his attackers, but his wound worsened, bringing on fevers and hallucinations. His health deteriorating, he had to resign his command, and on the 21st of February, 4AD, he died at age twenty-four.

For Augustus, the death of his second adopted son within a span of eighteen months was catastrophic. Most people expected him to fall into despair, but he was made of sterner stuff. Again, he made new plans.

Three days of mourning were designated for Gaius and an enormous funeral was held. Tiberius attended the service and sent a letter of condolence to Augustus.

Julia wasn't allowed to attend the funeral. Exiled in Pandateria, she was bereft; her two most promising sons were gone. Her third son, Agrippa Postumus was sixteen, but he tended to get into trouble and didn't seem to be a promising candidate for high office.

With the loss of her first two sons, Julia became a sympathetic figure, and Augustus showed her some mercy. He moved her exile from Pandateria to Rhegium, a busy port town on the toe of Italia, and allowed her to receive some pre-approved visitors, including her daughters, Julia the Younger and Agrippina.

Augustus also changed his attitude toward Tiberius. A month after Gaius' funeral, he summoned him to a meeting at the Julian-Claudian domus.

Tiberius asked Thrasyllus. "What do you think he wants?"

"He'll probably offer you the consulship."

"If he does, I won't take it."

"Why not?" Thrasyllus said.

"Do I want to be controlled by him again? You know, in one way I love him for what he's done for Rome; but in another I hate him for what he's done to me. Do I want to give him another opportunity to control my life?"

"He's already controlling your life. As long as you recognize it, you'll manage. You have no choice. Don't think you have to make some grand gesture of defiance. Just wait. I told you a long time ago, someday you will rule. Lucius and Gaius are gone. Rome needs you. It's your destiny. You're like the North Star—the steady beacon on which all travelers depend."

When Tiberius arrived for the meeting at the Julian-Claudian domus, Livia and Sejanus were outside Augustus' study. Livia told him that Augustus had been waiting for him.

"I'm not late, am I?" Tiberius asked.

"No, but you should have been early," his mother said.

Tiberius turned to Sejanus, "Have we learned anything else about Gaius' death?"

"Not yet. We're looking into several possibilities. It was probably some mysterious eastern disease. When he was wounded, he should have come back to Rome immediately."

"You're right about that," Tiberius said.

A slave opened the door to the study and Tiberius entered. He expected a great welcome after seven years, but Augustus didn't even look up from the large map he was studying on a table.

"Can you believe those incorrigibles in Pannonia are at it again?" Augustus said, talking down to the map. "They're causing trouble throughout Illyria, attacking towns. They even raided one of our camps when the troops were on a march. They stole the baggage train!"

Tiberius was surprised that Augustus skipped the expected salutations, but, under the circumstances, it was better to get right down to business.

"Have we been able to catch up to them?" Tiberius said.

"No, they strike quickly and then retreat across the Danube."

Tiberius leaned over the map. "Where were they last?"

Augustus pointed to an area on the map between Pannonia and Noricum where the Danube turned almost at a right angle. "It's a turbulent part of the river and they fled across it in boats they had hidden there. When our soldiers caught up, they couldn't cross the river quickly enough, and if they had, they would have been vulnerable as they landed."

"Yes, that would have been an untenable position."

"Let's sit down," Augustus said.

It had been seven years, but Augustus looked as though he had aged more than that. He was thin and gaunt, and looked very different from the robust and handsome statues of him that had been erected in every town of the empire.

"I'm so sorry for your loss," Tiberius said. "And I want to thank you for giving some relief to Julia."

"Of course," Augustus said, coldly. "So, when will you be ready to take over the legions in Illyria?"

Tiberius was not shocked by the question, or rather the order, and answered without hesitation, "Right away."

"Good. We've got a lot of work to do. And we're going to have to work together closely. The generals there are incompetent, missing in action, and troop morale is horrendous."

"We can fix that," Tiberius said.

The remainder of 4AD brought several momentous events. Augustus gave Tiberius command of fifteen legions and, for the third time he would lead a campaign into Illyria. The Senate gave him three years of proconsular imperium and tribunician power.

Most important for the empire, Augustus adopted him as his son. Augustus was sixty-seven, Tiberius, forty-five. With the adoption, Tiberius took the name Tiberius Julius Caesar Claudius Nero. This surely signaled that in the event of Augustus' death, Tiberius would succeed him as *princeps* and would be the heir to his fortune, a fortune that had grown twentyfold since Julius Caesar's death.

A condition of the adoption was that Tiberius would first adopt his nephews, Germanicus and Claudius, the sons of Drusus I, making them the adopted grandsons of Augustus. They were now in the line of succession after Tiberius, but the succession was meant seriously only for Germanicus who had great potential. Claudius, to the contrary, was lame, stuttered, and thought to be a fool, but he wasn't.

At Tiberius' adoption ceremony in the Temple of Apollo, Augustus made him swear an oath that when he became *princeps*, he would follow Augustus' policies as far as possible and would designate Germanicus as his own successor. Tiberius took the oath. While holding a stone in his hand, he said, "If I abide by this my oath may all good be mine, but if I do otherwise, in thought or act, let all other men dwell safe in their own countries under their laws and in possession of their own substance, temples, and tombs, and may I alone be cast forth, even as this stone."

He threw the stone out of the temple door. As he did, he realized that he had given total control of his life to Augustus. He had no choice; events had overtaken him. He realized that if things went badly, he could be as alone as the stone he had just cast.

Livia was immensely pleased as she became even more powerful than she had been already. As the wife of the *princeps* and mother of the future *princeps*, her will was to be obeyed, and her grandson Germanicus would be in position to succeed Tiberius if that became necessary.

Tiberius' adoption transferred him and his Claudian family, into the *paterfamilias* of Augustus. They would be under the *princeps' patria potestas*, the kind of absolute power that Augustus had used to banish Julia.

Now that Tiberius had transitioned from a son-in-law/step-son to adopted son, he lost his independence as the head of an old aristocratic family. He became a subordinate in Augustus' family, and now his family property would fall under the control of Augustus.

For Tiberius, this was an enormous price to pay in order to return to the favor of the *princeps*. He could have declined the adoption, but, after his years of desperation and humiliation, he willingly accepted it, believing that within a few years, he might inherit everything.

Augustus also adopted Agrippa Postumus, Julia's last son. The end result was that through adoptions, Augustus had replaced Gaius Caesar and Lucius Caesar with five new potential heirs—Tiberius and his son, Drusus II, Germanicus and Claudius, the sons of Drusus I, and Agrippa Postumus.

For Julia, it was good news that her son, Agrippa Postumus, had been adopted by Augustus, opening the possibility that he might attain an important post and even someday succeed the *princeps*. This would empower Julia to settle many scores.

Livia saw Postumus as a competitor to Tiberius, and she ordered Sejanus to keep an eye on Postumus and report everything to her.

Sejanus compiled a list of Postumous' fights, reckless gambling, and sexual indiscretions. He told Livia, "All indications are he's a brutal and promiscuous degenerate, not the kind of young man we could expect to be loyal or trustworthy."

"I guess he takes after his mother," Livia said. "What a disaster for Rome he would be!"

Livia passed on Sejanus' reports to Augustus, trying to persuade him to rescind the adoption, but Augustus resisted her, saying that Postumus was young and would grow out of his reckless behavior.

Livia wasn't deterred, and ordered Sejanus to step up his surveillance and investigation. "Find something to charge him with," she said. "His mother was banished, he can be banished, too."

Sejanus acted quickly and brought a long list of charges against Agrippa Postumus. One involved a made-up accusation of rape by a married woman who Postumus had slept with many times before the accusation. In addition, Sejanus brought other charges, so many that it was impossible for Postumus to mount a defense.

Augustus reluctantly agreed to banish Postumus because of the scandal to the imperial family, although he didn't rescind the adoption.

When Livia told Sejanus that the banishment was approved, he said, "I have just the place. Planasia, a small island next to Elba."

"Good. But take him quietly."

"He might resist."

"I'll have Augustus draw up a written order," Livia said. "You'll have the authority to use whatever force necessary."

The banishment sparked rumors that Livia was the one behind it. While that may have been true, other accusations were spread that she had also been behind the deaths of Lucius and Gaius to ensure that Tiberius would be the successor to Augustus. Outlandish rumors and slanders like this were common in Rome.

CHAPTER TWENTY-ONE

Augustus had picked the right man to lead the legions in Illyria, a territory enclosed by the Adriatic Sea, the Danube River, and the borders of Italia, Macedon, and Thrace. Tiberius was thoroughly familiar with the region having commanded five legions there between 11 and 9BC. Now he commanded fifteen legions, plus an additional fifteen auxiliary legions supplied by allies, for a total of about 150,000 soldiers. Energized by his restoration to power, he proved himself to be an excellent commander, instituting the same tough but fair discipline that he always had. He made sure that the soldiers had sufficient supplies, and though rations may have been short at times, they were distributed evenly so that they would last until they could be replenished. Drawing on his firsthand experiences and his study of all the previous wars in Roman history, Tiberius anticipated every action and reaction of the enemy, and never allowed the enemy forces to assume the offensive.

It was a hard-fought war. He didn't have to engage in hand-to-hand combat as he had in Pannonia eighteen years earlier, but was visible on the frontlines during all major battles. He knew that the pivotal moment in most battles was at the enemy's first all-out charge. If the front line of the legion withstood the charge, the battle would be won. He always had reinforcements at the ready to bolster the front line, and was sure to be there as well. It took three years of campaigning to reduce the whole of Illyricum to submission.

The timing of his victory was fortunate for Rome, because in 9AD, legions in Germany, under the command of Publius Quinctilius Varus, suffered a devastating defeat at the Battle of the Teutoburg Forest. The German disaster unfolded as Varus marched his three legions, with an additional 6000 allied German troops, from the Elbe River west toward the Rhine River, intending to set up camp there for the winter. The allied German troops who accompanied the Romans were from several different tribes, and were led by Arminius, a prince of the Cherusci tribe. Arminius was considered a Roman ally. He had lived in Rome, spoke Latin, fought alongside the Roman army, and negotiated with the other German tribes on behalf of Rome.

Varus, with so many men, and with the aid of Arminius, was confident that he had the province well under control. As he moved west toward the Rhine and approached the Teutoburg Forest, Arminius told him about a resurgent rebellion at the Elbe River. Varus didn't want his successful campaign marred by a last-minute rebellion, and turned his army around to find the rebels. He found none. If there had been any, they had disappeared. Varus turned back and again headed west toward the Rhine. This diversion delayed him well into the autumn.

The soldiers, tired from the long, fruitless march, moved in a mile-long column. Varus, not expecting any trouble, relaxed discipline, allowing the soldiers to load themselves down with their plunder. The soldiers weren't in an orderly formation but were intermingled with civilians, traders, slaves, mules, and oxen. The Romans were at the head of the column; Germans in the rear.

At one point, Arminius told Varus that he was going to a village for some additional supplies and would return right away. Instead, he went to join an army of Cherusci warriors waiting in the forest to ambush the Roman column. Arminius had planned the ambush long before, and had chosen a narrow choke point with a sinking bog on one side and a steep wooded hill on the other. On the hill, the Cherusci had built a long barricade.

When the Romans entered the choke point, the Cherusci unleashed the ambush. From behind cover, they launched arrows and spears at the exposed soldiers, who, in their untenable ground position, weren't able to organize a strong defense. Some Romans charged up the hill, but were unable to surmount the barricade; many were killed trying.

With the Romans disorganized, the Cherusci attacked furiously, screaming war-cries as they charged in full assault, and just at that moment, the allied German soldiers turned on the Romans, attacking them from behind. Varus realized that he was about to become the victim of one of the greatest betrayals in the history of warfare. As both the Cherusci and

Germans rampaged, Varus committed suicide, leaving his soldiers to be slaughtered. The Cherusci seized the standards of the three legions.

In Rome, unaware that this disaster was unfolding, the people were in the midst of honoring Tiberius for his victories in Illyria. Senators and a large crowd had assembled in the Forum. A high platform had been erected, and Tiberius climbed the steps and took his seat next to Augustus. From his place of honor, Tiberius waved to the assembly, and, as the people cheered, he thought again about how far he had come from the day he had hidden in the cave. Here he was, now standing before Rome, being heralded as the greatest general since Agrippa.

To further signify Tiberius' accomplishments, the Senate authorized a triumph for him and the minting of a *denaris* coin with the images of Augustus on one side and Tiberius on the other.

Two days later the celebration ended when news of the Teutoburg disaster reached Rome. Augustus was stunned and distraught. He banged his head against a wall and ranted, "Varus, bring back my legions!" He swore to stop shaving until the standards were recovered and the loss was avenged.

Tiberius postponed his triumph, and Augustus gave him command of the legions in Germany, in addition to those in Illyricum. All realized that had Tiberius not pacified the Illyrian tribes, the Germans could have made common cause with them, and combined, they could have mounted a formidable challenge to Rome.

Taking command in Germany, Tiberius faced serious opposition from Arminius, who not only led the Cherusci, but had enlisted other tribes to join him. The Roman troops wanted to confront the Germans immediately, but Tiberius moved carefully to avoid falling into any traps, instituting even more elaborate precautions than he had in his earlier campaigns. Some accused him of stalling and being overly cautious. He responded, saying, "The least risky strategy is the most glorious."

He camped his army on the Gallic side of the Rhine, and from there conducted raids into Germany. At every crossing of the Rhine, he strictly limited the amount of permissible baggage, and he wouldn't signal an advance until every transport wagon was inspected to make sure that none carried anything but what was permitted and necessary. It was extra baggage that had greatly contributed to the annihilation of Varus' legions.

Using a strategy of divide and conquer, he gained assurances of peace from most of the other German tribes. Those who refused, he threatened or attacked until they submitted.

The Cherusci dispersed, and Arminius fled east of the Elbe. By 12AD, stability in the German province was restored as well as could be expected when dealing with an untamed and barbarous people.

Arminius was not captured. Whenever opportunities presented themselves, he engaged in hit and run raids against the Romans. But he was no longer a major threat.

During these years, Augustus not only overcame any reservations about Tiberius, but embraced him. He wrote several letters to encourage Tiberius and establish a bond. In one he wrote, "Goodbye, my very dear Tiberius, and the best of luck go with you in your battles on my behalf." In another, he wrote, "Goodbye, dearest and bravest of men and the most conscientious general alive! If anything goes wrong with you, I shall never smile again!" In another, "Your summer campaigns, dear Tiberius, deserve my heartiest praise; I am sure that no other man alive could have conducted them more capably than yourself in the face of so many difficulties and the war-weariness of the troops. All those who served with you agree with me." In another, "When people tell me, or I read, that constant campaigning is wearing you out, damnation take me if I don't get gooseflesh in sympathy! I beg you to take things easy, because if you were to fall ill the news would kill your mother and me, and the whole country would be endangered by doubts about its leadership." High praise from the most powerful man in the western world!

In 13AD, the Senate granted Tiberius joint control of the provinces with Augustus, who was now seventy-six years old. Tiberius was also assigned the task of carrying out the next census, a task traditionally conducted by the censors.

With the German province relatively stable, Tiberius made frequent trips to Rome. In early spring, he took a route, not around the lower Alps as he usually would, But crossed over the western range, the route that Hannibal had taken with his elephants on his famous invasion over the Alps into Italy. The road reached three thousand meters above sea level, with spectacular and seemingly unlimited views of the world. Climbing up the road, Tiberius saw towering peaks, wide chasms, cataracts pouring into abysses, small villages nested into recesses in the mountains, and thick blankets of snow weighing down the branches of pine and fir trees. With every turn of the road, a new vista revealed either the Mediterranean, the Apennines of Italia, or the plains of transalpine Gaul.

At the highest point, Tiberius wandered away from the road, and sat on a rock ledge that jutted out from the mountain side. His guard followed him, warning, "Be careful, that ledge might not be safe."

Tiberius said, "It's been here for a thousand years. If it falls now, it was waiting for me. Go back to the wagons."

Tiberius wanted the solitude.

"I'm at the top of the world," he said to himself, "and in more ways than one."

He sat, enjoying the view and the quiet. No one was in his sight. It was a sublime view representing the grandeur of nature itself. An eagle flew below him, and a calm, ineffable feeling came over him. He tried to put words to it, but couldn't. Trying to stay immersed in the moment, to commune with nature, he succeeded for a time, but was unable to sustain it. His mind kept reverting to things he had to do. Even here, he couldn't leave behind the issues of his life. He'd need more time to fully experience this view. He promised himself that someday, he'd return to this spot. He took a deep breath, looked around one more time, and went back to the road.

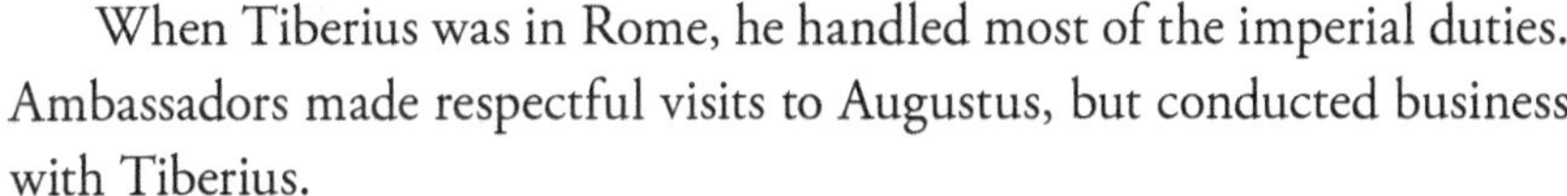

When Tiberius was in Rome, he handled most of the imperial duties. Ambassadors made respectful visits to Augustus, but conducted business with Tiberius.

His son, Drusus II, began spending his days with him to learn about the administration of the empire. In 14 A.D, when another rebellion broke out in Illyria, Tiberius took Drusus on the campaign there. But, on his way to Illyria, the Senate recalled him; Augustus had taken ill at his ancestral home at Nola.

Tiberius rode straight to Nola to be with him. When he saw Augustus, he was shocked by the sight. Augustus was gaunt, his body already wasting away; his voice was weak, and the godlike presence was gone. Nevertheless, Augustus continued working from his bed. Between spells of weakness, he sent out orders and messages. Tiberius marveled that he was still involved in the smallest details of the administration and still doing what he thought best for the nation. Augustus told Tiberius that the empire was not to be expanded any farther—he wanted only to protect the borders as they were.

In the middle of dictating a decree, Augustus suddenly gasped and stopped talking. When the doctor came into the room to examine him, he pronounced the *princeps* dead and closed his eyes.

Tiberius stared at the body. It was nothing but matter now, he thought, but what an extraordinary man Augustus had been. There was no one like him, no one who had accomplished more in the history of mankind. No doubt, he would be declared a god by the people. Maybe they would be right—the divine Augustus Caesar, like the divine Julius Caesar. Tiberius asked himself, "How am I going to follow in the footsteps of these gods? They believed in their own divinity; I'm not a god, far from it."

Livia came into the room. She kissed her husband's body on the forehead. She had no tears, and her voice remained as steady and commanding as ever. Turning to the doctor, she told him to keep the death a secret. Some matters had to be attended to before the death was announced.

"Are you alright?" she said to Tiberius.

He wasn't, but said that he was.

"We have to start making arrangements for the funeral," she said. "There's a lot to do."

At that moment, Tiberius thought that it was Livia who was made of the sternest stuff of all.

CHAPTER TWENTY-TWO

The death of Augustus shook Rome. He had been its absolute ruler for forty-five years, from his victory in 31 BC at Actium until his death in 14 AD. Not only had he won military victories, he had transformed the city-state into an empire powerful enough to control its far-flung territories. His reign saw great building projects, and he had earned the right to say, "I found Rome a city of bricks and left it a city of marble."

Livia made sure that the funeral was the most elaborate in history. At the temple of Apollo, next to the Julian-Claudian domus, Tiberius and Drusus II delivered eulogies, but neither could console the people. From there, the funeral procession moved down the Palatine Hill to the Via Sacra and to the Campus Martius. Crowds gathered all along the route to watch it pass. Women wailed and tore their clothes even though such conduct had been prohibited by the Law of the Twelve Tables.

Augustus' body was lifted high on an elaborate funeral pyre outside the Julian mausoleum. Prayers were said and the pyre was set ablaze. It burned for an hour before the ashes were collected, mixed with honey, and deposited in the mausoleum, joining the ashes of Marcellus, Agrippa, Drusus I, Gaius Caesar, and Lucius Caesar.

Funeral events continued for a week. Tiberius stayed with Livia to support her, though she needed less support than he did. He felt a void without the towering presence of Augustus, a presence that had controlled and dominated his entire life. It was hard to believe that the great man was dead, that he was now a pile of ashes in an urn; unless, as some apparently believed, he had become an immortal god.

At a Senate session, Tiberius went to the rostrum and unsealed Augustus' will. He began to read, but after a few words, he stopped, saying that his grief had taken his voice. He handed the scroll to his son, Drusus II, who finished reading it aloud. It began, "Since fate has cruelly carried off my sons Gaius and Lucius, Tiberius shall inherit two-thirds of my property."

Tiberius kept a stony, expressionless face. He thought that even in death, Augustus had diminished him. He was chosen to succeed the *princeps* only because Gaius and Lucius had died. He was the third choice.

But his disappointment passed as it began to sink in that his years of expectation were coming to an end. He was going to be the most powerful man in the world and would have the resources to do or build anything he desired. Augustus, during his reign, had built up an enormous surplus in the treasury and had amassed an un-heard of personal fortune. Tiberius would control it all.

In his will, August made Livia even more powerful than she had been already. She received the remaining third of his estate, and he adopted her as his daughter. He renamed her Julia Augusta, an unprecedented distinction that meant that she would have extraordinary powers. It was an odd arrangement because Livia and Tiberius became sister and brother by adoption. Some saw this as Augustus' final diminishment of Tiberius, making Livia his equal in prestige.

At the next senate session, the Senate consecrated Augustus as a god. They instituted his cult, and funded temples and priests for his worship. Many Romans were skeptical of the notion that the Senate could make any man a god, but many others truly believed it.

In any case, Augustus was immortalized by his accomplishments. Tiberius thought that Augustus would undoubtedly rank among the most influential men of history, earning his power while walking the tightrope of Roman politics. Always mindful of the fate of Julius Caesar, Augustus declined to openly make himself a dictator; nonetheless, he incrementally transformed Rome from a republic into what he called the *principate* with himself as the *princeps*, or first citizen of the Republic.

Tiberius also thought of the dark side of what Augustus had accomplished. By unique and ingenious deceptions and manipulations, Augustus had solved the problem of keeping the support of the people while leading them inexorably toward servitude. He repeatedly spoke of the

Senate's dignity and his respect for the Republic while his actions exhibited the opposite views. He didn't destroy the Republic by plunging it into a cauldron of boiling water. Instead, he gradually raised the temperature of the water so that the citizens wouldn't realize, until it was too late, that their rights had been eliminated. Tiberius thought that liberty is not lost all at once, but is taken from men by degrees, exactly as Augustus had done.

Tiberius would inherit what Augustus had built but knew he could never come close to matching his accomplishments or achieve his godlike status. He only hoped that he could maintain the empire and keep the political hyenas from tearing it apart. He would have to walk a tightrope between seizing power as a hereditary ruler and accepting power only by the will of the Senate. By inheriting the *principate* from Augustus, he was, in effect, transforming the Republic into an emperorship, but he would try to gloss over that fact by acting and talking as though the Republic still existed.

At a meeting of the Senate to transfer Augustus' powers to Tiberius, a bill was introduced confirming him as the new *princeps* and granting him all the powers that Augustus had possessed. Tiberius wanted to maintain the Augustan illusion that he was merely the first citizen of the Republic, a servant of the Senate, so he equivocated about accepting such authority, saying the empire was too large for one man to govern. A heated debate followed, and, in a charade of republicanism, Tiberius said that he was willing to take command of any part of the government that the Senate saw fit to entrust to him, but not all of it.

Senator Asinius Gallus Soloninus, Vipsania's new husband, sarcastically asked which part Tiberius wanted. Tiberius answered that it would not be proper to select or decline any part of a responsibility which he'd actually prefer to avoid altogether. This was an ambiguous and puzzling answer that might have been drafted by Theodore of Gadara, Tiberius' tutor of oratory at Rhodes. It left many senators uncertain of what position to take.

One exasperated senator shouted, "Oh, let him either take it or leave it!" Another taunted, "Some people are slow to do what they promise; you are slow to promise what you have already done."

Tiberius made mental notes of those who disparaged him, but most of the speeches amounted to sycophantic grandstanding by senators hoping to ingratiate themselves with him.

The bill confirming him as the new *princeps* passed by a wide margin. Ironically, the Senate granted him even more legal power than Augustus had enjoyed, because Tiberius' term was not limited to ten years.

Tiberius expressed reluctance but, in the end, accepted both the title and the responsibility, and assured the senators that his power would last only as long as the Senate thought necessary, saying, "I'll stay until I grow so old that you may be good enough to grant me a respite." He was fifty-six years old.

Several senators said that they would always give him their absolute allegiance, but Tiberius discouraged this kind of talk. When one senator addressed him as "My Lord and Master," he warned that he never wanted such an insult to be thrown at him ever again.

He said that he recognized his own fallibility and understood the role of the Senate to be above his, saying, "I should always be consistent and never change my ways so I am as I am in every sense, but for the sake of precedent, the Senate should beware of binding itself to support the act of any man, since he might through some mischance suffer a change."

This pleased most of the senators and they applauded as he left the Senate. A smaller group of senators gathered around Asinius Gallus, whispering among themselves. They complained that because Tiberius had inherited such enormous powers, he was really becoming an emperor, or a king, the first king of a nation that had sworn to never be ruled by a king again.

They were right. Soon, he would be openly called emperor rather than *princeps.*

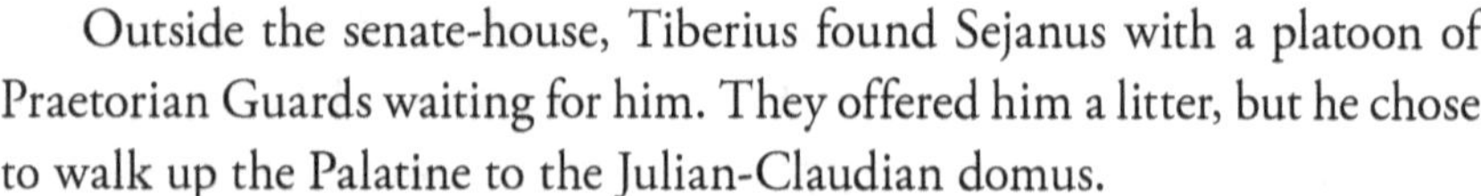

Outside the senate-house, Tiberius found Sejanus with a platoon of Praetorian Guards waiting for him. They offered him a litter, but he chose to walk up the Palatine to the Julian-Claudian domus.

Sejanus walked with him, assuming that he would have the same role with Tiberius as he had enjoyed with Augustus, and he offered information about events and upcoming matters.

When they arrived at the domus, Livia embraced Tiberius and asked, "How does it feel to be the ruler of Rome?"

"It feels like I'm holding a wolf by the ears," he answered.

That evening as Tiberius and Livia were having dinner, a military tribune arrived with a report that the exiled Agrippa Postumus, Julia's last son, had been found dead on Planasia, the island where he had been banished.

"How did it happen?" Tiberius asked.

"I was told that Postumus had been shouting and fighting and threatening people," the tribune said, "and he had to be restrained. He was forced into his room, and later found dead."

"This matter will have to be forwarded to the Senate for a full investigation," Tiberius said.

As the tribune left the room, Tiberius looked at his mother for her reaction. She showed none.

Rumors of murder began circulating among the people as was usual with a death of a potential heir. One rumor claimed that Livia had ordered the killing to eliminate a potential rival to her son. Other rumors spread that Augustus himself had left an order that, upon his death, Agrippa Postumus was to be eliminated for the good of the nation. After all, it was Augustus who had banished him. Nevertheless, most of the rumors blamed Tiberius.

Tiberius thought about whether this would be a problem for him. He hadn't ordered the execution, if that's what it was, but if people believed that he had, it was a problem, whether real or imagined. This became clear when Julia's republican friends demanded an investigation into the death. Sympathy for Julia spread, and her friends demanded her immediate release from Rhegium. Support for her cause grew quickly, and a cabal of senators used it to foment calls for Tiberius' removal.

These senators discussed possible successors to Tiberius. They proposed Germanicus, who had proved himself a capable military leader and was currently in command of legions in Germany.

Sejanus gave Tiberius a full report of these developments and about the public support for Germanicus and his wife, Agrippina, a couple who easily could be seen as emperor and empress. Sejanus also reported the growing number of accusations against Tiberius, including slanders, jokes, and lampoons that ridiculed him. He saw this as part of an organized, concerted effort to undermine him and make way for Germanicus.

Sejanus provided the information to the Senate, and in the Senate-house, several senators asked Tiberius what action should be taken against the offenders. His surprising answer was that the liberty to speak and think as one pleased is the test of a free country. "We cannot spare the time to undertake any such enterprise," he said. "Open that window, and you will let in such a rush of denunciations as to waste your whole working day; everyone will take the opportunity of airing some private feud. If so-and-so challenges me, I shall lay before you a careful account of what I have said and done; if that does not satisfy him, I shall reciprocate his dislike of me."

Whether his tolerance was genuine or merely a disguise for his real feelings about such critics wasn't clear. It had always been difficult to know what Tiberius was thinking. His reactions were unpredictable. Sometimes, as in this situation, he reacted as a dispassionate judge, making decisions and proclamations fairly and impartially for the overall good of the nation; other times, he seemed driven by anger at his critics, at those who disrespected or slandered him, and at those who undermined belief in the greatness of Rome.

Sejanus could read Tiberius' moods well, and usually timed his approaches and proposals according to the emperor's moods. At what he thought was a well-timed moment, he told Tiberius that he was investigating second-hand reports of a plot to free Julia, take her to join Germanicus' legions in Germany, and instigate a rebellion.

Tiberius instructed Sejanus to utilize all the resources of the Praetorian Guard to track the conspirators down.

"I have a suggestion to make," Sejanus said. "Your Praetorians are separated into four separate locations in the city. It divides them. I think they should all be housed in one place so that they'll be unified and we can have better control. They are your most loyal supporters, and you should have direct control over them."

"They're my most loyal supporters because Augustus raised their salary to three times that of the regular legions," Tiberius said.

"That, and they know of your reputation as Rome's greatest general," Sejanus said. "How you've always treated your troops fairly, and looked out for their interests. Most of all, how you never wasted lives."

"Where would we put them?"

"There are brick buildings at the northeastern wall that would be perfect for a Castra Praetoria. You could assemble the Guard there and speak to them on a regular basis."

"Give me an estimate of the cost, and if it's not too expensive, you can go ahead."

Sejanus gave Tiberius a low estimate of the cost to gain his approval, and began construction immediately. He knew a better organized Guard would strengthen Tiberius' hand against his opponents in the Senate. He also knew it would strengthen his own position. Next to the *princeps*, the emperor, he would become the most powerful man in Rome.

The camp would consist of a fortress, barracks, administration buildings, and a marching field. In all it would cover forty acres surrounded by a high concrete-and-brick wall with towers at each of its four corners.

As Sejanus built his Castra Praetoria, Tiberius began building his royal palace. He bought two buildings on the Palatine Hill that faced each other, one towards the east, one the west. He had them renovated with the finest marble, wood carvings, and mosaics that could be found in the empire. In the building facing east, he installed an altar to the Divine Augustus Caesar.

Between the buildings, now called the Domus Tiberian, was a long, elevated terrace supported by an enormous wall. From one side of the terrace, one could see the grand buildings, monuments, and temples of the Forum and the Capitoline Hill, from the other side, the Circus Maximus.

While both construction projects were proceeding, Tiberius did his best to govern, conducting affairs in the most judicious and even-handed manner that he could. He tried to balance the interests of all the competing factions, and took special consideration of the provinces that had suffered at the hands of dishonest governors. When one governor reported in the Senate that there had been a great increase in taxes collected in his province, Tiberius chastised him, saying, "It is the duty of a good shepherd to shear his sheep, not to skin them."

Rome was relieved that the transition of power from Augustus to Tiberius seemed to be proceeding smoothly and that the city was calm. But the calm didn't last, broken by the news of mutinies by the legions in the provinces of Pannonia on the Danube and Germany on the Rhine.

CHAPTER TWENTY-THREE

Mutinies

The mutiny in Pannonia began when the legion commander relieved the legionaries from work in recognition of Augustus' death. With no work to keep them occupied, trouble began. Instigated by an ex-actor, Percennius, the soldiers mutinied for better pay and conditions. They sensed weakness in the new emperor, and calculated that Tiberius would need the support of the legions against his enemies. Percennius turned his acting skills to demagoguery. Speaking to a crowd of legionaries, he asked, "Why obey, like slaves, a few commanders of companies, fewer still of battalions? You will never be brave enough to demand better conditions if you are not prepared to petition—or threaten—an emperor who is new and still faltering. Inactivity has done quite enough harm in all these years. Old men, mutilated by wounds, are serving their thirtieth or fortieth year. And even after your official discharge your service is not finished; for you stay on with the colors as a reserve, still under canvas—the same drudgery under another name! And if you manage to survive all these hazards, even then you are dragged off to a remote country and "settled" in some waterlogged swamp or untilled mountainside. Truly the army is a harsh, unrewarding profession! Body and soul are reckoned at two sesterces a day—and with this you have to find clothes, weapons, tents, and bribes for brutal company commanders if you want to avoid chores."

Percennius was a powerful speaker. He went on adding to the list abuses, "Heaven knows, lashes and wounds are always with us! So are hard winters and hard-working summers, grim war and unprofitable peace. Praetorian Guardsmen receive eight sesterces a day, and after sixteen years they go home. Yet obviously their service is no more dangerous than ours. I am not saying a word against sentry duty in the capital. Still, here are we among tribes of savages, with the enemy actually visible from our quarters!"

Percinnius convinced the legionaries to refuse to work and when the centurions attempted to restore discipline, the legionaries rebelled. They seized a hated, hard-driving centurion, loaded him with baggage, and drove him before them like a pack animal. Another centurion, nicknamed "bring me another," was notorious for flogging his subordinates with vine-sticks, first breaking them on their backs then asking for another stick. He was cornered and cut to pieces. The rest of the centurions were driven out of the camp and their belongings stolen.

Tiberius was enraged. The mutineers had broken their sacred oath of duty and had to be punished, but he couldn't afford to leave the city to deal with them. Instead, he designated his son Drusus II as proconsul and sent him to Pannonia along with experienced generals and advisors. He also sent two battalions of Praetorian Guards led by Sejanus.

When Drusus II first arrived at the camp on the Danube, he was jeered by the soldiers, and negotiations with them stalled. But Drusus fell into some luck when a full eclipse of the moon occurred; it was considered an ominous portent and unnerved the mutineers. Their enthusiasm for the rebellion began to wane, and it waned even further with the arrival of an early winter rainstorm. The rain was so cold and so fierce that the soldiers couldn't leave their tents, and it seemed to them that divine wrath was upon them. They saw the eclipse and the torrential rains as directly related to their criminal mutiny.

At that point, Drusus, on the advice of Sejanus, moved quickly to arrest and execute Percennius and the other ringleaders. Percennius was beheaded. Others who had begun the mutiny wandered outside the camp and were hunted down and killed by company commanders or guardsmen.

The soldiers went back to work, and Drusus II returned to Rome. Tiberius congratulated him, and personally thanked Sejanus for the help he gave his son so competently.

Meanwhile, Tiberius' nephew and adopted son, Germanicus, was in command of the legions on the Rhine. The mutiny there was unexpected because Germanicus was immensely popular, partly because of his handsome looks and generous nature, and partly because of his lineage. He was a son of Drusus I and Antonia. A decade earlier, the *princeps* had arranged his marriage to Agrippina, Julia's daughter, with the hope that it would produce offspring to continue the Julian bloodline. Over time, the couple had six children.

Agrippina traveled with Germanicus on his campaigns throughout the provinces. When the Rhine mutiny broke out, Agrippina was in camp with her youngest child, her one-year-old son, Gaius, who was nicknamed Caligula, or "little boots," for the miniature soldiers' uniform and boots he wore. The troops treated him as their mascot and lucky charm.

The mutineers in Germany made the same demands as those made in Pannonia, and the same pattern of violence, negotiations, and then more violence followed. Trying to put an end to the mutiny, Germanicus mounted a platform and spoke to the soldiers, sympathizing with their demands. Many of the soldiers began shouting and urging him to march on Rome and replace Tiberius. Germanicus knew better than to countenance treason. Raising his sword high for all to see, he shouted that he preferred death to treason. His advisors easily restrained him from plunging the sword into his chest. It seemed like bad playacting, and the mutineers derided him and dared him to do it. One soldier offered Germanicus his sword, saying that it was sharper.

Humiliated, Germanicus retreated to his tent where he and his advisors discussed what to do next. They decided to forge a letter in the name of Tiberius, promising to meet the demands of the soldiers. When the letter was read aloud, the soldiers were skeptical and demanded immediate payment of the bonuses or they would take their pay in plunder instead. Intimidated, Germanicus paid the bonuses out of his own funds. Now the mob was in charge. They conducted mock trials of allegedly abusive centurions, condemning innocent men to physical abuse and punishment.

Germanicus stood by and watched, hoping that the mutineers would grow tired. But the violence escalated, and he had to call for other legions to come and suppress the mutiny. With a clash brewing, he sent Agrippina and little Caligula away to an allied Gallic tribe to keep them safe. Agrippina, with her little boy in her arms, staged a procession out of the camp. She raised Caligula high so that the troops could see him and waved his arms at them, saying over and over that Augustus' great-grandson is being forced to leave for his safety. Apparently, this tapped into something visceral and caused a change of heart among the troops. The emotions of mobs cannot be explained by logic. The soldiers asked her not to go, and ended the mutiny.

Germanicus should have been condemned for capitulating to the mutineers, but, instead, he and Agrippina were lauded for resolving it, and they subsequently rode a wave of popularity. They were a glamorous couple who could easily have been seen as the rulers of Rome. People said that Germanicus, with his wavy blond hair, looked like Alexander the Great. He was certainly more attractive than the morose Tiberius, and Agrippina had the appearance and demeanor of a queen. She was beautiful, with the inherited large eyes of her mother, Julia, and the strong lower jawline of her father, Agrippa. She appeared as a woman as strong and forceful as any man.

Political operatives who supported the growing Julia-Agrippina party began working against Tiberius, some urging Germanicus to lead a march to Rome to restore the Republic.

Despite the encouragement, Germanicus did not march on Rome but continued military operations in Germany. In 16AD, at Idistaviso, in central Germany, he trapped and defeated Arminius' army, and recovered the standards Varus had lost at Teutoberg. Germanicus almost captured Arminius, but the betrayer of Varus escaped.

In 17AD, Germanicus went back to Rome to celebrate a triumph for his victories against the German tribes and the recovery of the standards. It was a spectacular event, with a million people cheering along the route. Germanicus' return of the standards was proclaimed more significant than Tiberius' return of the standards lost by Crassus at Carrhae. This was debatable point, but, in the enthusiasm of the moment, it was readily accepted by the people.

Agrippina and five-year-old Caligula rode in the triumphal chariot at Germanicus' side. His older sons, Drusus Germanicus and Nero

Germanicus, and his daughters, Agrippina the Younger and Drusilla, rode behind them in a second chariot.

Germanicus professed his allegiance to Tiberius, but both Julia and Agrippina continually undermined the emperor. Even in exile, Julia spread poisonous slanders about Tiberius' murderous character, while Agrippina, who was circulating among the nobles in Rome, was able to freely spread the same lies. Together, they fed the rumor that Tiberius was responsible for the death of Agrippa Postumus. They even hinted that Tiberius, with or without Livia, had arranged the deaths of Julia's other sons, Gaius Caesar and Lucius Caesar.

Aware of all this, Tiberius knew that Germanicus, as a military hero, could be the point of the spear for those plotting against him, and he knew that the mother-daughter pair, Julia and Agrippina, had the ability to launch that spear. But he was reluctant to take any further action against them without clear proof of treason.

Sejanus had attempted to obtain such proof but had collected only secondhand evidence. He reported to Tiberius at the palace, and they walked on the terrace so that no one could overhear them. Sejanus said that Julia and Agrippina were engaged in a seditious plot. He showed Tiberius dozens of anonymous pamphlets that were being circulated throughout the empire, pamphlets accusing him of a wide variety of misdeeds—including theft, embezzlement, sacrilege, murder, fratricide, and sexual degeneracy.

Tiberius shouted, "Find out who wrote this trash. Who's paying for it?"

"It's not one person," Sejanus said. "There are hundreds of these people; they call themselves observers, reporters, truth-tellers, speakers of truth to power."

"Truth-tellers! How about filthy liars? Where do they get the gall to slander me like this, to slander anyone with this wild talk? If they believe this trash, they should be forced to prove it. They should be forced to bring a prosecution," Tiberius said, as he picked up a large boulder and held it over his head with two hands, "and if they don't prove their case, they should be thrown from the Tarpeian Rock." He smashed the boulder against the terrace wall.

As Tiberius and Sejanus walked back and forth on the terrace, Sejanus took his arm. "I know you're upset but I have something else to tell you."

"What?"

"We've been told that Julia has been saying to her friends that you should suffer the same fate as Agrippa Postumus."

"That vile bitch. She not only destroyed my life, now she wants to end it."

"Coming from the daughter of Augustus, it's extremely dangerous," Sejanus said.

"Who did she tell?"

"We only have second-hand information now. When we get a first-hand witness, we can charge her with violating the *maiestas laesa*," Sejanus said.

The law of *maiestas laesa*, diminishing the majesty of Rome, was passed by the tribune Saturninus in 100 BC. It was an overbroad and vague statute that made any act damaging the greatness of the Roman people the equivalent of treason. It opened the door to arbitrary prosecutions, which were quickly applied to political disputes and accusations. In 88 BC, after the Social War, it was used against senators and equestrians who had sided with the Italians demanding citizenship. Since Augustus had come to personify the state, the law of *maiestas* could be aimed at anyone who expressed words, signs, or thoughts against him. Now, it was Tiberius who personified the state.

Tiberius glared at Sejanus. "How does she spread her poisons?"

"People come and go all the time, delivering food, clothing, letters. She has agents; she uses codes to send messages."

"Are these agents paid?"

"I'll find out."

"How much is her stipend?"

"Two thousand a month"

"Cut it to two hundred a month. Maybe when she doesn't have the money to pay her friends to pass on her messages, she won't have any more friends."

Tiberius ordered that Julia be confined to her house and not allowed any more visitors. This was a devastating sentence for Julia. She couldn't bare the solitude, stopped eating, and after five weeks, starved to death. Her death was called a suicide.

When Tiberius heard that Julia was dead and how she had died, his first reaction was volcanic. "How could they let this happen? Who in Hades was watching her? They should have force fed her? They've made her a martyr."

He shouted at Sejanus, "I want a full investigation. This could be a plot to discredit me. Do whatever you have to do to find out every detail. Torture the slaves if you have to."

When Sejanus left, Tiberius' mood changed. He felt sick. He should have handled it differently. He had overreacted to the slanders against him, and had taken it out on Julia. The poor girl, he thought. What an ending—the daughter of Augustus. If she had been a man, she would have used a sword. But her looks were everything to her. She couldn't mutilate herself. She starved herself, a crueler kind of death. As much as he had hated her, he felt some empathy for how tormented she must have been at the end.

Julia's death stirred up more calls in the Senate for Tiberius' removal. Julia's party shifted its allegiance to Agrippina as their new symbolic leader, and she absorbed the goodwill that had been attached to Julia. She was a natural leader with a knack for public display, as she had shown when she used little Caligula to shame the Rhine mutineers.

Many thought she would convince Germanicus to lead a rebellion. Sejanus told Tiberius that they should prepare for civil war. Tiberius hated the thought of a battle with Germanicus, the son of his beloved brother, Drusus I. He had sworn to Augustus that he would protect him. This was a dilemma he couldn't resolve. Tired and depressed, Tiberius felt an urge to get away from Rome, to return to Rhodes, or somewhere even farther away. But it was too late for that; he had to hold the empire together.

CHAPTER TWENTY-FOUR

Germanicus didn't lead a rebellion. Instead, he campaigned in Germany for three more years, hoping to win spectacular victories, extend Rome's empire, and enhance his own reputation. When he won battles, even small battles, his popularity in Rome soared. However, since his campaign was a drain on the treasury, Tiberius wanted to curtail it. He said that Germanicus was defying the deathbed order of Augustus that there should be no further expansion of the empire. Tiberius might have justifiably relieved Germanicus of command, but he was cautious not to insult the people's favorite who had legions loyal to him and ready to march on Rome.

In 17AD, to separate Germanicus from his troops, Tiberius shrewdly offered him a consulship. Accepting the consulship would mean that Germanicus would have to return to Rome and turn over his army to another general; this would be a recall without criticism. Germanicus had mixed feelings about it, but, after some hesitation, he accepted. The years of campaigning had been difficult, and he was relieved to be rid of the almost impossible task of pacifying Germany.

When he returned to Rome, Tiberius granted him another triumph for his victories, praising him lavishly in public while in private expressing doubts of his loyalty. Then, in 18AD, another opportunity to sideline Germanicus arose when a massive earthquake struck in Asia Minor, Tiberius sent Germanicus to the East to oversee relief efforts. He gave him command of the eastern empire, including the provinces of Greece, Asia Minor, Syria, and Judea. He reasoned that it was better that the young prince was occupied in the provinces rather than in Rome, where he could easily become the leader of a rebellious faction.

At that time, many such factions existed. Some hoped to restore the power of the senatorial oligarchy, some hoped to revive a genuine republic, and others wanted to install an emperor of their own choosing. Tiberius understood the desire to restore the Republic, but he believed that his enemies were disingenuously using the restoration movement as a means to replace him with one of their own as emperor. Germanicus would be the obvious choice.

Recognizing that Germanicus could build a strong power base in the East, Tiberius took measures to watch and constrain him. He removed the legate of Syria, a personal friend of Germanicus, and replaced him with Gnaeus Calpurnius Piso, the optimate aristocrat who, along with his brother Lucius, had visited Tiberius when he returned from Rhodes. Tiberius calculated that Gnaeus would be a counterweight to Germanicus' republican tendencies.

Livia was a strong supporter of Gnaeus Piso, whose wife, Plancina, was a close friend of hers.

Tiberius expected tension between Germanicus and Gnaeus Piso, but underestimated how much there'd be. They disagreed on every issue, and even though Germanicus had the greater imperium, Piso ignored or countermanded his orders. When Germanicus ordered Piso to lead an army of Syrian soldiers into Armenia, Piso refused, and the tension between the two men grew.

Making the situation more difficult, their wives fought. On several occasions, Agrippina insulted Plancina, who returned the insults.

In 19AD, Germanicus went to Egypt under the pretext of dealing with a grain scarcity, and Piso, in acting command, reversed or cancelled Germanicus' past orders. When Germanicus returned, matters came to a head, and they argued and insulted each other in public. Germanicus threatened charges of insubordination, and Piso left for Rome to present his side of the story.

Piso traveled to the city of Antioch on the Mediterranean coast, and while awaiting a ship, received news that Germanicus had become gravely ill and might be dying. He delayed his departure, waiting for news.

It appeared that Germanicus had been poisoned. The doctors tried antidotes, but his condition worsened. On his death bed, surrounded by his three closest friends—Vitellius, Serverus, and Vernius—he accused Piso and Plancina of having poisoned him. He asked his friends to exact his revenge. "Even if I were dying a natural death," he said, "I should have a legitimate grudge against the gods for prematurely parting me, at this young age, from my parents, children and country. But it is the wickedness of Piso and Plancina that have cut me off. I ask you to take my last requests to your heart. Tell my father and brother of the harrowing afflictions and ruinous conspiracies which have brought my wretched life to this miserable close. The chief duty of a friend is not to walk behind the corpse pointlessly grieving, but to remember his desires and carry out his instructions. If it was I that you loved, and not my rank, you must avenge me! Show Rome my wife—the divine Augustus' granddaughter. Show them our six children."

As he uttered the word "children," he closed his eyes and died. Each of his friends touched his right hand, swearing to seek vengeance.

Germanicus was only thirty-three. All Rome believed that he had been poisoned. Most people suspected that Piso and Plancina were responsible, and that they had acted on the orders of Tiberius and Livia. A rumor floated that when Piso heard that Germanicus had died, he threw a party.

◆

After the funeral in Syria, Agrippina sailed to Italy with the ashes of Germanicus. Arriving at Brundisium on the Adriatic Coast, she was met by throngs of supporters demonstrating their sympathy and loyalty to her and her sons—Drusus, Nero, and Caligula, the great-grandsons of Augustus.

A cohort of Praetorian Guards escorted her from Brundisium to Rome, and Agrippina's carefully staged entry into the city aroused the sympathy of the people. She played her part of the grieving widow superbly. The people recognized her and her children as the legitimate descendants of Augustus, and thought that she should be the regent of the next emperor.

Germanicus' ashes were interred in the Mausoleum of Augustus, but neither Tiberius nor Livia attended the ceremonies. People said that they didn't attend because the public would have seen how glad they were that Germanicus was dead. It was said that when Tiberius was asked about what effect Germanicus' death would have on the empire, he answered, "Princes die, but the empire remains."

The reason Tiberius and Livia didn't attend was because of information that Agrippina was planning a demonstration against them, using hundreds of organized street thugs to cause trouble in the way that Clodius and Fulvia Flaccus had used them in the past. Tiberius could have ordered the Praetorian Guards to deal with them but chose not to give Agrippina the public confrontation that she seemed to want.

Agrippina's supporters continued to spread rumors that Tiberius had ordered the murder of Germanicus, just as he reportedly ordered Agrippa Postumus' murder and Julia's starvation. The tense atmosphere grew even more tense when Vitellius, Serverus, and Vernius, the friends of Germanicus, brought charges of murder and treason against Gnaeus Piso and Plancina. The case captivated the public's attention with factions taking opposite sides and people arguing and fighting in the streets.

As the trial date drew near, Gnaeus' brother, Lucius Piso, asked Tiberius to transfer the trial from the Senate to the imperial court. He wanted him to do this in order to avoid the Senate being influenced by the street violence.

Tiberius told Lucius, "As much as I care for you and your brother, and as much as I would like to accommodate you, I can't. I have to remain impartial. If not, my position as emperor would be illegitimate. I'd be no better than the leader of a gang of bandits. I have to let the Senate hold the trial."

"I understand," Lucius said, disappointed. "But you'll be there?"

"Yes," Tiberius said. "But only in the capacity of chairman. I can't vote. My role will be to insure a fair trial."

Tiberius opened the trial with a speech designed to demonstrate his impartiality, saying, "Gnaeus Piso was my father's friend and governor, and co-consul with me, and I myself, with the Senate's approval, made him Germanicus' helper in his eastern duties. But these relationships must not influence the result. It must be decided objectively whether, having upset the prince by disobedience and quarrelsomeness, he rejoiced in his death, or whether he murdered him. For if he has exceeded his position, failed in respect to his senior, and exulted in his death—and my sorrow—then I will renounce his friendship and close my doors against him, but not use a ruler's power to avenge personal wrongs. If, however, there is proof of murder, a crime which would require vengeance whatever the victim's rank, it will be your duty to give proper satisfaction to his wife and children, and myself, his adoptive parent.

"I grieve for my son, and always shall. But I offer the accused every opportunity of producing evidence which may establish his innocence or Germanicus' unfairness, if there was any. And I implore you not to regard charges as proofs because my personal grief is involved. Those whose blood-relationship or loyalty to Piso have made them his defenders should help him in his peril with all the eloquence and industry they possess; and I urge the accusers to be no less industrious and determined."

Germanicus' friends presented the case for the prosecution; Gnaeus Piso's relatives, led by his brother Lucius Piso, presented the case for the defense.

The prosecutors produced little credible evidence that Gnaeus Piso or Plancina poisoned Germanius. What they did present was based mostly on speculation. However, they produced mountains of firsthand evidence that Piso had committed treason by refusing orders, countermanding orders, and undermining discipline. As the evidence came in, senators glared at Piso. Outside the Senate, the crowds shouted that if the Senate spared him, they were ready to lynch him. Piso bore it all without expression. After the second day of the trial, it became clear that he would be convicted. If that happened, he'd face a terrible choice. If convicted of treason, all his property would be confiscated and his family left destitute, but if he were to die before the guilty verdict was rendered, his property would be safe.

Piso went home and wrote a letter to Tiberius asking that after his suicide the case should be dismissed before a verdict could be rendered and that his son Marcus should not be penalized. He left the letter open on his desk. Later that night, he closed the door to his bedroom, and when dawn came, he was found dead with his throat cut and his sword lying on the floor next to him.

Still the prosecutors weren't satisfied, and, irrespective of Piso's death, they moved for his property to be forfeited to the state, depriving his son of his inheritance. Tiberius listened to the prosecution argument then read Piso's letter aloud to the Senate. He vetoed the proposed penalty, saying that Piso had not been convicted and whatever the father had done, his guilt should not be transferred onto the son.

At Livia's urging, Tiberius dismissed the charges against Plancina. Livia was angry at him for not interceding on Piso's behalf, saying that if he didn't support his most loyal friends, he wouldn't have any. He replied that, as emperor, he had standards to maintain. He couldn't let his personal feelings subvert the law. She disagreed, called him a coward, and accused him of being afraid of Agrippina. He tried to defend himself, and accused her of interfering in affairs of state. During a heated argument, she angrily showed him letters from Augustus complaining about Tiberius' "embittered and intractable disposition."

Tiberius knew that Augustus had not always cared for him, but what infuriated him was that his mother, instead of destroying such mortifying letters, had kept them for so long. He decided to avoid seeing his mother unless it was necessary for state affairs.

Piso's death didn't end the matter. Though no evidence of poisoning had been produced, the rumors continued to spread that Tiberius and Livia had been behind the alleged poisoning. Pamphlets were circulated and songs written extolling the bravery, good looks, charm, and republicanism of Germanicus. Other pamphlets and songs criticized Tiberius for his overly stern and strict policies, his aloofness, and his brutality. Additionally, they said that Tiberius avaricious, which did not enamor him to the people. Pamphlets were circulated that accused Tiberius of keeping treasury funds for himself, and refusing to spend funds on lavish spectacles and gladiatorial games, events others leaders often had used to win public approval. Tiberius responded by saying that the gladiator fights were a waste of both life and money. He said that if the people loved violence so much, they should join the legions.

However, he understood the value of keeping the public entertained, so, instead of gladiatorial games, he sponsored a weeklong tournament of chariot racing in the Circus Maximus. The races were Rome's most popular entertainments. On the first day of the tournament, he was amazed at the size of the crowd that had assembled even before the races had started. The stands that could hold 200,000 people were filled to capacity. Tiberius was pleased when the people cheered his appearance on the imperial balcony above the grandstand.

People in the stands and on the fields streamed in every direction. Vendors and bookmakers shouted, and groups of chariot team partisans sang songs. Trumpets announced the entrance of the chariots into the stadium, and two dozen chariots circled the race course in a colorful procession. The drivers, the chariots, and the horses wore the colors of the six competing teams: red, blue, green, white, purple, and gold. As a team passed, their supporters, wearing shirts of their team's colors, enthusiastically cheered, all trying to be louder than the supporters of the other teams.

When the trumpets sounded again, the first group of six chariots lined up behind the starting barrier and the crowd quieted down. The presiding officer let the starting flag drop, the barriers opened, and the horses burst out onto the track.

The race wasn't only about speed but more about making the seven turns around the course without crashing or colliding with a post or another chariot. After the last lap, the drivers took a straightaway to the finish line and, astonishingly, finished the day without a crash. This was an exception, usually there was at least one crash or pile up during a day's racing.

Sometimes, in the heat of the competition, drivers would cut off other drivers, and even lash them with their whips. This would make the crowd explode. Fans would curse a driver who cut off their driver. If a blue team driver cut off a red team driver, the partisans of these teams would curse and argue and even fight over the outcome of the race.

During the week, there were several of these arguments and fights, each getting more serious as the days passed. On the last day, a popular driver from the blue team was second from the lead behind a red team driver. On a turn, he tried to pass the red team driver on the inside. The red team driver swerved to cut him off. The blue chariot hit the rail, breaking its axle, and throwing the driver onto the track. Because he had tied the reins around his waist, he was dragged by the horses and severely injured.

Seeing this, blue team fans confronted the red team fans, and fights started throughout the stands. Others joined in, and a riot followed. Tiberius was disgusted, and called in the Praetorian Guard to quell the riot.

After the riot, Tiberius was in a sullen mood. He told Sejanus that the riot shows why we've had so many civil wars. People attach themselves to a team and act as though the team members were part of their family. If you insult their team, they'll attack you. "This might make sense if it were based on the merit or the skills of the drivers," he said, "but it's not. It's based on the color of a shirt. Have a charioteer from a green team whom everybody loves switch to a purple team, and those that loved him will now hate him. And those that hated him will now love him."

"You're right. Although it's only amusement, it shows you how irrational people can get," Sejanus said.

"And it applies doubly to politics," Tiberius said. "Partisans will view their own party members who steal from the treasury as merely doing business as usual. But, they see the same conduct by members of an opposing party as major corruption and call for their executions."

Sejanus nodded in agreement. "And quite often they're wrong about the person. People can be convinced, through a constant diet of false information to love a monster and hate someone who's looking out for their best interests."

Tiberius raised his eyebrows, "Which one am I?"

"The latter, of course," Sejanus said.

"That's right. But for some reason, they think I'm a monster. It's all made up."

Sejanus agreed and used the opportunity to tell Tiberius about all the rumors and accusations that had been circulating. He told him about the insulting graffiti written on Rome's walls and more about the abusive pamphlets, lampoons, and poems that were being distributed through the cafes and markets. One lampoon that was more provocative than most was a drawing of Tiberius and, under it, the lines:

Here is Sulla, men of Rome, surnamed
Sulla the Fortunate—to your misfortune;
Here is Marius come back at last
To capture Rome; here is an Antony
Uncivilly provoking civil strife,

His hands thrice dyed in costly Roman blood,
Confess: "Rome is no more!" All who return
To reign, from banishment, reign bloodily.

Tiberius began to get angry, but his mood changed quickly and he laughed, "Menelaus would have enjoyed the references to Marius and Sulla."

"I'm surprised you're taking it so lightly," Sejanus said.

"It's just a bunch of malcontents letting off steam. And it's nonsense. I was never banished. I took a voluntary vacation."

"That may be true, but you shouldn't let such slanders continue." Sejanus persisted. "The law of *maiestas laesa* forbids anything that brings disrepute on the people of Rome and you represent the people of Rome. Allowing this kind of thing encourages real conspiracies."

"Such as?"

"The most dangerous is centered around Agrippina's friends. They've been advocating for Germanicus; now they've switched their allegiance to his sons."

"Bring me some solid evidence," Tiberius said. "We'll deal with them all."

Taking that remark as a mandate, Sejanus embarked on a campaign to prosecute Agrippina's circle of friends and others for violations of the law of *maeistas laesa* or for whatever charges he could find. His plan was to find a weak link, a person who would inform on others, then work his way up the ladder towards Agrippina and her closest associates.

Sejanus was a master at building cases against people and exploiting the legal system to his advantage. In Rome, citizens could bring criminal charges against other citizens, and, if they prevailed, they would be entitled to a part of the fine imposed, and in some cases, they would be entitled to a substantial part of the defendant's property. This system worked effectively for centuries during the Republic; however, from the era of Marius and Sulla, abuses of the system became rampant. Professional informers, *delators*, proliferated, and working with ambitious lawyers, either uncovered or manufactured charges against wealthy targets. Both the *delators* and the lawyers claimed that their activities were for the public benefit, but most of them were working for their own benefit, and many became wealthy in the process.

The *delators* watched, not only for crimes or outright sedition, but also for a word spoken in a drunken moment against the emperor or an innocent joke made at his expense. Anyone could be denounced. People were terrorized. They said the walls had ears. Those who had whispered in confidence to friends, stopped whispering. The *delators* targeted senators and equestrians since they were the ones with the most wealth to confiscate.

Sejanus had a stable of *delators* whom he employed to bring charges against his political enemies or anyone he wanted to eliminate. He charged so many that most senators were afraid of him and would do his bidding to stay on his good side.

Tiberius gave him more and more authority, calling him, "My Sejanus," and authorizing him to speak on behalf of the emperor. Senators had to conduct business through Sejanus, and he leveraged his position to get information, establishing a network in which half the Senate was giving information about the other half, and the latter half was doing the same about the former half.

He also gathered information by befriending wives of senators and wealthy equestrians, using his good looks and charm to his advantage. Women loved to be around him, and they competed to bed him. He played hard to get, but when it suited his purposes, he'd engage in an affair, a dangerous game since his black-haired, dark-eyed Tuscan wife, Apicata, was violently jealous of his friendships with other women.

After the death of Germanicus, the most logical successor to Tiberius was his son, Drusus II. Tiberius gave him tribunician authority to prepare him for leadership. But Drusus needed discipline. He was known to get violent when he was drunk, and Tiberius had to chastise him repeatedly, once writing him a letter, saying, "You shall not behave like that while I am alive to prevent it; and if you are not careful, I will see to it that you have no chance of doing so after I am dead."

Tiberius disapproved of his avid interest in gladiatorial games, calling him bloodthirsty. Tiberius had tried to limit the games, but Drusus had publicly called for more, thinking, perhaps, that it would make him popular.

Drusus II loved a party, and with his best friend, Herod Agrippa, went from one to another, from one drinking bout to another.

While Drusus II caroused with Herod Agrippa, partying and chasing women, he neglected his wife, Livilla, whom he had married in 4AD in an arrangement made by Augustus after Livilla's husband, Gaius Caesar, died. She was the daughter of Drusus I and Antonia, and thus a cousin to Drusus II.

Livilla had reluctantly accepted the marriage, and in 11AD, she gave birth to a son, Gemellus, a surviving twin.

In the ensuing years, she matured into a remarkably beautiful, clever, and cultivated woman. However, she was not content. Either she sought out Sejanus, or he sought her. In either case, they had a torrid affair.

Drusus grew suspicious. One evening after a banquet where Drusus had been drinking heavily, he tried to slap Sejanus in the face. People jumped between them to prevent a fight, but Sejanus didn't have to be restrained. He backed off, knowing he couldn't strike the emperor's son. He'd find another way to get even.

When Tiberius heard of the fight and all the drinking bouts, he summoned Drusus. They sat on a marble bench. "What's going on between you and Sejanus?"

"That son of bitch thinks he's everybody's superior," Drusus said. "And I don't like the way he's cozied-up to my wife. Every chance he gets, he's whispering to her."

"Well, we can't have that. I'll talk to him about it," Tiberius said.

"I'll take care of it myself," Drusus said.

"Listen to me," Tiberius said. "Maybe if you weren't out drinking and carrying on every night, and maybe if you stayed home with your wife, he wouldn't have the chance to whisper to her."

"Who does he think he is? Even if I'm away for a year, he shouldn't be circling around her." Drusus slammed the bench, stood up, and shouted, "If he's not careful, I'll stick his head on the end of spear."

Tiberius was surprised by the outburst, but smiled because he knew where Drusus' temper came from. "Sit down, and listen to me," he said. "I know how you feel, but some of this might be your own fault."

"I don't see how you can say that," Drusus said.

"I can say it very easily. You have a beautiful young wife," Tiberius said. "You should be paying more attention to her instead of running around partying all the time. What is it that you want with other women? Livilla has everything you need. She's lovely. She's sweet. She wants your companionship. Maybe she's not getting it, and she's looking somewhere else. Sejanus pays attention to her and she's flattered. I'm not saying she's done anything, but women want attention."

Drusus remained silent, then said, "I suppose you're right."

"I know I'm right. Many men are out eating tripe when they have a delicious piece of lamb at home. You should appreciate her. There's nothing these other girls have that she doesn't have. If you treat her well, you'll find there's nothing better in the world than a loving wife, and a loving couple can make each other much better than they could be alone."

"You're right."

"You know I've never recovered from losing Vipsania. I was such a fool. I'm sorry for what I did to her, and I'm sorry for what I did to you. You deserved to have her as your mother."

"Yes. Maybe that's my problem. I was brought up by Julia instead of my real mother."

"Again, I'm very sorry. But don't repeat my mistake. Go out of your way to cherish your wife. The few years I had with your mother were the most wonderful years of my life; nothing was better then or since."

"I'm sorry," Drusus said as he hugged his father. "I'll try my best."

Meanwhile, Sejanus, without Tiberius' knowledge, used his most trusted cadre of praetorian guards to keep track of Drusus' movements. They let Sejanus know when Drusus left Rome or was away from his house. When the timing was right, Sejanus and Livilla would meet in one of his apartments. On occasion, he visited Livilla's house, asking for Drusus, knowing he wasn't home. The lovers would then retire to a back bedroom, which added to the thrill.

Livilla had a voracious appetite for sex, and she overwhelmed Sejanus. Usually, he was in control of his relationships, and could turn them on and off as he wished, but with Livilla it was different. He was completely enthralled. However, he was playing with fire. Under the laws of Augustus, adultery could be a capital offense. Sejanus, who prosecuted so many others, had made himself vulnerable to retaliation.

In 23AD, Tiberius appointed Drusus II as his co-consul, hoping to develop his son's abilities for the time when he would succeed him. However, Drusus became ill with a persistent fever. He had suffered the same illness several times during the year, but by September it became more serious. September was a dangerous month in Rome; mosquitoes were everywhere, and every year, many people died. At the end of the month, Drusus died, and all assumed it was from natural causes.

Although Tiberius had been hardened against death after living through the deaths of so many close to him, his son's passing overwhelmed him. He remembered Drusus as a newborn, a playful boy, a young man with so much potential. He thought about his success in Pannonia. What a terrible loss!

The funeral did nothing to ameliorate the pain. The weather was gloomy, and the mourners seemed angry, not sympathetic. They cursed Herod Agrippa for leading Drusus into a profligate life, even though that had nothing to do with the cause of his death. Thinking it better not to go to the funeral, Herod Agrippa left Rome.

Tiberius thought it was the end of the road for him. He had no one of his own family to continue his legacy. Now his successor would be a stranger. Feeling as though he had aged decades, he paced the rooms of his house cursing. He thought of the dead all around him: His cousin Marcellus, his mentor Marcus Agrippa, his brother Drusus I, his tutor Menelaus, his nephew and adopted son Germanicus, his friend Piso, and now Drusus II, his only biological son—all gone.

Bad news kept coming. Vipsania died, apparently of natural causes. When Tiberius learned of her death, he was too despondent to appear in public, and for days remained locked in his rooms, walking in circles, muttering his regrets, saying over and over, if only this, if only that. He wondered whether the death of their son Drusus had brought on

Vipsania's death. But, what did it matter now? He was almost ready to die himself. "I've suffered enough calamities for one lifetime," he said. "I've had enough."

When Tiberius emerged from his rooms, Sejanus did everything he could to console him. He invited people whom the emperor liked, hoping they would lift his spirits, but Tiberius was too dejected to care, and chased them away.

Eventually, nature took its course, and he slowly recovered. One morning, just as he had revived himself from his depression on Rhodes, he revived himself again. He began working harder than ever on his administrative and executive duties, motivating himself by keeping in mind his ultimate goal to be remembered as a capable and fair-minded emperor. Work was his solace. He attended all the Senate sessions and tried to rule with the benefit of the wisdom he had acquired through experience. But his nature and suspicions hadn't changed. He couldn't help listening carefully for those who seemed pleased that the succession would now pass to a son of Agrippina and Germanicus—either Nero Germanicus, Drusus Germanicus, or Caligula. True, they were the most direct descendants of Augustus, but he believed that a "new man" who had risen by merit should be the next emperor. Sejanus certainly would be more capable than any of Agrippina's sons.

Sejanus took on many of the emperor's duties, working to overcome a block of senators who continually resisted, complained, and obstructed Tiberius' administration. These senators opposed every measure designed to improve conditions or fix a problem, but they proposed no alternatives. Through treachery and slander, they poisoned the atmosphere, and it seemed they hoped that Tiberius would be a failure, even if that would damage the nation.

To fight them, Sejanus, used the best tool that he had—bringing charges of *maiestas laesa* against several of them or their associates. He stretched the application of this overly broad law far beyond its intended purposes, and applied it so frequently that Rome began to suffer a reign of terror, cloaked in legal language.

In one instance, at a time when Tiberius was away, Sejanus prosecuted a poet, Clutorius Priscus, a close friend of an opposition senator. Priscus had been highly praised for a poem he had written on the death of Germanicus. Then, upon hearing that Drusus II was seriously ill, he wrote a poem eulogizing him. Unfortunately for Priscus, Drusus had a temporary recovery, and the eulogy seemed premature. It was interpreted as being hopeful for his death. When Drusus eventually died, Priscus was charged with *maiestas*, and the poet was summarily executed.

When Tiberius returned to Rome and learned of the execution, he was surprised but did nothing to chastise Sejanus. The only action he took was to issue an edict that in the future no such executions should take place without a hearing to review the sentence.

Sejanus continued the prosecutions, increasingly exercising his power out of personal vindictiveness. A senator named Cremutius had insulted Sejanus several years earlier, and now made the mistake of writing a book in which he stated that Brutus and Cassius were the last of the great Romans. Sejanus called this an insult to both Augustus and Tiberius, and thus Rome itself. Cremutius was prosecuted and convicted of *maiestas*. He committed suicide.

Sejanus targeted the close friends of Agrippina. He prosecuted Votienus Montanus for slandering Tiberius with gossip alleging that the emperor engaged in perverted sex with his slaves. Tiberius was so incensed by the slander that he appeared at Montanus' trial, scowling at everyone, thus assuring that there would be a conviction and execution.

Sejanus charged another friend of Agrippina, Claudia Pulchra, with treason because she allegedly threatened the life of Tiberius, possibly with poison. However, because his evidence was weak, he added a charge of adultery, which he knew he could easily prove.

As her trial progressed and it was clear that Claudia would be convicted, Agrippina wrote to Tiberius asking for clemency on her friend's behalf. When he denied it, Agrippina went, uninvited, to see Tiberius. She burst into the domus, and found him praying at the altar of the Divine Augustus. Even more impulsive and brash than her mother Julia, she called Tiberius a hypocrite for praying to Augustus while persecuting his granddaughter. They shouted at each other, and when Tiberius stood over her in a rage and shouted that he'd had enough of her, Agrippina backed down and asked for peace between them. They agreed to have a dinner the next evening to discuss matters and the future of her sons.

Sejanus learned of the potential reconciliation and decided that it was not in his best interests. As Agrippina arrived for the dinner, Sejanus had one of his slaves whisper to one of her slaves a warning that Agrippina should be careful of what she ate. The slave whispered in Agrippina's ear, and she refused to eat anything, telling Tiberius it was because she had an upset stomach.

Tiberius saw this as an insult, and offered to switch plates with her. She still refused to eat. The insult was too much for him and his anger mounted. He had fought so many battles against Rome's enemies, faced them with honor, sword to sword, but was now being accused of the underhanded crime of poisoning. He wanted to strike her, but without saying anything, left the room. No reconciliation occurred. Sejanus had prevented it.

Tiberius and Sejanus met daily to discuss their enemies list, not only enemies from Agrippina's faction, but also from other senatorial factions. Tiberius considered them enemies because he saw them as obstructionists who prevented him from accomplishing his goals. He also saw many of them as warmongers. His policy, as Augustus had mandated, was not to expand the empire. But many senators and generals proposed new campaigns. They wanted either to cross the ocean to invade Britain, or attack Parthia, or colonize the Red Sea and the Arabian Peninsula. He wouldn't allow any of it. He believed, as Augustus had, that the Roman Empire should remain as it was, strong at its borders, and at peace.

He knew what Hannibal had said, "That when Rome had no more enemies abroad, it would find enemies within, and thus would destroy itself." The implication could be drawn that Rome should continue finding enemies abroad. But he was not going to be influenced by Hannibal; he would abide by the wisdom of Augustus. The empire was large enough.

Sejanus, of course, agreed, and since he was in such a favorable position with the emperor, he thought it was time to improve his circumstances. He divorced his wife, Apicata, and asked Tiberius for permission to marry

Livilla, the widow of Drusus II. He didn't tell Tiberius that he had been having an affair with Livilla for some time, even while she had been married to Drusus. Sejanus took this step despite knowing that Apicata would be angry and vindictive. He figured he would deal with her when the time came.

Tiberius turned down the request, saying that Sejanus had not held senatorial rank, making it inappropriate for him to marry into the imperial family. But not wanting to alienate him, he said that he would greatly reward Sejanus for his good work at some time in the near future, adding, off-handedly, that if Sejanus attained the consulship, he might reconsider. Sejanus smiled but saw the denial as an unfair rebuke after all he had done for Tiberius. He knew that the emperor could make him consul with a snap of his fingers. He didn't protest, but changed tactics and began expressing concern that Tiberius was working too hard and endangering his health. In a friendly way, he suggested that Tiberius should spend more time in the country as so many senators did. "Why should you be such a diligent workhorse while half the Senate is away on vacation? Your legates can do the routine work," Sejanus said. "This will give you more time to address the more important problems."

Tiberius thought seriously about Sejanus' suggestions, and in 27AD, at sixty-seven years of age, he left Rome, ostensibly to dedicate a temple to Augustus in Nola and a temple to Jupiter in Capua. He was accompanied by a group which included Sejanus, a contingent of Praetorian Guards, and Senator Marcus Cocceius Nerva, a renowned jurist, statesman, and diplomat whom Tiberius greatly respected. A man not only of words but a builder, Nerva had built aqueducts and a tunnel in the Campagna region between Puteoli and Neopolis.

After dedicating the temple to Augustus at Nola, the group traveled by wagon to Capua. On the way, they stopped at Tiberius' villa at Sperlunca where they admired the villa and the landscaping with its fountains, arbors, pavilions, and gardens. The villa also had a beautiful grotto at its seaside with an artificial island built near the mouth of a cave. Tiberius and his guests dined on the island. Apricots, pears, grilled pork, octopus, squid, olives, and pastries were served from small toy boats that floated across the water from the kitchen in the cave to the island. For hours, Tiberius, Nerva, and Sejanus discussed various topics as servants waited on them and poured wine. As the men talked late into the night, Tiberius seemed unusually relaxed and satisfied.

However, the next morning, his mood changed. He was scheduled to go to Capua to dedicate the temple, but was gripped by the same feeling that years ago had driven him to Rhodes. He said he didn't want to go to Capua to attend the dedication.

"But it's important for the people to see you," Nerva said.

"I don't care. I'm too tired," Tiberius said. "You go in my place."

Reluctantly, Nerva and Sejanus went to Capua without him. While they were away, Tiberius stayed at his villa admiring the sculptures he had brought years earlier from Greece and Rhodes. He was most proud of the group of sculptures that depicted the blinding of the cyclops Polyphemus by Odysseus. The mammoth statue showed Odysseus climbing toward the sleeping cyclops' massive head to make sure that the burning stake, held by his soldiers, would go directly into the cyclops' one and only eye.

Tiberius admired how the sculptor, using realistic and anatomical details, conveyed all of the drama and tension of the scene. The soldiers' strained muscles and terrorized expressions made them look almost alive. Odysseus' weathered face expressed all the hardships he had overcome and his indomitable determination. As he looked at the statue, Tiberius saw himself.

CHAPTER TWENTY-FIVE

When Nerva and Sejanus returned from Capua, Tiberius took them and several Praetorian Guard commanders to dinner at the Cavern, a well-known seaside cafe in Tarracina, a town north of his villa in Sperlunca. The café was in a beautiful setting, close to the shore at the bottom of a high cliff.

Tiberius' guests feasted on oysters and fresh fish soaked in garum fish sauce. After the meal, Tiberius said that he had announcement to make, but just as he said this, there was a rumble, and large boulders suddenly broke loose from the cliff above, falling on the café. The diners and waiters dove to the floor or under tables. Sejanus threw himself on his hands and knees across Tiberius' body to protect him. Several rocks struck Sejanus. Although some could have been lethal, he wasn't seriously hurt. Tiberius was unhurt but had difficulty getting up. Sejanus helped him up and led him away from the danger.

When it was over, three servants and one Praetorian guard had been killed.

"Let's get out of here," Nerva said.

The Praetorians helped Tiberius and Nerva into a wagon, and Sejanus drove it back to Sperlunca.

"Do you think someone intentionally caused the rock fall?" Tiberius asked.

Sejanus began to say that he doubted it because tremors were usual in that region, but it wasn't in his interests to say that; it was better for Tiberius to believe that he was the target of assassins. "I'll check the cliff to see if we can find anything, and as a precaution, I'll station extra guards around your villa"

"Double the guards," Tiberius said. "And question everyone around about whether any strangers have been seen in the area."

"Yes, Caesar."

"By the way, Sejanus. Thank you for saving my life," Tiberius said.

"It's my duty. I'll always protect you," Sejanus said.

The next morning, Sejanus asked Tiberius what the announcement was that he was going to make before the rock fall. Tiberius told him that he wanted to visit Capri, an island three kilometers beyond the peninsula of Sorrento in the Bay of Neapolis.

Augustus had bought the island, and visited it often with Livia. They had never taken Tiberius with them on their visits, and after hearing their descriptions of the island's beauty, Tiberius developed a fascination for it.

Tiberius told Sejanus that he had already arranged for two navy triremes to take his party to the island.

"Do you intend to stay long," Sejanus asked.

"I might."

Three days later, they boarded the triremes and headed across the bay to Capri. As Tiberius' ship approached the island, he stood at the bow, remembering the time he had sailed to Rhodes. The island of Rhodes was larger, but Capri was higher. He marveled at the height of the sheer cliffs, which rose 590 meters out of the sea. What a perfect place for a fortified citadel, he thought.

The triremes docked at the island's only landing site and were met by the governor of the island, who said he was used to getting surprise visitors, and offered to have Tiberius stay at his palace. Tiberius accepted the offer. After settling in, he spent several days touring the island. The weather was perfect, with warm sunshine and cool breezes. Abundant lemon trees were everywhere and superb, lush gardens on the island's southwest corner enhanced its beauty.

With local guides, Tiberius surveyed the entire island. It had two distinct hilltops, and he rode in a donkey cart up a steep trail to the top of highest one. From there he could see spectacular views of the Amalfi

Coast of Italia, Mount Vesuvius, the Islands of Ischia and Procida, and the peninsula of Sorrento.

A guide took him to an enormous cavern at the shoreline that could be accessed only by rowboat. The natives called it the blue grotto for its bright blue waters. Tiberius climbed out of the rowboat onto a natural stone ledge at the opening of the grotto. He sat watching the waves rush in and out, and listening to the soothing sounds of the water. He wished that he could sit there all day.

⸻ ◆ ⸻

After his survey, Tiberius picked a spot on the hilltop at the northeast corner of the island. He ordered tables and chairs to be brought there for an outdoor lunch, and invited the governor and other island officials. When everyone was seated, Tiberius stood and made an announcement. "I've decided to settle here on Capri. I'll build my villa on this spot with its magnificent views overlooking the sea."

An awkward silence followed until the governor spoke, "That would be wonderful." He said it as though he didn't really mean it and hoped it wouldn't happen. Clearly, the world as he knew it was about to change.

Nerva and Sejanus both looked stunned.

"What about Rome?" Nerva asked. "What about ruling the empire?"

"I can fulfill my responsibilities from here. Ships and mailboats will arrive and depart every day, and Sejanus can take care of routine matters in Rome."

"Shouldn't you get permission from the Senate?" Nerva said.

"I'll tell them to give me permission."

"What about urgent matters?"

"I can make decisions from here faster than the Senate can get themselves awake. They never make a decision unless they're sure it's safe."

Sejanus saw the opportunity that had just opened to him; he was ecstatic but didn't want to appear overanxious. "If that's what you think best," he said. "I'll continue to give you my unwavering support."

"I would expect nothing less."

⸻ ◆ ⸻

Tiberius said that he would return to Rome as necessary, but during the next months, the farthest he ever traveled was to his villa at Sperlunca. He was too occupied with his plan to convert Capri into a haven away from Rome, and with Nerva's help, he drew up a plan for several building projects. He would build an enormous villa, the Villa Jovis, for himself on the spot he had picked on northeast corner of the island. He would also a build a great lighthouse, and three new temples, one each to the gods Jupiter, Minerva, and Mars, and he would renovate or expand the twelve small villas that Augustus had built.

Beginning the work was like a new breath of life for him, and he thrived on dealing with the engineers and architects; it reminded him of his time with Agrippa and the construction projects in Rome.

He sent for the great architect, Vitruvius Pollio, to oversee the building projects. Vitruvius came to stay on Capri, but, because of his advanced age, could only give general advice. He left the calculations and drawings to Nerva and the younger architects. Nevertheless, Tiberius was thrilled with Vitruvius' company. He was the type of man that Tiberius admired—a doer, a builder, from the same mold as Nerva.

Vitruvius explained the principles of architecture. He explained the origins and the proper uses of the Ionic, Doric, and Corinthian styles, and he advised Tiberius to use pozzolana mud for his building projects, explaining that it was found in the region around Mount Vesuvius. "This substance," he said, "when mixed with lime and gravel, lends strength to buildings, and can be used for piers constructed in the sea. Since it sets hard under water, neither the waves nor the force of the water can dissolve it."

"It seems to have magical properties," Tiberius said.

Nerva said that he had successfully used pozzolana to build his tunnels and aqueducts.

The stone for the lighthouse, the villas, and the temples was excavated from the island, but special materials and marbles were transported from the mainland.

When completed, the Villa Jovis was forty meters high and had eight levels. It was like a fortress, with terraced gardens for growing vegetables, and a system for channeling rainwater collected on the roofs and stored in a giant cistern. On its eastern side, a sheer cliff dropped precipitously down to the rocks at the edge of the sea. It would be impossible to scale and anyone who fell from there would have no chance of survival.

Visitors to the island had to be cleared by Sejanus who screened them all along with all correspondence. He determined who and what Tiberius would see, and he made most of the routine administrative decisions. Tiberius called him "my partner in toil." Sejanus read the incoming mail, but wasn't allowed to read Tiberius' outgoing mail that bore the imperial seal. It was a capital offense for anyone but the addressee to open and read a sealed imperial correspondence.

At first Sejanus split his time between Rome and Capri, ten days in Rome, ten days on the island, but as time passed, he spent more time in Rome. He brought only the most important matters to the emperor's attention, and handled everything else himself. In Rome, he passed on messages from the emperor, but gradually the words became more and more his own.

When Sejanus was in Rome, his second-in-command, Sertorius Macro, took his place as praetorian commander on the island, and he was as efficient as Sejanus at handling security and administrative matters.

On the anniversary of the rock fall at the Cavern at Tarracina, Tiberius took the survivors there for a reunion. They toasted their survival and commemorated those who had been killed.

"You still don't know if the rock fall was an accident or not?" Tiberius asked Sejanus.

"I don't think it was an accident."

"If it wasn't an accident, who did it?"

"We don't know, but we haven't given up," Sejanus said. "We question anyone who gets arrested to see whether they have any information. Sooner or later, some criminal, wanting to save himself, will turn up."

"If you ever catch them, make an example of them," Tiberius said.

"Yes, Caesar. Examples are important," Sejanus said.

"Deterrence."

"You're right," Sejanus said, "I recently had a conversation with an Egyptian high priest about punishment and deterrence. He suggested that we do what they used to do in Carthage."

"What's that?"

"Throw criminals to the lions in the arena for all to see; that would be a powerful deterrent."

"This is Rome, not Carthage," Tiberius said. "We're not so barbaric. You know, they sacrificed infants to their gods rather than animals."

"Perhaps, we won't use the lions."

"Let's think of more pleasant things."

As the building projects progressed, Tiberius turned much of his attention to replicating the culture of Rhodes. He invited orators, poets, and philosophers to visit, and imported musicians, dancers, and actors.

In March of 28AD, Jason of Nyet, the Stoic philosopher whom Tiberius had met on Rhodes, visited the island. Tiberius welcomed him as though he were a long, lost son. Jason stayed for a month, and the two men spent most of their days talking about the big questions, questions that had nothing to do with contemporary politics. Jason was a master conversationalist with a talent for drawing people out in a discussion. Sometimes his conversations sounded like Socratic dialogues.

Tiberius greatly enjoyed their talks. Conversing like a Greek philosopher was the kind of thing that he enjoyed most, and he wished he could do it all the time. Often, while he and Jason were walking across the heights of the island or sitting on the veranda, they discussed Plato, Epicureanism, and Jason's stoic great-grandfather, Posidonius. Each day they continued the conversation from the day before. They philosophized about the meaning and purpose of life, and talked about how to live the best life.

One beautiful, balmy evening, seated on a veranda after having discussed many subjects, Jason asked Tiberius what more he wanted out of life. Tiberius didn't answer right away. He stood and walked about, then stopped and looked out to the sea. "I want to wake up and begin each day as though it's the first day of a new life," he said. "I want to forget what happened yesterday, and look at everything anew, like a young child seeing the world for the first time."

"What do you mean?"

Tiberius sat down again. "I mean just that; I want to appreciate the world. Nature, the rivers, the trees, the hills, everything. So many things are astounding. Once I sat at the top of the Alps, and it was like seeing creation, like being part of creation. I can't explain it. But we should try to experience and contemplate the world more. Forget all the pettiness of daily life—the politics, the arrests, the prosecutions. Forget who I am. Forget getting revenge."

"Is that possible?" Jason asked.

"Unfortunately, no," Tiberius said. "Not for me, anyway. I try, but within minutes, I'm crushed with problems and responsibilities. And, worse, I suffer with my regrets. I can't escape them; I can't escape from myself."

Jason waited for Tiberius to say more. When he didn't, Jason asked, "What regrets?"

"There are too many to count."

"What's your greatest regret?"

"There's no single one. They're all connected in a pattern, one leading to the next."

"Let me speak openly," Jason said. "Wasn't your divorce from Vipsania your greatest regret?"

"Of course, but it's hard for me to talk about it."

"I'm sure it is, but remember Posidonius," Jason said. "He taught that the rational man accepts his fate as part of the natural order of things. Our fates have been determined, and although we must act in the best way that we can, once it becomes clear what the results of our actions will be, a rational man accepts them. There's no point in tearing yourself apart, your actions and the results were meant to be."

Tiberius stared out at nothing. The sea was in front of him, but he didn't see it. He stood abruptly. "I can't accept that. You may be right that whatever is going to happen is going to happen, but I'm responsible for what I do. Just because my fate is preordained, it doesn't excuse me. Otherwise, a murderer could say it wasn't his fault, but fate's. That can't be. It's a contradiction. A man has to accept responsibility and suffer for his own mistakes."

"Perhaps we've talked in a circle," Jason said, "starting at different points and coming to the same conclusion. Only my approach alleviates suffering; yours causes more suffering."

"But suffering is part of the natural order of things. We can't escape it. Not until we're dead," Tiberius said. "Without suffering, we wouldn't do the things necessary to avoid suffering; we wouldn't make the effort to secure the safety of our families and our people."

"That's an interesting idea, Manichaean; there must be evil for there to be good."

Both men fell silent. Then Jason asked, "But where does evil come from? Is it an external phenomenon that intercedes into human affairs and controls the actions of men? Or is it within us?"

"Evil is not external," Tiberius said. "It's not an incorporeal idea. It's not separated from us. It's part of nature." He waved his arm. "Look around. Animals have to eat other animals. Driven by hunger, they have to kill something. And something has to be killed. The killer and the killed are both victims of evil. There's no way out for them."

"What if there were no carnivorous animals?"

"But there are. And even if there weren't, there's still man."

"Man doesn't have to be carnivorous," Jason said.

"But he has to kill or be killed, to dominate or be dominated," Tiberius said.

"You think it has to be that way?"

"Yes. It's in our nature," Tiberius said. "Even when we bond together in a social group, whether a tribe or a nation, we see other groups, not as fellow humans, but as natural enemies, competitors for scarce resources. That's what leads to war."

"So, there's no hope?" Jason said.

"Well, let's not give up yet," Tiberius said. "We have made some advancements. We're no longer barbarians taking each other's scalps. Societies have found better ways, and men have invented other means of battling one another. They've invented substitutes for war and substitutes for murder. They have prosecutions and elections, chariot races and games, and economic competition. These are less dangerous fields of battle to channel the instinct to kill."

"So, much of what we do is a substitute for killing our competitors?" Jason said.

"Yes. Animals do it. During mating season, two rams will batter each other to see who's the strongest. They don't fight to the death. When it's clear who would win, they stop. The winner gets the prize—a mate. We do the same thing. The winning athlete gets a trophy, the winning prosecutor gets acclaimed, the winning politician gets the office, and the best merchant gets the money. We stop there. We don't have to continue to the ultimate fight to the death to know who would have won."

"But sometimes we do continue," Jason said.

"It's still part of our nature."

"Is that why we make gladiators kill one another?"

"You might be right," Tiberius said. "The games express our murderous nature. They might satisfy a desire to kill. Reduce the desire for war."

"I thought you hated the gladiator contests."

"I do, but they still exist. I don't think I could end them without causing a revolution. If I had greater support and not so many detractors, I could do something about them." Tiberius stood, indicating that he had had enough of the discussion that was beginning to wander off the topic.

"Well, we certainly have given ourselves enough to think about," Jason said. "Perhaps, we should have some wine."

"On that we can agree," Tiberius said.

CHAPTER TWENTY-SIX

Tiberius felt that he had found his true home on Capri. He loved the island, the mild breezes, the lush vegetation, plentiful fruit, and ever-changing skies and sunsets. Intellectually stimulated by conversations with friends, visiting artists, and philosophers, he imagined living in Athens during the times of Socrates, Plato, and Aristotle. Each day, he thought, was a gift, and he made a conscious effort to enjoy them all. Feeling more content than he ever had in his life, he issued imperial decisions and proclamations marked by such tolerance and leniency that people wondered whether they were being issued by him or someone else.

Unfortunately, his contentment was interrupted by Sejanus' reports about treasonous and slanderous conduct. Tiberius had always been subject to mood swings, from energetic enthusiasm to moroseness; Sejanus' reports pushed them to extremes. He could be pleasant all day, immersed in his projects, but upon receiving a report of slander against him, he would start raging and threatening to exact severe punishments.

Sejanus told him that Agrippina and her allies were using his absence from the capitol as an opportunity to turn the people against him, spreading accusations and slanders that he engaged in debaucheries. They fabricated stories that he had imported dozens of young dancers, male and female, for him to watch as they engaged in titillating and lascivious performances. They embellished the lies by adding that Tiberius took part in the performances.

Sejanus delivered a particularly disturbing report while Tiberius was having dinner with Nerva and Vitruvius. He reacted by throwing objects against the walls, stomping back and forth, and ranting, "What kind of snakes would make up this nonsense? And those who repeat these filthy stories are no better. Is there anything wrong with watching young people dance? And the music and the singing? That's why I came here—for the beauty of the place, for enjoyment. Being around young people, it's good for the spirit. Sure, you always expect a certain amount of grumbling and criticism from the public, but these are venomous vipers. I've ignored them too long. I've been tolerant too long. My inaction has only encouraged them."

Slamming his fist on the table, he shouted, "They should have their tongues pulled out and their hands cut off."

"These buzzards are the scum of the earth," Sejanus said.

"Buzzards, yes, that's a good word for them. They'll spread lies about anyone. Remember they even ridiculed Julius Caesar, saying that when he became close friends with King Nicomedes of Bithynia, their relationship was sexual. Years later, the slanders were still the object of laughter, and repeated in songs by his troops. They sang, 'All the Gauls did Caesar vanquish, Nicomedes vanquished him.'"

"Caesar took it with good humor," Nerva said.

"The troops were only fools," Tiberius said, "but the slanderers were malicious weasels, and so were the ones who repeated the lies. Can you imagine some cowardly piece of slime demeaning the greatest general of all time?"

"Maybe, like Caesar, you should ignore it," Nerva said.

"No. Something needs to be done. It's not only slandering me; it's slandering my ancestors and my descendants. A hundred years from now, people will be repeating these lies. And it's not just about me. This kind of disrespect, the insults and defamations thrown back and forth, what does it lead to? Sedition and civil war."

"It's true," Sejanus said, "these buzzards get people hating each other. They should be prosecuted."

Vitruvius usually avoided politics, but spoke up. "I agree a thousand percent. Rome needs to be scrubbed of these troublemakers who criticize and demean everything and everyone, who deface and destroy monuments, and debase our ancestors."

"We have more critics than doers," Sejanus said.

"I'm reminded of king Ptolemy," Vitruvius said. "Ptolemy had spent years and a fortune advancing literature. In Alexandria, he sponsored a contest for original works. One of the contestants was Zoilus, a Macedonian, who pretentiously took the surname of Homeromastix. During the contest, Zoilus read his writings to the king. The writings were critical of *The Illiad* and *The Odyssey*."

"What did he expect to gain by criticizing Homer?" Nerva said.

"Who knows what goes through the mind of a reptile like that," Vitruvius said. "In any event, the king, hearing the father of poets and the captain of all literature abused, and his works, which all the world admired, was outraged."

"I suppose this Zoilus thought he could write a better epic himself," Tiberius said.

"Ptolemy said nothing because it was an open forum," Vitruvius said, "but when it was over and Zoilus requested that something might be bestowed upon him, Ptolemy gave him what he deserved. He exiled him."

"He should have done more than that," Sejanus said.

"A king only has to make his wishes known," Vitruvius said, "and sometime after, it's not clear how, Zoilus was killed. Some reported that he was crucified, others that he was stoned to death, and others again that he was burned alive on a funeral pyre at Smyrna."

"All of which he would have deserved," Sejanus said. "Those that tear down the foundations of a nation, whether in its arts, history, or religion, are committing forms of treason that precede and lead up to the ultimate political treason."

As Tiberius listened to the discussion, he was looking for something in a carton filled with scrolls. From his time with his tutor, Menelaus, and with Vipsania, he had collected scrolls of great speeches and writings.

"Here it is," he said as he unrolled a scroll of Cicero's that Vipsania had given him.

"No matter what you think of Cicero," he said, "his writings contain a lot of wisdom and he could make a convincing argument."

Tiberius read aloud. "A nation can survive its fools, and even the ambitious. But it cannot survive treason from within. An enemy at the gates is known and carries his banner openly. But the traitor moves amongst those within the gate freely, his sly whispers rustling through the alleys, heard in the very halls of government itself. For the traitor appears not a traitor; he speaks in accents familiar to his victims, and he wears their face and their arguments, he appeals to the baseness that lies deep in the hearts of all men. He rots the soul of a nation, he works secretly and unknown in the night to undermine the pillars of the city, he infects the body politic so that it can no longer resist. A murderer is less to fear."

"And we still have many treasonous scoundrels among us," Sejanus said.

"Right," Tiberius said. "When are you going to bring me their heads?"

"I have one for you."

"Who?"

"Titus Sabinus."

"He's a friend of Agrippina?"

"Yes, he is," Sejanus said. "After the death of Germanicus, he paid a lot of attention to her and her children, visiting their home and escorting them in public."

Sejanus explained that one of his agents, Latiaris, casually complimented Sabinus for his unwavering support of Agrippina and her family in its misfortunes. Sabinus responded by speaking highly of Germanicus and Agrippina. This conversation seemed to cement a close friendship, and Sabinus invited Latiaris to his villa where he talked openly of his grievances and his hatred of Tiberius.

"He showed Latiaris a slanderous pamphlet," Sejanus said, "and based on that we shadowed him and his clients. We saw his freedman coming out of a scribe shop where some of these pamphlets originated, and we were able to get one of the slaves to tell us everything."

"And what was that?"

"Sabinus had paid for the pamphlets to be written and distributed. But, more important, it seems there was a plot to poison you during one of your visits to the Cavern Cafe at Tarracina. That didn't work out; the rock fall interrupted their plans."

Nerva interjected, "What other evidence do you have?"

"Besides Latiaris, we have a *delator* who engaged Sabinus in an incriminating conversation that was overheard by others." Sejanus said. "That should be enough."

Tiberius signed and sealed an order charging Sabinus with conspiracy, treason, and *maiestas laesa*.

"I leave for Rome tomorrow," Sejanus said. "After his conviction, we'll question him to see what he has to say about his fellow conspirators."

"I want them all," Tiberius said. "Then we'll let them see our magnificent cliff from the top to the bottom."

"That'll be something to see," Sejanus said.

As Sejanus left, Tiberius walked him to the door and held his arm. "Let me ask you something," he said out of the hearing of the others. "Your man Macro, how is he?"

"Not the brightest, but you see the size of him, and those hands! He could kill any man with those hands. He keeps discipline in the ranks for me."

"Is he to be trusted with secrets?"

"He's quiet. I've never known him to divulge anything he shouldn't," Sejanus said. "As background, he's a very pious man, and prays to the gods daily, particularly Mars the Avenger. I heard he believes that Mars interceded on his behalf during a battle in Germany."

"Thanks for all your good work," Tiberius said. "Have a good trip and good hunting."

Two weeks later, Sejanus returned from Rome without Sabinus.

"Where is he?" Tiberius asked.

"He's dead. When your order was read in the Senate, they convicted him by voice vote and had him executed immediately."

"Immediately!" Tiberius shouted. "Without a trial?"

"Yes. No one objected," Sejanus said. "The voice vote was the trial, a mock trial. I suspect they didn't want him talking about his fellow conspirators."

Tiberius shook his head. "How did he take it?"

"Hard to tell," Sejanus said. "The guards threw a sack over his head and slung a rope around his neck. All you could hear were muffled cries. They strangled him in the jail."

"And they defied my order for a reasonable time to reconsider any death penalty," Tiberius said. "You remember the order that I issued after the execution of that poet Priscus?"

"Yes. I remember that. I think some of the senators were panic-stricken, thinking that Sabinus would implicate them."

"Who pushed for the quick execution?"

"Asinius Gallus Saloninus and a few others."

"Gallus, again."

"I hope you don't mind, but the senators insisted on sending a delegation to meet with you, so I took the liberty of agreeing and inviting them here to discuss procedures. I can cancel it, if you'd like."

"No. That's a good idea. I'd like to see their faces. I'll be able to tell who has a guilty conscience."

A delegation of three senators arrived at Capri. Tiberius, with Nerva at his side, received them in the Temple of Mars.

The senators, Publius Lollius, Asinius Gallus, and Sallustius Crispus Passienus, represented the three main factions of the Senate. The first faction, led by Agrippina's circle, wanted to keep the emperorship but replace Tiberius with a new emperor. The second hoped for the elimination of the emperorship and the restoration of the Republic. The third wanted to keep the emperorship and supported Tiberius, believing that his steady hand prevented the possible outbreak of civil war.

Publius Lollius represented the group that wanted a new emperor, ideally one of Agrippina's sons. Tiberius was astonished that Lollius had been chosen as their delegate. It was Lollius' brother, Marcus Lollius, who years earlier had so officiously delayed Tiberius' interview with Gaius on the island of Samos, and who had later committed suicide when he was found to have taken bribes from the Parthians. Publius Lollius closely resembled his brother Marcus Lollius, with his large nose and receding chin.

Disingenuously, Tiberius said, "I was sorry to hear about your brother's tragic end."

Lollius glared at him.

Tiberius was even more astonished that Gallus had been chosen as a representative of those who wanted to eliminate the emperorship. Gallus was Vipsania's second husband, and had claimed that Drusus II was really his son, not Tiberius' son. At the time, the claim infuriated Tiberius, but Augustus had ordered him to stay calm. Adding salt to the wound, Vipsania gave Gallus five sons. "How I would have loved five more sons," Tiberius had said, "but I lost the chance."

Gallus was loathed by many people, because he was snobbish and smug, always looking down his nose at people. He believed that he was smarter than anyone and was always ready with what he considered a witty retort to rebuke people.

Sallustius Crispus Passienus was from the third group that supported the emperorship without change. Tiberius had a favorable opinion of him.

As for the other two, Tiberius wondered whether someone had sent them as a subtle ploy to manipulate him, to play on his hatred of either Lollius or Gallus, hoping to incite him into a rash action that the Senate could use against him. He wasn't going to fall for that trick.

"You wished to see me," Tiberius said coldly.

Gallus spoke first. "The Senate sends you well wishes with the hope that our few misunderstandings can be cleared up."

"And what are those?" Tiberius asked.

"First, the law of *maiestas*," Gallus said. "We believe that law has been used too broadly. It should be reserved for more serious issues, for the issues for which it was first intended—for a general who surrenders an army, or for violating a sacred treaty, a violation that would stain Rome's honor and reputation. It shouldn't be used to punish citizens who merely make frivolous statements that are unflattering to you. Speaking freely shouldn't mean the death penalty."

"I can agree with that," Tiberius said, "but I'd remind you, after the execution of that poet Clutorius Priscus, I issued an edict that a reasonable time for review should intercede between a conviction and an execution. The review should separate the frivolous from the treasonous. And I also would remind you that it was the Senate that summarily executed Sabinus, not I."

"That's true," Gallus said. "But it was an action taken in the urgency of the moment." He smiled as he said, "And I'm sure Sabinus wanted to get it over with."

Tiberius didn't smile at Gallus' flippant answer. "He may well have," he said, "but why was my edict disobeyed?"

"The Senate didn't mean to disobey your edict, but we believed it was necessary to act swiftly."

"And what about the law that Clodius passed," Tiberius said, "the law that anyone who condemned a citizen to death without a trial should be executed, the law he aimed at Cicero for condemning the Catiline conspirators without a trial."

Gallus raised his voice, "The Senate used its traditional powers under a *Senatus consultum ultimum* to conduct an emergency trial to safeguard the nation."

"There was no emergency," Tiberius answered, speaking slowly, emphasizing each word, "And I'd like the Senate to provide me with the names of the ones who pushed for the summary execution."

Gallus looked as though he were going to argue further, but Sallustius interceded, saying, "The Senate was obligated to respond to the emperor's commands."

"I didn't command his death."

"But it was clear what you wanted," Sallustius said.

"So, the Senate can read my mind?"

Sallustius, trying to avoid an escalating argument, said, "We'll have those who pushed for the execution explain what their reasons were."

"Be sure to do so," Tiberius said. "Anything else?"

"Yes, there is," Sallustius said. "We've been hounded by calls from the people for a restoration of the Republic. And we've seen many signs of a brewing rebellion. We've debated the issue extensively, and while we don't endorse the idea, we think that perhaps some concessions should be made."

"What kind of concessions?"

"We've come to an agreement that the power to legislate should be returned to the assemblies. Since Augustus transferred the legislative power to the Senate, we've been stalemated over some very important issues. There are two sides in the Senate—reform and resistance—and they can't seem to compromise. If the assemblies were empowered again, the impetus would provide the momentum to get bills passed."

"Are you telling me that because the Senate can't do its job, we have to return control of the empire to the mobs in the streets?" Tiberius said.

Lollius interjected. "Not the mobs in the streets, but the lawfully constituted assemblies as it was during the Republic."

"I understand they want one man, one vote," Nerva said.

"Some have asked for that," Sallustius said.

"That's not how it was in the Republic," Nerva said. "Votes were weighted in favor of the propertied classes. Do you want to keep that system, or do you propose one man, one vote?"

"That should be discussed," Sallustius said.

"The people want one man, one vote," Gallus said, "like the Athenian democracy."

"Let me remind you," Tiberius said, "the Athenian democracy is long dead."

"Nevertheless," Lollius said. "Our citizens are capable of making good decisions. In the end, the people know best."

Tiberius abandoned caution and began to vent. "You mean the people who follow every demagogue who promises them gifts in exchange for their votes—free corn or bloody spectacles to wallow in? You mean the people who riot and kill each other over a chariot race?"

"That's a cynical view of our people," Lollius said.

"But an accurate one. Our people, the ones who show up for the assemblies, are no longer hardworking farmers," Tiberius said. "Too many are unemployed loafers on the dole, looking for the next handout, looking for the next circus, or the chance to watch the slaughter of gladiators and beasts. You can't even get them to join the legions, even when we're in serious jeopardy. In my opinion, if you don't serve in the legions, you shouldn't have a vote."

Lollius stood in front of Tiberius. "If they knew how you felt about them, they would hate you and wouldn't want you for their emperor."

Tiberius stood up and pointed his finger at Lollius. "Let them hate me, as long as they respect my conduct," he said. "They could do a lot worse. And if the Senate would do its job, I wouldn't have to be emperor. Remember, I took an oath to Augustus to carry forward his policies. Transferring the legislative power to the Senate was one of his most important changes. One man, one vote was not his wish. Do you want to disregard the Divine Augustus?"

The senators couldn't answer. To challenge the word of Augustus could be taken as *maiestas laesa*, so they said nothing. The meeting was over. Tiberius didn't offer them either a meal or accommodations.

Before the senators left the island, Sallustius had a private conversation with Nerva.

"What's going on here?" Sallustius asked.

"What do you mean?" Nerva said.

"We keep hearing all these reports of orgies and debaucheries. About forcing people into sex acts then throwing them off the cliff. Has Tiberius gone insane?"

"You believe that nonsense?"

"There's got to be some truth to it. Where there's smoke, there's fire. Reports from travelers and slaves never stop. The rumors are everywhere."

"Do you think that Tiberius, who had been a straight arrow his whole life, now, at his age, would suddenly begin to act like a satyr? He's the last person who would demean himself that way."

"People change," Sallustius said.

"No, they don't," Nerva said. "Tiberius was never promiscuous. His one love was Vipsania."

"You don't know what he did on the outside."

"When he led the legions on campaigns, he forbade prostitutes from traveling with them. No one was stricter with the troops, and he set the example. If he had been debauching himself while restraining them, they would have had his head."

"True," Sallustius conceded.

"Don't believe the rumors; they're slanders of the worst kind, spread by lying weasels, then taken up by ignorant and gullible rumormongers."

"So, you assure me, none of these rumors are true?"

"I assure you. Absolutely."

When news got back to Rome and that Tiberius had ridiculed the proposal to transfer the legislative power back to the assemblies, it sparked arguments everywhere about the emperorship. Agrippina's party used the controversy to stir up calls for rebellion, and to advocate for the designation of her children—Nero Germanicus, Drusus Germanicus, and Caligula—the great-grandsons of Augustus, as the true line of succession to the emperorship, with Agrippina acting as their regent. They instigated protests against Tiberius, held meetings, posted signs, and distributed more seditious pamphlets.

Sejanus recorded it all.

CHAPTER TWENTY-SEVEN

Livia died in 29AD, at the age of eighty-six. It was thought that Tiberius would return to Rome for her funeral, but he didn't. Some said it was because he was afraid of assassination; some said he was angry at his mother because she had kept the disparaging letters Augustus had written about him; others said that it was because he had quarreled with her about her support for Agrippina. Livia had opposed strong measures against Agrippina.

Now that Livia was gone, Sejanus, with Tiberius' acquiescence, intensified his efforts to discredit Agrippina and her party. To observers, it became clear that were Sejanus to succeed in removing her and her sons from the field, he would be the most logical choice to succeed Tiberius. The Senate, recognizing this possibility, turned to flattery, authorizing altars and statues in Sejanus' honor. Some senators saw him not only as a successor but as a replacement.

In the meantime, Sejanus built a case of *maiestas* against Agrippina on the basis of reports that she and her oldest son, Nero Germanicus, had spoken openly and contemptuously against the emperor, and also that she planned to retreat to the army of the Rhine, Germanicus' old army, and persuade the soldiers there to protect her. Sejanus gathered a substantial file of evidence, drafting an indictment with a long list of sedition and conspiracy charges against her, and adding charges against Nero Germanicus for immoral behavior.

Sejanus brought the indictments to Tiberius for his approval. Sitting at his desk, Tiberius waved to Sejanus to sit down. He studied the indictment then looked up and stared at Sejanus.

"She said these things?" he asked.

"Yes," Sejanus said.

Tiberius read more, his face turning red as he read more.

"And you have corroboration?"

"Yes. We do."

"Who are her contacts in the Rhine army?"

"Germanicus' friends, the ones who prosecuted Piso are involved. Vitelius for sure, if not all of them."

"You don't sound completely sure."

"I am. There's no doubt about it."

"You're positive about this?" Tiberius said, staring into Sejanus' eyes.

Sejanus calmly, and without expression, stared back. "I'm absolutely sure, and when they're arrested, we'll get more evidence."

Tiberius didn't go into a rage but channeled his rage, resolving that there was no choice but to prosecute Agrippina and all her followers, no matter the consequences. He signed and sealed the indictment and sent it to the Senate.

When the Senate, out of concern about the public's reaction, hesitated to prosecute Agrippina. Tiberius followed up with a threatening letter and another copy of the indictment with his seal circled in red. This time the Senate acted. They filed the charges and conducted a trial, using the testimony of *delators* to convict both Agrippina and her son. The Senate sentenced them both to death.

As he often did, Tiberius had second thoughts. He wondered whether he was letting his personal feelings influence his imperial responsibilities. He thought hard about it, and just before the sentences were to be carried out, he changed the death sentences to banishments.

He banished Agrippina to Pandateria, the same island where Augustus had banished her mother, Julia. Remembering that Julia had starved herself to death, he ordered that if Agrippina refused to eat, she should be force-fed. He banished Nero Germanicus to Pontia, an even smaller island.

When the banishments were announced, public protests in support of Agrippina and her son broke out and rumblings could be heard in the Rhine army. Tiberius was called a tyrant, and death threats against him were scrawled everywhere on the city walls.

Sejanus advised Tiberius to take the threats seriously, and convinced him to change the food-tasting procedure. Tiberius had always had a food-taster, but hadn't paid much attention to the process. Now he gave it a lot of thought. Poisonings were not uncommon in Rome; even those who had food-tasters were the victims of poison. The problem was that the poison might not take effect on the food-taster until after the intended victim ate the meal. Tiberius changed the procedure: the food-taster would take the food an hour before it was served to him and once again five minutes before. The food-taster and the food would remain in the emperor's presence. If the food had to be heated up, it would be heated in front of the emperor.

Sejanus reported daily about threats against the regime and any suspected conspiracies. He reported that Agrippina's middle son, Drusus Germanicus, had openly raged against the treatment of his mother and his brother and had made reckless statements against Tiberius.

"I feel sorry for him, but we can't allow that," Tiberius said.

Sejanus promptly charged Drusus Germanicus with *maiestas* and imprisoned him in the Castra Praetoria.

With this imprisonment of both Nero Germanicus and Drusus Germanicus, Sejanus had removed two of the three sons of Germanicus and Agrippina. They would have been Sejanus' competition to replace Tiberius. Only Caligula, the youngest son was still free, and he was smart enough, and cold-hearted enough, not to say anything or protest the treatment of his mother or his brothers.

Sejanus' position continued to grow stronger. He assumed even more of the emperor's duties, and intensified the purge of his perceived enemies. Fear of the Praetorian Prefect spread, and many informants tried to ingratiate themselves with him by providing useful information.

In 30AD, an informant gave Sejanus a letter written by Senator Asinius Gallus Saloninus, Vipsania's second husband. In the letter Gallus had written that Tiberius had physically abused Vipsania during their marriage. The letter went on to imply that Drusus II was not Tiberius' son, but was actually Gallus' son, and it alleged that Tiberius continued to abuse young women and exiled or executed wealthy men in order to get access to their property and their vulnerable daughters.

With this letter in hand, Sejanus had his Praetorian Guards bring Gallus to the Castra Praetorian for questioning. They put him in a windowless interrogation room where Sejanus and three guards sat across from him.

Gallus was indignant. "What's this about? I'm a Senator. I can't be treated like this."

"I have a few questions for you," Sejanus said.

"Tell me what it's about," Gallus demanded, confident in his status. "You can't question me without grounds."

"I have lots of grounds."

"What grounds?"

"I ask the questions here, not you. And, to be clear, you're not leaving here until you answer the questions."

Gallus waived his hand in disgust. "Alright, question away."

Leaning forward and whispering as though the conversation was just between them, Sejanus asked, "Did you ever say that Tiberius abused Vipsania when they were married?"

Gallus had not expected such a question. He thought he might be questioned about the execution of Sabinus or about some of his business dealings, but this was a surprise. His expression changed as he thought about how to answer. After a pause, he said, "It depends on what the definition of abuse is."

"It's a simple word," Sejanus said in icy seriousness.

"It still depends on what you mean by abuse," Gallus said.

"Alright. Did you ever say that Tiberius physically abused Vipsania?"

"No"

"How about emotionally?"

"No. But he made her life miserable."

"So, he abused her emotionally?"

"Yes."

"And you said that?"

"I might have."

"And you wrote that in a letter?"

"I did not," Gallus said. He began to say something else, but Sejanus abruptly cut him off. "Did you ever say that Drusus was your son, not Tiberius' son?"

"No," Gallus said. His senatorial bearing seemed to be crumbling. "It may have been a joke. It was a question of timing, the overlap of our marriages."

"That doesn't make sense, senator," Sejanus said. "Drusus was born while Tiberius and Vipsania were still married."

"True," Gallus admitted weakly.

"So, were you implying that you had sexual relations with Vipsania before she married Tiberius?"

"No," Gallus protested.

"Then you were implying that you did so while she was married to Tiberius?"

"No."

"Did you ever, in fact, have sexual relations with Vipsania while she was married to the emperor?"

"No, I did not."

"If you did, that would be adultery. Correct?"

"Yes. Of course."

"And possibly *maiestas*."

"It didn't happen."

"If it did, you would be subject to execution or exile."

The room was hot, and Gallus was sweating heavily. "I'm aware of that, but I didn't."

"But you implied it?"

"No."

"Did you ever say that Tiberius continued to abuse young women?"

"No."

Sejanus stood and raised his voice. "Did you ever say that Tiberius executed or exiled wealthy citizens so that he would have access to their property and their vulnerable daughters?"

Gallus looked wary. "I did not."

"Are you sure."

"Yes. I swear."

"You swear?"

"I swear on my mother's eyes," Gallus said, raising his right hand as though taking an oath.

Sejanus sat down, and took a folded letter from a pouch. He unfolded it and gave it to Gallus. "Read that," he said.

Gallus read the letter. His hands were shaking.

"Did you write that letter?" Sejanus asked.

Gallus stammered. "I don't know. I can't be sure. I don't remember this letter."

"Look on the bottom right. It has the initials 'AGS,' standing for Asinius Gallus Saloninus. Are those your initials?"

"I don't know."

"Well. Let me show you some other letters that we know you wrote. They are also signed "AGS." And the writing looks exactly the same. Do you see that?"

Gallus nodded.

"So, did you sign that letter?"

Gallus slumped in his chair. "I may have. I may have meant it as a joke."

"And in the letter, you say, 'And Tiberius abuses young women to this day.' Do you see that at the next to last paragraph from the bottom?"

"Yes."

"And you go on to say, 'Tiberius exiles and executes wealthy men in order to get access to their property and their vulnerable daughters.' Do you see that?"

Gallus slumped further into his chair. "I see that."

"So, you wrote those things," Sejanus asked.

"I guess I did." Gallus said.

"You admit it."

Gallus nodded again.

Sejanus suddenly slammed his palms on the table and shouted, "What about your mother's eyes?"

Gallus was startled. "What?"

"You swore on your mother's eyes," Sejanus shouted again. "Now you admit you lied."

Tears came into Gallus' eyes, and he put his face in his hands. "It was only a joke. Please. Give me a break."

Sejanus smiled. "I don't remember you ever showing mercy to anyone. But we'll see what Tiberius decides."

After hearing a detailed report of the interrogation, Tiberius told Sejanus to go ahead with charges in the Senate. Gallus was quickly convicted and imprisoned.

As a reward for Sejanus' good work, Tiberius designated him as his co-consul for 31AD, and granted his earlier request to marry Livilla, the widow of Drusus II.

Sejanus finally had what he had been striving for. As a consul, related by marriage to the Julian-Claudian family, he was no longer a mere equestrian. He joined the list of "new men" from outside Rome who had risen from obscurity to the highest office of the state. He joined Marius, Cicero, and Agrippa as the most acclaimed of all "new men." All he needed now was tribunician power—with such power, he could readily succeed Tiberius.

CHAPTER TWENTY-EIGHT

With Sejanus handling most of the government business, controlling access to the emperor, and screening all incoming correspondence, Tiberius had much less to do. At first, he enjoyed having the leisure time for his academic and recreational pursuits, but he began to feel isolated and out of touch with what was going on. He was uneasy and imagined what plots could be in progress against him. While he marveled at Sejanus' efficiency, he worried that Sejanus could be manipulating him, and, perhaps, maneuvering him right out of power.

Feeling so isolated, he thought about friends he no longer saw, and asked Sejanus to locate Narbo, the sea captain who had stayed with him at Rhodes. He asked him three times, but Sejanus said that his praetorians were unable to locate him. They said that he was most likely in the East.

A few weeks later, Pometius came to Capri to deliver his monthly accounting of the assets and properties. Tiberius greeted him with a hug as he usually did, and asked him question after question. How was his wife? How were the servants? He surprised himself by remembering the names of so many of them.

"How are the kitchen girls?" He asked, thinking of those who were there when he freed Pometius.

"Most everyone is well. We've lost a few, but that is to be expected," Pometius said.

Tiberius changed the subject, "Has Captain Narbo ever contacted you?"

"Yes. In fact, he has," Pometius said. "A month ago, he asked how he could get a message to you. I told him where and how to send it."

"I never received a message from him."

"Maybe he never sent it."

"If he said he sent it, then he sent it," Tiberius said. "Could you get in touch with him?"

"I think so," Pometius said. "He told me that he captains a merchant ship between Ostia and Sicily."

"That's interesting," Tiberius said, wondering why Sejanus hadn't been able to find Narbo. "I'd like you to contact him and ask him to come here. Nothing urgent, I'd just like to talk to him for old times' sake."

"I'll do that."

"But don't mention it to Sejanus or any of the Praetorians."

Pometius nodded. "Alright."

"Have him come with you on your regular reporting day."

Pometius easily located Captain Narbo and met him at Ostia on his merchant ship. Narbo had just unloaded a cargo of grain from Sicily and was waiting for a cargo of manufactured goods to be taken back.

"So, you're Pometius," Narbo said. "I've heard good things about you."

"And I've heard only good things about you," Pometius said. "Tiberius thinks you should be the admiral of the navy."

"That's flattering, but I'm thinking more about an olive grove."

"That sounds nice," Pometius said "I came because the emperor wants you to visit him on Capri. I have to deliver my monthly report to him in a few days, and he suggested that you come with me."

"I'll take it as a suggestion but I'll obey," Narbo said.

They both laughed.

Narbo took Pometius into the ship's cabin and served a lunch of cheese, grapes, and wheat bread soaked in olive oil. The enjoyed the meal, traded stories, and drank some wine. Narbo told Pometius that he had been worried about Tiberius because he had heard rumors that he was under the control of his minister, Sejanus.

"What you say has a lot of truth in it," Pometius said. "Sejanus screens his letters, and has his ear. Sejanus is very smart, very persuasive. He doesn't confront or make demands of Tiberius. Instead, he plants ideas in his head, and turns him against people. I don't think Tiberius realizes that he's being manipulated"

"The Tiberius I knew would not be so easily fooled," Narbo said. "Does anyone advise him?"

"Marcus Nerva is very close and gives sound advice, but Sejanus seems to have more persuasive powers."

"Thank you for telling me that," Narbo said.

On the reporting day, they sailed to Capri on Narbo's ship. When they docked, Praetorian Guards stopped them and searched the ship. The guards told Pometius that he could go up the pathway to the villa, but Narbo couldn't. He hadn't been preapproved. The guards said that they would have to check with Macro, since Sejanus was away in Rome. But just at that moment, Tiberius came down the pathway on horseback. He jumped down from the horse and greeted Narbo with open arms.

"My old friend. You look the same," he said.

"And you also," Narbo said. "We've been fortunate in our health."

Narbo wasn't being exactly truthful. Since he last saw him, Tiberius had aged quite a bit and had lost most of his hair.

"Come let me show you my modest little villa," Tiberius said, and ordered the guards to get another horse for Narbo.

As they rode up the trail, Narbo said, "This is even more beautiful than Rhodes."

"Yes, it is. Wait till you get to the top."

At the villa, they went up to the highest terrace and looked around in every direction. As they marveled at the view, Tiberius suddenly asked, "Why didn't you send me any letters?"

"I did. You didn't get them?"

"No. I get so many letters, maybe they were discarded," Tiberius said, although he already knew that his mail was being screened.

"I thought you didn't want to hear from me," Narbo said. "When Pometius contacted me, I was relieved."

"Well, from now on, we're going to stay in touch. Even if I have to send the navy to drag you back here."

At Tiberius' insistence, Narbo stayed an extra day, and they walked on the cliffs as they had done on Rhodes, reminisced about those days, and talked about what had happened since they last met.

"I thought you were going to retire on Rhodes." Tiberius said.

"Unfortunately, I invested in some merchant ventures. I'm a better captain than I am a business man, so, I'll be working for a while longer."

"That's too bad. But you could retire here. I've enough for the both of us and everybody else."

"Thanks. But no thanks. I like to pay my own way."

"It wouldn't be a handout. I'd give you a ship to sail around the island to watch for pirates and prevent trespassers."

"You have a navy for that."

"You could reenlist. I'll give you a whole fleet of ships."

"You could do that, of course," Narbo laughed.

"Yes. I could."

"I'll think about it."

After their walk, they had lunch on the terrace.

"As you can see," Tiberius said. "I'm isolated here. You visit a lot of port cities and probably know more about what's going on than I do. How are things throughout the empire?"

"Most people are content, the economy is good, and everyone—or almost everyone—is glad there's no war going on."

"That's good. What do they say about me?"

Narbo thought before answering. It would be difficult to say what he had heard, but he had to be honest. "They say you were a great general, but to be honest, they say you've deprived them of gladiatorial contests, and they say you've become a recluse. All sorts of gossip and stories keep going around. Ridiculous stuff. No one takes it too seriously, but they like to gossip."

Tiberius knew all that, but it was still difficult to hear it from his friend. "That drives me mad, but I can't seem to stop it. Even Sejanus can't stop it. He says we should start throwing the slanderers to the lions."

"I don't think we'll ever do that," Narbo said, then cleared his throat and whispered. "As for Sejanus, don't take offense, but I think you should know, people say he's in charge, and you're the emperor in name only. They say he's the emperor of Rome and you're the governor of Capri."

"They might be right."

"And statues have been erected in his honor in almost every port city and certainly in every town in Etruria," Narbo said. "In my opinion that's not a healthy situation for a ruler. You're too vulnerable. They fear him more than they fear you."

"Why is that?"

"They know that even if you didn't care for them, you would treat them fairly," Narbo said. "But Sejanus prosecutes people for his own purposes. He entraps them, twists their words, conjures false testimony, and threatens the most horrendous tortures to get slaves to say anything he wants. Senators tremble when Sejanus stares at them."

"Those jackals should tremble," Tiberius said. "And if Sejanus didn't do his job, who knows what they'd be up to. Augustus had an Agrippa; I need a Sejanus."

"You know best," Narbo said. "But he's ruthless."

"You can't hire lambs to catch wolves."

"A wolf can sneak up you and be ripping your throat before you know it's there."

"He's been loyal to me," Tiberius said. "When the rocks fell at the Cavern, he saved my life."

"Maybe he saved your life to protect his own position," Narbo said.

"I appreciate your concern, but he has always looked out for my interests. I can't act against him based on speculation only."

"Please, just be careful."

"I will," Tiberius said, embracing Narbo. "And whenever your ship passes this way, be sure to visit me."

"I will."

On the day Narbo left the island, Sejanus returned, but they didn't meet.

When Sejanus reported to Tiberius, he said, "I understand your friend Captain Narbo was here. That must have been pleasant for you."

"Yes. There's nothing like old friends. We picked up right where we left off."

Tiberius chose not to ask why Narbo's letters hadn't reached him. He wondered why the letters would be a problem for Sejanus, and he began to understand just how much control Sejanus had over him. He was living in quasi-exile. It was a voluntary exile, not like Agrippina and Nero Germanicus, but it had greater ramifications. He knew that he needed to regain control.

The next day, Senator Nerva returned from a visit to Rome, and Tiberius walked with him along the top of the cliffs. When they rested, they sat on a bench under an umbrella-shaped tree. "Caesar, I have something to tell you," Nerva said. "I was present in the Senate house and one of my aides overheard Sejanus telling a group of senators that when he prosecuted Agrippina and her friends, he had only been following your orders."

This alarmed Tiberius. Was Sejanus switching sides and aligning himself with Tiberius' enemies in the Senate? If he were, he would be a formidable adversary.

"What do you think about it?" Tiberius asked.

"I'm not sure, but I think you need to be on your guard. You may need to take action."

On the 5th of October, 31AD, when Pometius delivered his next monthly financial report, he asked the slaves in the room to leave.

"What is it?" Tiberius asked.

"Antonia, your brother's widow, sent a message to me. She said to tell you to beware. A slave had whispered to her that there's gossip going around that Sejanus plans to usurp you, even if he has to assassinate you."

"That's not new gossip."

"You have to take it seriously. The slaves hear a lot; they have ways of knowing what's going on before the Senate does."

"I have to be fair. I have to be sure. Sejanus has been loyal to me," Tiberius said. "I can't act against him based on slave rumors."

"I understand," Pometius said, "but please be careful."

Tiberius was skeptical of the warnings, but the more he thought about them, the more he understood their seriousness. Each night, he sat alone going over the possibilities. He didn't have proof that Sejanus was planning to supplant him or assassinate him, but it was logical that he would. He thought that to survive in this world one has to act on a combination of logic and instinct. He formulated a plan as though he were planning a military campaign, going over every detail of what he had to do and exactly how he had to do it. He had to be careful not to tip his hand. Sejanus controlled communications and had the power of the Praetorians on his side. They might be more loyal to Sejanus than to him, and if Sejanus felt threatened, he would act first.

At a time when Sejanus was away conducting government business in Rome, Tiberius began methodically laying the groundwork for his plan. He gave Nerva a sealed letter to deliver personally to Graecinus Laco, the commander of the Rome's urban military cohorts who policed the city. Laco had been Tiberius' best legate during the wars in Illyria and Germany.

"May I ask?" Nerva said.

"I'm going to make some changes, and it has instructions in the event I need his assistance in Rome."

After Nerva left for Rome, Tiberius summoned Macro and suggested that they take walks together. Macro was such a big, heavy man that it was difficult for him to keep up with Tiberius' brisk pace, so, instead, they began having lunches together. They talked, but Macro was reserved. He spoke carefully as though afraid to offend the emperor. Little by little, Tiberius got him to talk in a more relaxed, man-to-man way. They discussed families, governing, and trouble spots in the empire. Tiberius was sizing him up, testing him. He would bring up a subject one day and return to it another to see how well Macro remembered it. Macro remembered well. Tiberius concluded that in spite of what Sejanus had said, Macro was indeed very intelligent, and he was motivated by the same self-interest as everyone else.

A few days later, Tiberius put his plan into motion. He assumed that Macro would tell Sejanus everything he said, so he was careful not to divulge too much, telling him only what he wanted him to know. He swore Macro to secrecy and told him that he would soon grant Sejanus tribunician power, thus making him the equivalent of his co-ruler just as Agrippa had been co-ruler with Augustus.

"He'll be happy with that," Macro said.

"Yes. But he'll have to give up the praetorian prefecture. And, of course, I'll promote you to his position."

"Thank you. That's what I've wanted. I'll do my best for you," Macro said.

Knowing Macro's religious views, Tiberius told him that when the time came, Macro would have to swear before the gods an oath of loyalty to him.

"I'll swear that right now," Macro said.

"Tomorrow will be soon enough. We'll go to the Temple of Mars, and we'll have a ceremony with the temple high priest presiding."

"Thank you, Caesar," Macro said as he bent to kiss Tiberius' hand.

The next day was windy with clouds accumulating in the west. Tiberius and Macro rode in a wagon to the temple of Mars where the high priest conducted a secret ceremony, recited prayers, and sacrificed a goat.

Macro read his oath before the altar, "I swear by this my oath to Mars and all the gods who protect Rome, that my loyalty to the emperor, Caesar Augustus Tiberius Claudius Nero, will never waiver. I will obey his commands and always protect him and his emperorship. If I break this vow, I will be cursed in this life and the next, and my descendants will suffer for my sacrilege."

Macro saluted Tiberius and they embraced.

"Thank you, again, my emperor," Macro said.

"And thank you," Tiberius said, "I hope we have a long and prosperous relationship."

As they left the temple, Tiberius said, "And remember, we don't have to tell Sejanus any of this yet. We'll surprise him at the right time."

"Yes, Caesar."

Sejanus was scheduled to deliver a message from Tiberius to the Senate in Rome on the 18th of October 31AD. The session would be chaired by the consul, Publius Memmius Regulus, an old-line patrician known for his dedication to traditional protocols. Tiberius had handpicked him for the consulship.

Leading up to the scheduled date, Tiberius wrote two letters on official scrolls. He sealed them both with his imperial seal, and put a red ribbon around one and a blue ribbon around the other. Then he called Macro to his terrace. Making sure that no one was in hearing distance, he gave him instructions. "Go to Rome, and on the night before the Senate session, visit Consul Regulus. Show him this sealed imperial scroll with the red ribbon addressed to him from me. It is your appointment as the new Praetorian Prefect. Let him unseal and read it, but keep the scroll in your possession.

"Then tell Regulus that before Sejanus addresses the Senate, you will deliver another imperial scroll addressed to him from me. The scroll should be read aloud to the Senate. Tell him that at its conclusion the Senate should take appropriate action. Do you understand?"

"I understand."

"Then go to my old friend Graecinus Laco, the chief of the city police cohorts. He'll be expecting you. He knows what to do. He has instructions. Tell him that tomorrow when the Senate meets, the entrances and exits should be occupied by his military police. You understand."

"Yes. I understand."

"In the morning go to the Senate early. When Sejanus arrives, approach him on the steps and show him this sealed scroll, the one with the blue ribbon, that you are delivering to Regulus. He may question you about its contents. Tell him that it's about him, and that you believe its good news. Tell him you think it's his tribunician power. Give him a wink."

"What if he wants to see it?"

"He can't see it. It has the imperial seal and is addressed to the consul Regulus."

"I understand."

"Once he goes into the Senate, gather the Praetorians who escorted him, and show them the scroll with the red ribbon, the one with your appointment as the new Praetorian Prefect. Make them salute you, and then send them back to the Castra Praetoria. Tell them you'll have news for them about promotions and a bonus of fifty gold pieces for their loyalty to Emperor Tiberius."

"They'll like that."

"When they leave, you go immediately into the Senate and deliver the scroll with the blue ribbon to Regulus.

On the day that Sejanus was to deliver the message to the Senate, Macro did exactly as he had been instructed. He met Sejanus on the senate steps, showed him the scroll with the blue ribbon, and told him it was good news for him personally. Sejanus rushed into the Senate, expecting a grant of new powers.

Macro showed his appointment as prefect to the Praetorian escort. They saluted him, and obeyed his order to return to their camp. When they left, Macro delivered the scroll with the blue ribbon to Regulus, while Laco and his military police took their places outside the temple entrances.

Regulus began reading the letter aloud to the Senate. It began in a meandering way with Tiberius citing some good points about Sejanus but increasingly adding criticisms. It was a long letter, and as the words droned on, some senators became impatient. Some didn't understand at first, but as the criticism mounted, many began to sense what was coming.

As the reading of the letter continued, Laco and his military police entered the building. Senators noticed their entry, and those senators seated closest to Sejanus began moving away. Regulus continued reading: "Finally, certain information of the gravest import has come to my attention. Based on unassailable and fully-corroborated testimony, I charge Sejanus with treason for plotting to destroy your emperor. With my seal, I demand that action should be taken against him and his accomplices."

Sejanus, who minutes before had been expecting to be elevated in power almost equal to that of the emperor, sat stunned. He looked around for his Praetorian Guards, but saw only Laco's military police.

Regulus called Sejanus to stand forward.

"Are you speaking to me?" Sejanus said.

"Yes. Stand up."

The consul's lictors, Commander Laco, and several military police surrounded Sejanus. Then Regulus moved the senators for a resolution of imprisonment. When the motion carried, the lictors grabbed Sejanus. He flailed his arms and shouted "get your hands off me." When he tried to rush to the exit, the lictors knocked him down, then pulled him up. One held him by the hair, and the group dragged him out. Sejanus shouted, "I'll be back, and you'll pay for this!"

The Senate immediately adjourned, and the senators waited to see whether the Praetorian Guard would come to rescue Sejanus. They didn't, so the Senate re-assembled and, under their extraordinary *senatus consultum ultimum* power, quickly sentenced Sejanus to death without a trial.

The sentence was carried out without delay, and Sejanus was choked to death. His body was dragged through the streets to the Tiber and thrown in. The people celebrated, jeered at his corpse, and knocked down his statues.

CHAPTER TWENTY-NINE

The Senate didn't stop with the execution of Sejanus. With the tyranny that the senators had endured for so long lifted, they released the dogs of retribution: Sejanus' acolytes and accomplices were executed, their properties confiscated, their families condemned. It was a blood bath reminiscent of the days of Marius and Sulla.

Macro's Praetorians were let loose to summarily arrest or execute Sejanus' accomplices, and, within the ranks of the Praetorian guard, several praetorians who had been favored by Sejanus and who had abused their power were beheaded.

After the initial bloodletting, the *delators*, looking to profit from the crisis, brought charges against scores of other senators or equestrians who had allegedly colluded with Sejanus. Many of the *delators* had been informers for Sejanus against his enemies; now they informed for his enemies against his former friends. Prosecutions for *maiestas* and other crimes multiplied.

Exacerbating the toxic atmosphere, investigators extracted confessions by torture from the slaves of the suspects. It was difficult enough to distinguish between a true and a false confession, but when they were obtained by torture, it was nearly impossible. As a result, scores of innocent people were imprisoned, executed, or driven to suicide.

In the first trials, once evidence was produced that a defendant had worked with or even befriended Sejanus, no defense was accepted. But as the trials proceeded, Tiberius began having second thoughts. Although he had instructed Sejanus to find the slanderers and conspirators, when he learned the full extent of Sejanus' methods, he was repulsed, and began sending daily instructions from Capri to the Senate to keep the prosecutions evenhanded. The accused were given a fair chance to defend themselves. One, Marcus Terentius, spoke on his own behalf. "Yes, I was a friend of Sejanus; and so were you and so was Tiberius Caesar. Who was I, to investigate the virtues of Caesar's minister? I crawled, as you all did. It was fame, then, to be known to the hall porter of Sejanus, or to his servants. Let plots be punished and conspiracies suppressed; but as for friendship with Sejanus, the same argument must clear you, me and Caesar himself."

It was a powerful argument, and with Tiberius' approval, Terentius was acquitted.

Another defendant, Messalinus Cotta, a senator with an illustrious family lineage, was known for his jokes and sarcastic remarks. While everyone was whispering, he continued his usual habits and was overheard making a sarcastic remark about the emperor. Sejanus prosecuted Cotta for *maiestas*, but Tiberius sent a written defense of him imploring the Senate not to regard as a crime, words without any significance, words spoken during a convivial banquet. Cotta was acquitted.

Tiberius was in a dilemma: he wanted the trials and charges against those who deserved them aired publicly so that the purge could be justified to the people, but his reputation suffered terribly because many of the charges were based on slanderous accusations against him, accusations of sexual depravity and sadistic cruelty. The slanders were either exaggerations or total fabrications, but each time spoken, they'd be repeated. Lies, told over and over, became accepted as facts by those who wanted to believe them. He was called a monster, either for his supposed cruelty or for his supposed debauchery. The accusations and slanders would become the basis for many subsequent histories.

As the trials continued, Tiberius said that he would return to Rome to dispense justice to the remaining defendants and end the purge, but he kept postponing the trip and the purge continued.

Staying on Capri, he spent most of his days looking across the bay to the mainland. Under a canopied desk on his veranda shielding him from the sun, he read the reports of all the trials and senate debates, and marveled at Sejanus' deceit and at his own stupidity for trusting him and giving him so much power. As more information was uncovered about Sejanus' methods, Tiberius came to believe that Sejanus was evil incarnate, sent from Hades, devious beyond human comprehension. He began to fully understand how Sejanus had used the *delator* system to wipe out the descendants of Augustus, one by one, trapping them with legal tricks and trumped-up accusations.

Recognizing how destructive the *delator* system had become, Tiberius knew he had to bear the blame. Sejanus had used *delators* on his behalf, and he wondered how many innocent people had been destroyed on false or exaggerated charges. Reform was needed, and, although he wasn't sure that he had the energy left for it, he said he would head a reform commission. He told Nerva, "This could be more important than the wars that I fought to save the empire. Hannibal said we'd be destroyed from within, and these vultures might do it. They're ripping the flesh of Rome from its bones. I have to act right away."

But he still procrastinated. He had been mistaken so many times that he now examined every issue from several sides. It seemed that he had lost the confidence to pick a course of action and go with it. He practiced a speech to Nerva that he intended to give to the Senate, saying that Rome suffered with many evils, but the worst was spreading falsehoods that destroyed honest men. "The liar is worse than a thief or an arsonist," he said. "Worse still is the professional *delator* who profits from the destruction of another person's reputation. Even when the victim of the falsehoods and slanders is not a perfect person, destroying him by exaggerations and lies, leaving him ruined, is a villainous crime. Not only is the crime perpetrated against the individual victim, it is perpetrated against society, weakening the bonds and affinities of the people. When those slandered are the leading men of the nation, the crime is a thousand times worse, and infinitely worse when it's the emperor who is slandered."

Tiberius didn't go to the Senate in Rome to deliver the speech but stayed on Capri ruminating about past events, about what had gone wrong, what was still wrong. He thought about how alone he was. Although he had the friendship and loyalty of Pometius and Nerva, his position placed a barrier between them.

Thrasyllus remained on the island but was beginning to get senile. He wandered about, sometimes claiming that he saw something in the stars, but, except for the recall letter from Augustus, he hadn't predicted any of the major events that had occurred. He knew that his credibility was gone. When Tiberius, out of habit, asked his opinion of something, Thrasyllus often would answer, on the one hand "this," and on the other hand "that," until one day Tiberius told him that what he needed was a one-handed advisor.

Nevertheless, when the stars were bright, Tiberius and Thrasyllus would sit on the veranda gazing up, and Thrasyllus would name the constellations, describing their movements across the sky.

Tiberius marveled at the immensity. It made him feel like a speck in the universe. His position, his power, his wealth—all were nothing compared to this vastness. Why had he tormented himself, done such cruel things, just to gain power? He wished his life had gone differently, that he could have been a sea captain like Narbo, responsible for his ship and no more.

On a windy afternoon, Pometius delivered news that Herod Agrippa had returned from the East. He had landed at Puteoli and requested an audience with the emperor. Tiberius told Pometius to send for him right away.

It had been nine years since Drusus II had died and Herod Agrippa had left Rome. After Herod left, it was revealed that he had been deeply in debt and unable to pay his bills. While Drusus lived, the creditors gave Herod time and leeway to pay. Without Drusus, they demanded immediate payment, which in Rome could be devastating to a debtor, resulting in possible arrest and even bondage. To avoid an arrest, Herod fled to the East where he hoped to obtain financing.

Tiberius had mixed emotions about Herod. He had been angry at him for leading Drusus into bad habits, but also had a genuine fondness for him and had enjoyed their lively discussions. He had even contemplated adopting him, but couldn't because Herod was a Jew.

Now, as Herod arrived on Capri, the past was put aside, and Tiberius greeted him warmly. Herod explained that he had settled his debts. He told of his travails trying to avoid arrest, how he had been jailed in Judea and had bribed his way out, how he had fled to Alexandria, and went into hiding until his wife's relatives paid his debts.

"Why didn't you ask me for help?" Tiberius said.

"I assumed you were angry with me after your son's death."

"Perhaps I was at first, but Drusus was his own man. I couldn't blame you."

"I sent letters, but I assume, knowing what we know now, that Sejanus must have intercepted them."

"Please don't say that name again!"

Both men fell silent until Tiberius asked, "So tell me, what did you learn from your troubles?"

"I learned not to trust anyone."

"No one? Not even your family."

"No one."

"But your wife's relatives paid your debts."

"Only because they saw a benefit for themselves."

"You're even more cynical than I am," Tiberius said.

"I'm cynical," Herod said, "but I never give up hope that people will do what's right just for the sake of it."

Tiberius and Herod talked every day for weeks, covering a wide range of topics. Their conversations reminded Tiberius of his conversations with Jason of Nyet, although they were less philosophical and more practical.

Tiberius asked about the rebellions in the East and about the prophet Jesus of Nazareth, who had gathered such a large following among the Jews. "And I understand they still follow him even after his execution," Tiberius said.

"That's common with martyrs," Herod said.

"Was he a revolutionary?" Tiberius asked.

"No. In fact, he preached that the citizens should accept the authority of the state. When the Pharisees tried to trick him into saying that the Jews shouldn't pay taxes to Rome, he showed them a coin with your image on it and told them, 'Render unto Caesar the things that are Caesar's, and render unto God the things that are God's'"

"That made sense," Tiberius said. "If that's what he said, then he was unjustifiably executed."

"You're right," Herod said. "The Pharisees wanted him out of the way because he was a threat to them. They spread lies about him and accused him of immorality, trying to undermine his popularity. They called him 'a gluttonous man, a winebibber, and a friend of the tax collectors and sinners.' But the people knew those were lies."

"What made him so popular? Was he another one proposing to give away land to the poor?"

"No. Quite the opposite," Herod said. "His ideas were very unusual. He said to forget about land and money, that the quest for wealth and money was the root of all evil. It drives men to murder and plunder, inviting revenge and more murder and plunder. He said people should just accept their lot in life and live according to the laws of God."

"He was a Stoic?"

"In some ways, but he had a much more powerful message. It's paradoxical. He said that men should turn the other cheek rather than repay the insult."

"That would be nice if everyone would do it, but then they'd be like lambs to slaughter," Tiberius said. "The beasts of prey among us would take everything they had, including their wives and daughters."

"I suppose it's just a dream," Herod said, "but in the nightmare that most people live, a good dream provides hope for the future. Jesus preached that by living a good and true life, we'll be rewarded in the afterlife."

"We need help for the present," Tiberius said.

"It brings help in the present," Herod said. "Believing in the possibility of a glorious afterlife will cause people to do what's right in this life."

"It might be better" Tiberius said, "to preach that you will be horribly tortured in the afterlife if you don't do what's right in this life."

"Now that's real cynicism," Herod said.

Tiberius was struck by that remark. It had an emotional effect on him. He stood and turned away from Herod, and said, "You're right," he said. "My first reaction when I had to judge has always been to torture or execute. I've done it so many times, I can't remember them all. It was my duty to do it, but I've come to hate what I've become."

Herod didn't reply right away. Tiberius stood completely still, staring into space. There was an awkward silence until Herod said, "It's never too late to change."

"I'm afraid it is."

At that, Tiberius exhaled, turned, and put his hand on Herod's shoulder. "Well, my friend. I have an offer for you. It comes with a steady income, so you won't have to chase after that evil money," he said. "I'd like you to tutor Gemellus, my grandson, Drusus and Livilla's boy."

"That's quite an honor, thank you."

"I have a villa here for you to use now, and we can make arrangements so that by the time Gemellus grows up, you'll own the villa outright."

"That's very generous of you. I'll have to think about it."

"Do you have any better prospects?"

"Not really, but before I take your offer, I must go back to Alexandria to finish some business."

"That's fine," Tiberius said. "I have one condition."

"Yes."

"You're not to teach him to turn the other cheek. You're to teach him to trust no one."

"Of course."

On the night Herod left for Alexandria, Tiberius drank more wine than usual. It was an exceptionally clear night, so he tried to sleep on the veranda, but couldn't. The brightness of the moon and stars brought back his thoughts about the universe and existence. He thought about his discussion with Herod about the afterlife. Was it really possible or just a myth? He thought about his own existence, not about his status in society, but about his physical existence. It gave him an odd, uncomfortable feeling. He shook his body to get rid of the feeling. He tried to think of the future, but his thoughts kept sliding back to the maelstrom of his past and current life—the accusations, the trials, the executions. He wondered what had made the people do what they had done. He understood Sejanus— ambition and power were the natural elements of Roman life; but he couldn't understand Agrippina—why would she believe he had ordered the murder of Germanicus? What did she hope to gain by spreading slanders about him? Couldn't she wait for him to die? Her sons would have been his heirs.

Eventually he slept, but near dawn something in his dreams woke him up. He sat upright, his mind racing. *What if Sejanus hadn't been guilty? What if he was falsely accused like that preacher in Judea? What if Agrippina and her friends had manipulated me to turn me against him? I never had direct proof that he would assassinate me, only words and accusations. How reliable can that be? Maybe they passed false accusations to my friends knowing that my friends would pass them on to me. Falsehoods built on falsehoods. People feared and hated Sejanus, they hear what they want to hear. He may have been entrapped just as he entrapped others. Maybe I was wrong to condemn him. I could have been wrong.*

Thinking that he may have made a terrible mistake, he felt weak and sick to his stomach.

Later that morning, Macro announced, "You have a visitor."

"I'm not ready to see anyone."

"It's Antonia, your brother's widow. She said she'd wait. It's important."

"Alright, bring her in."

Antonia was the daughter of Octavia and Marc Antony. After Antony's death, Augustus arranged her marriage to Drusus I, and she had represented both the Julian and Claudian families well, carrying herself with dignity throughout the years. When Drusus I died in 9 BC, she dedicated herself to his memory and to their children, Germanicus, Claudius, and Livilla. She never remarried.

Antonia brought news. Apicata, the wife that Sejanus had divorced so that he could marry Livilla, had committed suicide.

"That's too bad," Tiberius said

"She left a note," Antonia said. "It's hard to read, but I've looked at it carefully. I'll come right to the point. She claims that Sejanus and my daughter Livilla slowly poisoned your son Drusus so that Sejanus could marry her and become part of the imperial family."

Tiberius was stunned. He stumbled and almost fell to the floor.

"Sit down, sit down," Antonia said helping him to a couch. He sat there for several minutes, staring at a wall, not saying anything.

Finally, he said, "Let me see the note."

Antonia gave it to him. He looked but couldn't read it. "I can't see it," he said.

She took the note back and read the first part of it out loud, "I, Apicata, swear to the gods of my ancestors that Sejanus, the Praetorian Prefect, and his paramour, Livilla, fed poison to her husband Drusus, the son of Tiberius, day by day until he died."

Tiberius couldn't catch his breath.

"You should lie down," Antonia said. "We should get a doctor."

"No. I'll be alright."

Tiberius was able to take several deep breaths to calm himself.

It was unusual for him not to explode at such news. When he was angered, he had often exploded like a volcano spewing rocks and red-hot lava. Now he just sat stupefied, feeling a cold, clammy sweat break out.

Antonio poured him some water, and after a few minutes, he asked, "What proof is there?"

"She goes on to say that two slaves will confirm it—Lydgis, the cup bearer, and Eudemus, the doctor. They gave the poison to Drusus over the period of a year. You remember how he kept getting sick. That was their plan: to make it look like he was sickly."

"How do we know Apicata isn't just getting revenge on Livilla for stealing her husband?"

"Anything is possible," Antonia said. "But I wouldn't be telling you this about my own daughter if I didn't believe it was true."

"How do we know these slaves didn't say whatever they were told to say?"

"I watched it myself. The interrogators didn't feed them any information. They were separated and told their stories voluntarily."

"Where is Livilla now?"

"She's locked in the basement of my house."

"What has she said?"

"She screamed through the door that she wasn't sorry."

Now Tiberius exploded. "Jupiter! How much more do we have to take?" he shouted. His strength coming back, he began to rage, "We've been plagued by the line of women spewed forth from Scribonia, that bitch Augustus married. She bore him that whore Julia, who bore Agrippina. Nothing but lust, jealousy, and contriving. And now your daughter has outdone them all."

"I hope you're not insulting me," Antonia said.

"No, Antonia, I have the highest respect for you."

He poured a cup of water for her and one for himself. "I can understand Sejanus doing it, but what made Livilla go along with it."

"You said it before—lust. As a young girl, all she could think about was Sejanus. It was as if he had magic powers over her. She'd sneak out to see him whenever she could. They even met around the corner from our house, and she had him in the house. The danger made it exciting."

"You knew this?"

"Of course not. If I knew I would have chained her in the basement. But I never knew. She learned all about secrecy from Sejanus."

"It's hard to believe that she would cheat on my son, my son who might have become the emperor," Tiberius said.

"She didn't care about emperors. She cared about the thrills, the excitement, the sex. She wasn't like Agrippina, who only cared about the power and pushing her husband to the top. Livilla was passionate, like Julia. The difference was that Julia dominated many men, Livilla was dominated by one man."

"Poor Drusus; he was no match for Sejanus," Tiberius said. "You know I was almost done in by Sejanus, but I was the only one who could match him. In an odd way, I'm glad you told me. Now I have no doubt that he was guilty. If I hadn't acted when I did, even without conclusive proof, I'd be dead now.

"Sejanus prosecuted Germanicus and Agrippina's sons to get rid of them, but he had nothing on my son, so he poisoned him. His plan was to kill me next. But I acted first. It wasn't the stars that protected me, it was my instinct for survival."

Tiberius sent Antonia's evidence to the Senate. Testimony was taken from the slaves Lydgis and Eudemis, who each confirmed everything that implicated Sejanus and Livilla in the poisoning. The Senate unanimously imposed the sternest sentences—Sejanus had already been executed, and now his children were sentenced to death.

His son and two daughters from his previous marriage to Apicata were killed. The older daughter screamed as two Praetorians dragged down the street. She didn't know what she had done but cried that whatever she'd done could be punished by a whipping. "I promise not to do it again."

The younger daughter was still a virgin, and, under Roman law, could not be executed. One of the guards overcame that obstacle before executing her.

Livilla was left to starve to death in her mother's basement. Her son Gemellus was spared as he was the son of the victim, Drusus II, and the grandson of Tiberius.

CHAPTER THIRTY

Tiberius, who had been robust throughout his life, was now seventy-two, and the stress of his years in power, the slanders and accusations, Sejanus' betrayal, and the revelation of his son's murder, all had taken their toll. He was tired and hardly walked the cliffs. He never returned to Rome again, though he kept track of events that effected the empire and the imperial family.

In 31AD, Agrippina's oldest son, Nero Germanicus committed suicide in prison. In 33AD, Agrippina starved herself to death on Pandateria, and the same year, her middle son, Drusus Germanicus, died of starvation in prison, not on purpose but from lack of edible food. Reportedly, he tried to eat the straw in his mattress to stave off his starvation.

When Tiberius heard about Drusus Germanicus, he said that no one should ever name a son Drusus. His brother Drusus was killed by a horse; his son Drusus was poisoned; and his grandnephew Drusus was starved to death in prison.

Also, in 33AD, Asinius Gallus Saloninus died in prison. Tiberius wondered whether Gallus regretted challenging him in the Senate, plotting against him, and marrying Vipsania. He wondered whether he married her to torment him with jealousy.

Macro asked Tiberius about the forty men who remained in prison for colluding with Sejanus. His first thought was to order their executions to end the whole tragic episode. He asked Nerva's opinion.

Nerva had become his new "ally in toil." Tiberius valued his advice and generally took it. In this case, Nerva said it would serve no purpose to execute the prisoners and Tiberius could turn the page by granting them clemency. This would be a popular move, and would lessen the divide within the nation. Nerva reminded him that Julius Caesar granted clemency to his adversaries, even after they fought on the side of Pompey against him.

Tiberius disagreed, "And what did that get him—twenty-three stab wounds from the people he pardoned."

"That was different. He was assassinated after he declared himself dictator."

"And what am I?" Tiberius said.

"You're the *princeps*, the emperor. Power was given to you by the people and the Senate. You didn't seize it."

"True, but clemency is out of the question. I don't enjoy this. In fact, I hate it. But I'm the minister of the laws. My duty is to punish wrongdoers—perjurers and those who file false charges. Worse are the weasels who spread filthy lies to poison the minds of our soldiers. If they're not stopped, they'll undermine the legions and destroy us all. I never forgot the speech of Appius Claudius Crassus. Remember, 'Death by cudgeling is the wage of the soldiers who forsake the standards or quit their posts; but those who advise them to abandon the standards and desert their camp escape punishment and are not touched.'"

"But after everything that's happened, we can be more moderate," Nerva said.

"No, those who advocate desertion deserve death by cudgeling, and worse," Tiberius said. "You have to pull out the weeds before they choke the garden."

"Yes, Caesar," Nerva said.

Determined to do his duty, Tiberius signed the execution decrees. It saddened him, not because of those being executed, but because of all the turmoil that had gone on, all the prosecutions that had destroyed so many, and the lives that were wasted. His generation was almost wiped out. Not only his generation, but the children of his generation. He asked himself how much of it was his fault? He asked Nerva the same question. He asked Pometius, and when Narbo visited, he asked him. Pometius and Narbo gave tactful answers and made excuses for him. Only Nerva was completely honest, saying that Tiberius bore much of the responsibility because he had retired to Capri, leaving Sejanus with too much power and his enemies with too much opportunity to sow discord. Nerva said that if Tiberius had stayed in Rome, many of the problems could have been avoided.

"You're probably right, but we'll never know," Tiberius said. "Staying in Rome may not have prevented anything. The ambitious will always find ways to cause trouble, and stab people in the back, all for personal power and profit. As no one man can stop war, no one man can stop the disease of fanatical partisan politics."

Tiberius began to feel stronger and began walking the cliffs again. Trying to forget politics, he stayed focused on what he enjoyed in life. He invited scholars and philosophers from around the empire to Capri to discuss interesting topics, and he was glad to be surrounded by his friends—Nerva, Narbo, and Pometius. He hoped they would stay with him until the end.

To free up his time, Tiberius delegated most of his proprietary duties to Pometius, and most of his political duties to Nerva. Both men were exemplary. Pometius continued to capably manage the properties and the staff. Nerva was as good as an administrator as Tiberius, and had the added advantage of getting along well with most of the senators. In addition to all his other accomplishments, he was a respected jurist, recognized as the head of the Proculian school of law, which advocated that provinces and local districts could follow their own laws as long as they didn't conflict with national policy.

Tiberius often walked the cliffs alone without guards or lictors. This gave him the chance to contemplate his life and to try to reconcile himself to his memories and regrets. He was able to put some behind him but could never fully escape them all. It was impossible. There was a constant fury smoldering inside him, a visceral hate for the conspirators, *delators*, and scandalmongers who had undermined his emperorship and poisoned his personal life. He wanted to see them get the justice they deserved.

On one of his walks, he thought about the wrongs that had been done to him, and also the mistakes he had made and the wrongs he had done to others. He thought about the men who had taken their own lives, Calpurnius Piso's trial and suicide. He was so engrossed in his thoughts that he hardly noticed his surroundings until he found himself on a high cliff overlooking the sea. There was a strong wind pushing him from behind, and he thought about jumping. He had heard that you die from the fall before you hit the ground. But that was a coward's way out, he thought. He shook his head and decided that he would fix what he could. He'd work to overcome the lies and slanders that he knew would be written about him.

He rushed back to his villa and began mapping out his plans. First, he would deal with the *delators*. They were destroying Rome. If he could get rid of them, it would be a favor to Rome's future.

The *delators* not only fabricated evidence, they also bribed jurors before and during trials. Jury tampering had become a serious problem. Cases that by any objective assessment should have been decided one way were decided the other way for no discernable reason. Only bribery could explain it.

To address the bribery problem, Tiberius changed the procedure for choosing juries. The procedure in effect at that time was that from a pool of five hundred jurors, the prosecutor would pick a hundred names. Then the defendant could strike fifty of the hundred, leaving fifty to hear the evidence and the summations, and render a verdict.

Tiberius changed the procedure for important cases, especially cases in which the *delators* were involved and stood to make a profit. Now the entire jury pool of all five hundred would hear all the evidence and the summations. Then eighty-one of them were randomly selected and the other jurors were discharged. Each side then challenged fifteen jurors, leaving fifty-one to render the verdict.

The jurors did not retire to deliberate amongst themselves, but immediately cast their votes. A verdict could be decided by a mere majority vote. Since those who would want to bribe the jurors would not know the composition of the jury until the very end of the trial, it would become extremely difficult to bribe enough jurors.

Tiberius knew he had designed a better method of jury selection because when the first trials were conducted in this manner, the *delators* paid mobs to protest in the Forum against the new procedure.

Next, he turned his attention to extortion by governors in the provinces, which he saw as a threat to the stability of the empire. Almost every rebellion in the provinces had been caused by abusive and rapacious governors enriching themselves at the expense of their constituents.

Knowing that any solution would have to solve the underlying causes of the problem, and not simply mask the symptoms, he reinstituted a policy that Pompey had enacted. Pompey had recognized that the extortion problem stemmed from the exorbitant debts that magistrates accumulated when they ran for elective office. To win the people's favor, it was customary for candidates to sponsor public games, gladiatorial contests, and chariot races. To fund these events, they often borrowed heavily, expecting to recoup their expenses later. Magistrates became wealthy not during their initial magistracies, but when they were assigned to govern provinces. Some governors stayed within the law, but too many used their positions, not for the public good, but to pay back their creditors and accumulate fortunes for themselves. Donations, gifts, and bribes from provincials for favorable decisions and preferences helped to line the governors' pockets.

Pompey broke the connection between campaign debts and extortion of the provincials. His policy mandated a five-year period between serving as a consul or praetor and serving as a governor of a province. Since, under the new policy, the consuls and praetors ending their terms couldn't be assigned provinces for the next year, the assignments would be given to solvent ex-consuls and ex-praetors whose magistracies had long since concluded and who presumedly wouldn't have crushing debts. The policy had its intended effect, and the number of prosecutions for extortion and bribery declined substantially.

The next problem Tiberius addressed was that of senators and equites using their enormous wealth for purposes that were against the interests of the state.

To address this Tiberius proposed to revive the Julian law, originally passed by Julius Caesar, that had fallen into disuse. Caesar's law limited the amount of capital that senators and equestrians might hold in their liquid accounts, and required them to invest the major portion of their assets in Italian land. Caesar's aim had been to restrain the use of liquid assets to finance private armies, conspirators, agitators, and street gangs, which was exactly what he had done himself to gain power. He said that he wanted to be the last to overthrow a government in that way.

Tiberius called Nerva to his villa to discuss his plan, saying that in today's Rome, wealthy and ambitious men used their assets to hire, not armies of soldiers and street gangs as Caesar had, but armies of *delators* and lawyers to prosecute their enemies and their competitors. He said their wealth would be better used by investing in land, buildings, bridges, and other projects.

Nerva objected on the grounds that forcing such a transfer of assets would cause a financial crisis. He was unable to dissuade Tiberius, although he convinced him to allow an eighteen-month grace period for accounts to be brought into compliance. Nerva wanted to moderate the law further, but Tiberius ordered him to send an imperial decree to the Senate announcing that the Julian law would be enforced again.

"Yes, Caesar," Nerva said, in the way he usually did when he disagreed with a ruling.

Despite the grace period, the announcement immediately precipitated a wave of debt recalls and a financial panic. The panic soon worsened, and Nerva convinced Tiberius to advance a hundred million sesterces to a fund, from which interest-free loans could be made to debtors who had sufficient security. The panic abated, and the markets stabilized.

An unintended consequence of the financial turmoil was that it uncovered many cases of illegal usury, and this gave *delators* new crimes to prosecute, and lawyers new deep pockets from which to enrich themselves. Allegations and prosecutions persisted, and some of the most unscrupulous moneylenders were convicted.

Nerva was disappointed at the continuing turmoil, but Tiberius told him, "It may not have been a perfect solution, but, at least, some of those moneybags got what they deserved."

"Yes, Caesar."

On a late autumn afternoon, Pometius told Tiberius that Nerva wasn't eating.

"Is he sick?" Tiberius asked.

"I don't think so. His servants think he's committing suicide."

Without putting anything on over his tunic, Tiberius raced to Nerva's house where he found him on a bed on his terrace. Tiberius was shocked at how white and drawn he looked.

"Are you alright?" he asked.

"I'm fine," Nerva said.

"You don't look well."

"I'm fine."

Tiberius sat on the edge of the bed. "No, you're not. Tell me the truth. You're not eating."

"The truth. The truth is that I'm finished eating."

"Why?'

"It's my time."

"No, it's not. You have so much to live for."

"I've lived my life. I want to go out on my own terms."

Tiberius knew Nerva's wife had died long ago, so he talked to him about his children and grandchildren. They were going to need his guidance. He talked about the high esteem in which he was held by all and how much Rome needed his foresight and good counsel.

"And I need you," Tiberius said. "We've accomplished so much together. What will people say when they hear that my chief counselor deserted me?"

"I'm not deserting you. We all have to make our own decisions."

Tiberius tried to find some issue to get Nerva talking about other matters.

"Is this because I wouldn't grant clemency to the prisoners that you said I should?"

"No."

"Because I passed the finance law over your objections?"

"No. You're the emperor. You have the ultimate authority and responsibility."

Tiberius sensed that rejecting Nerva's counsel had hurt his friend and, regardless of what he said, that was why he was doing this. The thought crossed Tiberius' mind to tell Nerva that he would resign and let him be the emperor. Instead, he said, "I'm sorry to have brought you to this."

"This has nothing to do with you," Nerva said.

"I think it does. I retreated here to Capri to get away from my responsibilities and I hoisted them onto you. That was unfair because you didn't have the final authority, which I'm sure frustrated you."

"That's not it. You spoke of my foresight. Well, my foresight tells me there's disaster ahead, and I'm too tired to deal with it anymore."

"Together we can overcome any kind of disaster. And I promise you, I'll listen to your counsel. Just don't do this."

"Listening to my counsel might not help. I don't know what counsel to give anymore. I feel like we're waiting for an earthquake. There have been tremors, but something far greater is coming, and we can't do anything about it."

Tiberius had always thought Nerva was an optimist. Now he was stunned by his pessimism. He tried to remain upbeat and waved to a servant to bring some food. The servant brought raisins and honey cakes.

"Please, eat something," Tiberius said.

Nerva shook his head.

"At least have some water."

Nerva waved the cup away.

Tiberius tried everything. "If you were in pain or sick with an incurable disease, I could understand. But you're in good health. Why not wait until you get sick? That may come sooner than you think."

Tiberius walked back and forth trying to think of what to say, of what to do. The thought occurred to him that he could have Nerva force fed. But that would solve nothing.

Instead, he said, "Marcus, you've been without your wife for too long. You need to take another wife. You're still young. You can find the most beautiful and intelligent woman in Rome. She would give you something to live for."

Nerva looked at Tiberius and smiled, "You've been looking for another Vipsania for a long time, and you haven't found her."

"True. But I'm a disagreeable, decrepit old man. You still look young."

"Thank you, but I'm not young. Rome has taken everything out of me. Those filthy *delators* destroyed so many good citizens. And the slanders you've endured. I felt them as though they were slandering me. Rome needs a cleansing. It needs a Sulla, but I'm afraid it will get another Marius, and I don't want to be here to see that."

"You're giving up without a fight," Tiberius said.

"I've already fought. I'm like a consul who's lost a battle and, rather than be taken by the enemy, falls on his sword. He dies with dignity, with honor."

Nerva turned on his side away from Tiberius.

Tiberius looked out over the terrace. The sun was falling below a band of clouds that had formed above the horizon, enlightening the underside of the clouds with glowing colors. He stared for a moment then went to the bed, pulled Nerva up, and half-walked, half-dragged him to a bench.

"Sit there and look around," he said, almost shouting. "Look at the sun. Look at the beauty; the incredible colors. What god painted this for us? I think a god far greater than our gods painted it. It's precious just to be alive. Forget everything else. Give up your position, and just enjoy the beauty of every day."

"I've seen it. The picture of it is imprinted in my mind. I don't need to see it again. It will be there long after I'm gone."

"When you're gone, where will you be?" Tiberius said.

"I won't be; I will have been. I will have lived. That's all."

Tiberius wanted to say something profound, but said only, "You've got more money than you could ever spend. You could change your name and find some other place to live. If you do it, I'll go with you."

"You couldn't do it," Nerva said. "You're trapped like I'm trapped. Our lives are done; the book is written. All that needs to be done is to beat death, to defy the horror of an unchosen death."

Tiberius knelt on one knee next to the bed and held Nerva's hand, "Marcus, please don't do this."

"My dear friend," Nerva said, "it's done."

Tiberius saw that it was no use and left without saying anything else. He walked home slowly, feeling shaken and drained.

CHAPTER THIRTY-ONE

After Nerva's death, Tiberius brought his grandson, Gemellus, to live with him on the island. He also brought Caligula, the last living son of Germanicus and Agrippina. He would raise them both and designate them as his heirs, giving Caligula preference because he was older.

Tiberius did not expect to live too much longer and hoped that the historians and philosophers he invited to the island would help him educate Caligula, and that Herod would educate Gemellus.

When Herod returned from Alexandria to tutor Gemellus, he asked Tiberius why he had given Caligula preference as his successor, a boy who often seemed capricious.

"I know he's unpredictable at times," Tiberius said, "but he'll grow up. He has the blood of Augustus, the characteristics of his father Germanicus, and he's the grandson of my brother Drusus, who was better than all of us."

"But he's also Agrippina's son," Herod said.

"Although she was my enemy," Tiberius said, "she did what she thought best for her family. And she never disgraced them."

"You've become very understanding in your old age," Herod said.

"We have to move on," Tiberius said.

"But Caligula isn't like anyone else."

"Maybe he'll be an improvement. Or maybe, next to him, the people will come to realize that I wasn't such a bad emperor."

Herod was taken aback by that remark and thought how cynical it was. He asked Tiberius, "Why not prefer Gemellus, he's your grandson?"

"To be perfectly honest with you, and this is in strict confidence," Tiberius said. "I want to wait. I want to make sure he doesn't grow up to look like Sejanus. I may be wrong, but he looks a little like him already. There is that possibility. Sejanus might have been seeing Livilla earlier than we know. What a victory for him that would be—the son of Sejanus as emperor."

"If it turns out that Sejanus is the father, not Drusus, what will you do?"

"I'll face that when the time comes."

Caligula was supposed to stay at Tiberius' side to learn the skills of generalship and administration, but he wasn't interested. He was more interested in entertainments and playing adolescent games.

His moods seemed to change on a whim, and on some days, he surprised everyone, spending a lot of time with Macro, who took him under his wing. Two very opposite people bonded, one large and morose, the other thin, airy, and always jesting. Although Tiberius had wanted Caligula to learn from philosophers, he was glad that Caligula was, at least, learning something from Macro about practical matters.

On other days, Caligula would be studious, and would sit in while Herod was tutoring Gemellus. When the lessons were over, Caligula would stay and talk with Herod, asking questions about the world. A friendship developed between them although there were subjects that they wouldn't talk about. Caligula never mentioned the fate of his mother or his brothers; Herod never mentioned his father murdering his other sons.

Herod was also careful in what he said around others, and about his relationship with Tiberius. But, as can happen with two talkative people, their conversations can go in unexpected directions. For Caligula, the more absurd or outlandish the conversation, the more he enjoyed it. Herod, with his experience and wealth of knowledge, was always able to provide entertaining anecdotes and stories.

One day, while riding in the back of a carriage together, with the driver up front pushing the horses to go fast, Herod and Caligula bantered back and forth. For some unexplainable reason, Herod disregarded caution and talked too much and too freely. He talked about all the political prosecutions, and about the emperor. Assuming their friendship was stronger than it really was, Herod told Caligula, "I pray every day that Tiberius will go to Hades and that you will become emperor in his place."

Caligula's reaction startled Herod. He told the driver to stop the carriage. He got out and threatened Herod with strangulation if he ever said such a thing again.

Herod stumbled for an answer. "I didn't mean anything, I just…."

"Never mind," Caligula said with an odd smile, then climbed back into the carriage.

Herod thought the incident would be forgotten, but the carriage driver, Eutichus, had overheard. Months later when Eutichus was arrested for theft, he bargained with the prosecutor for leniency and offered to testify about what he had heard. He told a convincing story.

Macro learned of this and brought the information to Tiberius, who summoned Caligula and asked him what had been said. Caligula remembered the words exactly and repeated them to Tiberius. He emphasized that he had told Herod that he would strangle him.

When Tiberius confronted Herod with the story, Herod couldn't deny it and tried to explain it away as a joke. Tiberius listened but his face looked frozen, like a death mask. He condemned Herod to prison to await possible execution.

"Take him away," he said to Macro and the guards.

To Herod he said, "Now, it's just a question of the method of execution."

Tiberius was surprised that as Herod was taken away, he didn't breakdown but stared defiantly back at him.

The effect on Tiberius was devastating. Condemning Herod was the last thing he wanted to do. He had thought that Herod was open and honest, but now decided that he was a schemer like all the rest. He guessed that Herod had tried to ingratiate himself with Caligula, who might become the next emperor, while forgetting that he had welcomed him back to Rome and had forgiven him for the death of Drusus. Again, Tiberius wondered whether there was anyone who could wait for him to die a natural death.

In March 37AD, at age seventy-seven, Tiberius left the island for his villa at Sperlunca where he was to meet with several senators. Macro and Caligula accompanied him. Once there, he felt ill and went to bed. While he slept, an earthquake shook the Bay of Neopolis, and the lighthouse on Capri that Tiberius had built toppled into the sea. Macro said that Tiberius should not be told, but Caligula told him anyway.

Tiberius was shaken by the collapse of his lighthouse, taking it as a sign that his time had come. He amended his will, named Caligula and Gemellus as his primary heirs, and left legacies to Pometius, Narbo, and all his staff members. He freed three hundred slaves to be selected by Pometius. He left legacies to Nerva's children. They didn't need it since Nerva had been quite wealthy, but Tiberius wanted to leave the legacies to show his gratitude to his loyal friend.

He left a legacy to the children of Vipsania. Her husband, Asinius Gallus, had died in prison without leaving anything for them. Tiberius, despite his hatred of Gallus, wanted to take care of Vipsania's children. She had been the one great love of his life, and her children should have been his.

After signing the will in front of witnesses, he said, "That's it. I think I can say, like Sulla, 'No friend has ever done me a kindness and no enemy a wrong without being repaid in full.' Let me rest now."

Everyone but Macro left the room to join the senators waiting outside. Tiberius lay still in his bed thinking about Rome and all the turmoil he had lived through; all the wars, the murders, the executions, the betrayals. He fell in and out of semi-consciousness. Opening his eyes for a moment, he said out loud, "People are driven to kill each other, not by hunger, but by senseless words and deeds." He closed his eyes and turned on his side, thinking that it was all such a waste of time, a waste of precious life. In his half-delirious state, he wished he could tell them how to stop. He wished he could bring them all to Capri, where no courtrooms or lawyers would be allowed. He wished that he could do everything over again. He'd do it differently. Perhaps that preacher in Judea was right—give up all this fighting—give up avenging every wrong—turn the other cheek—give up all these worthless possessions, give up the obsessive quest for power and glory.

He fell asleep and dreamed of archers shooting arrows at him as he ran, the arrows hovering close behind him, forcing him to run faster and faster. He saw Augustus in the Pantheon illuminated by a shaft of sunlight. Then he woke, and heard people in the room. Someone was taking his pulse. He heard someone say, "It's over," and he felt someone twisting the imperial signet ring off his finger. He forced himself to sit up. "Get away from me you scavengers," he shouted with a rasping voice. "I'm not dead yet."

He tried to swing his legs out of the bed but fell to the floor. He had no strength left and blacked out for a second. Macro picked him up and placed him back on the bed. "Oh, it's you Macro," Tiberius said. "Good, I thought it was somebody else. I thought it was Charon from Hades."

"No. It's just me," Macro said. "Lie back and rest."

Tiberius did as he was told. He was comforted. He closed his eyes and thought Macro would take care of everything until he got better. Perhaps I should make him the emperor instead of that silly boy, he thought. Perhaps I can change my will before it's too late. He tried to push himself up again. "I have to get up," he said. He felt his ring finger. The ring was gone. "Where's my ring? Bring me my ring."

"Lie back," Macro said, gently pushing him back down on the bed.

"But my ring."

"The ring is being cleaned. Don't worry, when you wake up, it'll be here."

Tiberius dozed into a delirious half-sleep, then a deeper sleep. The doctor felt his neck and his wrist, waking him. Tiberius heard the doctor say, "I think he's gone, but I'm not sure."

From outside, he heard the senators shouting, "Long live the emperor." Then he heard Caligula's high-pitched voice, "Thank you, thank you, senators. With this ring it will be my honor…"

Tiberius again tried to get out of the bed, but Macro held him down. Tiberius felt huge hands squeezing his neck; thumbs pressing into his throat. He realized what was happening and tried to pull the hands off. He couldn't breathe. He felt an urge to live that he had never felt so strongly in his life, and he tried again to pull the hands off, but couldn't. Everything turned black, and he passed out. Macro kept squeezing with all his strength, and then it was over. Tiberius was dead.